All the characters in this book are fictitious,
and any resemblance to real persons living
or dead is purely coincidental.

A CUCKOO IN CANDLE LANE

A powerful début novel...

When Elsie and Bert Jones move with their children, Ann and Arthur, to Candle Lane in Battersea, they are befriended by their new neighbour Ruth Marchant, whose husband Ken has never allowed her to forget he is not the true father of their child, Sally. Elsie and Ruth's friendship changes their lives, and Ann and Sally also become friends, growing up as teenagers in the swinging sixties. Family life is at the heart of Candle Lane, from childhood sexual abuse to maternal love so devoted that a mother will break a young girl's heart to protect her son...

This book is dedicated to my son
Michael Maynard who died in 1998
aged twenty-seven, and who is now
'Over the Rainbow'.

LM

A CUCKOO IN CANDLE LANE

by

Kitty Neale

Magna Large Print Books
Long Preston, North Yorkshire,
BD23 4ND, England.

British Library Cataloguing in Publication Data.

Neale, Kitty
    A cuckoo in Candle Lane.

    A catalogue record of this book is
    available from the British Library

    ISBN   0-7505-2294-1

First published in Great Britain 2003 by Orion

Copyright © Kitty Neale 2003

Cover illustration © Hulton Getty by arrangement with
Orion Publishing Group

The moral right of Kitty Neale to be identified as the author of this
work has been asserted by her in accordance with the Copyright,
Designs and Patents Act, 1988

Published in Large Print 2005 by arrangement with
Orion Publishing Group

Magna Large Print is an imprint of Library Magna Books Ltd.

Printed and bound in Great Britain by
T.J. (International) Ltd., Cornwall, PL28 8RW

Acknowledgements

With thanks to my family, friends and literary agent for their invaluable help, patience and support. Special thanks to Jean Vivian – she knows why.

Author's Note

Many places and street names mentioned in the book are real. However, others and some of the topography, along with all the characters, are just figments of my imagination.

Chapter One

Battersea, South London, 1953

Sally Marchant ran headlong down the street, arms and legs pumping like pistons and socks bagging around her ankles. Just before the corner she risked a quick glance over her shoulder, then scuttled round onto the main road where she leaned thankfully against the pawnbroker's window, skinny chest heaving as she dragged freezing air into her lungs. Why do they always pick on me? she thought, her eyes staring blankly across the busy main road, to where huge ugly factories flanked the dirty River Thames.

She set off again, walking rapidly and hoping she had lost her tormentors in the warren of streets and alleyways. It was just before she reached her own turn-off that they jumped out in front of her from the shelter of a shop doorway, and her stomach lurched as she braced herself for the confrontation.

The two girls straddled the pavement, hands on hips and arms akimbo to bar her way.

'Well, well, what 'ave we here? It's the ginger nut,' one of them jeered.

'My hair ain't ginger.'

'Yes it is, you daft cow.'

'It ain't ginger ... it's auburn.'

'Don't kid yourself,' she sniggered, her eyes

11

travelling pointedly down to Sally's feet. 'New shoes?'

'Yeah, but what's it got to do with you?'

The girl's pugnacious face glinted in triumph. 'You're a liar,' she shouted. 'We saw you on Saturday in Rosie's secondhand shop, and them shoes look like the ones yer mum fished out of a box of rummage.'

'Ugh!' The other girl's long thin face stretched into a grimace of distaste. 'I bet all yer clothes are secondhand – *and* full of fleas.' She scratched herself vigorously, turning to her friend. 'Are you itchy too?'

'Yeah, I am, now you come to mention it,' she replied, raking her nails through her hair. Then, grinning maliciously at Sally, she added, 'By the way, Spooky, 'ave you seen any ghosts lately?'

Sally clenched her hands into fists, nails digging painfully into her palms in an effort to hide her humiliation. I won't let them see me cry, she thought, I won't. Lowering her head she dodged into the road to pass them, running off with the sound of their laughter ringing in her ears.

A few minutes later she turned into Long Street, halting momentarily to catch her breath. Then, after a final quick check behind her, she darted left into Candle Lane where three doors down at number five she lifted the letterbox to grope for the key that dangled on a piece of string. Carefully pulling it through she opened the door and stepped into the narrow hall, eyes clouding when she saw her dad's coat hanging on the rack. Sick with disappointment she crept upstairs to her room, clambered into bed, and curled into a tight ball under the thin blankets.

Her feelings of isolation increased at the sound of children playing in the street below her window. Boys playing football or marbles, girls with skipping ropes, their voices high as they jumped in time to a chant...

PK penny a packet,
First you chew it, then you crack it,
Then you stick it on your jacket
PK penny a packet.

She longed to join in their games, to play outside as they did, but her dad would never allow it. After school she was forced to remain in her room, out of his way, and only allowed downstairs for dinner. When he went to the pub she could stay in the kitchen until bedtime, and picturing the lovely fire burning in the hearth, she prayed he would be going out tonight.

The noise in the street gradually became distant as she allowed her mind to drift, trying to escape the cold and loneliness by retreating to the elusive and beautiful place she saw only in her dreams.

At last Sally felt safe and warm, in an altered state, floating above the bed and gazing down at her own body wrapped in a cocoon of untidy blankets. She wasn't afraid; she felt light and free, happy to let this moment go on for ever.

The bedroom door was thrust open, her peace shattered as she was propelled violently back into her body, the sudden jolt leaving her feeling disorientated and blinking rapidly at the speed of the transition.

'Come on, Sally, yer dinner's ready. Didn't you hear me calling?' her mum asked, peering round the door.

'Oh, sorry ... I must 'ave fallen asleep,' she stammered.

'Well, get a move on. You know yer dad don't like waiting for his grub,' Ruth Marchant urged as she scurried away.

Reluctantly Sally crawled out of bed and padded downstairs, shivering in her thin clothes as she entered the kitchen. Careful not to make any noise she pulled out a chair, whilst glancing surreptitiously at her dad sitting at the end of the table. He was reading a newspaper, his dark greasy hair flopping onto his forehead.

Taking a deep breath and holding it, she sat down, relieved when he didn't look up. Please, she thought, as she turned to see her mum carrying two steaming plates across the room, please let him be in a good mood.

'Here you are, Ken,' her mum said quietly.

'About bloody time too,' he snapped. 'In future, see that me dinner's ready when I come home.'

'Yeah, all right love, it won't happen again,' she said meekly, placing their plates on the table.

Sally could sense the tension in the room and her stomach churned with nerves. His anger hung in the air ... palpable ... waiting to explode.

Lowering her eyes she looked at the grey mutton stew, thick with pearl barley, and felt a wave of nausea. Beads of perspiration broke out on her forehead. 'Mum,' she gasped. 'I'm sorry, I can't eat it. I feel sick.'

14

A chair was shoved back, screeching across the lino and she jerked with fear, eyes widening as her dad leaped to his feet, the chair crashing onto the floor behind him.

'What's this?' he ground out, leaning menacingly over the table. 'Feels sick, does she? Like mother, like daughter, is it?'

Ruth crouched low in her chair, cowering away from him. 'No, don't be daft, Ken, she's only ten.'

'What! Don't you dare call me daft, you bloody bitch,' he yelled, suddenly lunging forward to grab a handful of her jumper, the material straining as he yanked her roughly towards him. Drawing back his other hand he slapped her violently across the mouth, the force of the blow splitting her bottom lip. 'Now get that brat out of my sight, or else!' he screamed.

'Quick, go to your room, Sal,' Ruth sobbed, struggling to pull herself away from his grip, blood trickling onto her chin.

Sally hesitated, her body rigid with fear, but was suddenly galvanised into action when he turned, giving her a vicious sneer.

'Do you want me to give yer mother another slap?' he spat, raising his hand in a threatening gesture.

Heart pounding Sally ran from the kitchen, jumped the stairs two at a time and burst into her room, throwing herself across the bed. It's my fault, she thought, clutching her hands over her ears in an effort to drown out the sound of her dad's voice screaming obscenities. Mum's gonna get it now, and it's all because of me. 'Please God,' she whispered. 'Please, don't let him hurt her any more.'

After a few minutes a strange calmness began to penetrate her turbulent thoughts; she felt the lightest of breaths on her cheek, like an angel's kiss. Gentle hands caressed her hair and she opened tear-filled eyes to see the room glowing in a golden shimmering light. She smiled; it would be all right now. Her friend was here.

Ruth was peering in the mirror, gingerly dabbing at the blood on her lip, when the door burst open.

'Mum, are you all right?' Sally gasped, her face creased with anxiety. 'I heard me dad go out. Did he hit you again?'

Seeing the fear in her daughter's eyes Ruth tried to smile reassuringly, but ended up wincing as the cut re-opened. 'I'm fine, sweetheart. Come over here and sit by the fire. Do you still feel sick?'

'No, I'm all right now. My friend came and made me better.'

'You and yer friend, Sally. How many times 'ave I got to tell you? It's all in yer imagination.'

'But, Mum...'

'Now that's enough,' Ruth snapped. 'I ain't in the mood for your silly stories, I've got enough on me plate as it is.'

'I'm sorry,' Sally whispered.

Ruth's voice took on a softer note. 'I tell you what,' she said, trying to make amends, 'you must be hungry. I've still got some stew left, would you like it warmed up?'

'Yeah, thanks, Mum.'

When Sally had finished eating, she rose, taking her plate to the sink. 'Do you want me to wash the dishes, Mum?'

'No, it's all right, I'll do them later,' she answered, leaning back in the chair and widening her legs. 'Come on, come and sit on the floor in front of me and I'll do yer hair.'

Once Sally was settled it was blissfully quiet for a while, and as Ruth absently drew the brush through her daughter's thick, shiny red hair, she noticed how the flames from the fire reflected and enhanced the colour, turning it to a beautiful burnished copper. She smiled softly at the memories evoked, a face floating into her mind, but then Sally's voice intruded, startling her back to the present.

'Mum, are we going to see me gran tomorrow?'

'Yeah, of course we are.' Ruth looked forward to going to Tooting to see her mum and sister Mary, whose husband was a travelling salesman covering the North of England. Harry was a good-looking bloke and often away from home for long periods, but he earned good money so her sister wanted for nothing.

'Mum, why hasn't Auntie Mary got any kids?'

'I dunno, pet. Perhaps the stork will bring her a baby one day.'

Sally twisted around, looking up at her quizzically. 'Why don't she get one from the chemist's?'

'That's not where you get them from, love.'

'But, Mum, we saw a lady buy one last week, don't you remember?'

Puzzled, Ruth Marchant shook her head. 'No, darling. I dunno what you think you saw, but you can't buy babies.'

'You can yer know,' Sally said sagely, wagging

17

her head, her little face full of the importance of what she had seen. 'When we went to the chemist's, I saw Mr Brown putting a baby in his scales. He told the lady it was ten pounds, and a lovely little whopper.'

Ruth snorted, trying to hold back her laughter. 'Oh, Sally,' she finally managed to gasp, pressing the back of her hand to her sore mouth, 'you are funny. I dunno where you get your ideas from. Look, dear,' she added, fighting to keep a straight face, 'you can't buy babies by the pound, like potatoes.'

Sally frowned in consternation. 'But the lady paid Mr Brown for it ... I saw her.'

'No, the baby already belonged to her – she just wanted to check its weight, that's all.'

A stream of questions followed and Ruth did her best to answer them, until at last Sally leaned back contentedly, her curiosity satisfied for the time being.

'Mum, will you brush me hair again?'

Ruth smiled affectionately and it wasn't long before she noticed that Sally's head had begun to nod up and down with each stroke of the brush. 'Come on now, you're falling asleep and it's time you were in bed.'

'All right, Mum,' she yawned, rising slowly to her feet. 'Night, night,' she whispered tiredly, leaning over for a kiss.

Ruth washed the dishes, tidied up, and then gazed around the spartan room. Satisfied there was nothing Ken could find fault with, she flopped down in front of the fire, stirring the dying embers to life with the poker before adding a few more lumps of precious coal.

With a sigh, she remembered that there was still the grey pinafore skirt she had managed to find for Sally in the secondhand shop to alter. The hem needed taking up, but somehow she wasn't in the mood for sewing. Instead she dug into her apron pocket, fishing out a packet of cigarettes. These were her one luxury; she would buy only enough meat for Ken and Sally, just putting vegetables on her own plate. She smiled ruefully; they didn't notice and the few spare coppers enabled her to buy a couple of packets of Woodbines a week.

Perhaps I should stop smoking, she thought, then I could save up and buy new clothes for Sally. No, she shrugged, assuaging her guilt; there was no point in doing that. Ken would go mad if he saw Sally in new clothes. He resented any money spent on her, and in a perverse way, it seemed to please him when she looked scruffy.

Ruth took a nervous drag on her cigarette and glanced at the clock. He wouldn't be home for at least another hour and by then she would be in bed, pretending to be asleep. She grimaced. He was hitting her more and more lately – but then, after what she had done, it was no more than she deserved.

Chapter Two

'Hello, come on in,' Mary urged. 'Would you like a cup of tea before we go to the market, Ruth?'

'Yes, please, I'm parched.'

'Your grandmother's in the sitting room, Sally, if you would like to go through. Can I get you a glass of milk and some chocolate biscuits, my dear?'

Sally gazed up at her aunt, forming her lips into an unfamiliar shape as she tried to emulate her voice. 'Yes, please, I would love some, thank you sooh much. Is my Huncle Harry at home?'

'Hark at Polly Parrot,' her mum giggled. 'She's trying to talk like you, Mary.'

'Well, there's no harm in that. I soon realised that to gain promotion I would have to improve my elocution. No, Sally,' she said, turning to smile at her. 'I'm afraid your uncle is still away.'

Sally lowered her head in disappointment, but soon perked up as they entered the sitting room. Her gran's chubby face broke into a huge grin that revealed large gaps in her yellowing teeth.

''Ello, me darling,' Sadie Greenbrook said fondly. 'My, you're a sight for sore eyes,' she cried, holding out her arms. 'Come on, give me a kiss.'

Sally hurried across the room and kissed her gently on the cheek, then standing back, and with her eyes focused slightly off-centre, she gazed at her in concentration. 'Is your hip hurting you?'

Sadie's eyes widened. 'Well, I never. I dunno

how you do it, but you always seem to know where I'm hurting the most.'

'Your light don't look right in some places, that's how I know.'

'What do you mean, Sally? What's this light?'

'Nothing, Gran,' she answered quickly, glancing over her shoulder to see that her mum's face had tightened with annoyance.

'Sally, that's enough of that,' she snapped.

'What are you so angry about, Ruth? She ain't doing any harm,' her gran said, jumping to Sally's defence.

'I've told her a thousand times to stop all that nonsense.' She bristled indignantly. 'It's all in her imagination, Mum, so please don't encourage her.'

'All right, all right, calm down ... let's just forget it.' The older woman frowned, then peered at her daughter. 'Here, is that a cut on your lip? How did that happen?'

'I caught it on a door, that's all.'

Sally stared at her mum in astonishment. Why was she telling lies?

'Oh yeah, caught it, did yer?' her gran said, eyes narrowed suspiciously. 'And how's Ken? Working, is he?'

'Yeah, he's still doing delivery driving at Petersons. Look, I'll just go and give Mary a hand with the tea.' She turned to Sally, her hand on the doorknob. 'And you behave yourself, my girl.'

'Well now, ducks. How are things at home?' her gran asked as soon as her daughter was out of sight.

'Fine, everything's fine,' Sally answered,

21

gnawing her bottom lip.

'And how's yer dad?'

'Er ... he's all right.'

'So, yer mum cut her lip on the door, did she. How did she manage that?'

'I dunno,' Sally answered, hopping nervously from one foot to the other. 'Gran, I need the toilet,' she stammered, scurrying out of the room, desperate to avoid any more questions.

Blimey, Sadie thought, it's like trying to get blood out of a stone with those two. Perhaps she could get Sally to open up when her mum went out. She'd been suspicious for some time that things were not right with Ruth's marriage; for one thing, her daughter had lost a lot of weight. She shook her head worriedly, reluctant to involve her granddaughter in her subterfuge, but she was desperate to find out what was wrong.

The door opened and she peered at her daughters as they came in from the kitchen. Mary was carrying an elegantly laid tray. Why does that one always have to put on airs and graces, she thought. Just look at her swanking with the best china. Her eyes flicked around the immaculate sitting room. It had been hard when deteriorating health had forced her to move in with Mary and her husband Harry. Sadie's eyes clouded as she thought longingly of her old house with its cosy kitchen hearth.

Pouring out the tea, Mary passed a cup to her. Then, holding out a plate, she asked, 'Would you like a biscuit, Mum?'

'Thanks, I won't say no,' Sadie said and, taking

one, she promptly dunked it in her tea, masking a grin when she saw Mary purse her lips in disapproval.

Sally had scuttled back into the room just in time to witness the scene, bursting into giggles when Sadie lifted her biscuit, frowning in consternation when half of it remained in her cup. 'Oh, stone the crows,' she chuckled, giving Sally a cheeky wink and trying to fish out the soggy mess with her teaspoon.

'Honestly,' Ruth sighed, shaking her head. 'It's like a flippin' circus when you and Sally get together, Mum.' She gulped down the last dregs of her tea. 'Come on, Mary, let's go now. If we don't get a move on, all the decent stuff will be gone.'

As they put their coats on, Sadie couldn't help noticing the difference between them. Both were pretty, with brown hair and blue eyes. But Mary, her elder daughter, looked neat and tidy, with newly permed hair lying in tight curls around her face. Ruth, the shorter of the two, looked shabby and washed out, her greasy lank hair pulled back into a rough untidy bunch.

'Ain't it about time you got yerself a new coat, Ruth?' Sadie asked bluntly. 'That one looks fit for the dustbin.'

Her daughter's cheeks flushed. 'Don't start, Mum. My Ken don't earn the sort of money that Harry does.'

Sadie sighed. Her husband hadn't earned a lot either, but they used to be a darn sight better dressed. Perhaps Ruth wasn't any good at handling money. 'Why don't you get yerself a little part-time job to help out?' she suggested.

Ruth looked askance. 'Ken would go mad if I went out to work. It's a matter of pride with him – he thinks a woman's place is in the home.'

Sadie clicked her teeth. 'What a load of old-fashioned nonsense. Women went out to work during the war, they kept the country running and you worked on–'

'Oh Mum, don't go on about it, or we'll never get away,' Mary interrupted as she snatched up her shopping bag.

Ruth turned to Sally. 'We won't be long, love, look after your gran. Is there anything you want from the market, Mum?'

'Yeah, you can get me some snuff, dear,' she answered, ignoring Mary's grimace of distaste. She was fed up with her elder daughter's nagging, finicky ways.

'Did me mum really go to work during the war?' Sally asked when they were alone.

'Yes, dear, she was a bus conductress for a couple of years,' Sadie told her, smiling fondly at her granddaughter. Sally was the light of her life. There was something ethereal about her and she had a sensitivity that was unusual in a child. Wriggling into a comfortable position, and easing a plump cushion behind her back, she related all she could remember about Ruth's job. 'Of course, she had to leave when you came along,' she ended, fumbling in her mind for something else to distract Sally. 'Have I told you about yer granddad?'

'You told me that he drove a wagon, with big horses pulling it.'

'They were shire horses, huge bloody great things, but your granddad loved them. He worked

24

for the brewery, delivering barrels of beer all over London.' She smiled inwardly as a picture of Charlie arose in her mind. He always looked a proper dapper chap, sitting up on the dray wearing his bowler hat, a leather whip hanging loosely across his lap. She was sure he would still be alive today if they hadn't lost their only son during the war, convinced it was the shock of David's death that had brought on her husband's heart attack.

Sadie sighed deeply. Their son had been a tall laughing lad who, at the outset of war, had joined the Royal Navy, strutting proudly in his smart new uniform. He told her not to worry when he went to join his ship, reminding her of all the scrapes he had got into as a boy, and saying he was indestructible. Oh, but you weren't son, were you, she thought sadly, glancing at his picture on the mantelpiece. His ship was hit by a torpedo and sank in the cold waters of the Atlantic. There had been a few survivors, but David wasn't one of them, and she had thought her heart would break. Now, looking back, she wondered how she had survived the terrible grief of losing both her husband and son in such a short time.

With a sharp intake of breath she pushed away the bad memories, fumbling for a bag of sweets kept in her apron pocket. 'Fancy a Fox's Glacier Mint, Sal?'

'Yes, please.'

'What sort of sweets do yer get from your dad?' she asked, hoping to catch her out while she was distracted.

Sally, her hand reaching into the bag, snorted derisively. 'He wouldn't buy me sweets.'

'Oh, and why not?'

'Er, well, he just w-wouldn't,' she stuttered.

''Ave you been a naughty girl then, is that it?'

'No, of course I ain't. I hardly ever see him.'

Sadie was puzzled. What on earth did she mean? Had he left them – was that why they looked so downtrodden and scruffy? She leaned forward anxiously. 'Sal, has your dad left home?'

'Oh no, it's just that I 'ave to keep out of his–' Sally paused, clamping a hand over her mouth, eyes wide with fear. 'Please, Gran, don't ask me anything else. I'll get into trouble.'

Sadie closed her eyes against the frightened expression on her granddaughter's face; the poor kid looked terrified and was obviously hiding something. But what? And how could she find out?

When Mary and Ruth entered the bustling indoor market, their ears were assailed by the raucous voices of the market-traders as they shouted their wares, vying for custom in front of stalls piled high with colourful displays of fruit and vegetables. The two women looked around excitedly, pleased to see even more goods on display that hadn't been available during the war. There was still partial rationing, but it wasn't as bad, and rumours were abounding that the coupon system would be over with soon.

Mary tugged at Ruth's arm, raising her voice above the din. 'Come on, let's get our meat first.'

'Yeah, all right,' she shouted back as they pushed through the crowds to Tommy Porter's stall.

'I'm looking for a cheap bit of brisket,' Ruth told her. 'If I cook it really slowly there should be a bit left over to 'ave with bubble and squeak on Monday.'

Mary nodded; she had seen a nice shoulder of lamb and haughtily raised her arm to catch the butcher's attention.

'Well, well, it's the duchess,' he said, grinning widely. Then with his smile encompassing them both, he added, 'And what can I get you two lovely ladies?'

'Wotcher, Tommy,' Ruth said on a laugh. 'Duchess – yeah, that's a good one, and it suits me sister down to the ground.'

'If you two have quite finished, I'll have that shoulder of lamb, please,' Mary indicated, holding her head high and refusing to be baited.

'And I'll 'ave that piece of brisket over there,' Ruth pointed.

Tommy chuckled as he reached for the beef. 'My, don't yer sister speak proper. Shows us Cockneys up, she does.'

'We ain't Cockneys, Tom, we wasn't born within the sound of Bow bells,' Ruth told him.

'Yeah, I know – yer don't sound like proper Londoners. Now me,' he said, thumping his chest proudly, 'I was born and bred in Stepney.'

'You cheeky sod, Tommy,' Ruth laughed. 'I'm just as much a Londoner as you are. I'm a South Londoner, and proud of it.'

'All right, keep yer shirt on,' he grinned. 'But what about yer sister then? Does she come from somewhere really posh, like Mayfair?'

'I don't think so, Tommy, at least me mum has never said so, but–'

'Oh, get a move on, Ruth,' Mary snapped,

interrupting her mid-sentence, 'and where I come from is none of your business, Tommy Porter.'

Ruth raised her eyebrows. 'Blimey, what's the matter with you? Did you get out of bed on the wrong side this morning? There's no need to be so bloody miserable – we was only having a laugh.'

Mary turned to her sister, bristling with indignation. Couldn't she see that she was showing her up? 'Just shut up, Ruth,' she hissed, before completing her purchases.

They were making for their favourite vegetable stall, having learned which ones gave short measures or put a few rotten potatoes amongst the good ones, when Mary spotted a rack of children's clothes and paused as a dark green coat caught her eye. She fingered the thick wool material, thinking that it would look lovely on her niece, but dare she buy it? Looking up, she saw that Ruth had forged on ahead, and acting on an impulse she yanked the coat off the rack and gave it to the stallholder.

'Quick,' she said breathlessly. 'Put it in a bag.'

Having paid for it, she hurried to catch up with Ruth as her sister joined the queue at the fruit and veg stall.

'What's in there then?' Ruth asked.

'Oh, nothing much. Just a jacket I fancied.'

'Well, let's 'ave a look at it.' Ruth's hand made a grab for the bag.

Mary thrust it quickly behind her. 'Not now, for God's sake. Stop making a spectacle of us ... it can wait until we get home.'

'All right then, misery guts. I dunno what's got into you today,' Ruth said irritably.

Mary rubbed her forehead; she didn't know

what was the matter with her either. Her life was just so empty, but how could she explain that to her sister? Ruth thought she had the life of Riley – nice home, fashionable clothes, a good husband. Huh! If only she knew the truth.

'Me arm feels like it's dropping off,' Ruth complained, as they entered the hall and thankfully put down their laden shopping bags.

Mary hurried into the kitchen, and as she laid the tea tray to her meticulous satisfaction, she worried about Ruth's reaction to the coat. She had tried in the past to buy her niece new clothes, and though she didn't understand why, her sister always refused. Oh, what the heck, she thought, I'll just have to get it over with. Taking a deep breath she drew herself up to her full height, and snatching up the bag, marched purposefully into the sitting room.

'Here you are, my dear,' she said, beckoning to Sally. 'I've got a little something for you. I hope you like it.'

Sally's face lit up with excitement. She peeped inside the bag, gasping in disbelief and then looked up, her eyes like saucers. 'Is it really for me?'

'Yes, of course it's for you. Why don't you try it on,' she urged.

Almost reverently Sally took the coat out of the bag, her fingers stroking the soft material. 'Oh, Auntie Mary,' she whispered. 'It's lovely. I've never had a new coat before.'

'Hold on a minute,' Ruth demanded. 'What are you playing at, Mary? I've told you before, we don't want no charity.'

Mary felt her temper flare. 'Look here, this is not charity. Surely I can buy my niece a present if I want to. After all, she's the only one I've got.'

Sally rushed across the room, the coat clutched protectively to her chest. 'Oh please, Mum,' she begged. 'Please let me keep it.'

'For Gawd's sake, Ruth, what's the matter with you?' Sadie cried. 'You ain't too proud to dress the kid in secondhand gear that makes her look like a bleedin' ragamuffin.'

Ignoring her mum, Ruth glared at Mary, eyes blazing. 'How many times 'ave I told you not to buy us things. You just don't listen.'

'But it's only a coat – why are you so angry?' Mary asked in genuine puzzlement, watching as her sister floundered for a reply.

All eyes were on Ruth as she sat with her head lowered, their breath held as they waited for her to answer. She finally raised her eyes, and with tight lips, said, 'Oh, all right then, she can 'ave it.'

Sally yelped happily and rushed back across the room. 'Thanks, Auntie Mary! Thanks for buying it for me,' she cried.

'It's my pleasure, dear. Now come on, let's see what it looks like on you.'

Smiling she put the coat on, raised the fur-edged hood and began to pose comically, turning this way and that, her chin held high.

Mary thought she looked beautiful. The fit was perfect and the colour enhanced her lovely green eyes. Gone was the untidy urchin who had arrived that morning. How she envied Ruth her daughter. Look at her, she thought, she's like a colt, all arms and legs, and that beautiful hair. 'You look very nice, Sally,' she said.

'My, she looks a proper treat,' Sadie grinned.

'There's something else in the bag that you've missed,' Mary told her.

Eagerly opening the bag again, Sally pulled out a matching fur muff, a cord attached to hang around her neck. 'Oh, Auntie Mary,' she whispered.

'Come on, get that coat off now, and put yer old one on,' Ruth ordered. 'We're going in a minute.'

'But you haven't had a cup of tea yet,' Mary protested.

'I know,' her sister said belligerently. 'But it's late and Ken will be home soon.' Picking up her shopping bags, she announced, 'Right, we're off now. See you next week, Mum.'

Sally ran across the room, the bag holding her carefully folded coat clutched tightly in her hand. 'Bye, Auntie Mary. Bye, Gran,' she said, giving them both a quick hug.

Mary watched her sister as she marched stiffly from the room. 'Well, that's nice isn't it,' she said indignantly, when she heard the front door bang. 'All I did was buy Sally a new coat, and Ruth didn't even have the decency to thank me for it.'

'Now, don't get all huffy,' Sadie placated. 'There's more to Ruth's behaviour than meets the eye, and I ain't too happy about that cut on her mouth neither.'

'That's no excuse for being rude, Mum,' Mary retorted, lifting the tea tray. 'Trust you to stick up for her.'

'For crying out loud, Mary, that girl's got a

31

hard life compared to you. Can't you show a bit of compassion for once?'

She stared coldly at her mother, trying to swallow her anger and biting back a retort. Christ, Mum, she thought, you have no idea how awful my marriage is, and if you did, would you show the same concern for me?

Chapter Three

The van rumbled slowly down the street and Elsie Jones, sitting in the passenger seat, stared at the dingy area with dismay. It was awful! There was nothing of beauty in these streets of mean terraced houses. No tree-lined avenues, no green fields just scrubby grass struggling to survive amongst the rubble of old bomb-sites.

How could she live here after the lovely leafiness of Wimbledon? Oh Bert, she thought, glancing at her husband in the driving seat, what have you brought us to?

'Here we are, love,' he said cheerfully, turning into a narrow lane and pulling into the kerb. 'This one's ours.' Switching off the engine he jumped out, hurrying round to the passenger door, a frown creasing his brow when he saw the expression on his wife's face.

'Come on, Elsie, it's not that bad, and if things go well we may not have to rent the place for long.' He was a huge man and the muscles rippled in his arms as he lifted her gently down onto the pavement, her short stocky body looking diminutive beside him.

Elsie's eyes roamed over the gloomy façade of the house, and then the identical one next door. A small white face surrounded by beautiful coppery-coloured hair was peeping out of the window, and as their eyes locked Elsie felt a jolt, as though a part of her had reached out and touched a spark within the girl.

Startled by her feelings she found herself unconsciously walking towards the window, but then the curtains fell back into place and the girl was hidden from view. Puzzled, but hearing the shouts of her own children, she turned to see that Bert had opened the back of the van and Arthur and Ann came tumbling out, laughing excitedly, only to pull up short when they saw their surroundings.

'Blimey, what a dump,' Arthur complained.

'What's that awful smell, Mum?' Ann asked, wrinkling her nose.

'I don't know,' she answered, sniffing the pungent air. 'It's horrible though.'

'Hello. Moving in, are yer?'

Elsie turned to see a tall thin woman, wearing a cotton turban over her steel curlers, peering into the back of the van.

'You'll soon get used to the stink, love,' she added, moving to stand by their side. 'Some people say it comes from the brewery, others the glucose or candle factory. It's only people new to the area, or just passing through, that notice the smell. Welcome to Battersea,' she said with a grin, before strolling away and disappearing into a house a few doors down.

Anxious to get away from all the prying eyes, Elsie held out her hand. 'Bert, give me the key and let's get inside.'

The door squeaked in protest as she pushed it open and stepped into a dank narrow hall. Well, at least it's clean, she thought, as she slowly wandered from room to room. Of course it wasn't a patch on her old house, but for the time being at least they would just have to make the best of it. 'Come on, let's get our stuff unloaded,' she said resolutely.

The evening was drawing in before everything was arranged to Elsie's satisfaction. She was exhausted, yet there was still the meal to finish cooking. It was only a scratch one of sausages and mash, not their usual Sunday roast, but it would have to do.

Ann was upstairs unpacking her prized collection of books, Arthur was in the back yard kicking a football about, and Bert was in their bedroom, putting the wardrobe together.

She looked around at her familiar things that somehow looked out of place in this poky kitchen, then sank down onto one of the kitchen chairs for a much-needed rest. She was tempted to get the cards out; something was nagging at her, plucking at her mind. But would they tell her anything? Had she been put in this dreary place for some special reason? No, she mentally shook herself. She was tired and over-dramatising her feelings – they were here because of Bert's new business, that was all.

Snapping out of her reveries, Elsie rose to finish

off the dinner, and as she poured thick gravy over the sausages, she called her family to the table.

'I've got to take the van back to the yard after dinner,' Bert mumbled, stuffing a chunk of sausage into his mouth. 'We've got our first big job tomorrow and Frank wants to check it over to make sure everything is running smoothly. We don't want to take any chances.'

Elsie tried to smile, but found her lips trembling instead. She pulled out a handkerchief, pretending to blow her nose in an effort to hide her feelings.

Was it only three months ago that Bert's mum had died and their lives had changed overnight? The time had flown by. The old lady had left them a bit of money, not a huge amount, but enough for her husband to think about setting up his own business.

Part of Elsie wished that Bert had stayed with the removals firm he'd been with for over ten years and she sighed, shifting in her chair. Yet she couldn't deny that everything had fallen into place quite nicely with the new business, especially Frank wanting to come in with him like that. Not that he had much money to offer, she thought. Still, Bert was grateful for his expertise, and she could see that it would be useful to have a motor mechanic on board.

Her husband had been so excited about starting up his own furniture removals company, and she recalled how delighted he'd been when they found the secondhand van. But how she wished they had been able to find an affordable yard in Wimbledon instead of having to move to Battersea. Now stop it, she sniffed, mentally giving herself a shake and glancing up at her husband. If Bert was willing to take the gamble and throw away ten years of security on this venture, she wasn't going to stand in his way. No, she'd support him, and offer as much help as she could.

The first hurdle had been overcome now, but she hadn't realised how hard it would be to leave the house she had lived in for so many years. Not only would she miss her friends, she also wouldn't be there to see her pretty garden burst into bloom in the spring. She glanced out of the kitchen window, seeing the drab back yard that was just a concrete patch, and shuddered.

Bert stood up, his bearlike physique filling the small room. He placed his cap at a jaunty angle on his thick dark hair, smiling at her gently as though sensitive to her feelings. 'I'll be back as soon as I can, love,' he said, bending down to kiss the top of her head.

Elsie sat back in her chair, replete after the makeshift meal, and tried hard to rid herself of the gloomy mood that was casting a dark cloud over her normally cheerful demeanour. Glancing at her children she knew that it was going to be difficult for them to settle in this new area too. Ann and Arthur were sitting quietly, with no sign of their usual bickering. Seeing their long faces, she realised she would have to make an effort for their sakes.

Drawing a deep breath, she rose stiffly to her feet. 'Right, let's get this table cleared,' she chirped, fighting off her tiredness as she bustled around stacking the empty plates, trying to give an illusion of normality.

'I don't like it here, and I want to go home. I don't know anyone around here and I miss my mates!' her son cried, glaring at her accusingly.

'Arthur, we've talked about this and it was all explained to you. This is home now and we'll just have to make the best of it. Anyway, you'll soon make friends when you start your new school tomorrow.'

His bottom lip stuck out belligerently. 'Well, I hate it!' he yelled, rushing out and slamming the back door.

Elsie winced as the glass panes rattled, and it wasn't long before she heard the sound of his ball thudding repeatedly against the kitchen wall, the noise reverberating in the small room. She rubbed a hand tiredly across her brow as she looked at her daughter. Would it be better here for her, she wondered. God, she hoped so. The kids at her last school had been so cruel and it had taken Ann a long time to deal with the unrelenting name-calling. Now she might well have to start all over again.

'Have you finished unpacking your books, Ann?' she asked.

'Nearly – I've just got a few more to do. I think I'll go and finish them off now, if that's all right?'

Elsie nodded distantly. Had they done the right thing moving here? She wasn't normally so pessimistic, but she just couldn't shake off these vague feelings of disquiet.

Chapter Four

Sally awoke early. Something had disturbed her, but she was reluctant to open her eyes and let go of her dream. She had been flying, free as a bird, skimming low across the sky with the dawn light casting a glow on the rooftops below. A small smile played across her face as she recalled the joyous feelings of weightlessness that had held her enthralled.

The sound of a door banging penetrated the thin walls and she heard muffled voices, then laughter. Of course – it was the new neighbours. The house next door had been silent since old Mrs Richardson died and now the unaccustomed noise had woken her.

I wonder what they'll be like, she thought, remembering the lady who had stared at her so strangely and the brief glimpse she had had of two children, one of them a girl of about her own age.

Stretching out, her ears were pricked for sounds of movement from below. The front door slammed and she scrambled across to her window, just in time to see her father striding down the road.

'Mum, can I wear me new coat to school?' she asked later, gulping the last of her porridge.

'Oh, I don't know. If yer dad catches you wearing it, he'll go mad.'

'Please, Mum. The other kids are always taking

38

the mickey out of me 'cos I'm so scruffy. I'll come in ever so quietly, and if Dad's home I'll go straight to me room as usual.'

'Well...' Ruth pondered as Sally widened her eyes in mute appeal. 'All right then, but please be extra careful,' she added worriedly.

Sally leaped to her feet, anxious to get the coat before her mum changed her mind. She rummaged in the back of the cupboard, pulling it from its hiding place and shrugged it on over her old school clothes. Then, grabbing her satchel, she made a dash for the door, running outside to find the Lane suddenly, and almost totally, engulfed in a thick, choking smog.

It took her ages to get to school. She fumbled along in the grey, eerie atmosphere, only able to see about eighteen inches in front of her face, heart jumping when people occasionally loomed up in front of her, most clutching scarves or handkerchiefs over their faces. At last she reached the main road and could hear the muffled sound of traffic as it crawled slowly along, headlights barely piercing the gloom.

The bell was clanging when she finally arrived at school, thankfully joining a queue of children in the playground as they filed into the building.

The classroom was quiet and she was struggling with maths, her most hated subject, when the door opened and Mrs Brooks came in, followed by a girl who kept her head shyly lowered.

Sally's jaw dropped. Was it the girl she had glimpsed yesterday?

The headmistress handed her over to Miss

Penfold and her teacher's eyes scanned the room before coming to rest on the empty seat beside Sally.

'This is Ann Jones and she is starting school today. I'm going to sit her next to you Sally. Will you help her to settle in, please?'

When at last the new girl lifted her face, there was a gasp of surprise and muffled sniggers. One of her eyes was lodged in the corner of the socket and the other appeared to be leaning drunkenly towards it.

Oh, the poor thing, Sally thought, her feelings of pity deepening when the sniggers in the room rose to loud laughter.

'That is enough!' Miss Penfold shouted. 'I will not have this behaviour in my classroom.'

The room fell silent and heads bent over desks again, with only a slight titter to be heard as Ann took her seat. Sally smiled encouragingly, leaning towards her and placing the arithmetic book between them. She pointed to the section they were working on and heard a whispered, 'Thanks.'

For the rest of the morning they worked companionably together, until the dinner bell broke the silence. Then there was a cacophony of noise. Desk lids banged, chairs screeched across the wooden floor, and a stampede of feet rushed for the door drowning out Miss Penfold's shout of, 'Quiet! Quiet!'

Sally waited, as she usually did, for the classroom to empty. 'I 'ave school dinners,' she told Ann who was still sitting quietly beside her. 'Would you like to come with me?'

'Well, I'd like to, but it would be better if you

40

went on your own,' she answered doubtfully.

'Oh, why's that?'

'I always get picked on, and if you're with me they might start on you too.'

Sally shrugged her shoulders. 'Don't worry about me, I get picked on too, yer know.'

Ann looked puzzled. 'But you haven't got anything wrong with you.'

'Huh, they think I'm a right scruff. I get called Spooky and Weirdo too.'

'Spooky? Why do they call you that?' Ann asked, her eyebrows raised.

'I dunno,' Sally prevaricated, reluctant to tell her the truth.

'Perhaps you're psychic, like my mum.'

'Psychic?' she wrinkled her nose. 'What does that mean?'

'Well, she can read the cards, or your palm, and look into your future.'

'No, I ain't like yer mum then,' Sally said emphatically. 'I can't do that.'

'Do you really want me to come to the dinner hall with you?' Ann asked quietly.

'Yeah, of course I do. Anyway, I think we might be next-door neighbours. Did you move into Candle Lane yesterday?'

It was the start of a friendship that grew as the week progressed, and Ann amazed Sally with her stoicism. She was teased mercilessly in the beginning, but just walked past her tormentors with her head lowered. 'Ignore them,' she would say, and after a few days this attitude paid off. Most of the kids grew tired of her lack of reaction,

41

and the name-calling almost petered out.

Sally found that it worked for her too. The bullying she had suffered was reduced to the occasional jeer from the other side of the road.

'Do you want to come into my house?' Ann asked hopefully as they made their way home from school on Friday.

Sally stared at the ground. She had been making excuses all week and realised how lame they sounded. She was desperate to keep Ann's friendship, but knew that, like other girls in the past, Ann would soon get fed up with a friend who wasn't allowed out to play.

With a gentle tug she pulled her to a halt, wondering if she dared confide in her. Ann was a loner too and so far she hadn't seen her playing outside very often. Would that make a difference? 'Look,' she began hesitantly, 'I've got something to tell you.'

'What's that then?' Ann asked.

'Well, you might not want to be my friend when you hear it, but it don't matter. I'm used to it,' Sally said defensively, kicking a small stone into the road.

'What do you mean? Why wouldn't I want to be your friend?'

''Cos I'm not allowed out to play after school,' she said, holding her breath as she waited for Ann's reply.

'Crumbs – is that all? I get kept in too if I'm naughty. Never mind, come round tomorrow and I'll show you my books; you can borrow some if you want.'

'No, no, that's not it. I can't come round

42

tomorrow either. I'm never allowed out.' Tears pricked at Sally's eyes. 'Me dad won't let me.'

Ann looked at her in surprise. 'Did you do something really, really naughty then?'

Sally shook her head. 'I haven't done anything. He just makes me stay in me room, out of his way.'

'But why does he do that?'

'I dunno,' she said, shrugging her shoulders dejectedly.

With her head tilted to one side and a thoughtful expression on her face, Ann asked, 'What about when he goes out? Couldn't you come round to my house then?'

Sally felt a surge of excitement. Could it work? He would be going to the pub tonight – but would she be able to persuade her mum?

That evening Ann opened the door with a grin and beckoned her friend inside. Leading her to the kitchen, she said, 'Mum, this is Sally.'

Elsie looked at the girl hovering shyly in the doorway. 'Hello, dear. Come on in,' she urged.

Large green eyes gazed back at her and once again Elsie felt that strange tugging sensation. She could see the girl was nervous and tried to put her at ease. 'Come and sit down, love. It's nice to meet you at last, and I'm so pleased you and Ann have become friends.'

Sally took the seat opposite her and Elsie smiled gently, glad to see her shoulders beginning to relax. 'Do you like jigsaw puzzles?' she asked, pleased when Sally nodded her head. 'Here, Ann, why don't you go and get that new one. It looks really good, and we can all have a go at it.'

Her tactics worked and for the next half an hour they sat happily fitting the puzzle together. Then when Sally reached into the box, rummaging about for another piece of blue sky, Elsie decided to seize the opportunity and took her hand, turning it palm up and gently unfurling her fingers.

'What are you doing?' Sally asked nervously, trying to pull her hand away.

'It's all right, don't be frightened,' Elsie said. 'I'm just reading your palm.'

'But I ain't got no writing on it,' Sally said, a bewildered expression on her face.

'No, dear, it's not that sort of reading,' Elsie told her, trying to stifle a laugh. 'I just look at the lines on your hand and they tell me things about you.'

As Elsie gazed at Sally's palm she was shocked by what she saw. This girl was special and she had rarely seen such lines.

'What can you see then?' the girl asked curiously.

Elsie's heart went out to her. She felt they were destined to meet and there would come a time when Sally would need a lot of guidance, but for now she would have to tread carefully. 'Well now, let me see. Hmm, your lifeline shows me that you're strong and healthy and this line here tells me that you're a clever girl. What do you think of that then?' she ended with a chuckle, trying to lighten the atmosphere.

Ann reached across and touched Sally's arm. 'Don't take any notice of my mum. You should hear my dad making fun of her. He calls her an old witch, and if she's been out shopping, he asks her where she parked her broomstick.'

'Oi, you cheeky moo, that's enough of your lip,' Elsie laughed. 'Anyway, it's nearly nine o'clock and time you girls were in bed. By the way, Sally, would you ask your mum to pop round one morning for a cup of tea? I'd love to meet her.'

Sally nodded, her head turning quickly as the kitchen door opened.

'Hello you lot,' Bert called as he walked in, with Arthur trailing behind him. 'You must be Ann's new friend from next door,' he smiled as he stepped towards Sally, startled when the girl backed away nervously.

'It's all right, love, I don't bite,' he told her, his soft voice at odds with his huge build.

Elsie saw Sally's reaction and frowned. What was the girl so nervous about? Bert was a gentle giant and wouldn't hurt a fly.

'Mum, I'm starving,' Arthur whined, breaking into her thoughts, sniffing loudly and cuffing his nose with the back of his hand.

'How many times have I told you to use a hanky,' Elsie complained as she bustled over to the bread bin. 'Right, I'll make you a sandwich, then it's off to bed.'

'That's not fair. Ann's still up and I'm older than her,' Arthur complained.

'You're both going to bed,' Elsie told him shortly.

'But–'

'Don't argue with your mother,' Bert ordered.

'Sorry, Dad, but it's still not–'

'Goodbye,' Sally whispered, before Arthur had finished speaking.

'Bye love, see you again,' Elsie called as she lathered margarine onto thick slices of bread.

Does her mother know, she wondered, recalling what she had seen in Sally's palm. And if not, should I tell her?

Chapter Five

Ruth guided her threadbare sheets through the mangle, her mind distracted. She had realised the time would come when Sally would rebel against being confined to her room, but hadn't expected it to happen so soon.

It had started on Friday evening when she had begged to go next door. When Ruth refused, Sally had bombarded her with questions. Why did she have to stay in her room? Why couldn't she go to her friend's house? Why did she have to keep out of her dad's way?

As in the past, Ruth tried to evade the answers, but this time Sally just kept on and on until she felt as though her head was splitting. Unable to tell her the truth and running out of excuses, she allowed her daughter to go next door, but her nerves had jangled the whole time. What if Ken came home? It would be her that got a belting, not Sally.

With a sigh she picked up her basket of washing. Why, oh why did that bloody lot have to move in next door? she thought, making her way outside to the yard.

'Hello. I've been hoping to see you.'

Her mouth full of wooden clothes pegs, Ruth looked up to find her next-door neighbour grinning at her over the fence.

'If you've finished your washing, why don't you come round for a cup of tea,' she invited. 'I don't know about you, but I could really do with one.'

Ruth looked into a round friendly face that beamed at her invitingly and found herself grinning back. She liked Elsie on sight and was sorely tempted to accept her invitation. When Ken and Sally were out all day she often felt alone and isolated, sometimes longing for another female to talk to, but dare she take a chance?

They had lived in Candle Lane for a long time now, but she hardly knew any of the other residents. They probably thought her snobbish, but Ken was adamant about not letting anyone know their business, and he refused to let her mix with them.

Yet as she looked into her new neighbour's merry twinkling eyes, Ruth wondered if it would hurt, just this once. Before she knew it she spat the clothes pegs out of her mouth, and found herself agreeing.

Now she sat at Elsie's kitchen table, her eyes roaming around the room, unable to help feeling envious at what she saw.

There was a beautiful Welsh dresser against one wall, crammed with blue and white striped china. The gingham curtains at the window were also blue and matched the tablecloth. Her eyes turned to the fireplace and she had to withhold a gasp when she saw the lovely brass companion set in the hearth, with a matching coal-scuttle glowing like copper as it reflected the flames from the huge fire. She sighed; the whole room was in stark contrast to her own dingy and uninviting kitchen.

As Elsie bustled round putting the kettle on the hob, and getting out cups and saucers, she was surreptitiously studying her neighbour. The other woman's clothes looked washed out and drab, thin wrists poked out from the sleeves of a shapeless cardigan and her dark brown hair was scraped back unbecomingly from her face. Feed her up, she thought, put her in some decent clothes, and she'd be a right beauty.

As they chatted together she was surprised at her reaction to Ruth. When Ann told her that Sally was forced to stay in her room, she had found it disturbing, unable to understand why the child was treated so badly. But now she wondered if Ann had exaggerated, finding that not only did she like the woman, she somehow felt sorry for her too.

'So what brought you to Battersea?' Ruth asked.

'Well, it's a long story but I'll try to cut it short,' Elsie told her, whilst pouring tea through a strainer into the cups. 'You see, my husband has always wanted to start up his own furniture removals business, and when he got left a bit of money, he decided to give it a go.'

'Blimey, he's got his own firm then?'

Elsie chuckled. 'I wouldn't call it a firm, he's only got one van. Still, as he said, it's a start, and if things go well we'll be able to expand in the future. Now tell me, what does your husband do?'

'He does delivery driving for a builder's merchant.'

'Then we've got something in common – both

48

our husbands are drivers,' Elsie said, smiling across the table at Ruth.

'Yeah, but my Ken would give his right arm to work for himself.'

'Oh, I don't think it's all it's cracked up to be. At least you know you've got a regular wage coming in each week. Until Bert gets himself established I'll be worrying myself sick most of the time in case he doesn't get any work.'

Ruth nodded slowly. 'Yeah, I suppose you've got a point.'

'How long have you lived in Candle Lane, Ruth?'

'For about seven years now.'

'Well, I must say, people are friendly here. I had no end of offers to help when we moved in, and Mrs Green, who lives opposite, kindly carried over a tray of tea while we were unloading the van, which made us feel welcome.'

'That's nice,' Ruth told her, then abruptly changed the subject. 'My daughter tells me that you read palms.'

'Yes I do, but I'm also a medium. It runs in my family – my mother was a clairvoyant.'

Ruth's face was alight with curiosity. 'I've never met a medium before. If you don't mind me asking, what do you do?'

'Oh, I don't do much, just a bit of palm-reading and I occasionally read the cards. It's a hobby and I don't do it professionally. I tell you what, I'll give you a reading if you like.'

'You don't go into a trance or anything, do you?' Ruth asked nervously.

'No, don't worry, I'll just do your palm.'

Reaching across the table, Elsie took Ruth's hand, examining the lines and mounts. Hmm, she thought, this lady has been through a lot. 'You've had a hard life, but it will be a long one,' she told her. 'There was someone in your past who meant a great deal to you, but for some reason you broke up with him.' Seeing something else, her brow creased and she looked up sharply. 'I see a child from this relationship too.'

Ruth snatched her hand away, her face pale. 'How do you know that?'

Before she could form an answer Elsie felt as though she was being drawn into a vortex, and her senses heightened. She could feel a presence and heard a name. 'Who's Charlie?' she asked.

Ruth jerked. 'Ch- Charlie?' she stuttered nervously. 'Me dad's name was Charlie.'

'He's warning you about something ... something to do with your daughter.' Elsie closed her eyes, listening to the voice. 'There's a man who may harm her, a man she should keep away from.'

Elsie could feel the presence fading, drifting away as she struggled to hold onto it. The room slowly came back into focus, and she opened her eyes to find that Ruth was visibly trembling. 'Oh I'm sorry, love, I didn't mean to frighten you, but the message must have been important for a spirit to come through so suddenly. Do you know what it means?'

White-faced, Ruth shook her head. 'No, I don't know what you're talking about.'

Scrutinising her through half-closed eyes, Elsie could sense this wasn't the truth, but despite that she liked Ruth and didn't want to spoil their

50

budding friendship. 'Well, I think you should listen to the warning,' she told her. 'The message was very strong.'

Ruth just nodded, her lips compressed. It was obvious from her expression that the subject was closed, and whilst pouring them both another cup of tea, Elsie found herself thinking about Sally's palm, wondering if she dare talk about the child's gifts. Deciding to trust her instincts, she sat forward in her chair and spoke earnestly. 'Do you know that your daughter is special, Ruth?'

'Special? What do you mean?'

Elsie groped for the right words, praying inwardly that she could make her understand. 'Some people are born with natural psychic abilities and your daughter is particularly gifted. She could grow up to be a spiritual healer.'

'No, no, not my Sal. You must be mistaken,' Ruth protested.

Giving a gentle smile of encouragement, Elsie urged, 'Think carefully. Haven't you noticed anything different about her?'

'No, not really. She does come out with some funny stories at times, but she's just a kid with a vivid imagination, that's all. Anyway, what sort of things should I 'ave noticed?'

'Well, has she talked about seeing imaginary people? It sometimes manifests itself like that.' Elsie watched Ruth's reaction and saw that something had struck home; she was staring at her now, as though transfixed.

'Her friend,' she whispered. 'She's always talking about her friend, and I've told her time and time again that it's all in her imagination.'

51

'What has she told you about this friend?' Elsie asked.

Ruth rubbed the pads of her fingers across her eyes. 'It started last year after she had emergency surgery for a ruptured appendix. Oh Elsie, it was terrible. The surgeon told me that they nearly lost her during the operation and that she had to be resuscitated.'

'How awful for you,' Elsie consoled. 'But please, go on.'

'When she came round from the anaesthetic she started to say strange things, they sounded so daft that I thought she was delirious. She went on and on about the place she'd been to, saying she wanted to go back to the lights and to see the lovely lady again.'

'Did you ask her about this place, Ruth?'

'Yeah, but it didn't make any sense. She said that she floated through a tunnel and at the end of it there were beautiful shimmering shapes. Even as she recovered from the operation it didn't stop, and I remember getting quite cross with her. There I was, her mum, but she didn't want to know. All she wanted was this other lady and I didn't have a clue what she was talking about.'

As she listened to the story unfolding, Elsie realised that Sally must have had a near-death experience. She had heard similar stories before, but such things were little understood, and rarely discussed.

'When she came home from the hospital,' Ruth continued, 'she gradually stopped talking about it, but sometimes when she's upset or not feeling well, she tells me about this friend who comes and makes her better.' She stopped, her eyes suddenly widening in fear. 'Oh God, Elsie, are you telling me that my Sally's talking to ghosts?'

'No, at least not yet. But by the sound of it I think she has a spirit guide, or what some people call guardian angels.'

Ruth sat quietly for a few moments, before a look of denial crossed her face, and shaking her head, she said, 'I don't know about all this, I need time to think.' Pushing back her chair and rising abruptly to her feet she added, 'I had better be off now, I've still got a lot to do. Thanks for the tea.'

'You're welcome. Why don't you pop round again in the morning? Or I could come round to you.'

There was a pause, followed by a sigh as Ruth said, 'Look, I had better be straight with you from the start. My husband won't allow me to make friends with any of our neighbours. I took a chance coming round here today and if he found out, he'd go mad. I'd love to return the favour and invite you round to my house, but I'm sorry, I just can't risk it.'

Oh, the poor woman, Elsie thought. Fancy having to put up with a husband like that. 'It doesn't matter,' she said cheerfully. 'You're welcome to come round here any time, and your husband doesn't need to know anything about it.'

'Thanks, that's good of you, but I'll 'ave to think about it,' Ruth said with a tremulous smile.

Closing the door behind her visitor, Elsie returned to the kitchen and slumped onto a chair. She felt drained of energy and sat absentmindedly twiddling the edge of the tablecloth, thinking about her new neighbours. She had been concerned about Sally, but after looking at Ruth's palm she was worried about her too. There were some strange goings-on next door, and it was obvious her neighbour was hiding something. But what?

When Ruth returned home her mind was reeling. She had never met anyone like Elsie before and didn't know what to make of it all. Her new neighbour was a clairvoyant, but she looked so normal, short and dumpy, with a kind, chubby face.

She held onto the back of a chair, wondering what on earth had come over her, talking so openly to a complete stranger. Yet there was something about Elsie that inspired trust, a sort of deep wisdom in her eyes.

Ruth looked critically around the kitchen and grabbing a duster, flicked it halfheartedly along the mantelpiece, unable to stop a picture of Elsie's lovely, cosy room from filling her mind. If only Ken would give her a bit more housekeeping money she could make it nice in here too.

Stop it, she told herself, count your blessings. After all, most men wouldn't have forgiven her as Ken had. He had stayed with her, which was more than she deserved. No, she was lucky, and lifting her shoulders she attacked her housework with renewed vigour.

At five o'clock Ken flung open the back door and stomped into the kitchen. Yanking a chair closer to the fire, he slumped down, yawned, and stretched out his legs to rest on the fender. Look at the state of her, he thought, watching Ruth scurrying around. The scrawny cow, she was getting like a bag of bloody bones.

'What's for dinner?' he snapped.

'We've got toad in the hole and it's nearly ready,' she answered, looking at him warily.

'Well, get a move on, yer lazy cow,' he snarled, smirking at the fear in her eyes; it was no more than the bitch deserved.

Arms raised and stretching his upper body, he grimaced as his muscles screamed in pain. Christ, it had been a hard day; his deliveries had weighed a ton. His boss, Jimmy Peterson, must be raking it in, the jammy git. There was an increasing demand for construction materials and today he'd been lumbered with delivering a large consignment of bricks to a building site across the river.

Still, it had been a bit of luck bumping into Billy Bushell, so there had been some compensation. Billy had offered him some cheap whisky, saying with a sly wink that it had fallen off the back of a lorry, and persuading him to meet at the King's Head in Balham later on to buy a few bottles.

Ken relaxed in his chair, shaking out the evening paper, and for a short while the only sounds to be heard were the scraping of a spoon against the side of a saucepan, and the rustle of the newspaper as he turned the pages.

At last, he thought, when Ruth called him to the table.

He sat in his usual place, gulping his food, anxious to get to the pub. Mopping up the last of his gravy with a chunk of bread and stuffing it into his mouth, he stood up, belching loudly.

'Christ, ain't it about time you learned how to cook a decent meal? You're bleedin' useless,' he sneered, as he stamped out of the room.

After a quick wash he flung on his coat, scowling at the thought of his destination. He had been born in Balham and it was where he and Ruth had started their married life, but now, if it hadn't been for the pull of cheap whisky, he would avoid it like the plague.

As he left the house and hurried down the Lane, he saw a bus just pulling into the stop on Long Street and sprinted to catch it. Flopping breathlessly onto the nearest seat, his thoughts were still on Ruth, recalling how after the war he had returned to their small flat, happy, optimistic, and willing to give their marriage a chance. And he had tried, by God how he had tried. But it was no good, he just couldn't stand it: every time he looked at the ginger brat it was a reminder.

Things might have worked out if Ruth had given him the son he wanted so desperately, but no ... she had failed him in that too. He was determined to make her pay, and nowadays the only pleasure he got was from the power he wielded over her. She didn't stand up to him, she wouldn't dare, and the only time she showed any spunk was when he threatened the kid.

The bus pulled up only a few steps from the King's Head and as he pushed open the door, a thick cloud of cigarette smoke billowed out into the cold night air. Glancing quickly around he was pleased to see there were no familiar faces about, and then strolled nonchalantly up to the bar.

'Well I never! It's Ken Marchant!'

His eyes lit up in recognition as he stared appreciatively at the blonde and busty barmaid. 'Barbara! Well, I'll be blowed. How are you, and how's Bob?'

'Blimey, where 'ave you been? Didn't you hear – Bob didn't make it. He copped it in Normandy.'

'Gawd, I'm sorry to hear that, Babs.'

'Thanks, Ken. I still miss him, he was such a smashing bloke.' She gave a little shake of her head. 'All those hundreds of boats that sailed to Normandy to pick our troops up from the beaches, and my Bob didn't manage to get on one.' She smiled sadly. 'He always was last in the queue, wasn't he? "Slow but steady" I used to call him.'

'Christ, what rotten luck,' Ken said sympathetically.

Barbara shrugged her shoulders and in a dismissive manner, said, 'It was a long time ago and life must go on. So come on, what can I get you?'

'I'll have a pint of bitter please, and 'ave a drink yourself.'

'That's nice of you. I'll 'ave a drop of gin if that's all right.'

'Yeah, of course it is.' He leaned forward, resting his arms on the bar. 'I'm looking for Billy Bushell. Have you seen him?'

She grinned widely. 'I've seen him all right. Seen him getting his collar felt.'

'What! When was that?'

'No more than an hour ago. He was in here flogging knocked-off booze to some geezer who, unluckily for Billy, turned out to be a copper. The landlord ain't too happy about it, I can tell yer. If the brewery finds out, he could lose his job.'

Ken's eyes widened; bloody hell, if he'd arrived any earlier the police could have nabbed him too.

Barbara looked at him shrewdly. 'Don't tell me you was going to buy his dodgy gear?'

'Well, yeah – I was, as it happens,' he said, grinning ruefully.

'Oh, you naughty boy,' she said, looking at him with a coquettish glint in her eyes.

By closing time he had drunk more than usual and was enjoying chatting to Barbara as she leaned across the bar, her bust surging over the top of her tight, low-cut sweater.

'Hang about, Ken, I'll soon 'ave this lot cleared up, then you can come back to my place for a drop of whisky if you like.'

'Now then, love, you know I'm a married man,' he told her, holding up his hands in mock horror.

'But Ken, it's only whisky I'm offering,' she said, her smile belying her words.

Chapter Six

Ruth was on her hands and knees, vigorously scrubbing the kitchen floor. Palms flat, she pushed herself up, resting on her heels, back arched as she massaged the base of her spine. Phew, she thought, I could do with a break. Hearing a sudden rat-a-tat on the dividing wall she smiled at Elsie's signal that the kettle was on, and bent forward with renewed vigour.

The last few months had brought many changes in her life and she had become close to her next-door neighbour, making it a habit to pop round for a cup of tea after her morning chores were finished. Life had become so much easier since Ken's boss had put him on long-distance driving. Somehow, being away from home for one or two nights a week had softened him, and it had been a while now since he had given her a clout.

Thankfully rinsing the last strip of lino, she stood up, pursing her lips as she rubbed her sore knees. Now for a cup of tea, she thought, returning Elsie's knock to let her know she was on her way.

'Wotcher, Elsie, is the tea made? I'm spitting feathers,' she called, stepping through the back door into the kitchen.

Elsie paused in the act of lifting the teapot. 'Yes, it's ready,' she said with a grin. 'You and your tea – I should have brought an urn when I moved next door to you.'

Ruth chuckled as she sat down at the table. 'How's things?'

'Fine, but did you hear the almighty racket my Arthur made this morning? He was in such a hurry to get downstairs for his breakfast that he slid the last five steps on his bottom. The whole street must have heard him yelling and he did his best to get out of going to school. We weren't fooled though, and it didn't stop him stuffing his face. I don't know where he puts all the grub. Bert said he must have hollow legs.'

'No, I didn't hear him, but I did notice your husband leaving early. Has he got another removals job?'

Spooning sugar into the cups, Elsie slid one across the table towards Ruth. 'Yeah, a family moving to Devon, lucky devils. The firm's doing well and Bert said if things keep up like this, they might be able to buy another van next year. Not that I see any benefits yet, as most of the money gets ploughed back into the business. Still, I mustn't complain. At least I get my housekeeping money every week.'

Ruth picked up her tea and took an appreciative sip. 'You're lucky, Elsie, you get a darn sight more money than me.'

'I know, but your husband's started doing long hauls so he must be earning more. Why don't you ask him for a rise?'

'You must be joking! I wouldn't dare do that. Anyway, now that he's away a couple of nights a week I don't have to buy so much food, so I'm that much better off.'

Elsie bit her lip, a strange expression on her face, but before Ruth could ask her what was wrong, she said, 'By the way, me and Peggy Green are going for a game of Bingo this evening. Do you fancy joining us?'

'I can't, Ken's due home tonight.' Ruth drank the last dregs of tea. 'In fact, I had better be off, I'm all behind today. I've got a stew to put on and there's still the ironing to do. I'll see yer tomorrow, Elsie.'

After seeing Ruth out, Elsie returned to the kitchen and sank onto a chair, her mind distracted. She had sensed for some time now that

60

Ruth had trouble coming, and only last week when her husband was supposed to be on a delivery job in Portsmouth and staying overnight, Bert had seen him in Balham. She suspected he was up to something and perhaps had another woman, but how could she tell Ruth that, and anyway what if she was wrong?

Elsie was so deep in thought that she jumped when there was a loud knock on the front door. Her brow creased, wondering who it could be as she hurried to answer it. Opening the door, she saw Arthur standing on the step, a policeman behind him.

'Mrs Jones?' he asked, resting a hand on Arthur's shoulder.

'Oh God, what is it? What's wrong?' she cried, gawking at the policeman, her knees turning to jelly.

'I would like to talk to you about your son,' he told her, sternfaced.

'You had better come in,' she said weakly.

He followed her into the kitchen, removing his helmet and tucking it under his arm as he stood officiously in front of her. 'Mrs Jones, did you know that your son wasn't at school today?'

'No, of course not. What's going on, Arthur? What have you been up to?'

His face crumbled. 'It's this rotten place, Mum. I hate living here. I hate my new school too, so I went back to Wimbledon.'

The Constable cleared his throat. 'I'm afraid there's more, Mrs Jones. He was also caught trying to steal sweets.' He forestalled Elsie's retort, adding, 'However, your son has been lucky. The

61

shopkeeper doesn't want to take the matter any further so he's been let off with just a caution.'

Elsie felt as if all the air had left her body. God, my son bunking off school and stealing, she thought. What on earth is his dad going to say?

'Right,' the policeman said tersely. 'I'll leave you now. I'm sure the lad has learned his lesson and won't do it again.' He turned to Arthur. 'I hope I'm right, young man.'

Arthur, looking shamefaced, just nodded and hung his head.

Once they were alone Elsie gazed at her son, unable to find words to convey her distress. She just couldn't believe it of him. 'Arthur ... why?' was all she could manage.

'I just miss everything, Mum. My mates, playing on Wimbledon Common, climbing trees, fishing in the ponds – and how can I play football on my own?'

'But why haven't you made friends at your new school?'

'Oh Mum, the other boys have always lived around here. They all know each other and don't want me muscling in on their gangs.' He stuck out his lower lip, adding despondently, 'I'm just the new boy, the odd one out, and they're always picking on me.'

Her heart swelled when she saw his unhappiness. He stood before her, socks bunched round his ankles, knees dirty and grazed, grey eyes shadowed. His thick, dark hair, so like his father's, was sticking up like a brush and she felt a surge of maternal affection. She just wanted to grab him, to hold him in her arms and protect him. 'Come here, son,' she appealed, but as her arms reached out, he backed away.

'Get off, don't be daft, Mum,' he protested indignantly. 'I'm not a baby, you know. I'm nearly eleven and a half.'

'I don't know what to say,' she floundered, her empty arms falling back to her sides. 'We can't go back to Wimbledon and you've just got to accept that. We have to make the best of it here.'

'I know, Mum, but I still hate it.'

'What about the stealing, Arthur, how could you do that? I thought we had taught you right from wrong.'

'I'm sorry, but I spent all my school dinner-money on the bus fare and I was starving,' he wailed.

Elsie just couldn't bring herself to punish him; he looked so miserable and somehow she couldn't blame him – she missed her old home too. This was such a heavily industrialised area with huge factory chimneys etching the skyline, belching out thick smoke that tainted the air. If she hadn't met Ruth and some of the other women in the Lane, she would have gone mad in this dismal area. Surely Arthur would settle down too if he could make some new friends.

It was then that a thought struck her and she lifted her head in silent thanks. The Boy Scouts! She had seen a lad further up the road in uniform so there must be a local troop nearby.

'I think I've got the answer, son,' she said, jumping up with excitement and chuckling at his bemused expression. 'You could join the Boy Scouts.'

Arthur frowned, staring at his mum doubtfully.

'Think of all the things the Scouts do, love,' she urged, 'and you know you've always wanted to go camping.'

His face lit up at that. 'Yeah, you're right, Mum. How do I find out about joining?'

'We can sort that out later, but first you must promise me that you'll stop bunking off school and that you will never, *ever* steal anything again.'

After gaining his promise, Elsie sent him to his room. What a strange day, she thought. There she was worrying about Ruth's problems, when trouble had come to her own door.

Yet later as she stood at the sink peeling the potatoes, her hands immersed in cold water, she again felt a shiver of intuition. A picture of Sally flooded her mind, and somehow she felt that it wasn't just Ken that Ruth had to worry about – it was her daughter too.

Chapter Seven

Sally was pulling on her mum's hand, urging her along and skipping beside her with excitement.

'Slow down, love, I'm going as fast as I can,' Ruth complained.

'I can't wait to see me Uncle Harry. He's lovely. Do you remember the last time he was home? It was ever so funny when I sat on his back and he pretended to be a horse.' She frowned suddenly, peering up at her mum. 'Why don't me dad play with me?'

Her mother's face tightened with annoyance. 'Will you stop asking questions, I'm fed up with it! Now move yourself, there's a bus coming and if we run we may be able to catch it.'

Sally sat beside her mum on the bus, looking disconsolately out of the window, wondering why she would never answer her questions.

When they arrived at her aunt's house, she ran across the sitting room, yelling, 'Uncle Harry!' and throwing her arms around his waist.

'Hello, princess,' he grinned. Then taking her hand he sat down on the sofa, pulling her onto his lap. 'How's my favourite girl then?'

'I've got a new friend and her name's Ann.'

'That's nice, dear,' he said, smiling indulgently.

'Where's me gran?' Sally asked, looking at her empty chair.

'She's got a nasty cold and is upstairs in bed. But don't worry, you can pop up to see her when she wakes up.'

'Harry, do you mind staying in and keeping an eye on mum while we go to the market?' Mary asked anxiously.

'No, of course not. I'll keep Sally company.'

As the door closed behind her mother and aunt, Sally sighed contentedly and snuggled closer to her uncle. It was lovely to have him all to herself. 'I wish you was me dad,' she told him wistfully as he stroked her hair.

'Now then, Sally, your father wouldn't like to hear you saying things like that,' he gently admonished.

'He wouldn't care. He doesn't like me,' she told

him sadly.

'Of course he does. You're a lovely girl and I'm sure he's very proud of you.'

She nibbled her thumbnail. If only I could tell him what me dad's really like, she thought. He would never let me sit on his lap like this. 'Uncle Harry, will you tell me a story?'

'All right, darling,' he said, giving her a fond squeeze. 'Once upon a time...'

The warmth of the fire, the gentle ticking of the clock and her uncle's soft voice soothed her, and as she lay curled in his lap, her eyelids grew heavy.

'Hey, are you going to sleep?' he joked, sitting forward and tickling her playfully under the arms.

She chuckled, wriggling away from his touch, arms tight to her sides. 'No, no, I was listening, honest. Oh don't, Uncle Harry, don't tickle me.'

He stopped abruptly and she frowned, sensing his change of mood. He wasn't laughing now as he clutched her around the waist, pressing her down and writhing beneath her, groaning softly. She stiffened with fear when his hand went under her skirt, moving up her leg, touching her.

'What are you doing? Stop – I don't like it!' she cried, closing her legs tightly together.

'Come on, princess,' he urged. 'You love me, don't you?'

Terrified, she tried to squirm away from his probing fingers. 'Ouch! Let me go! Please, let me go,' she begged. This was wrong, her uncle was doing naughty things, hurting her, and she fought to get off his lap.

He suddenly removed his hand and shuffled to

one side. Then, before she had time to react, he picked her up and abruptly crammed her into the small space beside him. 'It's all right, darling, I'm just showing you how much I love you,' he panted, his hands fumbling with the front of his trousers.

She sat rigid with fear, staring with wide-eyed horror as he got his thing out, holding it clenched in his fist as he thrust it towards her.

'Here, Sally,' he urged, his eyes glazed and dark. 'You hold it.'

'No!' she yelped, frantically trying to move away, but finding herself trapped as he leaned over her.

'Come on, Sally,' he cajoled, while his other hand began to travel up her leg again.

She opened her mouth to scream – and the door opened.

Ruth stood rooted in the doorway, frozen in disbelief. No, it couldn't be, her eyes were deceiving her. A surge of hot, intense rage suddenly infused her mind, freeing her feet and propelling her across the room. She grabbed Sally's arm, yanking her out of the chair with such force that she landed in a heap on the floor.

'You dirty bastard, you animal, she's only ten years old!' she cried, as her hands lashed out, beating Harry again and again around his face and head, while he cowered, his arms held up protectively.

'Ruth, Ruth, stop it, what on earth are you doing?'

Mary's voice penetrated her wall of fury and she could feel hands tugging at her clothes. 'Get off me!' she yelled, arms flailing. 'I'll kill him!'

'That's enough, Ruth. For God's sake, what's come over you?' Mary demanded.

Her shoulders heaving, and gasping for breath, Ruth gawked at her sister in disbelief. 'What's come over me? It ain't *me*, you soppy cow, it's *him!*' she shouted, her fingers stabbing at Harry. 'The dirty bastard was trying it on with Sally. He should be locked up, the disgusting pig.'

Harry buried his face in his hands. 'I'm sorry, Ruth. Look, it wasn't what you thought.'

'What! Do you think I'm blind? I imagined seeing you with your dick in one hand and the other up my Sally's skirt, did I?'

'What was that you said, Ruth?' Sadie croaked, standing in the doorway.

Sally whimpered like a baby when she heard her gran's voice. She crawled across the room on all fours to reach her, throwing her arms around one of her legs and clinging on like a limpet. 'Please, Gran, get me out of here,' she pleaded.

Sadie threw a look of disgust at Harry before painfully reaching down to her granddaughter. 'Come on, love,' she urged. 'Come upstairs with me.'

'No, Mum, I'm taking her home, and I'll call in at the police station on the way.'

'No, no, don't get the police,' Mary begged. 'Look, I must talk to you. Please, Ruth, come into the kitchen, let me explain.'

'Explain what! No, there ain't nothing you can say to make me change my mind. How can you even think of defending him, for God's sake? Men who interfere with children are the lowest of the low.'

Mary grabbed her arm. 'Please, just five minutes, that's all I ask.'

'I'm taking Sally upstairs, Ruth, she shouldn't be hearing all this,' Sadie said.

Distracted, Ruth nodded as her mum left the room with Sally clutching her hand. Then, throwing a look of scorn at Harry, and indicating that Mary should follow her, she marched into the kitchen. 'Well come on then,' she snapped. 'Spit it out.'

Mary closed the door and leaned against it, her hand on the doorknob. 'Please, Ruth, don't get the police involved, there's no need. You see, Harry couldn't have gone any further.'

'There's no way of knowing how far he'd 'ave gone.' She swallowed rapidly, bile rising in her throat. 'Bloody hell, Mary, we only came back because you forgot your purse!'

'No – look, you don't understand.'

'What's there to understand, you soppy cow? I know what I saw and I notice he ain't rushing to defend himself.'

'Please, listen to me, Ruth. Harry ... well, he couldn't have gone any further, because ... because he's impotent,' she blurted out, her face flooding with colour.

Ruth said disgustedly, 'Don't give me that. There ain't nothing wrong with him, not from what I saw. How can you lie for that sick pig?' Pushing Mary aside she yanked open the door. 'I'll never forgive you for this, and I'm still getting him nicked,' she warned, stomping upstairs and thrusting open her mum's bedroom door. 'Come on, Sally, we're going.'

Sally had never seen her mum so angry and edged closer to her gran as they lay side by side on the bed.

'Ruth,' Sadie urged, 'before you think about going to the police, 'ave you thought about a certain person having to give evidence?'

Was her gran talking about her? Sally worried. Was her mum going to take her to the police station? She burrowed her head into her gran's side as she listened to their conversation.

'What do you expect me to do, Mum – let him get away with it?'

'I don't know, but I think you should sleep on it before you make any decisions.'

'Oh, it's no good, I can't talk about it now. My head's splitting and I can't think straight. Look, I'll see you next... Oh no, Mum! What are we going to do? I ain't coming round here again.'

'No, Ruth, please don't say that. I couldn't bear it if I didn't see yer both. Can't you come round when Harry's away?'

Sally lifted her head slightly, peeping up out of the corner of her eyes. Her gran sounded so sad and her mum's face was stiff with anger. She held her breath, waiting for her reply.

'It ain't just Harry, it's Mary too,' she answered, her voice shrill. 'For God's sake, how could she stick up for him? No, I'll never forgive her, and I don't ever want to see her again.'

Tears filled Sally's eyes and she hunkered up closer to her gran, throwing an arm around her waist.

'Look at this poor kid, Ruth. God knows what effect this will 'ave on her. I really think you should take her home now.'

'Yeah, all right, Mum. Now come on, Sally,' she added tersely, 'get yourself up.'

'Ruth, don't talk to her like that. It ain't the child's fault,' Sadie admonished.

'I know that, Mum. But I'm just so bleedin' angry.'

Sally sat up reluctantly, cuffed her wet face on the sleeve of her cardigan, and dragged her legs over the side of the bed, too frightened to look at her mum.

'Listen, ducks,' her gran said, as she lifted Sally's chin with her forefinger and gazed into her eyes. 'You didn't do anything wrong and I want you to remember that.' She then gave her a quick hug. 'Bye for now, sweetheart, and don't you worry. I'll see you soon, I promise.'

As they went downstairs Sally saw her mum glaring icily at auntie Mary as they passed her in the hall. She had a brief glimpse of her uncle, still sitting in the chair, and then they were outside, her mum slamming the door behind them.

She ran and stumbled, dragged up the street as her mother's heels beat an impatient tattoo on the pavement.

'For Christ's sake, Sally, will you move yerself. Your dad will go mad if I don't get something for his dinner and I haven't done any shopping yet.'

In a daze Sally was hauled onto a bus where she huddled as far away from her mother as possible, gazing miserably out of the window. She shifted uncomfortably, sore from where her uncle's

71

fingers had probed. Why had he touched her like that? He said he loved her, but he had hurt her, frightened her.

As they passed over the railway bridge at Clapham Junction a train chugged through the tunnel beneath them, belching out a cloud of smoke that momentarily engulfed the bus, giving the illusion of time suspending for a few seconds. Sally turned as the mist cleared, finding her mum glaring at her, tight-lipped.

'Move yourself,' she snapped. 'We're getting off here.'

Startled, Sally lurched down the aisle, and as they got off the bus the police station loomed into view. Her breath caught in her throat and she dragged her heels as they drew near to the entrance. 'Mum, please don't take me in there,' she begged, frantically trying to pull out of her grasp. 'I'm sorry. I won't sit on me uncle's lap again – honest, I won't.'

'Bloody hell, Sally, what on earth's the matter with you! Take you in where? We're going to the shops, that's all.'

Her body slumped with relief. 'I ... I thought you was taking me to the police.'

'Don't be daft, why would I do that? Now come on, I must get some shopping.'

'But you told gran you were going to the police station.'

'Well I'm not, so just shut up about it.'

They dashed from shop to shop. The greengrocer's, the butcher's, then the baker's, her mum grumbling about the prices as her bags gradually filled, until at last they were on their way home.

Sally stood behind her mother, watching as she opened the front door. Stepping inside, Ruth turned swiftly, her fingers to her lips as she pointed to the coat-rack.

'Quick, Sal,' she hissed. 'Go upstairs, yer dad's home.'

Ken looked up in surprise when the kitchen door opened and Ruth stumbled in, looking pale and agitated. She dropped two full bags of shopping on the floor, dragged out a chair and sat with her elbows on the table, head buried in her hands.

'Ken, something terrible happened at Mary's,' she groaned.

'Oh yeah? Something's happened to your stuck-up sister, has it? Oh, my heart bleeds,' he sneered sarcastically.

'Please, Ken, please don't be nasty,' she begged, bursting into a torrent of tears. 'I just can't take any more.' Shaking violently as reaction set in, she sobbed, 'It ... it was H-Harry, he was trying it on with Sally. I ... I caught him with his hands up her skirt.'

'What!' he exclaimed, flabbergasted by Ruth's words. Bloody hell – fancy Harry being a nonce. His thoughts raced. Part of him was disgusted, and yet another part was wondering how he could turn this to his advantage.

'I wanna report it to the police, Ken, but I'm worried about Sally. Will they make her give evidence in court?'

'Why ask me, how would I know?' he answered irritably, rubbing the back of his neck, his mind turning over the possibilities. He was desperate

73

for some extra cash and might be able to use this knowledge to get some money out of Harry, but that would mean keeping the police out of it. I'll have to play for time, he thought. String Ruth along until I can think things through.

Feigning concern he walked across to the table, and standing behind his wife, he placed his hands on her shoulders, massaging them gently. 'Come on, love, you can't make any decisions while you're in this state. Why don't we talk about it again tomorrow when you've calmed down a bit. I tell you what, don't bother to cook anything, I'll pop down the road and get us some fish and chips.'

Ruth looked at him gratefully through her tears. 'Oh Ken, thanks ever so much.' She grabbed her handbag, fumbling for her purse. 'Here, I'll give you the money.'

'No, it's all right. I'll treat yer,' he said, hiding a smirk at her look of amazement.

He reached the chip shop, rebuking himself for offering to pay. Money was a bit tight at the moment because Barbara was costing him a fortune. His groin stirred as he remembered the previous night. God, she had been insatiable, and he couldn't wait to see her again. Blimey, it was lucky that Ruth was such a gullible twit. She had swallowed it without question when he told her he was taking on long-distance deliveries. He chuckled – it had been a great idea coming up with that one and it gave him the perfect excuse for his nights spent with Barbara.

'Cod and chips twice,' he ordered, reaching the front of the queue. He wasn't getting anything for the brat, she could share her mother's portion.

Chapter Eight

Barbara stood in front of the mirror putting the finishing touches to her make-up. Hmm, not bad, she thought, smoothing her platinum-blonde hair into a sleek bob, but me roots could do with a touch-up. She bared her teeth to check they weren't smudged with lipstick, then turned her head at an angle, imitating a seductive pout. Yeah, she thought happily, remembering what one of the regulars in the pub had remarked. I do look a bit like Diana Dors.

Her eyes flicked to the clock and she grimaced. It was nearly time to start her Sunday lunchtime shift. Glancing over her shoulder, she looked at the backs of her legs, pleased to see that her stocking seams were straight, and then ran a cursory glance around the room.

Not much longer, she thought, and I'll be out of this dump, with Ken as my meal ticket. Her brightly painted lips curved into a smile as she pictured his dark, gypsy looks. She fancied him rotten, and that was a bonus after some of the sleazy gits she had put up with during the last few years.

Time was running out though; her last boyfriend was due out of prison in three months. He was a nasty piece of work, and she wanted to be away from Balham before his release. I'll just have to push Ken a bit harder, she thought.

It was nearly one o'clock before Ken turned up at the pub, and her eyes widened as he approached the bar. There was an air of suppressed excitement about him and his dark eyes sparkled with mischief.

'Give us a pint, Babs, and 'ave a drink yourself,' he grinned, giving her a cheeky wink.

'You're looking pleased with yourself. Come up on the Pools, 'ave you?'

'No, but something else has turned up, and if things go well, we could be away soon.'

Her heart skipped a beat. 'Oh Ken, do you really mean it?'

'Oi, Babs, how about serving down here? That's if you can tear yourself away from Lover Boy,' a customer shouted.

'Sorry, darling,' she whispered. 'Back in a minute. Yeah, what can I get you?' she asked the customer impatiently, barely giving him a glance.

'I'll 'ave a pint of me usual, and you'd better watch your step if you don't want yer pretty face ruined.'

'What did you say? Are you threatening me?'

'Oh, ain't you heard the news? It's not like you to miss out on the grapevine, Babs.' He grinned maliciously. 'No, it ain't me you've got to worry about. Your bloke's been paroled. He's due out next week, and from what I've heard, he don't like his birds playing fast and loose with him.'

Barbara's fingers tightened involuntarily on the glass as she forced her mouth into a smile. 'Yeah, of course I've heard,' she lied. 'Here you are, one pint of bitter, that'll be one and tuppence, please.' Snatching his money, she threw it into the till,

76

then with her head held high and trying to look unconcerned, she rejoined Ken at the other end of the bar.

'You look a bit pale. Was that bloke giving you stick?' he asked.

'No, it's all right, I can handle the likes of him. I'm just a bit tired, that's all. Thank God me shift's nearly over. You are coming back to my place, aren't you?'

'Yeah, of course I am, and I've got something to tell you, but I don't want to talk about it in here.'

Barbara's right, Ken thought, as he hurried to Mary's house. She had told him to strike while the iron was hot, pointing out that even though he'd persuaded Ruth not to go to the police, she might change her mind.

'I wanna see Harry,' he demanded when Mary answered his knock, staring at him in panic.

'You had better come in,' she said, her voice trembling.

'No, I ain't coming in. Get him out here – and now!' he shouted when he saw her hesitate.

'All right, I'm here,' Harry said, appearing in the doorway. 'Mary, go inside. It would be better if you leave us alone,' he urged.

Ken smirked. 'Yeah, off you go, love. This might be a bit delicate for your sensitive ears. Now come on, Harry, get yer coat on. You and me are going for a little walk.'

'Please, Ken. Please don't hurt him,' Mary begged.

'It's all right, dear,' Harry said, pushing her gently inside and grabbing his coat from the hallstand. 'I won't be long.'

As they walked along side by side, Ken decided to keep quiet until they reached Tooting Common; it would build up the tension to let Harry sweat for a while.

The street was deserted, the sky grey with a hint of rain in the air as they reached the Common. Ken walked across the damp grass to sit on the nearest bench, glancing around to make sure nobody was in earshot. 'So, what 'ave you got to say for yourself?,' he demanded.

Harry sat down beside him, saying earnestly, 'Ken, listen, this whole thing has been blown up out of all proportion. I think the world of Sally and I was just giving her a little cuddle.'

'Don't give me that! From what Ruth told me, it was more than a cuddle... Anyway,' he added, turning the screw, 'she's going to report it to the police.'

Harry turned, his expression agonised. 'To tell you the truth, I've been expecting them. Mary and I hardly slept a wink last night and I'm surprised that they haven't been round already.'

'Well, you've got me to thank for that. Ruth was in such a state that I persuaded her to wait until today.'

'Please, Ken, think about the effect it will have on Mary, and Sadie. Can't you do something to stop her?'

'If you was only giving Sally a cuddle, why are you so worried? No, don't bother to deny it again Harry.' He smiled sardonically, adding, 'However, there may be a way to keep the police out of it.'

'How? Just name it, I'll do anything,' Harry

said eagerly.

Ken folded his arms and leaned back nonchalantly, his legs stretched out. 'Well now, let me see ... what's it worth to keep Ruth quiet?'

'Money!' Harry looked at him in disgust. 'You want money?'

'Don't look at me as if I'm something that crawled out from under a stone. After all, it ain't me that fancies little girls. Yeah, they love your sort in the nick,' he threatened.

'Oh God!' Harry buried his face in his hands, his voice muffled as he finally said, 'All right, how much do you want?'

Ken smiled – before going in for the kill.

Meanwhile, Barbara lounged on her bed, waiting anxiously for Ken to return. If it worked and he managed to get some money out of his brother-in-law, her troubles would be over. Less than a week, she thought, that's all the time I've got left to get out of this area. She reached across to the bedside table and picked up her nail varnish. Come on, come on, hurry up, Ken, she thought impatiently, as she painted another coat of bright red varnish on top of the old one.

At last there was a knock on her door and she jumped off the bed excitedly, rushing across the room to open it. Ken stood on the threshold, a wide smile on his face.

'It worked, Babs. I'm getting five hundred quid out of him.'

'Oh Ken, you're wonderful,' she cried, throwing herself into his arms. I've only got to persuade him that we need to leave straight away, she

79

thought, and I'm home and dry. 'Well done,' she crooned, rubbing against him suggestively. 'Oh, I can't wait for us to be together all the time. Can we go as soon as you get the money?'

He kicked the door shut with his heel, tightening his arms around her and nibbling her earlobe as he mumbled, 'What's the rush? I might be able to bleed some more out of him later.'

'Well, there is that, I suppose,' she said, thinking frantically. 'But it could be a bit risky, darling. What if Ruth still decides to go to the police? Harry's bound to tell them you've been blackmailing him.'

He stiffened, stepping back abruptly. 'Christ, you may be right. Look, I can't stay the night now. I'll 'ave to go home and make sure Ruth keeps her mouth shut.' He paused, brow furrowed in thought. 'All right, here's what we'll do. I'll pack me gear tonight and take it with me when I meet Harry at his bank in the morning. Then, once I've got the money, I'll meet you at Clapham Junction Station and we can leave straight away.'

'Yeah, all right, Ken. What time will you be there?'

'Let's say at around eleven o'clock.'

'Ken, we ain't decided where we're going yet,' Barbara reminded him. 'Where do you fancy?'

'I dunno, I ain't given it a lot of thought. North or South, Babs? It's up to you.'

She closed her eyes momentarily. South ... no, that would be too obvious. North would be better; nobody would expect them to head in that direction. 'How about Blackpool, Ken? I've always fancied going there.'

'Whatever you say, love. We can always move on if we don't like it.'

She smiled in satisfaction, he was so easy to manipulate and pushing her way back into his arms, she husked, 'Eleven o'clock at the Junction. I'll be waiting, darling.' She began to grind her hips, pushing herself closer and closer, feeling him stir and harden against her.

'Oh Barbara,' he groaned, picking her up and crossing to the bed, his eyes dark with lust.

Their lovemaking had been passionate, and now Barbara lounged satiated against the headboard, one arm thrown back supporting her head, and deep in thought. Ken was getting five hundred quid from Harry, but would it be enough? She had always wanted to live by the sea and dreamed of having a little bed and breakfast place of her own, but until Ken mentioned his scam that was all it had been – a dream.

She thought about the King's Head and the years spent grafting behind the bar. The landlord was a lazy bugger, leaving her to do most of the work and only showing his face when she wanted a barrel changed. He even left her to do the cashing up after every shift, trusting her to put the money in the safe, and just checking it before paying it into the bank every week.

An idea began to form and she narrowed her eyes. It was no more than the lazy git deserved; after all, she was the one who did all the work.

Chapter Nine

Sally awoke to the sound of raised and angry voices. She stumbled sleepily out of bed, rubbing her eyes with her knuckles as she crept nervously onto the landing, listening to the row downstairs.

'No, Ken, no! You can't leave me!'

'Get out of my way, you silly bitch.'

'No I won't, you can't go!'

'Move, Ruth. I won't tell you again.'

There was a scream, followed by a scuffle, and her dad appeared in the kitchen doorway, carrying a suitcase in each hand. Sally ducked down, terrified he would see her.

She peeped over the banisters again, just in time to see her mum grabbing his arm, her face twisted in anguish.

'No, no, please don't leave me!' she cried. 'What will I do without you? Please, Ken, why are you going? What 'ave I done?'

'Done! You ask me what you've done?' he spat. ''Ave you looked in the mirror lately? You're a bleeding mess. But worst of all you landed me with a cuckoo in the nest and I'm sick to death of the pair of you.'

He jerked his arm violently, trying to loosen her grip. 'As for what you'll do without me, you can get yourself a job or sell your body – though looking at the state of you there won't be many customers,' he said cruelly. 'Now, let go of me arm, or you'll be sorry.'

Sally watched anxiously as they tussled together. Her mum was hanging on desperately, refusing to let go. 'Get off me, or I'll smash yer bloody face in!' he yelled.

To Sally, her dad suddenly took on the form of the devil. His face, contorted in anger, looked dark and evil. He was going to hit her mum again – she had to stop him!

A surge of anger and hate suddenly catapulted her down the stairs and she flew across the hall. 'Leave her alone, you bully!' she yelled, running up and kicking him, feeling agonising pain as her bare foot connected with his shin. His arm came up, and the last thing she remembered before blackness descended, was the feeling of flying through the air.

Ruth stood paralysed looking at her daughter lying crumpled on the floor; her eyes still filled with the sight of Ken lashing out at Sally before he slammed out of the door. Oh, my God, she thought, she's dead, he's killed her! What sort of mother am I? Why didn't I protect her? Oh my baby – my beautiful baby. She slumped down onto the floor, reaching out to touch Sally's face. It felt cold, so cold.

With a hand covering her mouth in horror she stumbled to her feet and staggered into the kitchen, half-falling onto a chair.

Leaning forward, arms wrapped around her waist, Ruth rocked back and forth, oblivious to the keening, wailing sounds that were torn from her throat. Tears cascaded unchecked down her face. She was wrapped in a nightmare, an agony of self-recrimination. It should be me that's dead, she thought, over and over again. I ain't fit to live.

Gradually her thoughts became still, and numbness permeated her mind. She felt as though she was sinking into a black tunnel of oblivion, and went willingly. It was safe there; nothing could ever touch her again.

Elsie impatiently drummed her fingers on the table. 'I don't care what you say, Bert, I'm going round there. Something's wrong, I just know it.'

'Don't interfere, Elsie, it's none of our business.'

'I can't just leave it, love. First there was that terrible row, and now for over half an hour it's been deathly quiet. I'm worried sick.'

'All right, all right,' he said, holding up his hands in a gesture of surrender.

She scurried out anxiously. 'Ruth, Ruth, are you there?' she called, banging loudly on the door. 'Come on, Ruth, let me in!'

Peggy Green and Joan Mason appeared at her side, their faces concerned. 'We heard the commotion earlier on. What's going on, Elsie?' Joan asked.

'I don't know, but I'm worried,' she told them, bending down to look through the letterbox. Elsie couldn't see much, just the bottom of the stairs, but then, as her eyes adjusted to the gloom, she saw what looked like a leg.

'Bert, Bert!' she screamed, rushing back to her own front door. 'Come quick, I need your help.'

'Yes, you're right,' he said, peering through the letterbox. 'I don't like the look of it.' He stood up, turning to Elsie with concern in his eyes. 'We need to get in there – and quick by the look of it.' Lifting his foot he ordered, 'Stand back, I'm going to break the door in.'

Glancing around, Elsie saw Arthur and Ann hovering behind her. 'Get inside, you two,' she snapped, noticing other neighbours standing on their doorsteps, watching the scene with avid interest.

There was a loud crash when Bert kicked the door, and as it flew open Elsie rushed in, her face paling at the sight of Sally lying crumpled on the floor like a broken doll. 'Sally, Sally,' she cried, rushing to kneel at her side, heaving a sigh of relief when she heard a faint groan. Oh God, where was Ruth? She wouldn't leave her daughter like this. 'Bert, look after Sally. I must see if Ruth's all right.'

As Elsie entered the kitchen, her eyes stretched in amazement. Ruth was sitting in a chair, a glasslike expression in her eyes as she stared into the dying embers of the fire. 'Ruth, are you all right?' Elsie asked anxiously, hurrying to her side, her face creasing with concern when there was no response.

'Elsie, I don't like the look of Sally, I think we should call the doctor.'

'What? Yes, all right, Bert, but something's wrong with Ruth too. Look, can you carry her into our place? I'll bring Sally. We can't leave them in here, it's freezing, and anyway Ken might come back.'

'That bastard had better not show his face around here again. I can't stand a man who hits women and children,' Bert said darkly, bending to pick Ruth up. 'Christ, there's nothing of her, she's all skin and bones.'

Elsie was shocked to hear Bert swear, but didn't blame him; she'd like to get her hands on Ken too. Gently lifting Sally and holding her close to her chest, she followed her husband out of the house.

Earlier, in Balham, Barbara had quietly opened the side door of the pub. With bated breath she crept into the hall, padded to the bottom of the stairs and strained her ears for sounds of movement from above. Her nerves were taut and she sighed with relief at the sound of rumbling snores. It was seven o'clock in the morning, and just as she thought, the lazy git was still asleep – he didn't usually surface until after ten.

Creeping into the back room, she closed the door softly behind her, leaning against it for a moment while her eyes adjusted to the gloom.

Every sound seemed accentuated as she knelt in front of the safe. The noise of the dial spinning sounded like the rattle of a roulette wheel. The clang of the handle as she yanked it down appeared to echo loudly in the small room.

Tensing, she paused, her heart thumping as she gazed up at the ceiling. Then, drawing in a deep gulp of air in an effort to compose herself, she pulled open the heavy door, eyes gleaming as she grabbed the small stack of notes. Ignoring the coppers, she stuffed bags of silver into her shopping bag, pleased that two darts matches in the bar that week had swelled the takings. Lowering her head, she gave the bottom shelf a cursory glance that revealed a metal box secreted at the back, partially covered by a black cloth. Her eyes narrowed. I haven't seen that before, she thought, snatching it and stuffing it quickly into her bag.

She left hurriedly, anxious to pick up her suitcase from the flat. It was far too early to meet Ken, but she couldn't risk hanging about. The sooner she got away the better.

With her case in one hand and the heavy shopping bag slung over her shoulder, she hurried to Clapham Junction, making her way to Joe's Café. Ordering a cup of tea, she sat dragging nervously on her cigarette while glancing anxiously at the clock. Bloody hell, she had ages to wait yet, and her nerves were jangling.

She stared absentmindedly at the scene behind the counter. Joe was busily cooking a batch of sausages with a fag sticking out of the corner of his mouth, and every time he took a puff, the ash on the end grew longer and longer. To distract herself she counted the seconds, trying to anticipate when it would break off and fall into the frying pan. It dropped, smack in the middle, and she blinked as Joe just carried on turning the sausages. The dirty old sod, she thought. He should be shut down.

Raising the thick white cup to her lips, she grimaced with distaste at the bitter acrid tea. One more hour, that was all, and they would be on their way. Finally, unable to sit any longer, she left the café and went outside.

'Ken, Ken, over here,' she called from her vantage point on the corner, thankful that at last, he had arrived. Picking up her suitcase and heaving her shopping bag over her shoulder again, she rushed to meet him. 'Is everything all right? Did you get the money?'

'Yeah, it was a piece of cake. He was putty in me hands.'

'I've asked at the enquiry desk and we 'ave to go to Euston to catch a train to Blackpool.'

'Good girl. Come on then, let's go. I don't want to hang about round here.'

They made it to Euston just as a train was due to depart, and running down the platform jumped into a compartment, surprised but pleased to find it empty.

Now, sitting beside Ken, Barbara watched the scenery changing from town to countryside. She took a deep breath, turning to face him, wondering what his reaction would be. 'Ken, I've got something to tell you.' Fidgeting nervously in her seat she added, 'I ... I er ... I done something before we left.'

'Oh yeah?' His eyes narrowed. 'Spit it out then.'

'I turned over the King's Head, had it away with the week's takings.'

'You what?' Ken spluttered.

'The money's in me shopping bag.'

'You stupid bleedin' cow!' Jumping up in agitation, he gripped the luggage rack to steady himself as the train swayed, saying hoarsely, 'Christ, Barbara, don't you realise what you've done?'

'But, Ken, I thought it would help us. If we pool our money we could buy a house and start a bed and breakfast business. We could make a bomb in Blackpool.'

He flopped onto the seat opposite her, raking

his fingers through his hair. 'My God, you silly bitch. Don't you realise we was in the clear, with nobody after us.' He raised his eyes then, asking hopefully, 'Did you make it look like a break-in?'

She shook her head. 'Well, no. I had the keys, didn't I.'

'Yeah, and now when the landlord reports the robbery, who do you think the police will be looking for?' he asked sarcastically.

Barbara closed her eyes, slumping in her seat. Why didn't I think of that, she thought. Oh flaming hell, what have I done.

Chapter Ten

'Well, Mrs Jones,' the doctor said, closing his black bag, 'the little girl will be fine, just a slight concussion, and if she doesn't show any signs of disorientation or nausea she should recover in a few days. However, her mother is in some kind of shock, and unless she snaps out of it shortly she will have to be admitted for psychiatric care. I will need to discuss it with her husband. Do you know where he is?'

Psychiatric care? Over my dead body, Elsie thought. She'd heard some terrible things about that loony hospital. 'I've told you, Doctor. I think he's left them and I don't know where he's gone.'

'Do you know if she has any other relatives?'

'She's got a sister who lives in Tooting, but I don't know her address.'

'Hmm, well, she will need constant care until I can review her in a day or two.' He picked up his bag, adding, 'As we can't get in touch with her family, I had better make arrangements for her to be admitted straight away.'

Elsie shook her head frantically. 'There's no need for that. She can stay here and I'll look after her.'

He peered at her thoughtfully over the top of his half-moon glasses. 'Are you sure it won't be too much for you, Mrs Jones?'

'No, of course not. I can manage,' she assured him.

After a slight pause, he nodded slowly. 'Very well, but if she doesn't show any signs of recovery by Wednesday, she will have to go into hospital.'

Elsie heaved a sigh of relief and after showing the doctor out, she went back upstairs. Finding Sally asleep, and tucking the blankets around her, she crossed into Arthur's room to see Ruth. 'Sally's going to be fine,' she told her. 'Now can I get you anything, love? A cup of tea perhaps?'

There was no response. Ruth was staring into space, the glasslike expression still in her eyes. 'Come on, talk to me,' Elsie begged, but there was no answer, and not even a glimmer of movement.

Shaking her head sadly, the chubby little woman sat on the side of the bed, gently stroking the hair back from her friend's forehead.

By early afternoon Elsie's legs were feeling the strain as she trod heavily up the stairs again. Peggy had called earlier offering to help, and soon after that Nelly Cox. She tightened her lips. A few others had been round, but it soon became obvious that they were only after gossip.

Christ, she thought, it hadn't taken long for the news to spread that Ruth's husband had run out on her. Still, there were some good neighbours in Candle Lane, the salt of the earth most of them, but knowing what a private person Ruth was, she had assured both Peggy and Nelly that she could manage.

Now she quietly entered Ann's room and sat down beside Sally, gently bathing her forehead with a damp cloth.

'Mum, my head hurts,' she whimpered, her eyelids beginning to flicker.

'Shh, darling.' Elsie soothed. 'You've had a nasty bump, but rest quietly and you'll soon feel better.'

Sally turned her head, groaning with pain at the sudden movement. 'Where's me mum? I want me mum.'

'It's all right, darling, you'll be able to see her soon. She's not far away, just next door in Arthur's room.'

'Why can't she come in here to see me? Is there something wrong with her?' she asked anxiously, struggling to sit up but falling back on the pillows, her face contorted with pain.

'There, there, it's nothing to worry about,' Elsie crooned. 'Your mum's just a bit poorly, that's all.'

She watched Sally trying to fight the exhaustion that clouded her eyes, relieved when with a sigh she sank into her pillows, almost immediately falling asleep again.

Poor little love, she thought, quietly closing the door and making her way to Arthur's room, wrinkling her nose at the smell that assailed her nostrils as she entered. Shaking her head sadly, Elsie approached the bed. 'Come on, dear, let's get you nice and dry,' she urged, gently raising Ruth's arms to take off her wet nightdress.

There was no resistance when she rolled her first to one side, then the other, deftly whipping away the sodden sheet. The same procedure was carried out in reverse and, as she lowered one of her own ample nightdresses over Ruth's head, she tried to get some response from her friend. 'Sally woke up just now, she looks a lot better and I think she'll be able to pay you a visit soon.'

'She just stares into space, Bert!' Elsie exclaimed on returning to the kitchen, the sopping sheets tucked under her arm. 'I'll give these a soak. Poor Ruth, she must be in a bad way to wet the bed.'

'Elsie, are you sure you're not taking on too much? How are you going to cope if Ruth carries on like this?'

'I'll manage, and anyway, I'm sure she'll be all right soon. What else could I do, Bert? She's my friend and I couldn't let her go into the loony hospital, I'd never forgive myself.'

'I'm sorry I can't be of more help, but I've got to go to Richmond this evening. We've been asked to give an estimate for quite a big job.' He shook his head worriedly as he studied her face. 'You look tired, love.'

'I'll be fine, stop worrying.' She stood on tiptoe, snaking her arms around his neck, and holding her face up for a kiss.

Bert grinned, and putting his hands under her arms, he lifted her up effortlessly. With her feet dangling about nine inches from the floor, Elsie pounded playfully on his chest. 'Put me down, you brute,' she joked.

He pulled her towards him and planted a smacking kiss on her lips, before lowering her to the floor. 'There, you little spitfire,' he laughed, patting her on her backside. 'I'm off, I'll see you later.'

Elsie sat by Sally, deep in thought. It had been two days now and Ruth was showing no signs of improvement. She had just changed the sheets again and had managed to get her to drink a little soup, but there was still no response. It was like looking after a rag doll. If Ruth didn't snap out of it by tomorrow, she feared the doctor would insist that she be admitted to the psychiatric hospital. She felt helpless. How could she protect her friend?

Puffing out her cheeks, she glanced at the bedside clock. The kids would be home from school soon and she still had to get the dinner on. 'Hello,' she smiled, as Sally suddenly opened her eyes. 'Are you feeling any better?'

'Yeah, me head doesn't hurt so much now,' she answered, struggling to sit up. 'Can I see me mum?'

Elsie looked into Sally's worried eyes. It had been the devil of a job to keep her in bed for the last forty-eight hours and she was running out of excuses. 'Look, pet, your mum still isn't very well, but I'll take you in to see her. Don't worry if she seems a bit strange, she may not talk to you or anything, but that's because she's very tired. Now come on, I'll help you up, you may feel a bit giddy at first.'

'There now,' Elsie said as they stood beside Ruth. 'She's asleep, so we had better not disturb her.'

'But she's got her eyes open. Can I stay in here, please? I'll be ever so quiet, honest,' Sally appealed, her voice high.

Ruth stirred and Elsie's heart leaped. Was that a flicker of response in her eyes? Was it Sally's voice she was responding to? 'It looks like your mum's waking up, Sally. I tell you what, sit in that chair and you can talk to her. She might be a bit muzzy-headed, darling, but don't let it worry you.'

'Mum, it's me, are you all right?' Sally asked worriedly as she leaned over in the chair, grasping her mother's hand.

Elsie watched as Ruth turned her head, her face no longer glazed but filled with confusion. 'Sally,' she croaked. 'Sally, is it really you?'

'Yes, Mum, of course it is.'

There was a choking sound followed by a loud wail, and tears spurted from Ruth's eyes. Her voice rose in anguish. 'You're alive!' she cried. 'Oh, my baby, you're alive!'

'Mum, Mum, don't cry,' Sally begged, throwing herself onto the bed and into her mother's arms.

Elsie felt a lump in her throat as she watched them clinging to each other, her own eyes filling with tears. Thank God, she thought, thank God.

A week later Sally was sitting at the kitchen table, and other than the sore bump on her head, she was fully recovered.

'So your mum's all right now, Sal?'

'I dunno, Ann, she still won't get out of bed and

she just wants to sleep all the time.'

'Yeah, and it's my bed she won't get out of. I'm fed up with sleeping on the sofa.'

'You selfish pig, Arthur, no wonder you can't make any friends,' Ann snapped, glaring at her brother.

'Well, that's where you're wrong, clever clogs. I've got lots of friends now and mum said I can go camping with them in August – so there!' he shouted, sticking out his tongue and wagging it at his sister.

'Oh, you make me sick,' Ann said huffily, rising from her chair. 'Come on, Sally, let's go upstairs to my room.'

'Huh, well at least you've got a room to go to, even if you are sharing it with her. It's all right for you.'

'Arthur,' Sally placated, 'I'm sorry that you've got to sleep on the sofa, but I'm sure it won't be for much longer.'

He lowered his head, avoiding her eyes. 'Yeah, right,' he mumbled.

Following Ann upstairs, she wished her mum would get out of bed so they could go home. She liked being with Ann, and Elsie was lovely, but when Bert came home she felt sick with nerves, especially when he pulled Ann onto his lap. Her heart would pound uncomfortably, wondering if he would do the same naughty things as Uncle Harry.

'Arthur really gets on my nerves,' Ann said grumpily, plonking herself on the side of the bed. 'Still, mum said the doctor's due in the morning and he might let you come back to school.'

Sally hung her head as she perched beside her friend. She didn't care about school; she just wanted her mum to get better. It was worry and shock that had caused Ruth's illness, she had overheard Elsie telling Bert. And that's my fault, she thought guiltily. First I sat on me uncle's lap so he did naughty things, and Mum was really upset about that. Then soon after me dad left because he can't stand the sight of me.

Her mind grappled with the memory of something her dad had shouted, something that had puzzled her. She played the scene over in her mind and at last the memory returned. 'What's a cuckoo, Ann?'

'It's a bird, I think. Why do you want to know?'

'Me dad said he was landed with a cuckoo in his nest and I think he was talking about me.'

Ann scratched her head. 'What a funny thing to say. Why would he call you a cuckoo? Here, hold on a minute, I've got a book about birds somewhere. Perhaps we can look it up.'

She scurried across the room; her neck craning as she surveyed the rows of neatly laid out books. 'Here it is,' she said, returning to sit on the bed and flicking the pages, 'slim and long-tailed like a medium-sized falcon. It inhabits woodland, farmland, heath and scrub.' She turned to gaze at her friend. 'Well, that's not much help, is it?'

The door opened and Elsie poked her head into the room. 'Your mum's gone off to sleep, Sally, so don't disturb her. I'm just going down to get the dinner ready.'

'Wait a minute, Mum,' Anne called. 'Do you know anything about cuckoos?'

'They're birds.'

'We know that, but what does it mean if someone says they've got one in their nest?'

'What! Where did you hear that? Who said it?' Elsie asked, her voice high.

'Me dad,' Sally answered. 'He told Mum he was leaving 'cos she'd landed him with a cuckoo.'

Elsie ran a hand over her face before lifting veiled eyes, and gulping audibly she said, 'I don't know what he meant, but I'm sure it's nothing to worry about.' Her head then disappeared abruptly, and it wasn't long before they heard her heavy tread going downstairs.

Sally sat swinging her feet, gazing at the floor, her hands clutched between her knees. Why had Elsie acted so strangely? She looked almost frightened by her question.

'I've got something to tell you, Ruth' Elsie said later that evening, sitting on the side of Arthur's bed. 'It's something Sally asked me about, and I didn't know what to say.'

Ruth sighed wearily, wishing that Elsie would leave her alone. She was constantly coming in to chat to her, trying to arouse her interest, but she didn't want to talk, didn't want to think. All she wanted to do was sleep – it was her only escape.

'Did you hear what I said, Ruth?'

'Yeah, all right, Elsie. What did Sally want?'

'She asked me what it means if you've got a cuckoo in your nest.'

Ruth stiffened. 'Oh no ... please, I don't want to talk about it. I'm tired, just let me sleep.'

'Now come on, snap out of it, love. You heard

what the doctor said. If you don't pull yourself together he'll have you admitted to the psychiatric hospital. Is that what you really want? You've got to talk – get it all off of your chest, and who would you rather talk to – me, or a psychiatrist?'

Lying quietly, Ruth found that Elsie's words were penetrating the lethargy that clouded her mind, making her limbs feel like leaden weights. Would it help? she thought. Would talking about her secret make it any easier to bear? 'Sally ain't Ken's child,' she suddenly blurted out, and somehow just saying the words lifted the burden a little.

'I think I'd already guessed that. Would you like to tell me about it?'

'Yeah, I think so, but you're going to be disgusted with me. I'm a bad person, Elsie.'

'No, you're not. We all make mistakes, Ruth, and nobody's perfect.'

'But I'm really bad. You see, it happened when Ken was posted overseas during the war. I hadn't had a letter from him for nearly eighteen months and it was awful, Elsie, I didn't know if he was dead or alive. I was so lonely too. Then one of the girls I worked with on the buses persuaded me to go to a dance and I ... I er ... met a bloke.' Her fingers picked at the blankets nervously, too ashamed to look Elsie in the eye. 'His name was Andy and he was lovely. Tall, with curly red hair and a sprinkle of freckles across his nose. And his smile, it was so cheeky and infectious.' She sighed, her eyes clouding. 'We went out together a few times while he was on leave, and ... well, one thing sort of led to another.'

'And you got pregnant,' Elsie murmured.

'Yeah, but by the time I found out, he'd rejoined his unit.' Shaking her head sadly she added, 'And I never saw him again.'

'Did he know you were pregnant, Ruth?'

'I wrote to tell him, care of his regiment, but just after that Ken came home on leave. There was no way I could hide it from him, Elsie, I was starting to show.' Her voice rose. 'Do you know, he was lovely then. Of course he was furious at first, and we had a huge row, but in the end he said he couldn't live without me. He promised that he'd take the child on and bring it up as his own.'

'What did you do about Andy?'

'When Ken's leave was over I sent another letter to Andy. I lied – told him that I wasn't pregnant, that it had been a false alarm. He must 'ave been relieved because he confessed that he was married too, with a small son, and like me he didn't want to break up his marriage.' She slumped back onto the pillows. 'That was the last contact I had with him, and I don't even know if he survived the war.'

'What happened when Ken came home again?' Elsie asked.

'When Sally was born a redhead I didn't realise the effect it would 'ave on Ken. He didn't see her until he was demobbed, and after just one look at her, he went absolutely mad. He was convinced that nobody would believe she was his child and he became really deranged. Every time anyone looked at her he imagined they were smirking. Then he started saying his friends were making sly innuendoes. In the end he insisted that we

99

move away from Balham.'

'And that didn't help, I take it?' Elsie observed.

'No. He did try for a while, but just looking at Sally used to wind him up. There was one occasion when he hit out at her. The poor kid, she was only three years old, and ran up to him when he came home from work. He shoved her violently away, as if she was poison. But I wasn't going to stand for that, Elsie. I told him that if he ever touched her again, I'd leave him.'

'Is that why she has to stay in her room when he's around?'

'Yeah, it was safer to keep her out of his way.' Ruth frowned. 'It became like an obsession with him and he wouldn't let her play out in the street either, wanting her kept out of sight as much as possible. Christ, it's lucky the law says you 'ave to send your kids to school, or he'd 'ave stopped that too.'

'Poor Sally,' Elsie whispered.

'I always thought that if I could 'ave given him a kid of his own, he might 'ave softened, but I never got pregnant and that made him even more bitter. He used to scream at me, asking me over and over again if Sally's father was better in bed than him.'

Elsie leaned forward, stroking the back of her hand soothingly, and at her touch Ruth was unable to stop the avalanche of emotions. 'Oh God, what am I gonna do? He's left me, how can I manage on me own?'

'Shh, calm down,' Elsie soothed. 'You'll manage, love. We'll find a way, so stop worrying.'

'But what will I do for money?'

'Well, you could get a job. I can have Sally after school, she's no trouble.'

Ruth finally found herself able to look into her friend's eyes, and seeing the depths of her compassion, flung herself into her arms. 'Oh Elsie, I want me mum. I miss her so much,' she sobbed.

'Come on now, you'll soon be up and about and able to visit her.'

'Elsie, I can't, you don't understand.'

'Understand what, Ruth? Tell me,' she urged.

She told her about Harry's assault on Sally, seeing her friend's eyes darken with horror, then added hopelessly, 'So you see, I can't visit me mum.'

'Oh, poor Sally,' Elsie cried. 'No wonder she's nervous of Bert whenever he comes into the room.' She sat quietly for a while, deep in thought, then said eagerly, 'Look, I've got an idea. How about asking your mum to come and live with you now? I should think she'd be glad to get away from that Harry. It must be awful for her, having to live in the same house.'

Ruth looked at Elsie in wonderment. 'Yes – oh yes! That would be smashing and Sally would love it. 'Ave you got some paper and a pen? I want to write to her straight away and...' She paused, deflated as realisation hit her. 'But she couldn't get here. She's been housebound for years, with terrible arthritis. And there's her things – she would never leave her dresser, bed, and her other bits and pieces. They're all she's got left of her old home.'

'Well, that's nothing to worry about, is it?' Elsie grinned. 'Have you forgotten my Bert's a removal man? He'll pick up your mum, and her furniture.'

Ruth gripped her hand, her voice cracking as she said, 'Oh Elsie, I'm so glad that you moved in next door. I dunno what I'd do without you.'

'Go on, don't be daft, what are friends for? Now come on, how about some dinner. I've kept yours in the oven – are you hungry?'

'Do you know, I really think I am now,' Ruth answered. 'Will you ask Sally to bring up the pen and paper? No, wait,' she called, throwing back the blankets. 'I think I'll come downstairs.'

'Careful love, you may be a bit wobbly,' Elsie said, hurrying to her side. 'Come on then, I'll help you down. Your Sally is going to be thrilled.'

Chapter Eleven

Mary watched the tail end of the van as it rumbled down the street, only going inside when it turned the corner.

Feeling listless she climbed the stairs and entered her mum's room, empty now except for a chest of drawers. The silence of the house felt oppressive and she shivered. What was the matter with her? She had railed against her mother's disgusting habits, dunking biscuits in her tea, stuffing that revolting snuff up her nose and her interfering, always interfering. She had dreamed of having the house to herself again, but now that it was a reality, she felt bereft.

It had been dreadful since it happened, the atmosphere tense, and her mother refusing to be in the same room as Harry. She had wanted to tell her, to try to explain, but somehow she could never find the words; it was too embarrassing, too personal. Dejectedly she closed the door and went into her own room, curling on her bed in a foetal position, the memories flooding back...

It was her wedding night and she and Harry were in Brighton for their honeymoon. They had just finished dinner in the hotel, smiling at each other across the table, his hand covering hers.

She had refused any intimacy with him before their marriage; it had meant a lot to her to walk up the aisle a virgin. Of course she knew it had been hard on Harry, and during their two-year courtship there had been many moments when he had nearly exploded with frustration. Yet looking at him now and seeing the love in his eyes, she was glad she had waited. Tonight would be so very special.

'Why don't you go on up, darling,' he urged. 'I'll follow you after I've had a quick drink in the bar.'

She smiled gratefully, nervous yet excited too. Harry was so thoughtful, giving her this time to herself, and she loved him so much. He was a perfect gentleman, kind and considerate, and so handsome too with his dark brown hair and eyes.

Wallowing in a bath filled with rose-scented crystals, she felt some of the tension ease. It would be all right, she told herself; she trusted Harry, sure that he would alleviate her fears.

Stepping out of the bath she dried herself and slipped a pretty new nightdress over her head. Then, after brushing her hair, she climbed into bed to wait for him. Where was he, she wondered, her eyes growing heavy with sleep. Why was he taking so long to come up to their room?

Her next memory was of waking up to a nightmare. The room was in darkness and hands were tearing frantically at her nightdress. There was the strong stench of sour whisky as a wet mouth devoured hers, making her stomach heave. She twisted her head away, opening her mouth to scream, but a hand was placed brutally over her lips, cutting off the sound.

'Come on, you're my wife now, stop struggling.'

She froze momentarily in shock. It was Harry! Her legs flailing and her fists beating his chest, she fought to throw him off. With a swift movement he dragged her to the edge of the bed and turned her over, face down. One of his hands held both her wrists, pinning her arms above her head, while she writhed ineffectually beneath him. Then there was pain. An agony of excruciating pain, that seemed to tear her apart...

She pushed away the awful memory now and sat up, shivering. Her eyes felt gritty and she rubbed at them impatiently. Leaning back against the headboard she thought about their marriage and the sham it had become.

Harry had been so ashamed when he awoke the next morning to find her sitting awkwardly hunched in a chair, still wearing the shreds of her stained and bloody nightdress. She had reared back from him in terror when he approached her, refusing to listen when he tried to explain that the whisky he had drunk to steady his nerves had made him lose control.

After that, every time he tried to touch her she became hysterical, fighting him off like a wildcat, never able to forget the pain of being sodomised.

Thankfully as the years progressed, he tried less and less. Until one last final attempt.

She fought him off as usual, but this time it was different; instead of anger he had broken down and cried, saying her rejection and hysterics made him feel like an animal. He was ruined, less than a man now. Assuming he'd become impotent, she hadn't cared. After all, it was no more than he deserved. And anyway, it was a relief to settle down into a platonic relationship.

Now, shaking her head, she got off the bed, smoothing the covers automatically behind her. Walking slowly into the bathroom she stared at herself in the mirror, seeing her own pain-filled eyes staring back. Perhaps it was thinking about the past that caused it, she didn't know, but the realisation of what she had done suddenly hit her, and her face stretched in horror.

My God! It was her fault that Harry had lost control with Sally. If only she hadn't rejected him for all of their married life, if only she had tried to get help... Gazing at her reflection she was filled with shame and self-hatred. She deserved this – deserved this empty house and empty life.

Turning on the taps she filled the sink with water, then snatching the nailbrush she began to scrub her hands violently. They were dirty, so dirty; she had to get them clean.

Finally, exhausted, she looked with dispassion at her red, raw flesh, before her eyes scanned the bathroom. It was filthy too; she had to clean it, just look at the muck. She hurried downstairs and filled a bucket with hot, steaming water. Then, adding a liberal amount of soda, she bent down, grabbing a scrubbing brush and cloth from under the sink.

Chapter Twelve

In Blackpool, Barbara and Ken were walking along the front. A cold easterly wind was blowing, snatching at her scarf, and she impatiently tightened the knot under her chin.

I hope this one's better than the others we've seen, she thought, hooking her arm through Ken's. According to the agent's details the house sounded perfect. Six bedrooms, a large reception and dining room, with the bonus of a basement. A snip, he said, at eighteen hundred pounds. Why was it so cheap, she wondered, when all the other properties of this size were way beyond their budget, despite the treasure trove they had found.

She smiled, remembering their arrival in Blackpool. It had been pouring with rain and Ken was still hardly speaking to her. They had tramped the back streets, looking for an out-of-the-way bed and breakfast, their shoulders drooping wearily when they found that most were closed until the start of the summer season.

Eventually they had come across a seedy-looking house with a board declaring *Vacancies* in the window. The sour-faced landlady had begrudgingly booked them in, and they'd sunk onto the rickety bed gratefully, too tired to bother about the state of the grubby room.

It had been the cash box she'd found in the safe that changed everything. Ken had forced it open, gasping at the large rolls of notes that spilled onto the bed. A small book remained at the bottom and she smiled, remembering how Ken had pulled it out, eagerly flicking the pages.

'The crafty old sod,' he'd chuckled. 'Look, he's been on a right old fiddle.'

She hadn't understood the neat rows of figures, until Ken had pointed out that the landlord had two other barmaids listed as working in the pub.

'But there weren't any other barmaids,' she'd protested.

'That's just it. Don't you see, Babs,' he had cried excitedly, 'he's claiming for non-existent staff and copping their wages. Christ, looking at the amount of dosh here, he must 'ave been at it for years.'

Oh, she'd been furious. She had worked like a slave in that bleeding pub, and all that time the landlord had been building himself a nice little nest egg for his retirement. She was glad then, glad that she had turned him over, nicking his hoard of cash.

It was even better when they realised that they were in the clear now. The police wouldn't be looking for her, as they feared. After all, the landlord daren't report the robbery. They had the evidence right there that he'd been cheating the brewery...

'Are you all right, Babs? You're a bit quiet,' Ken

said now.

'Yeah, of course I am. I just hope this won't be another blind alley. I'm beginning to think we'll never find the right house.'

'Perhaps we're aiming too high. If this is as hopeless as the others, we may 'ave to look for something smaller.'

'I suppose so,' she sighed. 'But if we don't get a place with a decent number of bedrooms, we won't make much money.'

Leaving the seafront they turned into a wide road lined on each side with tall imposing houses. 'This looks promising,' Ken said, a hint of excitement in his voice as they walked briskly along, looking for number seventeen.

They found it halfway along, sandwiched between two immaculately decorated houses, where it stood out like a sore thumb.

Barbara gazed at the tall Victorian house with its filthy marble stairs leading up to a battered-looking front door, and her mouth drooped. 'It looks a bit rundown.'

'Nothing a lick of paint couldn't put right, but it all depends on the state of the inside. Come on, the agent's supposed to be waiting for us.'

They followed behind the portly figure as he extolled the virtue of each room. Their eyes darkened with dismay as they took in the filthy chipped paintwork, the wallpaper stained and hanging from the walls, and the smell! It was awful, a mixture of damp wood and mildew.

'The owner died recently and her heirs are anxious for a quick sale. They may be open to a reasonable offer,' the agent said, his eyes roaming over them.

'What! Recently, you say? This place looks like a bloody pigsty,' Ken scoffed.

The agent stiffened, but his manner remained polite as he said, 'From what I understand, she was elderly and only used the basement flat. Apparently she had become somewhat eccentric in recent years. If you would like to come this way, I'll show it to you.'

They trailed down the stairs behind him, perking up as they entered a spacious and well-equipped kitchen.

'As you can see,' the agent said, indicating the area with a sweep of his arm, 'this part of the house is in very good order. There is also a double bedroom and bathroom.'

'Yeah, but the rest of the house is a dump,' Ken told him.

'Just think of the potential, sir. The rooms are beautifully proportioned and the property is structurally sound. I can assure you,' he added pompously, 'that the condition of the house is reflected in the price.' He took a fob-watch out of his waistcoat pocket, flipped open the lid and stared pointedly at the dial.

'Well, what do you think, Barbara?' Ken asked, turning his back on the agent.

Barbara's eyes were misty; she could just see the refurbished bedrooms, cream walls and pretty chintz curtains, a vase of fresh flowers on each bedside table to greet the guests on their arrival. Oh yes, her bed and breakfast was going to be the best in Blackpool. 'Let's make them an offer,' she said excitedly.

Chapter Thirteen

In Battersea, Sally was jumping about with excitement. Any minute now and her gran would be here. She wrapped her arms around her waist, hugging herself with delight, and for the umpteenth time rushed into the front room to peer out of the window. It was strange to see the room empty now, except for two fireside chairs. A fire glowed in the grate and the pink curtains, donated by Elsie, cast a warm glow into the room. Would her gran like it, she wondered. Would she stay?

It had been a frantic week. Gran's letter had animated her mum and for the first time there was a sparkle in her eyes. She had rearranged the front room, moving the sofa into the kitchen to make room for gran's bed, and disposing of the old sideboard.

It was here, the van was here, and as it pulled into the kerb, Sally rushed into the street. 'Gran, Gran!' she yelled excitedly, yanking open the passenger door.

'Hello, ducks. I look like royalty sitting up 'ere, don't I?'

Sally couldn't help it. She clamped her hand over her mouth trying to choke it back, but it was impossible, and she burst into hysterical laughter. She had never seen anything so funny.

Gran's battered black hat had fallen askew, the large tatty feather that adorned it bent in half and dangling drunkenly over one eye. Her black coat with its motheaten fur collar was gaping round the middle, the buttons straining to cover her ample tummy. But funniest of all was the sight of her short dumpy legs, spread wide and exposing long pink flannel drawers, the elastic ending just above her knees.

'What's so funny?' she asked indignantly as her feet swung back and forth, unable to reach the floor.

'Nothing, Gran,' she gulped, trying to compose herself as Bert came round from the driver's side.

'Come on, Sally, move out of the way. Let me get your gran down.'

He tucked his arms under her lap and despite her bulk, managed to lift the old lady gently from the vehicle, standing her on her feet. Sadie swayed unsteadily for a moment as Bert doffed his cap and gave a little bow. 'There you are, Mrs Greenbrook, delivered safe and sound.'

'Sadie, love, call me Sadie. Thanks for fetching me; it's the first time I've been in a van and I really enjoyed it. When my husband and me moved into our first little house, we only had a handcart to carry our bits and pieces.'

'You're welcome, Mrs Gree ... sorry, Sadie. Now then, Sally, help your gran inside and I'll unload her things.'

Sally scurried to her side. She's so tiny, she thought, why haven't I noticed that before? As she took her gran's arm the pungent smell of mothballs assailed her nostrils, making her cough.

'I know, Sal, awful ain't it, but this coat ain't seen the light of day in years. Come on, let's get inside, these shoes are too tight and me bunions are killing me.'

Sally felt an overwhelming surge of affection. 'Oh Gran,' she whispered. 'I'm so glad you're here.'

Sadie's heavy iron-framed bed had been bolted together and placed against the far wall. Her oak dresser was under the window, the top covered with a white crochet runner, and her pretty rug added a splash of colour to the grey lino. 'It looks lovely, Ruth, I'll be fine in here. Though it's a shame that you've got to give up yer sitting room for me.'

'Nah, it doesn't matter, Mum. We never used it anyway.'

Sadie smiled at her daughter, and after another quick glance around, said, 'Now come on, Sally's in bed, so you and me can have a good old chinwag.'

They returned to the kitchen, Sadie smiling sadly at the shabby room. An old grey sofa sat in front of the fireplace, with a worn fireside chair on each side of the hearth. At the other end of the long room a rickety kitchen table and chairs, ancient gas cooker and a battered kitchen cabinet filled the space. There was no Ascot, just a cold tap over the square sink in the corner. Poor Ruth, she thought, what a difference from her sister's elegant home.

Ignoring the sofa, Sadie made herself comfortable in one of the chairs, leaning towards her daughter. 'Right now, let's 'ave it, Ruth. All your letter said was that you haven't been well and that Ken's left you. There's more to it than that, ain't there?' she added shrewdly.

Ruth raised her head and Sadie was heart-broken to see the depth of pain reflected in her daughter's eyes. 'Oh Mum,' she began.

When Ruth's story came to an end, Sadie sat back, closing her eyes momentarily. My God, she thought, I didn't realise how bad it was. 'How 'ave you managed for money, sweetheart?' she asked gently.

'I've got a job in the grocer's shop on the corner. The pay's only five quid a week, but if you don't mind chipping in a bit, we'll manage.'

'What!' Sadie sat up indignantly. 'Did you think I was gonna let you keep me? No, I've got me pension and a nice little bit of dosh tucked away too. Mary wouldn't let me give her any money so I've got a fair bit in me Post Office book.' She kicked herself when she saw Ruth's face flush. 'Now then, don't look at me like that. I hated it when she wouldn't let me pay my way. It always made me feel so beholden.' She leaned forward earnestly, adding, 'Honestly love, I'd prefer to give you some of me pension.'

Ruth nodded, looking reassured. 'Thanks, Mum. Elsie next door has been wonderful too. She nursed me and Sally back to health, then lent me enough money to get by on until I got me first wage-packet, and Bert, well, he even put a few bags of coal in the bunker.'

'Yeah, you've got smashing neighbours, but tell me how much you owe them and I'll give you the money to pay it back.'

'I can't let you do that, Mum.'

113

'Don't be daft, Ruth. Look, I've got the money and I want to help. This is a new beginning for us, so let's start as we mean to go on.'

When Sally awoke the next morning she hurried downstairs, grinning as she entered the kitchen. 'Gran, you're still here!' she cried happily.

'Well, of course I am,' Sadie told her. 'I'm here to stay.'

Sally sat opposite her gran, unable to stop smiling. She was glad her dad had gone away. No more violence, no more being stuck in her room all the time. And now, with gran living with them, life was just perfect.

'What do yer want for breakfast?' her mum asked.

'Can I 'ave toast, please?' she answered, unable to tear her eyes away from the halo of light surrounding her gran. Frowning, she focused her eyes, noticing darkness in places. She felt a strange tingling sensation in her palms and there was an overwhelming urge to reach out – to touch the dark areas, and to smooth them away.

'What's the matter? Why are you looking at me like that?' Sadie asked.

Sally shook her head, not understanding these new feelings in her hands, but was distracted when her mum put a plate of toast on the table, saying, 'Now, what are you going to do with yourself today?'

Forcing her eyes away from her gran, the tingling in her palms diminishing, she asked, 'Can I go to Battersea Park with Ann?'

'Oh, I dunno, Sally, it's a long walk.'

'Let her go, Ruth. The poor kid's had her wings clipped for years and it's about time she had a bit of freedom.'

'Mum, she's still only ten.'

'For Gawd's sake, she's old enough to look after herself. It ain't that far, and you went to the park often enough at her age.'

Sally looked from one to the other, then her eyes settled appealingly on her mum. 'Please,' she begged.

'Oh, all right,' she huffed. 'But I shouldn't count your chickens yet, Sally. Don't forget that Ann's only just got over another bout of tonsillitis so Elsie may not want her going far.'

She hurriedly swallowed the last of her toast. 'I'll go and ask,' she said excitedly, rushing next door.

Elsie agreed, saying that a bit of fresh air might do Ann good, but only if they promised to be home by two o'clock.

The two girls eagerly made their way to the park, but finding that the sixpence they had between them didn't stretch far enough to visit the funfair, they went off to the swings. Their disappointment soon forgotten as they vied to see who could swing the highest, whooping together on the seesaw, and becoming thoroughly giddy on the roundabouts.

With her newfound freedom Sally became inseparable from Ann, and they spent all their free time together. The spring weather was gentle and as the season changed to early summer, there was a buzz of excitement in the Lane. There was talk of Queen Elizabeth's Coronation on 2 June, with neighbours in and out of each other's houses, and kids being told to go out and play while their parents made plans.

On Saturday Sally was sitting beside Ann on her doorstep, both trying to decide what to play. Hopscotch, skipping, and dabs had already been suggested, when Sally's eyes were drawn to the roof of the house opposite. 'What do you think that is?' she asked Ann, pointing to the funny H-shaped thing attached near one of the chimneys.

'It's a television aerial, and we'll have one soon,' Ann answered.

'What! You're getting a television?'

'Yes, next week. Dad said he's getting one so we can watch the Coronation.'

'Blimey,' Sally sighed. 'You're lucky.'

'Don't worry, you'll be able to watch it with us,' Ann consoled.

Turning her head, Sally saw Nelly Cox bustling along the Lane, knocking at one door after another. Now that she was allowed to play outside she had come to know many of the residents, and Nelly was one of her favourites. She was short and dumpy like her gran, and always seemed to have a cheery smile on her face. With no children of her own she made a great fuss of all the local kids, many calling her Auntie.

After getting no reply when she knocked on Joan Mason's door, she now approached them, saying, 'Hello, you two. Is yer mum in, Ann?'

They both stood up, moving to one side. 'Yes, go on in, Nelly.'

'Bless yer, love, but I ain't got time. You know

116

what will happen if I go inside, don't you?' she chuckled, giving them a cheeky wink. 'Yer mum will put the kettle on, then we'll 'ave a chat, and before you know it an hour's gone. I've got the whole Lane to call on this morning, so can you just give yer mum a shout for me.'

When Elsie came to the door both Ann and Sally listened in amazement to the conversation, grinning at each other with delight.

'I'm collecting for the street-party, Elsie.'

'But when we had the meeting last week I thought we'd decided to all muck in to provide the food.'

'I'm not collecting food money. It's for booze for the adult party in the evening.'

'Oh right, how much do you want?'

'Whatever you can spare. Me old man's gonna order a couple of barrels of beer from the off-licence, and maybe some port or sherry for the ladies. What do you think?'

'Sound all right to me, Nelly.'

'Oh, and another thing. We need bunting and flags – 'ave you got any?'

'Christ, the last time anything like that came out was at the end of the war, and God knows where it is now. But don't worry, I'll have a rummage around to see what I can find.'

'Other streets will be having parties too, don't forget, and we don't want them putting on a better show than us.'

'I'm sure that with all the planning that's gone into it, the Lane will look wonderful,' Elsie assured her.

'I hope yer right, love. Well, I'd best be off and

thanks for yer contribution.' Turning, her eyes alighted on Ann and Sally, and with a grin she said, 'Are you looking forward to the fancy-dress competition, girls?'

Ann gawked. 'What competition?'

'Oh blimey, 'ave I put me foot in it, Elsie?'

'No, it's all right, they had to know some time.'

The day of the Coronation dawned chilly and wet, with rain threatening as Sally, with her mum and gran, rushed next door to join their friends. Nelly Cox and her husband George arrived shortly after, followed by a few other neighbours, and the small room became packed.

They all gathered in front of the television set, children sitting on the floor, gazing in wonderment at the black and white picture on the small flickering screen.

'Cor, look at that huge coach, Ann,' Sally gasped. 'It's just like Cinderella's.'

'Yes, it's lovely, and doesn't the Queen look beautiful?'

'That coach is gold, girls,' Bert told them.

'What! Made of real gold?' Sally squealed.

Bert laughed, 'No, love, it's just gilded, but if it was real just one of the spokes from those enormous wheels would set us up for life.'

Sally sighed, her imagination alight as she stared at the Queen waving to the crowds that thronged the streets.

The huge procession finally reached Westminster Abbey for the ceremony. The majestic music, the pageantry, with Richard Dimbleby's commentary, held them all enthralled, with only

Sally finding the long ceremony boring at times. Her eyes were slowly closing, and her head beginning to droop, when she felt a tap on her shoulder from behind.

'Wake up, girl,' her gran admonished. 'You're missing a bit of history. This is the first time a Coronation has ever been televised, and it will be something to tell yer kids about one day.'

Sally forced her attention back to the screen and found she was just in time to see the crown placed on Queen Elizabeth's head.

The next morning preparations for the street-party were already in progress as Sally jumped out of bed and scrambled to her window. Long trestle tables, covered with an assortment of white tablecloths and sheets, lined the Lane. Streamers of colourful red, white and blue bunting swayed in the gentle breeze and balloons were in evidence too, attached to front doors and lampposts.

She hugged herself with excitement. Her angel costume was ready for the competition. The white dress, with a top layer of net, had sequins sewn all over it that sparkled in the sunlight, and the wings, fashioned out of wire coat-hangers, were covered in silver tinsel.

Dressing quickly and running downstairs, her eyes popped at the assortment of delights strewn across the kitchen table. Nearly everyone had agreed to contribute food for the party and her mum had made red and yellow jellies, fairy cakes covered with bright pink icing and a huge bowl of trifle.

'Mum, can I put me fancy-dress outfit on

now?' she asked, her voice high.

'No, Sally, it's far too early. The competition ain't starting until three o'clock.'

'Can I go round to Ann's then?' she begged, fidgeting from one foot to the other.

'Yeah, all right, but eat yer breakfast first.'

Sally gulped down her porridge and as she hurried next door, her mum shouted, 'Oi, and don't get under Elsie's feet. She's still got lots of sandwiches to make.'

Ann opened the door, grinning as she drew Sally inside. 'We'll have to go up to my room, Mum's running around like a blue-arsed fly.'

'What did you say!' Ann's dad bellowed as he stepped into the hall.

Sally peeped at him from the corner of her eyes, noticing that he was fighting the urge to laugh as he added, 'And what sort of language is that, my girl?'

'Yours, Dad,' Ann said cheekily. 'I've heard you saying it to mum when she's rushing around.' She dodged by him, running up the stairs, Sally in her wake, both giggling when he pretended to chase them, roaring like a lion.

They were breathless when they reached Ann's room and collapsed onto her bed. 'My dad's a proper nut, isn't he?' Ann said, a wide smile on her face.

'He's lovely,' Sally said. And he was, she thought, as long as he didn't come too close. She was unable to bear it when men even brushed against her, glad that she didn't have to live in a house with a father and brother like Ann. It must be awful having to avoid them all the time.

Sally hadn't won the fancy-dress competition, but she didn't mind. The three-year-old Mason twins, a boy and girl, had taken the first prize. They looked so sweet dressed as a King and Queen, holding hands as they paraded in their outfits, their crowns made of cardboard covered with gold paper and brightly coloured jewels, which to Sally's disappointment on closer inspection, turned out to be wine gums.

Ann came second, dressed as Little Bo-Peep, and to Sally's delight she won the fourth prize, a book by Enid Blyton.

Now she and Ann were sitting on her doorstep, watching the men as they carried out barrels of beer in preparation for the adult party. A battered old piano had been wheeled out onto the pavement, courtesy of Mrs Edwards from number seven, and Mrs Mason's husband had volunteered to play the mouth organ.

As Sally watched the preparations she realised how different the day would have been if her dad hadn't gone away. Instead of joining in, she would have been stuck in her room, watching the party from her window.

'Wasn't it great, Sally?' Ann said.

'Yeah, it was, and I wish we could stay up for the adult party.'

They grimaced at each other when, as if on cue, they heard their mums calling them in. 'It ain't fair,' Sally protested. 'It's only eight o'clock.'

'Ann, did you hear me! I said it's time to come in,' Elsie shouted.

'I'd better go, she said, rising slowly. 'I'll see

121

you tomorrow.'

'All right,' Sally replied, standing up too and wandering indoors, her jaw dropping when she saw her mum. Ruth looked beautiful; her newly washed hair hung in soft waves onto her shoulders, parted on one side with a Lana Turner quiff. Her blue and white floral dress was clinched in at the waist with a wide belt, and she had a lacy white cardigan slung around her shoulders.

'Mum, you look lovely,' Sally told her, eyes wide in wonderment.

'Yeah, she scrubs up well, don't she, Sal?' her gran grinned. 'That dress was a really good find and looks hardly worn.'

'Thanks for knitting this cardigan, Mum. It fits a treat,' Ruth told her. 'Now then, Sally, get yerself ready for bed, and no arguments.'

'But, Mum, it's too early. Can't I stay up for a while?'

'No, definitely not. Yer gran's staying in to look after you so I can go to the party, and I ain't having you giving her a hard time.'

'It's all right, Ruth,' Sadie intervened. 'She can stay up for a while to keep me company.'

Sally hid a smile. Ever since her gran had moved in with them she had found she could play one off against the other, usually resulting in her getting her own way. 'Please, Mum,' she begged.

'Oh, all right. But I want her in bed by nine o'clock, Mum.'

'Whatever you say,' Sadie answered, giving Sally a sly wink.

''Ave you had a nice day, Sal?' her gran asked as soon as Ruth had gone to the party.

'It was smashing. The best time I've ever had,' Sally told her dreamily. 'Everything is so different since you came to live with us, Gran. Mum's made friends with people in the Lane and she smiles all the time now.'

'I know, it's good to see her so happy.' The old lady crossed to the window, drawing the net to one side. 'Blimey, the party's kicked off already. Come and see this, Sal.'

Sally saw Mrs Wilson and Nelly Cox, skirts held up showing their knees as they danced, Mrs Green and a few other women joining in. Their voices were loud and she smiled as her gran joined in the song...

Any evening any day, when you come down
  Lambeth way,
You'll see them all – doing the Lambeth Walk.

She strained her neck, giggling when her mum strolled up and began to dance with them, 'Oh Gran,' she whispered happily, 'it wouldn't 'ave been like this if me dad was here. Mum wouldn't 'ave dared go to the street-party. I hope he never, ever comes back.'

Chapter Fourteen

With all that had happened that year, her uncle's assault, then her father leaving, followed by her own and her mother's illnesses, Sally failed her eleven plus examination. Ruth, working fulltime and coming home tired each evening, just shrugged her shoulders when she saw the results, saying little about it, much to Sally's relief.

Ann failed too, much to her parents' surprise and disappointment. They blamed it not only on the change of school, but on the many times she had been unable to attend due to recurring tonsillitis.

Both girls now attended the same Secondary Modern School, and as it was only a short walk from home, they settled in easily, being put in the same class.

After a couple of years they began to blossom, turning into teenagers and shedding their puppy fat. Ann, though still short like her mother, developed a large bust and narrow waist. Sally was taller and slim with a small bust that to her disgust, was just beginning to burgeon. She hated it when boys began to look at her, doing her best to hide her figure by wearing baggy blouses.

Their interests only began to differ, when at fourteen, Ann, like their other friends, became interested in boys. Pictures of her idol, Pat Boone, began to appear on her bedroom wall and she started to experiment with make-up.

Wonderful new fashions were now available, especially aimed at teenagers, and young girls no longer had to wear the same style of clothes as their mothers. Ann suited the tight sweaters and circle skirts that she had taken to wearing when out of school, complete with layered net petticoats underneath that peeped out when she sat down. Sally, however, stayed in her baggy blouses and wore mostly straight skirts, determined not to attract too much attention.

'Come on, don't look so pessimistic, it'll be great,' Ann told her as they got ready to go to the local youth club. It had taken a lot of persuasion on her part to convince Sally to go, but at last her friend had agreed.

Sally stared at her reflection in the mirror. Ann had dusted her face with powder and insisted on applying a thick coat of mascara to her eyelashes. Spitting on the block and rubbing at it vigorously with a small brush, she had carefully stroked her lashes with the resulting black gunk. Then came the lipstick, bright orange to finish off the effect.

I look like a clown, she thought, blotting her lips to remove some of the colour. Ann didn't look much better, the make-up emphasising her squint.

As they stepped into the youth club, their ears were immediately assailed by the loud music blaring from a record player just inside the door. 'Oh, it's Elvis,' Ann enthused, beginning to jig about to the strains of 'All Shook Up'.

Sally's heart sank when she saw Ann's brother Arthur walking towards them from the other end of the hall, a wide smile on his face.

'I can't believe it,' he said, his eyes flicking up and down over her body. 'You look great, Sally.'

She squirmed uncomfortably. Ann had convinced her to wear one of her outfits and the stiff net petticoat scratched her legs. Her face flamed when Arthur's eyes settled on her bust, and rounding her shoulders protectively, she wished that she was wearing her usual baggy blouse, instead of the sweater that Ann had insisted looked better with the skirt.

Turning from Arthur's gaze she looked desperately at Ann, only to find her eyeing a boy who was selecting another record to put on the turntable.

As though aware of her scrutiny, he turned, his eyes quickly passing over Ann to settle on Sally. 'Well, well, who's this, Arthur?' he asked, putting the record down and advancing towards them.

'Bugger off, Billy,' Arthur growled, putting his arm around Sally's shoulders, his hand inadvertently brushing her breast. 'She's spoken for.'

Sally felt her heart thumping in her chest as panic set in. Twisting away from Arthur, she turned and fled from the hall, her heels skidding on the polished wooden floor.

'Wait, Sally, wait!' Ann called, rushing out after her friend. 'What on earth's the matter?'

'I don't want boys touching me,' she gasped, her chest heaving.

'It was only Arthur. Didn't you realise that he fancies you, Sally? He's had his eye on you for months.'

She stared at her friend in astonishment.

'Fancies me?' she squeaked. 'No, of course I didn't notice.'

'Calm down, love. I know he's huge like my dad, but he wouldn't hurt a fly.'

'Keep him away from me, Ann. Please ... don't let him touch me,' she begged.

'Christ, Sally. Take a deep breath, you're shaking like a leaf,' Ann urged, a puzzled expression on her face. 'Why are you so frightened?'

'I dunno, but tell him to leave me alone ... please!'

'All right, all right, I will. Now come on, we had better go home. We can't go back in there now, we'll be a laughing stock,' she said, a hint of reproach in her voice.

'I'm sorry, Ann. Look, you can go back in. I'm sure I saw Jenny Jackson and her friend Betty in there, so you needn't be on yer own.

'Are you sure you wouldn't mind?'

'No, of course not. I know how much you were looking forward to it. I'll be fine.'

'Well, all right then,' Ann said after a moment's hesitation. 'That bloke sorting the records was rather dishy, wasn't he?'

Sally forced a smile. 'Yeah, he looked all right. Bye, love, I'll see you tomorrow,' she called, moving off hurriedly, not giving Ann a chance to change her mind.

Ann watched her friend until she was out of sight then, shrugging her shoulders, she stepped back into the hall.

'What's the matter with Sally? Did I do something wrong?' Arthur asked. 'Isn't she coming back in?'

'No, she's gone home,' his sister told him brusquely. 'She isn't interested in you, Arthur, so keep your hands to yourself and leave her alone in future.'

'I only put my arm around her shoulders,' he replied indignantly as Jenny Jackson ambled up towards them.

'Wotcher, Ann,' she said. 'Why did Sally leave in such a hurry?'

'She wasn't feeling well,' Ann lied.

'It looked more like she was running away from you, Arthur,' Jenny said, hooking her arm through his. 'Don't yer know she ain't interested in boys? Maybe she prefers girls, if you know what I mean,' she sniggered.

'Well, that's her loss, isn't it,' he said, shrugging his arm out of Jenny's grasp, his eyes on the other end of the hall. 'Right – it looks like it's my turn on the billiard table,' he added, walking off, his shoulders stiff.

'Cor, your brother's gorgeous, Ann. Can't yer put a word in for me?' Jenny urged.

'If you keep throwing yourself at him like that, I won't need to,' she snapped. 'And in future keep your snide remarks about Sally to yourself.'

'I was only joking, yer silly cow,' Jenny retorted, and turning around she sashayed up to Billy who had returned to the record-player, her hips swaying suggestively.

Ann watched his eyes light up as Jenny approached him, and her heart sank. She was stupid, stupid! What chance did she have against someone who looked like Jenny? She turned away from the scene, and seeing that Betty was on her own, decided to join her.

Walking towards her she passed a group of boys lounging against the wall, and they all turned to look at her. One of them whispered something and they roared with laughter, another replying, 'Yeah, you're right, she's got a good figure, but you'd have to put a bag over her head to cover those weird eyes.'

Ann felt herself redden and her shoulders hunched. Stricken, she turned on her heels, scurrying back down the hall and out of the door.

Why had she expected it to be any different? Just because she had put make-up on and worn nice clothes, it didn't change anything. It was always the same – one look at her eyes and boys dissolved into laughter. Oh it wasn't fair, it really wasn't. Why couldn't she look normal like other girls?

As she turned the corner into Candle Lane, she wasn't surprised to see Sally sitting on her doorstep, and drawing near, forced a smile.

'Are you all right?' Sally asked. 'I had a funny feeling about you on the way home so I thought I'd wait outside for a while, just in case.'

'You always seem to know when I'm upset. It was just some of the boys in the youth club, taking the mickey out of my eyes as usual.' She sighed heavily. 'You'd think I'd be used to it by now, wouldn't you?'

Sally smiled consolingly as she gazed at her friend, her eyes slightly unfocused. 'Ann, your mum is going to start teaching me to read auras next week. Would you let me practise on you? You never know, I might be able to find out what's wrong with your eyes.'

'You already know what's wrong with them, Sally. They're crossed, and nothing can be done about it. Mum took me to a specialist years ago, and he told her that the damage is permanent.'

'Please, Ann, it won't hurt to try.'

'Oh, all right then, but it won't do any good,' she insisted.

Sally focused on Ann's eyes again. There was something wrong, she could sense it. But what?

Chapter Fifteen

The following Easter, 1958, when both Sally and Ann were fifteen, they left school, delighted at the thought of going to work. Wrapped warmly against the sharp wind they were now hurrying along the main road.

'I can't believe it, Ann! Fancy us both getting jobs in Arding & Hobbs.'

'Yes, but you're lucky – at least in the record department you'll be able to listen to the Top Twenty all day. Me, all I'll be doing is washing hair and sweeping up.'

'But, Ann, you'll be learning a trade. Think about when you're a fully qualified hairdresser.'

'Huh, that's years away yet and I'm getting paid a pittance in the meantime. I wish I was earning as much as you.'

'I'm only getting two pounds ten, and after giving me mum two pounds, I'll just have ten bob left.'

'But that's not fair,' her friend objected, her voice indignant.

'Me mum needs the money, Ann. It's been hard on her for the last five years. She's had to bring me up on her own with just her wage and a bit of gran's pension money.' Shrugging she added, 'I'll manage. I got me uniform on tick and I'll take a packed lunch each day.'

Ann grabbed her arm excitedly as they neared the entrance. They didn't start work until the end of April, but they couldn't resist having a look around the Department Store. Pushing open the large glass doors they found themselves in the perfume and makeup department, their noses wrinkling with delight as they sniffed the air, heavy with a combination of expensive aromas. Beautifully made-up sales assistants stood behind each counter, and seeing their sophisticated and haughty faces, both girls looked at them in awe, too frightened to approach them.

'Come on, Sally. Let's go and look at the record department,' Ann suggested.

'Yeah, all right.'

They eagerly passed through the electrical department, not interested in the display of gramophones, televisions and radios, and stepping down a short flight of stairs, entered the small but busy area tucked at the back of the store. There were several racks of LPs, a few listening booths, but other than that, just a long counter.

'It's a bit small really,' Sally said, unable to hide the hint of disappointment in her voice.

'It's all right,' Ann placated, giving her a nudge. 'Look at those boys buying records. You'll meet loads of blokes in here.'

Sally grimaced, feeling uncomfortable at the attention they were receiving from a group of teddy boys. They had their hair slicked back with Brylcream, leaving a quiff hanging low over their foreheads, and wore long jackets with tight drainpipe trousers. Crepe-soled shoes completed the look, and as one of them grinned at her she tugged Ann's arm, urging, 'Come on, let's go to the hairdressing department.'

With a quick glance over her shoulder and receiving a cheeky wink from one of them, Ann reluctantly followed Sally to the escalator. Stepping onto the slowly moving staircase they passed fashions on the first floor, furniture, household and bedding on the second, before reaching the third.

Losing their way slightly they followed the signs until they came upon a lush area, deeply carpeted, with a small counter beside a curtained section. 'Hairdressing's through that curtain,' Ann whispered. 'I was shown around after my interview and the manager told me that his customers want privacy when they're having their hair done. This is just the waiting room.'

Sally saw white wicker chairs, small glass tables topped with magazines, and huge pictures of glamorous models with the latest hairstyles, displayed on walls painted a soft shade of lavender. The whole department appeared uncluttered, calm and elegant. 'It's lovely,' she breathed.

'Yes, it's nice isn't it?' Ann whispered back. 'But come on, let's go, I don't want them to see me hanging about. Let's go across to Woolworth's. I need a new lipstick and somehow I don't think the make-up department in here will stock Gala.'

When they returned home, Sally sat in front of the dressing-table mirror applying a coat of Ann's new lipstick. 'Does it look all right?' She asked as her friend came to stand behind her.

'Oh no,' Ann grimaced. 'Pink just isn't your colour. A soft shade of coral would be better.' She gathered Sally's thick red hair into a bunch. 'Can I have a go at putting it up?'

'Yeah, of course, but what's the time? I don't wanna be here when Arthur comes home.'

Ann glanced at her watch. 'He's not due for another half hour yet. Look, why don't you just tell him that you're not interested instead of running off every time he shows his face?'

'I 'ave, but he just won't listen. Can't you talk to him, Ann?' she pleaded.

Ann deftly folded the back of Sally's hair into a sleek French pleat, securing it with grips and teasing a few tendrils from the side to curl round her cheeks. 'I've tried,' she said, 'but he still fancies you, Sally, and he's not used to girls running away from him. I think that makes you a sort of challenge.'

'Yeah, I've seen the way those two over the road throw themselves at him, especially Jenny. I just wish he'd catch one and leave me alone.'

'I expect he'll give up eventually,' Ann told her, putting down the comb and standing back to survey her efforts. 'There now, what do you think?'

Sally turned her head this way and that, deciding that she looked older with her hair up. 'It looks great. See, you'd be wasted in the record department: you've got a natural talent with hair.' She looked at her friend's reflection in the mirror, struck by how pretty Ann looked. 'Your eyes are much better now. All you've got is a very slight cast.'

'Yes, thanks to you. How did you do it, Sally? How did you know that my muscles were weak?'

'I dunno, it's hard to explain. I've always been able to see people's auras. When I was a little girl I used to call them lights and thought everyone could see them. Do you remember last year when your mum starting teaching me to read auras?'

At Ann's nod, Sally continued, 'Well, after a while I began to understand not only what I was seeing, but what I was sensing too. Somehow when I looked at you I could feel that the muscles in the back of yer eyes were weak. Now don't forget I only told your mum what I thought was wrong. It was her that came up with the idea of using exercises to strengthen them.'

'It's so bloody boring and she keeps me at it for ages. I have to sit in front of her following her finger with my eyes for what seems like hours. First one way, then the other, then up, then down. She's relentless, Sal.'

Sally smiled gently. 'I know, but it's worth it. Just look at the difference it's made.'

Ann hung her head. 'I sound ungrateful, don't I, but I'm not, honest. You can't imagine how wonderful it is, Sally. No more teasing, no more pitying looks. It took a bit of getting used to when boys started giving me the eye. I kept waiting for them to crack jokes.'

'Well, they're almost straight now, so you should be able–' Sally stopped abruptly. 'Did you hear the front door, Ann? It must be Arthur. I've got to go.' Jumping up in agitation, she made a dash for the door, heading down the stairs.

'Hello, gorgeous.'

Sally froze; she was only halfway down and Arthur was standing at the bottom, looking up at her. She felt trapped, unable to move as he slowly ascended the stairs, a soft smile on his face.

'Please, Arthur, let me pass,' she appealed as he reached her.

'Give me a kiss, Sally, and I might.'

'Arthur, just let her go. When are you going to get it into your thick head that she's not inter-ested in you?' Ann shouted from the top of the stairs.

'Shut up, Ann. I'm only talking to her,' Arthur retorted, glaring up at his sister.

Sally seized the opportunity, and while he was distracted she pushed past him, flying downstairs and out of the house, rushing into her own door breathlessly.

'Hello, love, been running, 'ave you?' Ruth asked, turning from the sink and rubbing her hands dry on the tea towel. 'Your hair looks nice like that, it really suits you. Do you know, I can't believe you're fifteen and starting work soon.'

Sally frowned, her eyes flicking around the room. 'Where's me gran?'

'She's not feeling well. Her arthritis is giving her a lot of pain so she's 'aving a little lay-down. You can go and wake her now. I said I'd give her a shout when dinner's ready.'

Sally went into the downstairs front room, where her gran had lived for the past five years, and studied her as she lay dozing.

The old lady's eyes suddenly shot open and Sally blinked with surprise when she winked cheekily, saying, 'You're giving me one of them funny looks again, ain't yer? Now stop worrying, I'm fine. I was just having a little rest, that's all.'

'Oh Gran, I can see you're not fine, so don't bother to pretend.'

She chuckled. 'I never could fool you, could I. You and yer lights.'

'Listen, Gran, I've got an idea. Elsie told me that I've got healing hands, and if she's right, I might be able to relieve some of your pain.'

'Well, I'm game, Sal, but you had better talk it over with yer mum.'

Elsie watched Ruth wringing her hands, a sure sign that she was agitated. There had been times when her nerves, as she called them, got on top of her again, but thankfully never as bad as that first time.

'What's up?' Elsie asked gently.

'It's about Sally and this psychic stuff. I'm just not sure about it.'

'Ruth, I've told you before, I won't do anything to guide Sally's gifts without your consent. We agreed that I would help her to understand the ability she had to see auras, and I haven't done anything more than that, but she's already able to sense illnesses. She's an amazing girl.'

'But she said you're going to teach her to do spiritual healing.'

Elsie sighed and leaned forward in her chair, gazing intently at her friend. 'I think there's been a bit of a misunderstanding, Ruth. Yes, I admit, I did tell Sally that I think she's got healing hands, but I didn't say I would help her to develop her skill, and I won't until we both agree that she's ready.'

Ruth shook her head worriedly. 'I'm just so confused about it all, Elsie. Some people say it's wrong to use psychic powers, and I'm frightened.'

'Look, all I can tell you is what I believe. You must make up your own mind.' Elsie stood up, walking slowly over to the window as if to gather her thoughts. 'Ruth, I believe that God created us, and that He endowed us with psychic abilities, or what some people call spiritual gifts. Why would He give us these abilities if we weren't meant to use them?'

'Well, yes, I see what you're getting at, but why does the Church say it's wrong?'

'I don't know, Ruth, it has never made sense to me. When they say it's wrong to use spiritual gifts, it's like saying God made a mistake in giving them to us in the first place.' She sighed deeply, adding, 'All I know is that Jesus could prophesy, and heal the sick, sending His disciples out to do the same. He taught that anything He could do, we could do also, and that's good enough for me.'

Ruth sat quietly mulling over her friend's words, and had to admit they made a lot of sense. She thought about her mum and the constant pain she was in. If Sally could help her, surely that couldn't be wrong. 'Elsie, do you think Sally is ready to develop her healing powers?'

'Yes, I think so, but I won't help her without

your agreement.'

'All right then, if she really wants to try, I won't stand in her way.'

The following week, Sally held her hands over her gran's body, raising her head in a silent prayer. Could she really help by doing this? Was she imagining the tingling sensation radiating from her palms? She allowed her mind to drift as Elsie had taught her, finding that her hands moved unconsciously, hovering over Sadie as if led by an unseen force.

'I think fifteen minutes is enough,' Elsie said, interrupting her concentration.

'How do you feel, Gran?' she asked, surprised that the time had passed so quickly.

Standing up, Sadie began to walk tentatively across the room, an expression of amazement suddenly crossing her face. 'The pain's almost gone – I can't believe it,' she cried.

Sally stared. Her gran's limp was barely visible. Surely it's not possible, she thought, unable to believe her eyes.

'I don't know where you get this power from, love, but to me it's like a miracle,' her gran said excitedly.

'Perhaps my real father's psychic,' Sally mused, remembering when at the age of thirteen she had finally found out what a cuckoo in the nest meant. It had been a shock to find out that Ken wasn't her father, yet somehow it was a relief too. So many things that had happened in the past had fallen into place, and she finally understood why he had always rejected her.

She shivered, remembering his violence, glad that he had gone out of their lives. After a shaky start, her mum was so much happier now. Oh, she bickered now and then with gran, which wasn't surprising, the old lady being such a dominant character. When gran had first moved in with them it must have driven her mum mad when she had played them off, one against the other. Sally smiled; it had taken them a long time to work that one out. What a horrible little brat I must have been, she thought.

'Yes, perhaps your father was psychic too,' Elsie said, breaking into her thoughts.

Sally smiled distantly, still thinking about her father. She had tried many times to imagine what he looked like, but all her mum could tell her was that his name was Andy, he came from Scotland and that she'd inherited his red hair. For a long time she had dreamed of finding him, fantasising about how wonderful it would be to have a father who loved her. Eventually of course she had come to realise that with so little information, it was impossible.

She shook her head, berating herself for wool-gathering, and turned to her gran, saying, 'Are you sure you're not imagining it? Do you really feel better?'

'Of course I'm not imagining it, Sally. I'm telling you ... the pain's almost gone.'

Ruth, who had been sitting quietly while all this had been taking place, suddenly spoke. 'Elsie, can you inherit psychic powers?' she asked.

'It does tend to run through families. But I've met many gifted mediums where it doesn't, so who knows,' she said, shrugging her shoulders.

Sally yawned, suddenly feeling exhausted. Her limbs ached and her head was beginning to thump.

'Sit down, Sally,' Elsie advised. 'You look worn out, and I think I know why.'

Once seated, Elsie sat opposite her, resting her forearms on the table as she spoke. 'One of the most important things you have to learn, Sally, is how to act as a channel. If you're tired it's because you're giving out your own energy, but don't worry, you did marvellously well for your first attempt and I'm amazed at the results. All you've got to do now is to learn how to let the energy flow through you, and not from you.'

'Why don't you get yourself off to bed,' her mum urged, looking at her worriedly.

Glancing at the clock, Sally saw that it was only nine thirty, but she didn't argue. Her headache was worsening and all she wanted was to sleep. Standing up, she rubbed her forehead. 'Yes, I think I will go up. Night, all,' she added as she made her way upstairs.

She lay in bed, her face turned towards the window, watching the clouds scudding across the face of a full moon, still unable to believe the sight of her gran walking across the room with hardly a limp showing.

Her eyelids then began to droop, but she was still aware of her aching limbs as she snuggled further down in the bed. It was as she slowly drifted off to sleep that she became aware of a presence, smiling softly when she felt a light, almost gossamer touch on her cheek.

Chapter Sixteen

I can't believe we've already been at work for four months,' Ann said as she and Sally made their way home from the store one evening. 'How are you getting along with your manageress now? Is she any better?'

'Oh, all right I suppose, but she's still so stiff and formal. It's "Miss Marchant do this, Miss Marchant do that".' Sally grimaced; she was a little in awe of Miss French, who always looked so elegant and sophisticated. She wore her dark, sleek hair combed back from her face into a neat chignon, emphasising her beautiful bone structure and perfectly applied make-up. Her white blouse was always crisp, and there was never so much as a speck of fluff on her black pencil skirt.

Sally looked critically at her own uniform; the blouse was going slightly grey after so many washes, and her flared black felt skirt, that she had thought so grown-up when she bought it, now hung unevenly at the hemline. She smiled ruefully at Ann. 'I got told off for saying *ain't* again today. "Miss Marchant," she said. "How many times have I got to tell you, there is no such word in the dictionary".'

Her friend's mimicry made Ann giggle. 'She sounds awful. My manager isn't too bad; he only gets angry if I don't sweep up as soon as he's finished a cut. Here, Sal, do you fancy coming to

141

the pictures tonight? *Cast A Dark Shadow* is on at the Odeon, starring Margaret Lockwood.'

'I can't, I'm absolutely skint. We can go on Friday when I get paid if you like.'

Ann shook her head. 'I can't make it then. Some of the stylists have entered a hairdressing competition, and when they said they needed a junior to assist them, I jumped at the chance.' She gave a little skip, grinning with delight. 'I'm so excited, I've never been to a competition before.'

Sally remembered how Ann had hated the thought of hairdressing, but now she had taken to it like a duck to water. She fingered her fringe. 'I've been thinking about having me hair cut short.'

Ann gazed at Sally's face. 'It would probably suit you, but I hope you're not asking me to do it. I wouldn't have the nerve.'

'Oh go on, Ann, I can't afford to go to the hairdresser's. I must get my club money paid off so I can buy another skirt and blouse for work, and that only leaves me five bob a week.'

'I just couldn't, Sally. Your hair's too long and I wouldn't know where to start. A trim, yes, but not a full cut.' She raked her fingers through her own short hair. 'Here, I tell you what, I could ask the stylists if they need a model for the competition.'

'Thanks, Ann, that would be great.' Sally suddenly winced in pain. 'I'm glad we're nearly home, my feet are absolutely killing me.'

'Mine too. My soles feel like I've been walking on hot coals.'

They smiled at each other in sympathy, parting outside Sally's door.

Later, when Sally and her family were sitting round the table having just finished their dinner, there was a light knock on the back door. 'Can I come in for a minute?' Elsie asked, poking her head inside.

'Of course you can. What can we do for you?' Ruth asked, gesturing her friend to a seat and reaching across the table to stack the empty plates.

'I wanted to have a word with you about Nelly's husband, George. He's in a terrible state and I wondered if Sally could help him with some healing?'

'Oh Elsie, I don't know. Helping her gran is one thing, but I don't know about anyone else...' Ruth shook her head doubtfully.

'Mum, please let me try,' Sally urged. 'I'd like to find out if I really can do healing.'

'But you know you can. Look at the difference you've made to your gran. She's in hardly any pain these days.' Turning to Sadie she added, 'isn't that right, Mum?'

'Yeah. It's worked a treat,' Sadie agreed.

'Please, it can't do any harm,' Sally begged.

She watched as her mother drummed her fingers on the table, a sure sign she was agitated, relieved when she finally said, 'Oh, all right then, but just this once, and no more. I mean it, Sal, so don't bother to argue with me.'

The following evening Sally watched George Cox as he struggled across the kitchen, his back bent and breathing laboured. She focused her eyes on his aura, feeling a prickle of tears behind her eyes as she realised that there was nothing she could do to help him, except perhaps to ease his pain. 'Please, take a seat,' she gulped, hurrying out of the room. 'I'll be back in a minute.'

'What's the matter?' Elsie asked, scurrying out of the room behind her.

Sally sat on the stairs, her head in her hands and fighting back the tears. 'He's dying, Elsie. I can sense that he's dying.'

Elsie lowered herself onto the stair beside her, wrapping an arm around her shoulders and drawing her close.

'He probably came here thinking that I can cure him, Elsie, and I can't. Oh God, I wish I had never started this now.' Her thoughts then flew to Nelly and she was unable to stop the tears from falling. She was such a lovely old lady, and so popular in the Lane – the first to offer help to anyone who needed it. But now that she needed help herself ... oh, it wasn't fair, it wasn't.

'It's all my fault, Sally,' Elsie cried. 'I didn't realise you'd be able to foresee terminal illness. This is awful for you – would you like me to send him home?'

'No, I can't just turn him away.' She hadn't had much to do with Nelly's husband. George Cox was a quiet man who mostly kept himself to himself, but when she did bump into him he always gave her a kindly smile. Drawing in a deep breath and gathering her strength, she dashed the tears from her eyes, saying with a tremor in her voice, 'Come on, let's go back in there.'

As she entered the room, the old man's rheumy eyes met hers and she was surprised at their depth of wisdom and compassion.

'Come here, ducks,' he beckoned, and as she reached him he took her hand, squeezing it gently. 'Don't worry, I know there's nothing you can do for me.' He smiled ruefully. 'Nelly insisted that I came to see you, but I know me number's up, love, so don't upset yerself.'

'Will you at least let me try to ease your pain?' Sally urged.

'Yes, of course, though I don't think you'll be able to do much.'

She stood behind him, closed her eyes, and offered up a silent prayer. Moving her hands slowly over his body, she was aware of being led to his lung area. The familiar feeling radiated from her palms and she prayed it was giving him some relief. 'How's that?' she asked, after about fifteen minutes.

He inhaled, a look of surprise crossing his wrinkled face. 'Why, that's wonderful, duck. It really has eased the pain and I can breathe a little easier.'

Sally smiled sadly, knowing that all she had achieved was a temporary respite. 'I'm glad it's given you a little relief, Mr Cox, but I don't know how long it will last. Me gran's arthritis plays her up again unless I give her regular healing.'

'Listen to me, gel, anything that makes my going a bit easier is enough for me. Can I come to see you again?'

It wasn't far to walk, but she knew what a huge effort it must have taken for him to get here. 'I tell you what,' she suggested. 'How do you feel about me popping into your house on my way home from work, perhaps a couple of times a week?'

'That's very good of you. Just one thing though – don't let on to me missus how bad I am. She doesn't need to know yet.'

On Friday evening the hall buzzed with the sound of voices as Sally stared at her reflection in the mirror, fingering her short hair that fell in wisps around her face.

'I can't believe it, Sally, it looks absolutely fantastic,' Ann said, standing behind her. 'Do you like it?'

'I dunno, it feels strange. My head feels so light.'

'You look sort of elfin-like and your eyes look even bigger. It's a shame your hairstyle didn't win the competition. Still, second place is great, isn't it?'

Sally nodded, still feeling unsure about the new style, asking as she twisted her head to look at the sides, 'Will we be able to leave now?'

Ann frowned. 'Well, yes, but do you mind going home on your own? I said I'd stay behind to help with the clearing up.'

'No, that's all right. I'll see you later.'

It wasn't far to walk, but at Candle Lane she pulled up short. Arthur was standing on the corner and there was no way to avoid him.

'Hello, Sally, I like your hair,' he said, smiling as she approached.

'Thanks,' she answered, her fingers tugging unconsciously at the wispy fringe as she edged past him. 'See yer then.'

He grasped her arm. 'Hang about, don't run away. Do you fancy coming to the pictures tomorrow?'

As he gazed at her intently, his grey eyes darkening, Sally found herself shuddering. 'I can't, Arthur, I'm busy. Let go of my arm, please.'

'Christ, what's the matter? Why do you always look at me like a frightened rabbit? I'm only asking you to come to the pictures.'

'Arthur, I'm sorry, I don't want to go out with you. Anyway, you've already got a girlfriend. Haven't I seen you with Jenny from across the road?'

'Bloody hell, Sally, I just take her out occasionally, that's all, it's nothing serious. If that's all that's stopping you going out with me, I won't see her any more.'

'No, don't do that,' she said hastily. 'I'm sorry, I just don't want to go out with you ... or anyone,' she added.

'Sod you then, you frigid cow,' he spat, spinning round and stalking off in the opposite direction, his back stiff.

She watched until he was out of sight, his words playing over in her mind. Frigid, he had called her frigid, yet she couldn't help her body tensing with fear when he came near. It was something in his eyes that frightened her, a look she could remember from her childhood that always made her shrink in terror.

'Blimey, Sally,' her mum said when she went indoors, 'you don't half look different.' She walked across the room, reaching out to touch her hair. 'It's so short, I'm not sure if I like it.'

'I'm not sure either, Mum, but I can't do much about it now, can I?'

Arthur found himself walking around the block, kicking himself for losing his temper. He just couldn't understand why Sally recoiled the way she did every time he came near her, almost as if she was terrified of him. Even as children she had avoided him, but it hadn't mattered then, she was just his kid sister's friend.

When had he first noticed how gorgeous she was? He couldn't remember. But one day he suddenly saw that she had changed from a gangly scruffy kid, into a beautiful teenager. Her new hairstyle looked great too, but he couldn't forget the fear in her huge green eyes as she looked up at him. Yet all he had done was to ask her for a date.

As he turned the corner, back into Candle Lane, he looked across at Jenny Jackson's house. She was the complete antithesis to Sally. Hot, passionate, and always throwing herself at him. Yes, he had taken her out a few times, but it wasn't serious and he'd drop her like a shot if Sally would go out with him.

He wasn't vain, but knew he wasn't bad-looking – the amount of attention he got from girls had shown him that. So what was it about him that Sally found so distasteful? He had tried asking his sister, but as usual she hadn't taken him seriously and had laughed, joking that Sally had better taste than to go out with him.

Perhaps I should give it one more try, he thought as he reached his own front door, deciding that he might as well turn in. They had a big job on tomorrow needing two vans, and were starting work early in the morning. He'd been working for his dad for over eighteen months now and enjoyed the work. It had been hard at first, as some of the furniture weighed a ton, but now his muscles had hardened and it had become a lot easier.

'Hello, son,' his mum said as he walked into the kitchen. 'You're a bit earlier than usual.'

'We're starting at six in the morning so I thought I'd better turn in.'

'Yes, your dad's already gone up. By the way, how's that new lad getting on, the one that you took on last week?'

'He's doing all right, but I'll be glad when he passes his driving test. I could do with a break when we're on a long haul.' He yawned widely. 'I'm going up, good night, Mum,' he called as he left the room.

Lying in bed, he touched the wall beside him, knowing that Sally was just on the other side. Yet this barrier was nothing compared to the one she had erected around herself. One more time, he thought – I'll ask her out one more time, but if she says no, I'll never ask her again.

Chapter Seventeen

The August sale was in full swing and Arding & Hobbs was packed with customers eager to find a bargain.

In the record department, Sally had a thin veil of perspiration on her forehead as she ran back and forth behind the counter, serving one customer after another. Her blouse felt as though it was sticking to her back, but Miss French looked as cool and immaculate as ever.

Stifling a yawn she glanced up at the clock, pleased to see that it was time for her break. 'Can I go to lunch please, Miss French?'

'Yes, but make sure that you are back on time. We are very busy, as you can see.'

'Yes, miss,' she answered, hurrying from behind the counter before another customer could waylay her, and heading for the staff staircase.

'Hello,' a voice said softly as she entered the canteen and joined the queue. 'You're from the record department, aren't you?'

'Er, yeah,' she whispered shyly, finding herself gazing up into a pair of soft brown eyes.

'I thought so. I work upstairs from you in the electrical department. My name's John, by the way.'

'I'm Sally.'

'Yes, I know.'

She raised her eyebrows. How did he know her name?

'I asked someone,' he said, as though reading her mind. 'I've been hoping to get a chance to talk to you. I ... I wondered if I could take you out one night?'

Sally saw that his face had turned slightly pink and found herself drawn to him. She loved the way his eyes crinkled in the corners when he smiled and his dark brown hair that flopped onto his forehead. But a date? She hunched her shoulders defensively, still gazing up at him.

'Go on,' he urged. 'I don't bite, honest.'

It was impossible not to smile; he looked like a little boy asking for a sweet, and she wondered how old he was. The queue moved forward and she found herself at the front. 'Just a cup of tea, please.'

After paying at the till she made her way to an empty table, not able to resist a glance behind. He had paid for his food, and yes, his eyes were scanning the room as though looking for her. She sat down quickly, her head lowered.

'Do you mind if I share your table?'

Looking up she saw him smiling appealingly. 'No, that's all right,' she answered, her voice trembling.

He put his tray on the table, taking the seat opposite her. 'Aren't you eating anything?' he asked, digging into a meat pie.

'I've got a packed lunch.' Feeling her face flushing, she pulled a sandwich out of her bag, taking a nervous bite and finding that her throat felt dry, making it difficult to swallow.

'I love your new hairstyle,' he said softly. 'It suits you.'

She touched her fringe. 'I think it's a bit short.'

'No, it's perfect, but you haven't answered my question yet. Will you come out with me?'

Sally picked up her cup of tea, quickly swallowing a mouthful and choked as the hot liquid hit her throat. Mortified, she felt tea dribbling onto her chin. 'I'm sorry,' she gasped, endeavouring to wipe it away with the heel of her hand.

'Here,' he said, holding out a handkerchief. 'It's awful when that happens, isn't it? Please, don't be embarrassed.'

151

It was his kindness, and the soft, concerned expression on his face that decided her. She wiped her chin and handed back the handkerchief, then, with a deep intake of breath, she agreed to go out with him.

'Tonight?' he asked eagerly.

She looked down at the table, endeavouring to hide her panic. How could she go out with him that evening – she didn't have anything to wear. 'I'm sorry, I can't, not tonight.'

'Tomorrow then,' he urged.

'I usually 'ave a lot to do on a Sunday,' she prevaricated, already regretting her impulsive decision.

'Couldn't you spare some time in the afternoon? We could just go for a walk or something.'

As she hesitated he tipped his head to one side. 'Please,' he said with an irresistible lopsided grin.

His smile was gorgeous, and her heart leaped. 'Yes, all right,' she found herself saying, smiling back at him.

It was only when she left the canteen to go back to her department that panic set in. What had she done? Yes, he seemed different from other boys, softer somehow, but what about when they were alone? What if he tried to touch her? Stop it, she admonished herself. They were only going for a walk – what could happen? No, it would be all right, and all she had to do now was to ask Ann if she would lend her something to wear.

Sally walked slowly home after work; her feet were aching, and she felt exhausted. She was anxious to tell Ann about her date with John, but

152

knew she had to call in to see Mr Cox first. She had been giving him regular healing, but sadly the relief was short-lived.

'Hello, how is he?' she asked as Nelly Cox opened the door.

'Oh, I'm so glad you're here,' the woman said, drawing Sally inside. 'He's having a really bad day and can't even get out of bed. Do you mind going upstairs to see him?' She looked closely at Sally. 'You look tired, ducks. Would you like a cup of tea or something?'

'Yes please, I'd love one,' Sally answered, mounting the stairs.

Creeping into the bedroom and crossing to the side of the bed, she focused on George's aura, gulping in distress at what she could see.

'Here you are, Sally,' Nelly said as she came bustling in carrying a cup of tea with a few biscuits balanced in the saucer.

'Has he seen the doctor?' Sally whispered.

Nelly shook her head. 'He saw him yesterday, but he won't let me call him today. He thinks the doctor will 'ave him admitted into hospital.'

'Perhaps that's the best place for him,' Sally said, lifting the cup and taking a sip of the hot sweet tea.

'No, it ain't.' The hoarse voice came from the bed and they turned, startled, as the sick man struggled to sit up. 'I want to die in me own house ... and in me own bed ... so I ain't seeing the bloody doctor again,' he gasped, sinking back with exhaustion.

'Oh, George,' Nelly cried. 'Don't talk like that. You ain't gonna die.' She turned her strained face

153

towards Sally. 'Tell him, love, tell him that he's gonna be all right,' she begged.

Before she could answer he raised his hand, touching his wife's arm. 'Nelly, can I 'ave a drink?' he croaked, his voice weak.

'Of course you can, I'll be back in a tick,' she told him, scurrying from the room.

'Sally, come here. I want to tell you something,' he whispered urgently.

Edging to the side of the bed, she took hold of his hot dry hand. 'What is it, Mr Cox?'

'I keep smelling lavender. My old mum loved it and used to place dried sprigs of it amongst her clothes. It feels like she's here, Sally, and that she's come to fetch me.'

Sally gulped as a large lump formed in her throat, but she couldn't hold back the tears, and they streamed unchecked down her face.

'Don't cry, sweetheart. I ain't sorry to go.' His voice weakened and she had to lean over the bed to hear him as he asked, 'Will you keep an eye on my Nelly for me? We never had any kids and she'll be all on her own.'

'Of course I will, don't worry.'

'Thanks, ducks,' he managed to pant, fighting for breath.

'Just rest now, she said, holding her hands over his body and praying for healing. With relief she saw his body relaxing, his breathing a little easier. Standing back she cuffed angrily at the tears dripping from her chin, feeling utterly helpless and useless. He was beyond her limited healing powers.

When Nelly came back into the room, she took

one look at Sally's wet face and the tumbler in her hand shook, water splashing onto the lino.

'It's all right, he's asleep,' Sally quickly assured her. 'Look, I'll just pop home and tell me mum where I am. Don't worry, I'll be back soon.'

'Leave the door on the latch. I'll stay with him,' Nelly told her.

Back in number five, Sally hurried breathlessly into the kitchen and said, 'Can you put me dinner in the oven, Mum? I'll 'ave it later.'

'You've been crying, love – what's the matter?'

'Mr Cox is really bad, Mum, and I'm gonna sit with him for a while.'

'But you needn't do that, Sal. Tell Nelly to get the doctor in,' Ruth said indignantly.

'He won't 'ave it, Mum. Now I've got to go, I'll see you later.'

'Hold on a minute, what time will–'

Sally didn't give her mum time to finish speaking; she was already on her way out again.

She drew up a chair beside Nelly, and they sat holding hands, listening to George's laboured breathing. The tortured rise and fall of his chest became hypnotic, and Sally lost all track of time.

Gradually, sitting in the dim room, her head began to droop with exhaustion. It was as she blinked her eyes furiously in an effort to stay awake, that she became aware of a light hovering at the foot of the bed. She lifted her nose, sniffing the air. It was unmistakable. The overpowering scent of lavender.

There was a gasp and she turned to see Mr Cox struggling to sit up, his arms outstretched as

155

though reaching out to someone. He opened his mouth, whispering just one faint word, before slowly sinking back, the breath leaving his body in a strange rattling sound.

'No, no!' Nelly wailed, throwing herself across the bed and sobbing hysterically. 'George, oh George, don't leave me, darlin'! Come back, please come back!'

Sally stared at his grey face, her body rigid with shock. It's like looking at an empty shell, she thought, as though the essence of the man she knew had gone. Then it hit her, like a blow to the stomach. He was dead.

Nelly turned anguished eyes towards her. 'Help me! Please, help me! He can't be dead – he can't!' she screamed.

Feeling overwhelmed, Sally sat rigidly, her mind frozen before panic set in. I need help, she thought, and desperate to get away, she made a sudden bolt for the door. 'I'm gonna get me mum, I won't be long!' she yelled, running from the room.

'Mum, Mum, come quick,' she shrieked, running into the kitchen.

'Wha ... what's the matter,' Ruth stammered, already half-asleep in a chair.

'Quick, Mum, it's Mr Cox, he's dead and Nelly needs you.'

'What's the time?' Ruth asked, running her hands over her eyes and glancing at the clock. 'Sally, where 'ave you been? It's nearly eleven o'clock.'

'Oh, for God's sake, will you listen to me,

Mum. Nelly needs you.' She shouted now, emphasising each word. 'Her husband is dead!'

At last it seemed to penetrate her mother's foggy mind and she jumped to her feet, eyes darting wildly around the room. 'All right, I'm coming. Now, where's me shoes?'

She felt her temper rising. 'Mum, just come in your slippers.'

'What's going on?' Sadie asked, appearing in the doorway, her dressing-gown slung around her shoulders and blue hairnet askew. 'What's all this racket?'

'Mr Cox is dead, Gran,' she answered, bursting into a fresh flood of tears.

'Ruth, get yourself along there, I'll see to Sally,' the old lady ordered.

'Yeah, all right, all right, I'm going ain't I,' her daughter said irritably as she hurried out.

Sally sank onto the sofa. 'Oh Gran, it was horrible. I've never seen anyone die before. I didn't know what to do and I ran away.' She buried her face in her hands. 'I feel so ashamed. How could I do that to Nelly?'

Her gran drew her close, saying, 'Now you listen to me, my girl. There ain't many fifteen-year-olds that could have stayed to watch someone die. All right, so you ran off afterwards. Bloody 'ell, it's not surprising that you panicked – and anyway, she's not on her own now. Your mum's with her.'

Sally felt drained. Her eyes were swollen and sore from crying, and her head was beginning to thump. 'I'm so tired, Gran,' she whispered, 'and what's the point of doing this healing? It didn't help Mr Cox, did it – and I'm sure Nelly expected me to save him.'

'Look, love, you can't perform miracles. He was already terminally ill when he came to you and at least you helped to ease his pain. Now come on, you've been out since early this morning and must be starving. I'll get you something to eat.'

Unable to stomach the thought of food, Sally said, 'No, I don't want anything, Gran.'

'All right, but I'll make you a cup of cocoa and then you can get yerself off to bed.' She squeezed her arm, adding, 'Things will look different in the morning, Sal. They always do.'

Chapter Eighteen

When Sally awoke the next morning she lay sleepily gazing at dust motes dancing in a shaft of sunlight that streamed through her window. Her eyes felt sticky and she rubbed at them impatiently with her knuckles, groaning as memories of the previous night came flooding into her mind.

'Sally,' her mum shouted from the foot of the stairs. 'It's gone ten o'clock. Do you intend getting up today?'

'Yeah, I'm coming,' she called despondently, groping for her slippers and throwing an old cardigan over her nightie.

Padding into the bathroom she looked dispiritedly at her reflection in the mirror, seeing a drooping mouth, eyes that were puffy slits and hair standing up on end like a hedgehog. Bending over the sink she splashed cold water onto her face, and with wet hands tried to smooth her hair before attacking it with a comb. Oh, what does it matter, she thought, slinging the comb impatiently back on the shelf and heading downstairs.

'Sal, you look awful,' her mum said as she walked into the kitchen.

'Leave the girl alone, Ruth, she's had a rotten time,' her gran intervened, coming to her defence as usual.

'Christ, Mum, all I said was that she looks awful and–'

'How's Nelly?' Sally interrupted, in no mood to listen to them bickering.

'Not too bad, considering. I went down to see her first thing this morning and now Peggy's with her. They're going to the undertaker's tomorrow to sort out the funeral. Joan Mason is dealing with the catering, and I told her we'd all muck in. Oh, and Mrs Edwards is arranging a collection for flowers.' She shook her head sadly. 'It's a shame really. Nelly ain't got any family left so there will only be friends and neighbours at the funeral.'

'Blimey,' Sadie said. 'It didn't take long to get that lot sorted. The poor sod only died last night.'

'You know what it's like around here, Mum. Everyone loves Nelly, and as soon as word got out that George had died, they all wanted to help.'

'Yeah, I know, but bleedin' hell, if Joan Mason's arranging the catering she'll be bossing everyone around as usual.'

'I know, but she volunteered and we didn't 'ave the nerve to say no. Oh, by the way, Sally, Nelly wants you to pop down to see her.'

She gaped in horror. 'Oh no ... I can't face her.'

'Why ever not? She's grateful that you stayed with her.'

'I should think so too,' her gran snorted. 'She should've had more sense and sent for one of us.'

Sally hung her head, unable to blot out the sight of Mr Cox's face lying lifeless and grey on the pillow. She remembered her promise to him and knew she had no choice – but not yet; she couldn't face it yet. 'I think I'll get dressed now and pop round to see Ann. I'll go to Nelly's later, Mum.'

'Hold yer horses, my girl. What about breakfast?' Ruth asked indignantly.

'Not now, I'm not hungry.' She saw her mum and gran exchange glances, and they both pursed their lips in disapproval. 'Look, I'll have something later,' she promised, hurriedly leaving the room, knowing that if she didn't escape she would get a nagging from both of them.

Now, sitting on Ann's bed, her friend listened without interruption as Sally told her about Mr Cox, her face full of sympathy, and only changing expression when she came to the bit about her date with John that afternoon.

'What's he like, Sally?'

'He's lovely, really nice-looking and ever so polite. He even offered me his hanky when I was choking on a cup of tea. Honestly, I was mortified, and must have been crimson with embarrassment.' She shook her head sadly. 'But I can't face going out with him now, and anyway, just look at the state of me.'

'Don't be daft, Sal. I could soon fix your hair,

and a bit of make-up will take care of the rest.'

'I'm too upset, Ann. I keep seeing Mr Cox over and over again in me mind.'

'Going out with John might be just what you need – it'll take your mind off it.'

'I dunno,' she said doubtfully. 'We're supposed to be meeting at Battersea Park, but I'm just not in the mood.'

'Well, you can't leave him standing there like a lemon, waiting for you. How would you face him at work tomorrow?'

Sally knew Ann was right and drummed her fingers impatiently, unconsciously mimicking her mother's habit. She drew in a deep breath. 'Bugger it, I'll just 'ave to go then, won't I?' she said, exhaling loudly with exasperation.

'Come on, it won't be that bad,' Ann cajoled. 'From what you've told me, he sounds really nice. Wait till Arthur hears about this,' she added gleefully, 'it'll bring the big head down a peg or two.'

'Ann,' Sally asked hesitantly, 'Er ... could you lend me something to wear?'

'Don't be daft, of course I can. I tell you what, how about that pencil skirt I bought last week and my beige blouse to go with it?'

'Not that lovely brown one! But you haven't worn it yourself yet.'

'It doesn't matter, this is a special occasion. My goodness, the ice maiden is going on a date.' She gawked at Sally, her face turning pink with embarrassment. 'Oh God, I'm sorry, it just slipped out. That was an awful thing to say.'

Sally stared at her friend. First Arthur had

called her frigid and now Ann was saying she was an ice maiden. Was it true? Was there something wrong with her?

'Please, don't look at me like that,' Ann begged. 'I didn't mean it, honest. It's just that you usually run a mile if a boy shows the slightest interest in you. Look at Arthur, for instance – he's been after you for ages.'

Sally could see how upset her friend was, and forced a smile. 'I know, you're right, but there's something about John that makes me feel I can trust him. He's different somehow.'

Ann uncurled her legs and stood up, patting Sally on the arm. 'Let's get you sorted out then.' She walked across the room, opened her wardrobe, and pulled out the skirt and blouse.

Sally left Ann, returning home in time for Sunday dinner, her thoughts on both Nelly and her date with John later that afternoon.

'Sally, you didn't want any breakfast and now yer hardly eating any dinner. What's the matter?'

'I'm nervous about going to see Nelly. I just don't know what to say to her, Mum.'

It was her gran who leaned forward and touched the back of her hand. 'Just let her talk about her husband if she wants to. I remember when our David died, and then yer granddad. Nobody would let me talk about either of them and it really upset me. It made me feel like they'd never lived. I wanted to talk, to relive my memories; it somehow brought them alive again in me mind.'

'I didn't know you felt like that, Mum,' Ruth said.

'No, I don't expect you did, love. I hid most of my feelings from you and Mary – you were both grieving too, don't forget. Anyway, people were only trying to be kind.'

Sally saw the sadness on their faces and rapidly changed the subject. 'Mum, I've got a date this afternoon.'

'What! A date, you've got a date? And when was this arranged? You're a bit late telling me, my girl.'

'I'm sorry, Mum. I met this bloke in the canteen on Saturday. He's ever so nice, but then Mr Cox died, and I forgot to tell you.'

'Hmm, and where are you going on this date?'

'We're only going for a walk.'

'All right, Sal, but I want you home by eight o'clock, and no later mind.'

'I'll be home well before that, Mum,' she assured her.

Sally had been to see Nelly, and as gran advised, had let her talk about her husband. She had been so sweet, saying that the healing *had* helped – but Sally knew she was just being kind. After all, what good had it done? It hadn't been able to save George.

Now she was reluctantly on her way to meet John, and as she got off the bus, her eyes scanned the road ahead. He was standing by the gates and when he caught sight of her, his face lit up.

'You came then,' he said, smiling gently.

The sound of his soft, husky voice made her stomach flutter, and she smiled back shyly.

'You look lovely, Sally,' he said, placing his hand on her elbow and guiding her through the gates into Battersea Park.

She tensed nervously at his touch, but steeled herself by gazing at the flower borders just inside the entrance. The rows of brightly coloured blooms – yellow dahlias competing with bright red geraniums – lifted her spirits and she smiled in pleasure, beginning to relax.

As they strolled along she could see several families sitting on the grass, picnics spread on gaily-patterned rugs, and their children playing in the dappled sunlight that filtered through the leafy canopy of huge oak trees. 'It's lovely here,' she murmured.

'Haven't you been to the park before?' John asked, a hint of surprise in his voice.

'Not for a long time. Do you come here a lot then?'

'Yes, I live just across the road and use the tennis courts a lot. Do you play?'

'No, of course not. Tennis is only for toffs.' As soon as the words left her mouth she was stricken, feeling the heat of embarrassment as her face coloured. God, she thought, what an idiot. What must he think of me!

'No, Sally,' he said, sounding unconcerned, 'tennis is for everyone and I certainly wouldn't call myself a toff. I could teach you to play if you like.'

'Er, I dunno ... maybe,' she stuttered, still cringing as they walked along a path that led to a small tea-room.

'Well, have a think about it,' he said, drawing her to a halt. 'Would you like something to drink?'

'I'd love a Coke,' she told him as he led her

towards a table under the scant shade of a small silver birch.

Sally studied him as he entered the tea-room, already chastising herself for agreeing to meet him. John was different from her first impression, more sophisticated somehow. He was also very well-spoken, and somehow that made her feel gauche and out of her depth. She raked her fingers through her hair, then frantically tried to smooth it down again, realising she had probably mucked up Ann's careful grooming.

'Here you are,' he said, placing two bottles on the table and sitting down opposite her.

'Thanks,' she mumbled, grabbing her Coke and sucking deeply on the straw, her eyes averted.

'Do you like working in the record department, Sally?'

'Yes, it's all right, but I'm not keen on Miss French, my manageress,' she told him, trying to be careful with her diction.

'Why is that?' he said, a slight frown creasing his brow.

'She's just so stuck-up. Sort of prim and proper, if you know what I mean.'

He let out a low laugh. 'Yes, I can see how you got that impression. What sort of music do you like, Sally?' he asked, abruptly changing the subject.

'Oh,' she enthused, her diction already forgotten, 'I love Elvis. Mind you, he didn't half look different when he went into the army. Don't you think it's a shame that he had to 'ave his gorgeous hair cut so short?'

'Yes, I suppose so,' John said hesitantly.

165

'Who's your favourite singer then?' she asked.

John grinned lopsidedly. 'To be honest, I prefer classical music.'

Sally grimaced. This date was getting worse and worse and it seemed they had nothing in common. As though sensitive to her thoughts he reached out, placing his hand over hers.

She jerked away nervously, seeing a puzzled look in his eyes as he leaned slightly towards her. 'I'm sorry, I didn't mean to alarm you,' he said softly.

Ashamed of her reactions she sank down in her seat, hunching her shoulders defensively.

'I play the piano,' he continued, as though trying to reassure her. 'My aunt taught me, and I think that's where my love of the classics originates from. That's not to say I don't like some modern music – I love jazz for instance.'

Unable to think of anything to say, Sally smiled wanly, wishing the ground would open up and swallow her.

'Come on, finish your drink,' John urged, and as she stood up he gestured to a small shaded path. As they ambled along she saw a set of gates ahead and sighed with relief. Thank God, she thought, they were leaving the park, so perhaps he was as unhappy in her company as she was in his.

They emerged onto a wide tree-lined avenue, crossing towards tall elegant houses, each with intricate wrought-iron balconies surrounding large windows that glinted in the sunlight.

John gestured to one of them. 'I live here, Sally, and I know this is unusual on a first date, but would you like to come in to meet my aunt?'

'Oh no, I couldn't,' she stammered shyly, her

eyes roaming over the large, affluent-looking houses.

'Please,' he urged. 'I've got a special reason for wanting you to meet her and we won't stay long.'

Before she could think of any further protest he led her up the wide steps and, opening the door, ushered her into a large square hall.

'Our flat is on the first floor,' he said, indicating the rich blue carpeted stairs with highly polished brass rods gleaming at the back of each tread.

Sally had never seen such a beautiful hallway and was unable to keep the surprise out of her voice. 'A flat? You live in a flat?'

'Yes, of course,' he said, his voice slightly puzzled as they mounted the stairs. 'This house is divided into four and I've lived here with my aunt since my parents died.'

When they reached the first floor, John opened the door facing them. 'It's only me, Lottie,' he called as he led her inside. 'I've brought someone to meet you.' He turned to Sally, a wide smile on his face, saying, 'Be prepared for a surprise,' as he led her into a large room that seemed to be filled with light.

The sun was blazing through two large windows, and for a moment Sally was blinded by the glare. She blinked rapidly and as her eyes adjusted, she saw a tall, slender lady with long, dark hair, standing in front of an easel, her back towards them and a paintbrush poised in her hand.

As she turned, Sally's eyes widened with shock. No, it couldn't be! She saw a face devoid of make-up, a large smudge of green paint across the nose. Her gaze travelled downwards and she looked with amazement at the woman's peculiar, scruffy outfit. She was wearing a man's shirt, liberally spattered with paint, that almost reached her knees and covered most of the faded denim jeans. Bare feet completed the bohemian look.

'Miss French,' she gasped.

Charlotte French smiled at the expression on Sally's face. She had studied her young sales assistant carefully and had seen the way she reacted to male customers, almost as if she was frightened of them. She was convinced that Sally was a virgin, perhaps with something in her past that had turned her off men. Realising that she would be ideal for John, she had suggested that he ask her out.

'Hello, my dear,' she said, advancing towards her. 'I can see you're surprised by my appearance. I wear these old clothes when I'm painting. Now, can I get you something to drink, a sherry perhaps?'

Sally's mouth opened, her voice coming out in a squeak. 'Er ... no, thanks.'

Lottie grimaced; they would have to do something about the child's voice. Her diction was awful. What would her friends think if they heard that awful Cockney twang?

'How about you, John? Would you like a sherry?'

'Yes please, Auntie.'

'Do sit down, Sally,' Lottie urged as she walked across to the drinks cabinet, glancing back to see Sally perched on the edge of the sofa, looking overwhelmed and biting nervously on her bottom lip. Pouring the drinks she hid a smile;

the girl was so innocent and just what John needed – but it would do no harm to gently probe her background. 'Now, Sally, tell me something about yourself. We don't get a chance to talk socially at work, do we?' she said, handing John his glass of sherry.

'Er, what do yer wanna know?'

'Well now, what are your hobbies for instance?'

'I ain't got any hobbies – well, except for reading that is.'

'Reading is a marvellous hobby, Sally, it can broaden the mind,' she told her. 'What about your father? What does he do for a living?'

Sally's face turned slightly pink and lowering her head, she said softly, 'My dad left me mum years ago.'

'How awful for you!' Lottie exclaimed, but with a small smile at John. It was even better, she thought, without a protective father in the background.

'Do you go to church, Sally?' John asked. 'I mean, are you Church of England or Roman Catholic?'

'No, I don't go to church, but I think I was christened Church of England. I do believe in God though, and just recently I've been learning how to do spiritual healing.'

Both Lottie and John froze, their glasses half-raised to their lips, looking at each other in horror.

'What's the matter?' Sally asked worriedly.

'Oh, my dear, you really shouldn't be doing things like that. It goes against the teachings of the Church,' Lottie told her, a frown creasing her brows.

'But it helps me gran,' Sally protested. 'It's taken her pain away.'

Lottie bit back a retort; it wouldn't do to alienate the girl. They would have to tread softly, perhaps introduce her to their church, and slowly show her the error of her ways. My goodness, who would have thought it? This innocent-looking child mucking about with spiritual forces. It didn't bear thinking about.

'Let's talk about this another time,' Lottie said, shaking her head at John, who still had a frown on his face.

They chatted for about another fifteen minutes, avoiding the subject of religion, until Sally told them that she had to go home. Lottie watched them leaving, hoping that she had made the right choice for John. The girl seemed pliable, her opinions unformed, so perhaps it would work out. It must, she thought fiercely, it must. At all costs, John must be protected, otherwise what sort of future would he have?

Chapter Nineteen

'I'm worried about Mary,' Sadie said, folding the letter and shoving it back into the envelope.

'I ain't interested, Mum.'

'For Gawd's sake, Ruth, she's yer sister!'

'Not any more she ain't. Now look, Mum, I said I would never forgive her for defending Harry, and I meant it.' Ruth stood up, walking across the room to look out of the window, her arms folded defensively.

'Look, it's been over six years now, don't you think you've punished her enough? Please love, come with me the next time I go to meet her. There's something wrong, I know there is.'

'No!' Ruth yelled, turning sharply to glare at her mother. 'How many times 'ave I got to tell you! And now you're trying to make me feel guilty. That ain't fair, and you know–' She paused, hearing a knock on the back door.

'Hello, it's only me. Have you got the kettle on?' Elsie asked as she poked her head into the room. Then, as if sensing the atmosphere, she added, 'What's up?'

'Oh, nothing,' Ruth said, taking a deep breath to compose herself. She was sick of arguing with her mum over Mary, and was glad of the distraction. 'How's things, Elsie?' she asked.

'All right, except for Bert's back that is, it's really playing him up. With all the heavy lifting he's done over the years it's starting to take its toll. Thank God it's Sunday so he can give it a rest.' Elsie pulled a chair out from under the table and plopped down, her ample rear bulging over the sides of the small wooden seat. 'By the way, Ruth, is Sally in? Ann wants a word with her.'

'No. She's gone to church with John.'

Elsie turned to Sadie, smiling sadly. 'Is she still refusing to give you any healing?'

'Yeah. John's convinced her that it's wrong to use her psychic gifts and there's no talking to her. I told her that my hip was starting to give me a lot of pain again, and do you know what she

171

said?' Sadie blinked her eyes, close to tears. 'She said I'm in God's hands.'

'What does your Ann say about it, Elsie?' Ruth asked.

'She doesn't say a lot, but I think she feels that John's got a bit too much influence over Sally.'

Ruth sighed unconsciously. Sally had been going out with John for over nine months now, and was becoming like a different girl. She was absolutely besotted and did everything she could to please him. She had already improved her elocution, changed her hairstyle and the way she dressed, saying that John wanted her to look more sophisticated.

She shook her head worriedly. If he loves Sally, why does he want to change her? Turning towards her friend, an appeal in her eyes, she asked, 'Elsie, do you think you could 'ave a talk with her? We've tried, but she just won't listen.'

'I'll give it a go, love, but I don't think it will do any good. She goes out of her way to avoid me these days.'

Sally tried to listen to the service, forcing her mind to concentrate on the sermon, but it was no good. The strange feeling of foreboding refused to go away. No, she thought, I must ignore it. John had told her that she had to fight these psychic episodes, insisting they were the work of the devil.

Closing her eyes she clutched her hymnbook tightly, a prayer on her lips, but the feeling just became stronger, filling her with an impending sense of doom. She knew something was terribly wrong when a message, urgent and compelling, rushed into her consciousness.

'John,' she whispered frantically, standing up abruptly, 'please let me pass. I've got to go home.'

Lottie was sitting on the other side of John and she turned, her face stiff with disapproval. 'Sit down, Sally,' she hissed.

'No, I must go!' she insisted, her voice now loud in panic as she struggled to push past John's knees.

The vicar faltered in his sermon and those nearest to them in the congregation turned in their pews, straining their necks to see who was causing the disruption.

John was forced to stand up, acute embarrassment showing on his face. 'Excuse me, Auntie,' he urged, and as she stood to let them pass he took Sally's hand, almost dragging her up the aisle.

On the steps outside the church he turned, and instead of annoyance on his face, she saw sympathy. 'What's wrong, darling, are you ill or something?'

'I haven't got time to explain, John. I must go home, but you go back in for the rest of the service.'

'Please, Sally, you can't just rush off without an explanation!'

Sally floundered. She couldn't tell him the truth and somehow she had to stop him coming home with her. 'Oh, for goodness' sake, John. It's just a woman's thing,' she lied, feeling her face flooding with colour. 'Now I really must go. I'll see you tomorrow,' she called, running off and praying that he didn't pursue her.

'Mum, Gran,' she gasped, rushing into the

kitchen. 'Quick, we've got to go to Auntie Mary's house. Something's dreadfully wrong.'

Three pairs of eyes stared at her, mouths agape, but it was Sadie who spoke first, her voice sharp with concern. 'Oh Sally, has something happened to my Mary?'

'I don't know, Gran. But please, we've got to hurry.'

'Hold on, my girl,' Ruth snapped. 'How do you know something's wrong? Who told you?'

'Nobody told me, Mum. It's just a feeling, but it's very strong.'

'Sally, what are you talking about? You're not making any sense.'

How could she explain? How could she make them understand? she thought desperately. 'Look, it's more than just a feeling. When I was in church something happened. I heard a voice whispering in my head, urging me to go to Aunt Mary's.'

Elsie jumped up, scurrying to the back door. 'That's good enough for me. I'll go and rouse Bert, he can drive you there.'

'Thanks, Elsie,' she said gratefully. 'Come on, Mum, get your shoes on, there's no time to lose.'

'No, Sally. I ain't going to your aunt's, and neither are you!'

'For goodness sake, Mum. What if I'm right? What if something terrible has happened and you refused to help. How will you live with that?' she asked impatiently.

Sally recoiled as her mum's face suffused with hatred. Ruth reared up, hands flat on the table, and leaning forward with her chin thrust out aggressively, she yelled, 'What if that sod Harry's

174

there – 'ave you thought of that?'

'What do you think he can do, Mum? I'm a grown woman now and I can look after myself,' Sally said quietly, trying to defuse her anger. Seeing Sadie struggling into her coat, she added, 'Look, we must go with Gran. How can we leave her to deal with this on her own?'

'All right,' Ruth capitulated. 'But this had better not be a wild-goose chase, my girl.'

Elsie bustled in again, puffing with exertion. 'Right, are you all ready? Arthur has just come in and he's taking you in his car.'

'I didn't know he had a car!' Sally exclaimed.

'He only got it yesterday,' Elsie told her. 'Now come on, he's waiting outside.'

Sally was ushered into the front seat, while Ruth and Sadie crawled into the back. Elsie waved them off, urging her son to drive carefully, her face creased with anxiety.

Sadie started shouting directions from the back, her voice booming in Arthur's ear. 'Turn left here, Arthur, then go along the Northcote Road.'

'It's all right, old girl, you don't have to shout,' he gently admonished. Then turning to Sally and smiling widely, he asked, 'What do you think of my car then? It's a Morris Minor. I got it off Dad's partner so it's in really good nick.'

'It's lovely,' she answered distantly as the feelings of foreboding returned, threatening to overpower her mind. 'Can't you go any faster, Arthur,' she pleaded.

The journey seemed to take for ever, but at last they pulled up outside Mary's house.

Sally was the first to clamber out of the car and

she rushed to her aunt's door, banging loudly on the knocker. 'There's no reply,' she said, turning to the others as they came to stand by her side, 'but she's in there. I just know she is.'

Sadie fumbled in her bag, her fingers trembling. 'Here,' she said, handing Sally a key. 'I didn't give it back to her when I left. I must 'ave known it would come in handy one day.'

Pushing open the door, her nostrils wrinkling at the clinical smells of carbolic and bleach, Sally called, 'Are you in, Aunt Mary?'

Sadie struggled past her, flinging open the sitting-room door. 'She's not in here. Try the kitchen,' she shouted.

Ruth rushed down the hall and called, 'No, she's not in here either.'

It was Sally who was first up the stairs, her fear leading her straight to her aunt's bedroom. 'Mum, Mum, quick! Up here!' she cried.

She barely recognised her aunt. Mary's face was gaunt and chalky white, while her body, lying sprawled across the covers, looked almost skeletal.

Sadie, limping into the room behind Ruth, immediately took charge. 'Arthur, quick, go and get me a glass of water with plenty of salt in it.'

'What's wrong with her, Mum?' Ruth asked, her voice quavering.

'It's bleedin' obvious ain't it. Look, what do you think that is?' Sadie shouted in agitation, pointing to the empty pill bottle lying on the floor.

'Oh, God,' Ruth whispered.

Arthur came in, a glass in his hand, filled to the brim and murky with salt.

'Thanks, love,' Sadie said. 'Now help me to sit

176

her up. We've got to make her drink this; it should make her sick. Sally, you go and get a bucket.'

Sally rushed downstairs, scrambling around in the kitchen until she found what she was looking for.

When she returned, they had her aunt sitting up and were forcing the liquid down her throat. She saw Mary choke, then heave, and rushed over with the bucket, nausea rising in her own throat at the sight of her aunt being violently sick.

'That's it,' Sadie crooned. 'Get it all up, darlin'.'

'Christ, Mum, how did you know what to do?' Ruth asked, her face pale.

'It's not the first time I've had to deal with this. I had a neighbour during the war who lost both sons and...' She shook her head. 'This ain't the time to talk about it. Come on, we've got to get Mary walking. Help me to stand her up.'

They took it in turns to support her, walking round and round the room. Sally could see that her gran was near to exhaustion and begged her to rest.

At last her aunt appeared to revive a little and they sat her on the bed. 'Leave me alone,' she slurred, trying to lie down again.

'No, Mary. Come on, sit up,' Sadie urged, shaking her by the shoulders and asking, 'Where's Harry?'

'Gone ... he's gone,' she mumbled.

Sadie turned to Ruth, her face etched with worry. 'Look, you can see that she can't be left on her own. Can we take her home with us?'

Sally watched her mum chewing on her lower lip as she stared at her sister. 'We ain't got much choice, 'ave we?' she said at last.

Arthur had to make two journeys; his car was too small to hold them all. Sally had offered to make her own way home, but he insisted on coming back for her.

It was strange sitting beside him in the car, watching his hands as they changed from wheel to gearstick so competently. She was finding conversation difficult and felt the atmosphere was strained, but Arthur didn't seem to notice. He gave her a quick glance, saying, 'It was touch and go there for a while wasn't it, Sally? Your aunt must have been in a right old state to try something like that.'

'Yes, you're right, but thank God my gran knew what to do.'

'Well, making her swallow salty water certainly did the trick.'

'I just hope she's going to be all right,' Sally said worriedly.

'I'm sure she's over the worst now,' Arthur said reassuringly as he manoeuvred the car through some heavy traffic. 'How's your boyfriend?' he asked, changing the subject abruptly. 'Still courting strong, are you?'

'He's fine, and yes, we're still going out together.'

The traffic-lights ahead changed to red, and pulling up he turned to face her. 'Do you think it's going to be a long-term relationship, Sally?'

'I hope so,' she told him, smiling softly.

'I see,' he said. Then with a deep sigh, he added, 'I'm thinking of asking Jenny to marry me.'

'Oh Arthur, how wonderful,' she enthused, yet puzzled by the slight pang she felt.

'You don't mind then?' he asked, as the lights turned to green.

'No, of course not,' she told him, surprised by the question.

They turned off the main road then, the traffic thinning as they drove down Long Street. 'Nearly there,' he mumbled.

'Thanks for all you've done, Arthur. We couldn't have managed without you.'

'Glad to help,' he said as they drew up outside her door. 'Will you let me know how your aunt is, Sally?'

'I'll do that, Arthur,' she answered. 'And thanks again. I'll pop round later and if you're not in, I'll leave a message.'

He flashed her a smile and Sally realised for the first time how good-looking he was. She forced her eyes away from his, and fumbling with the door handle, scrambled out of the car.

Perhaps it was something he saw in her expression, she wasn't sure, but her face flamed as Arthur walked to her side. 'You know don't you, Sally, that Jenny is my second choice,' he said, his pupils darkening as he gazed earnestly at her.

Sally reeled back, her stomach tightening. It was that look in his eyes again, a look that repelled her. 'Don't be silly, Arthur,' she gasped, turning away from him and rushing indoors.

Hurrying into the kitchen, and forcing Arthur from her mind, Sally asked, 'How is she, Mum?'

'Still groggy. We've put her to bed in my room

and yer gran's sitting with her.'

'Why do you think she did it?'

'I dunno, Sal. It may be because Harry's buggered off and left her. But somehow I think there's more to it than that. Perhaps yer gran can get her talking.'

'If anyone can it'll be Gran. Thank goodness we got there in time.'

'Yes, and that's due to you. I don't know how you do it, Sally. You spoke about a voice in yer head. What does it sound like?'

'I can't describe it, Mum. It's a sort of urgent whisper that becomes more compelling if I try to ignore it.'

'Doesn't it frighten you, Sally?'

'No, I've never been scared. But that doesn't make it right. I don't want it to happen any more. It's wrong – very wrong.'

'I don't understand how you can say that. Whatever happened to you in church, I thank God for it. It saved my sister's life.'

'Mum, can you manage without me for a while? I want to go next door to see Ann,' Sally said, not wanting to carry on with this conversation.

'Yeah, of course. I'll give you a knock on the wall when tea's ready.'

'Is Ann in, Elsie?' Sally asked, popping her head around the back door.

'Yes, she's in her room, go on up. Oh, wait a minute, Sally. Arthur told me what happened. How's your auntie? Is she going to be all right?'

'Yes, I think so. We got there just in time.'

'Well done, Sally. Your powers must still be developing, and according to the cards you should reach your full potential by the time you're eighteen.'

She felt the blood rush to her face. 'But I don't want them, Elsie. I just want to be normal!' she cried, rushing upstairs.

'What's wrong?' Ann asked, as she entered her room.

'Oh, everything. I hate being psychic,' Sally answered, flopping down onto the bed beside her friend. 'Why me? Why do I have to be different? And I'm dreading seeing John. I lied to him, Ann. He thinks I left church because I was ill.'

'Can't you just tell him the truth? After all, it sounds like you saved your aunt's life.'

'No, he says it's wrong to use psychic powers.'

'But why do you believe everything John tells you? What about my mum? Are you saying she shouldn't read palms or use the Tarot cards?'

'Well, yes I am. You see, John said she's misguided, and doesn't realise that she's being misled by the devil.'

Ann reared up, her eyes blazing with indignation. 'How dare you say that! Who are you to pass judgement on my mum? My God, you've changed into a sanctimonious little bitch. All I hear now is "John says this, John says that". He's brainwashed you and you're too besotted to see it.'

'That's not true,' Sally retorted, jumping off the bed. 'I'm not listening to any more of this. I'm going home.'

'Good,' Ann snapped. 'My mum's a wonderful woman and you seem to have forgotten how good she's been to you, and your family. Now go on – clear off – and in future stay out of my way!'

Sally ran downstairs and through the kitchen, ignoring Elsie's shout as she yanked open the back door, her emotions a turmoil of anger and misery.

'Wait!' her mum called as she rushed indoors, bolting for the stairs. 'Come back here, Sally.'

'Just leave me alone,' she sobbed.

Slamming her bedroom door she sprawled across the bed, going over and over her confrontation with Ann, I didn't mean it the way it came out, she thought. I didn't mean that Elsie's a bad person. She closed her eyes, hating herself for what she'd said. Oh, what am I going to do? she fretted. Surely I haven't lost Ann's friendship!

If only they understood. When John explained why she shouldn't use psychic powers, it all made perfect sense, especially when she told him about Mr Cox. As John said, she hadn't been able to save him and had just given his wife false hope, making his death harder to bear. Ever since he'd said that she had been wracked with guilt, realising that she must never use her healing powers again. John said that what happened in life was God's will, and she had no right to change it. She felt her eyes filling with tears and prayed that God would forgive her for what she had done.

Unbidden, her mind began to swim, and the room began to glow in a soft golden light. She felt a feathery touch on her cheek. 'Sally,' a voice whispered.

'No! Go away!' she screamed, burying her head in the pillows.

Chapter Twenty

The beach was crowded with holiday makers and scattered haphazardly with brightly striped deck-chairs. Small children splashed by the sea or knelt in the sand with buckets and spades, their backs turning pink as they competed to build bigger and better castles. The occasional father could be seen enthusiastically joining in their endeavours, while mothers sat in deckchairs, daringly exposing their knees.

Ken walked briskly along the promenade, puffing with exertion. The last six years had been prosperous and showed in his amply proportioned body. It was Barbara's scathing comments about his beer belly that had piqued his vanity and sent him out on this excursion.

He scowled as he slowed his pace, thinking about the bed and breakfast and the endless jobs waiting for him when he got back from his walk. Barbara had changed from the lovely sensuous woman he had left his wife for. Now she was nothing but a bloody old nag, he thought. Perfect, everything had to be bleedin' perfect. Even though it was early in June, every room was full and they had advance booking for the rest of the season – but did that satisfy her, oh no. She was already planning for next year and talking about having the whole house redecorated.

A small black and white dog suddenly dashed

across his path, causing him to stumble. 'Naughty boy, Patch,' a woman called as she walked towards him, a man at her side.

As Ken recovered his balance he noticed a curly-haired toddler clinging to her hand and stumbling along on podgy little legs. He was a beautiful child, bright with laughter, and Ken felt a pang of envy as his eyes moved to the boy's father.

'Blimey,' he gasped in recognition. 'What are you doing here?'

Harry put his arm defensively around the young blonde woman at his side. 'Ken,' he spluttered. 'Fancy bumping into you, and in Blackpool of all places.'

Ken narrowed his eyes suspiciously. 'Aren't you going to introduce me, Harry?'

'Er ... yes, of course. Sheila, this is Ken Marchant.'

'Hello, I'm pleased to meet you. Do you live in Blackpool too?' she asked as the child plopped down on his bottom beside her. Not waiting for a reply, she bent down and swept him up into her arms, saying, 'This little chap is Daniel. Here, darling, go to your daddy.' She smiled at Ken. 'My husband's ever so good with him.'

Harry's eyes met his, mute with appeal, before he turned to take the toddler.

'Well, you sly old dog,' Ken grinned, suddenly enjoying himself. 'What happened to Mary then?'

'Um ... Mary and I were divorced years ago,' he stammered, his face reddening.

Oh, this is lovely, Ken thought gleefully. It was obvious that Harry was lying and he was going to enjoy making the pervert squirm.

He was just about to turn the screw when the baby lifted two chubby little hands and held them to Harry's cheeks. 'Da-da,' he gurgled, bending his head to plant sloppy kisses all over his daddy's face.

Something pierced Ken's heart as he watched the scene. His own father had died when he was about the same age as Daniel, and his mother, left in hardship to bring him up on her own, had turned into a cruel, cold and bitter woman. He had tried to forget the misery of his childhood – the beatings, the hunger, the lack of love and affection. Now, looking at this child's happy smile, he wondered how he could even think about destroying his small world. Bloody hell, he thought, what sort of man am I?

'Are you all right, Mr Marchant?' Sheila asked, concern in her voice.

'What? Yes ... sorry,' he apologised. 'Look, I must go. I own a little B and B close by and I must get back. It was nice to see yer again, Harry.' He held out his hand. 'Take good care of your son. You're a lucky man.'

'Yes, I know,' Harry said softly, relief flooding his face. 'Thanks, mate.' He stepped towards him ready to shake his hand, but the child leaned forward and reached out chubby arms. 'I think he wants you to hold him, Ken.'

Holding the small body close to his chest, Ken felt a lump in his throat as he too was given a wet kiss on the cheek. 'Da-da,' the child said, touching his face.

'No, not me, mate.' He said sadly, adding,

'More's the pity.' Handing him back to Harry he turned to walk away. 'Well, bye then. Nice to 'ave met you, Sheila. See you again some time, Harry.' Ken hurried off then, smiling ruefully. Blimey, he thought, I must be going soft.

'Barbara!' he called, when he returned to the B&B. She was in the kitchen peeling a mound of potatoes, and walking up behind her he placed his arms around her ample waist, saying, 'Listen, love, I know we've talked about this before, but can't we try for a baby before it's too late?'

She spun around, placing her hands on his chest and pushing him away. 'Get off me, you daft bugger. Can't you see I'm busy? We've had six bookings for dinner.'

'Forget the bloody guests for five minutes, Babs. Didn't you hear what I said?'

'Yes, of course I did. But I've told you before, and I meant it. I ain't bringing a bastard into the world.'

'All right then,' he said, taking her back in his arms. 'As soon as the season's over I'll go and ask Ruth for a divorce.'

'Is this your idea of a proposal, Ken Marchant?'

'Yeah, it is. Will you marry me, Barbara?'

'Of course I will, you daft sod. Now bugger off, I've still got these flippin' spuds to peel.'

Meanwhile, Harry, still holding his son in his arms, ushered Sheila to the car. He was still reeling from his confrontation with Ken, and unable to believe his luck. Christ, it could have ruined everything, he thought. It was unbelievable really; both he and Ken had walked out on their wives,

186

and both had ended up in Blackpool. He had been so sure it would be safe living in the North of England, never expecting to bump into anyone he knew from London. Realising what a close call it had been, a slight sheen of sweat broke out on his forehead.

Could he trust Ken to keep his mouth shut, he wondered now, and what if they bumped into him again? He could inadvertently give the game away to Sheila, who was already looking at him with a frown on her forehead.

'Who was that chap, darling? He was a bit odd,' she asked, once settled comfortably in the back seat, Daniel on her lap and the dog by her side.

'He's just someone I used to work with,' he lied, anxious to change the subject. 'Look, we had better get a move on. Linda's due out of school soon and we don't want to be late.'

Driving faster than usual Harry drew up at the gates. 'Stay there, dear,' he urged, smiling at Sheila over his shoulder. 'I'll get her.'

Climbing out of the car he stood watching the children as they came tumbling out of the main entrance, eyes alert for Sheila's eight-year-old daughter. A smile curled his lips when he spotted her skipping along, blonde hair bouncing on her shoulders. God, she was beautiful, and he was determined not to lose her, even if it meant persuading Sheila to move to another area.

'Here, Linda, come to Harry,' he called, crouching down and holding out his arms.

She hesitated when she saw him, her bright blue eyes darkening as she spun her head this way and that, as though looking for an escape.

'Come on, princess,' he urged, a frown on his face. 'We don't want to upset Mummy, do we? She's still not well and you know how sad she gets when you behave like this.'

She stepped tentatively towards him and he pulled her stiff little body into his arms. 'There's a good girl,' he said, giving her a gentle squeeze. 'Now come on, get into the car.'

Only five minutes later they pulled up outside their neat little house on the main road, just on the outskirts of town. Harry got out of the car, and walking round to the passenger door, he took Daniel from Sheila's lap, saying, 'Come on, big fella, we're home.'

Later, when they had nearly finished their tea, Sheila was trying to wipe away the thick coating of strawberry jam that was plastered all over Daniel's cheeks. 'I don't know how he does it,' she groaned. 'There's more on his face than went into his mouth. Hold still you little devil,' she laughed, as he twisted his head this way and that, doing his best to avoid the damp sponge.

Harry heaved a sigh. 'It's been nice having an extra day off, but it's back to work for me tomorrow.'

'How long will you be away for?' she asked, finally removing the last trace of jam from her son's cheeks.

'Only for a week this time,' he told her, and pushing himself to his feet, added, 'Now come on, give that little hooligan to me.'

He swung him high in the air, laughing as Daniel chuckled with delight. 'Now, what do you reckon, Danny boy – shall we go into the garden to play for a while? With any luck it might wear you out before your bedtime. Coming, Linda?' he called, his face tightening when he saw her eyes slide away from his.

'No, I'll help Mummy,' she whispered.

Lowering Danny to the floor he walked over to her side, caressing her soft, shiny hair. 'There's a good girl. She does look a little tired doesn't she? I think I had better give you a bath tonight, your mummy needs to rest.'

Chapter Twenty-One

Sally looked anxiously at the clock, unable to do anything with her hair. She'd be late if she didn't get a move on.

'Mum,' she begged, rushing anxiously into the kitchen. 'Please, can you do something with my hair? I'm meeting John, in the park at three o'clock.'

'Sal, you know I like a doze after me Sunday dinner.' Ruth yawned widely. 'Anyway, it looks all right.'

'Oh Mum, it's a mess.'

Ruth clicked her tongue impatiently. 'Come here then. When are you gonna make it up with Ann? It's been months now and I'm fed up with looking at your long face.'

'I've tried, Mum, but she doesn't want to know.'

The door opened and Sally gazed at her aunt as she walked across to the table, tapping it six times with her knuckles before sitting down. It was this bizarre ritual, along with the way Mary constantly washed her hands, which had finally forced Sadie to admit that her daughter needed professional help.

She had been seeing a psychiatrist for eight weeks now and he had diagnosed something called OCD, an obsessive-compulsive disorder. There were signs of improvement, but Mary was still too fragile to return to her own home.

'Are you going out, Sally?' her aunt now asked, eyes dulled by the effects of the antidepressants she'd been prescribed.

'Yes, I'm meeting John.' Sally glanced in the mirror. 'Thanks, Mum, that looks much better.'

Her aunt suddenly leaned forward and clutched her arm. 'Is everything all right between you and your chap?'

'Yes, of course, we're fine,' she told her, puzzled by the question.

'Sally, are you sure? I need to know that things haven't been ruined for you.'

'I don't know what you mean, Auntie, but I really must go now. Perhaps we could talk later.'

'Sally, do you know what the date is?' John asked as they sat on the grass under the shade of a large willow tree, enshrouded by the graceful draping fronds.

She stared across the lake, fascinated by a pair of swans as they glided regally across the surface of the water. 'They're so beautiful,' she murmured.

'Yes they are, darling, but did you hear what I said?'

'What?' she teased. 'Oh yes, something about the date.'

'It's the fifth of August – doesn't that mean anything to you?' he asked quizzically, leaning back against the thick tree trunk.

Sally twisted round to meet his eyes. 'Of course it does, darling. How could I forget that we met a year ago today?' She chuckled. 'Do you remember how I choked on my cup of tea?'

'Yes,' he laughed. 'Still, it broke the ice didn't it?'

He picked up his neatly folded jacket and Sally smiled affectionately at his fastidiousness. She had never seen him looking less than immaculate. Taking something from the pocket, he came to kneel at her side, his expression solemn. Her eyes widened as he opened a small box, and holding it out towards her, asked, 'Sally, will you marry me?'

The large diamond solitaire sparkled in the sunlight and she gasped: it was gorgeous.

'It was my mother's engagement ring,' he whispered as he took it from the box, and lifting her hand, slipped it onto her finger. 'Look, it's a perfect fit.' He then tilted his head to one side, giving her the lopsided grin that she loved so much. 'You will say yes – won't you?'

'Oh John, of course I will,' she cried, flinging herself into his arms.

He held her gently for a second before kissing her lightly on the cheek. 'Come on,' he said, grasping her hand and pulling her up. 'Let's go and tell Lottie.'

They hurried to the flat and as soon as they entered the sitting room, Sally proudly held out her left hand, twiddling her ring finger.

'Congratulations,' Lottie said, smiling with delight. 'Now come on, this calls for a celebration.' She opened the drinks cabinet, and poured three liberal glasses of sherry. 'I'm sorry it isn't champagne, darling, but you didn't warn me, you naughty boy,' she said girlishly, patting him gently on his cheek.

Sally still found John's aunt an enigma. There was the haughty, prime and efficient Miss French, her manageress, who attended church twice a week and helped with fund-raising events. But at home she was Lottie, transformed, like a butterfly that had broken out of its chrysalis: Lottie, who would play the piano for them, pounding out Brahms and Beethoven with passion, and producing paintings that were bold splashes of colour that screamed at you from the canvas.

'Well now,' she asked, breaking into Sally's thoughts. 'Have you fixed a date for the wedding?'

'Hold on, Auntie, we've only just got engaged,' John answered, laughing softly.

Feeling hot and sticky, Sally decided to freshen up, and placing her glass of sherry on the coffee-table, she said, 'Please excuse me, I'm just going to the bathroom.'

Leaving the sitting room, she started to walk along the hall, her eyes drawn to one of Lottie's newly hung abstract paintings. She peered in fascination at the vivid daubs of yellow, orange and red swirling across the canvas, finding herself thinking of a Spanish dancer, arms held high and spinning in a frenzy of wild passionate movement.

Then, becoming aware of John's voice drifting from the sitting room and hearing her name

192

mentioned, she pricked up her ears.

'Yes, I know, John, she's perfect – so innocent and pliable. I'm glad that you're so fond of her, but are you sure you'll be able to deal with it when you're married?'

'Don't worry, it won't be a problem.'

'Very well. I was right about her then and she'll be a good cover. But be careful, John; it would be a disaster if anyone found out.'

Sally frowned. What were they talking about? It didn't make sense, and what would be a disaster?

'Ah, there you are, Sally,' Lottie said, her eyes narrowing suspiciously as she stepped into the hall. 'I see you're looking at my painting. Have you been to the bathroom?'

She felt her face flush. 'Yes, thank you, I was just on my way back,' she lied, not wanting Lottie to know she'd been eavesdropping.

'Well, what do you think of it then?'

'What? Oh, the painting. It's wonderful, it reminds me of someone dancing the flamenco.'

'How marvellous,' Lottie smiled. 'That's just what it is. Well done, Sally, my technique must be improving. Now come on, I've poured you another drink.'

The reception they received at Sally's house was in complete contrast. Her mother stared at them in horror. 'But she won't be seventeen until February,' she spluttered, her eyes on John. 'She's far too young to get married.'

'We aren't planning to get married straight away, Mrs Marchant. We thought perhaps when Sally is eighteen.'

193

Ruth did a rapid calculation on her fingers, 'Hmm, and that's in about eighteen months. Yeah, well, I suppose that'll be all right,' she said begrudgingly. 'But I still think it's too young.'

'Oh, for goodness' sake, Mum,' Sally said indignantly. 'You were married at nineteen; there's only a year's difference. Please, can't you just be happy for us?'

'All right, I'm sorry, but I don't know what you expect – it was a bit of a shock springing it on me like that. Well, come on then, you might as well show me yer ring.'

Sally could see the tight expression on her mum's face and sighed, longing for the closeness they had once shared. It was the same with gran; since she had been going out with John there was a constraint between them. She held out her hand, the ring sparkling as it caught the light.

Ruth gave it a cursory glance. 'Yes, very nice,' she said quietly.

'It belonged to my mother, Mrs Marchant,' John told her.

She didn't make any comment, just smiled grimly, her manner dismissive as she sat down.

The strained atmosphere made conversation impossible. Sally squirmed with embarrassment, relieved when after a short time, John said he had to go. She saw him out, lifting her lips for a kiss that was as light as a feather as his mouth skimmed across hers.

'Bye, darling, see you tomorrow,' he murmured.

Standing on the doorstep she gazed after him as he sauntered down the Lane, only turning her head when she heard a car pulling into the kerb.

Her aunt was the first to climb out, followed by Arthur, hurrying round from the driver's side to assist her gran as she struggled stiffly onto the pavement.

Sally went across to help. 'Was everything all right at your house, Auntie?'

'Yes, and I've brought a few more things back with me.' She turned to Arthur. 'Thank you so much for taking us, it was very kind of you.'

'That's all right, it was no trouble. Hello, Sally,' he grinned. 'How's things?'

'Fine, thank you,' she told him, smiling happily. 'In fact John and I have just got engaged.'

'What!' her gran yelped. 'Don't tell me you've got engaged to that poncy git?'

Glaring at her gran, Sally felt her happiness draining away. How could she say that, and in front of Arthur too! Turning on her heels, she marched indoors.

Now, sitting gazing out of her bedroom window, she wondered what was wrong with her family. Why didn't they like John? He was wonderful. Gentle, kind, and not at all like Arthur who made her shiver with fear every time he looked at her, his eyes dark with lust.

She ignored the soft knock on her bedroom door, not even turning her head when her aunt came into the room.

'Sally, can I talk to you?'

'No, not now. I'm sorry, I just want to be on my own for a while.'

'Please, dear, we really do need to talk. There's something I want to tell you, something that

195

nobody else knows – except for my psychiatrist, that is. Can I trust you to keep it confidential?' she added softly.

Despite her unhappiness Sally found that she was intrigued, and twisting around to look at her aunt, she said, 'Yes, you can trust me.'

'Sally, I'm sure you know the facts of life, so you must know what happens between a man and woman when they get married.'

She shivered. Yes, she knew a little, but she was mainly in ignorance of what really happened. It was something she preferred not to think about and always pushed to the back of her mind.

'This is so difficult,' her aunt murmured, taking a deep breath before continuing, her hands clenched so tightly together that the knuckles gleamed white. 'You see, Sally, even though I've been married to your uncle for twenty years, I'm still a virgin. Yes, I can see by your face that you're surprised, aren't you?' She paused, the parody of a smile on her face. 'The reason I'm telling you this, is because I don't want you to end up like me.'

Sally averted her eyes, embarrassed by her aunt's revelations and suddenly nervous about where this conversation was leading. She folded her arms across her chest defensively, shrugging in an effort to look nonchalant. 'Why should I end up like you?'

'Because like me, you've had a bad sexual experience. Mine made me frigid, terrified of sex. I just want to make sure that you haven't been affected in the same way by what your uncle did to you.'

Her breath caught in her throat; she felt herself

go hot, then cold. It had never been discussed before; it had been buried, like her shame. Why did her aunt have to bring it up after all these years? 'I don't want to talk about it,' she croaked.

'But not talking was the cause of my breakdown,' Mary said urgently. 'I understand that now. I've never spoken about my feelings, I've always been too proud. Always worried about people's perceptions of me, and to cry in front of anyone would have been anathema for me, a sign of weakness. So you see, I never had an outlet for my pain.'

'Is that what caused your illness, this OCD thing that you've got?'

'Well, partly I suppose. But what really caused it was guilt, Sally. Guilt and self-hatred, and that's why I keep washing my hands all the time. My psychiatrist said it's the root of my illness.'

She stared at her aunt. 'I don't understand: what have *you* got to feel guilty about?'

'Oh, my dear, I was feeling guilty about you, of course. I thought that if I'd been a proper wife to Harry he might not have turned his sexual attentions towards you.'

Sally placed her elbows on the windowsill and rested her head in her hands as she contemplated her aunt's words. She sighed deeply, raising her eyes at last. 'Do you know, Auntie, I too have always felt guilty for what happened. I thought it was my fault that Uncle Harry did those horrible things to me.'

Her aunt advanced across the room, placing a hand on her arm. 'Oh, how awful. I didn't realise that you felt like that,' she said, her voice deep with compassion. 'Hasn't your mother talked to you about it?'

'No, it's never been discussed.' She smiled ruefully. 'Until now.'

'Well, I'm glad we're bringing it into the open at last. I've learned a lot from my psychiatrist, some of it not very pleasant. But one of the things I've come to realise is that your uncle is a paedophile. Do you know what that is?'

'No, is it an illness?'

'Huh, he's sick all right, but not in the way you mean,' Mary answered, her face grimacing in distaste. 'A paedophile is a person who is attracted to children sexually. I know, disgusting, isn't it? But you see, when my psychiatrist explained that my rejection would not have turned him into a paedophile, it was such a huge relief. He told me that I wasn't to blame for what Harry did to you. A normal man would have looked for a sexual relationship with another woman – not a child.'

She stared hopefully at her aunt. 'So if he's a paedophile, does ... does that mean it wasn't my fault either?' she whispered.

'No, of course it wasn't, and it's awful to think that you've carried this burden for so long. But now, I must ask you a very difficult question.'

Her aunt began to pace the room, head down as she walked back and forth in agitation. Then, suddenly coming to a halt she blurted out, 'Are you frightened of sex?'

Sally bristled. 'John is wonderful. He doesn't expect sex before we're married.'

'That's nice, dear, but it isn't what I asked. All right, perhaps I have no right to ask you such a personal question. But please, I just want you to know that if you do have a problem, it is possible to get help.'

'I don't need any help,' Sally protested, squirming with embarrassment. 'I'm fine.'

'That's all right then. Please forgive me for probing into your personal life, but you see I just wanted to make sure that your uncle didn't cause you any lasting damage.' Mary smiled tenderly. 'I'll leave you in peace now, but I'm glad we had this little chat.'

As the door closed behind her aunt, Sally turned back to the window, going over the conversation in her mind. For so long she had shied away from thinking about her uncle, but now that her aunt had brought the whole thing into the open, she found herself relieved that it hadn't been her fault after all. Now, as she gazed down into the Lane she let out a long sigh, feeling that a huge weight had been lifted from her shoulders.

She was about to turn away when she saw Jenny crossing the road, tottering on high stiletto-heeled shoes, a tight skirt clinging to her hips. Arthur was polishing the chrome bumper on his car and smiled as she draped herself seductively across the bonnet. He threw down his duster, reaching out to pull her into his arms, their bodies merging passionately.

Sally averted her eyes, clicking her tongue with disgust. Ugh, she thought. Thank goodness John doesn't hold me like that. Unable to resist another peep, she saw that their lips were now fused together in a long and ardent kiss. Her stomach lurched, and though she didn't want to acknowledge the feeling, she felt a surge of jealousy.

Chapter Twenty-Two

Sally found that the months following her engagement were something of an anti-climax. The subject was rarely mentioned at home and though her gran had apologised, there was still a constraint between them.

One Friday as she walked home from work, the sun low in the sky and an autumn chill in the air, she was once again realising how much she missed Ann. She desperately wanted someone to confide in about her relationship with John, but who? Mum and Gran made it obvious that they didn't like him, and somehow she thought her auntie was still too fragile.

She hunched her shoulders. Perhaps she was worrying about nothing. Yet John rarely held her in his arms and had never really kissed her, except for an occasional peck on the cheek. It had been wonderful at first, she had felt so safe, but lately she had begun to notice how much he avoided touching her, almost as if he found her repulsive. Should it be like this, she wondered. Did he really love her?

Turning into the Lane, she was surprised to see Nelly Cox standing on her doorstep. Her steel-grey hair was pulled back into an untidy bun and although the evening was chilly, she only had a thin cardigan over her faded cotton dress. Since her husband's death she had become very frail, almost as if she had lost the will to live, and every time Sally saw her, she was wracked with guilt.

'Hello, Nelly, are you all right?' she asked worriedly as she approached.

'Yeah, I was looking out for you. Do you fancy coming in for a cuppa?'

Sally sighed inwardly; she wasn't in the mood, but how could she refuse? 'Yes, all right, I'd love one. I can't stay for long though, Mum will have my dinner ready.' She followed Nelly inside, wrinkling her nose at the sour smell. It had been so different when George was alive, the house had been immaculate, but now, sitting at the kitchen table, Sally couldn't help but notice how grimy everything looked.

'What's up? You look a bit down,' Nelly said, spooning condensed milk from an encrusted tin into her tea.

Sally averted her eyes from the dirty cup, and balked at the thought of drinking from it. 'Nothing's up, Nelly, I'm fine. I've just had a hard day, that's all.'

'How's that boyfriend of yours?' she asked shrewdly. 'Is he treating yer right?'

'Yes, of course he is.'

'Well, I hope he turns out to be a good husband like my George. Do you know, we hardly had an argument in nearly fifty years.'

Sally touched the old lady's hand where it lay on the table, remembering the day when she had apologised for using healing powers on her husband. Nelly had been so kind, dismissing her apology and saying that it had made his last few weeks less painful. It was obvious that she was just trying to make her feel better, and Sally had come to love this brave old lady.

Realising that Nelly wanted to talk about him now, she settled back in her chair to listen patiently. 'Yes, he was a lovely man,' she told her.

'My only regret is that we didn't 'ave children, Sally. I know he'd 'ave been a smashing father, he loved kids.' She chuckled, adding, 'Blimey, we tried hard enough. Thank God there was nothing wrong in *that* department, if you know what I mean.'

Feeling her cheeks burning, Sally lowered her head. Fancy Nelly saying a thing like that.

'I'm sorry, I didn't mean to embarrass you, it just sort of slipped out. Though I'm surprised to see you blushing. I thought you youngsters knew it all nowadays.' She grinned at Sally across the table. 'Things were different in my day. When George and me got married I knew nothing about – well, you know, sex. My mother just told me to lie back and to think of England until my husband's base desires were satisfied. Base desires, I ask you! I didn't have a clue what she was talking about. Still, it was fun finding out,' she added with a saucy little wink.

Sally felt a lump in her throat. Somehow as Nelly talked about her marriage it increased her worries about John, making her realise even more strongly that something was missing in their relationship.

'Come on, Sally, spit it out. I can see you're upset. Is it me talking about my George?'

Shaking her head vigorously, she said, 'No, Nelly, of course not. It's just ... well, you see ... I don't think my boyfriend really loves me.'

'Now why would you think that? He's asked you to marry him, ain't he, and surely he wouldn't do that unless he loves you?'

'Yes, maybe, but he never really shows me any affection and sometimes there's a strange expression on his face when he looks at me, almost as if he finds me distasteful.'

'Are you sure you're not imagining things? I seem to remember yer mum telling me that he's a very religious chap, is that right?'

'Yes, he is,' Sally told her.

Nelly smiled in satisfaction, folding her arms under her drooping bust. 'There's yer answer then. He probably doesn't trust himself. You see, once men get started, it's sort of difficult for them to stop. I mean, just look at you – you'd be a temptation to any man. Perhaps he's frightened that he might go too far before you get married.'

Sally gazed across the table, feeling a surge of hope. 'Do you really think that's what it is, Nelly?'

'Of course. You should count yourself lucky, my girl. After all, more and more girls are getting pregnant before they've got a wedding ring on their finger. Look at that Judy Wilson at number ten, for instance. Six months gone by the look of her, and no sign of the father. I don't know what things are coming to, I really don't,' she added, shaking her head.

'Oh Nelly, I'm so glad that I've talked to you,' Sally said, a smile on her face. 'You have really eased my mind.'

'That's nice to hear, ducks. Perhaps I ain't so useless after all. Now how about another cuppa?'

Sally, happier now, glanced at the clock. 'I'm

sorry, but I really must go. Mum will be wondering where I am.'

She kissed Nelly gently on the cheek, pleased to see that a little spark had returned to her eyes. Perhaps our talk has done us both good, she thought, as she hurried home.

Sally had just sat down when the back door flew open and Elsie staggered into the room, her face white and drawn.

'What is it?' Ruth asked anxiously, rushing forward, her arms outstretched as though she expected Elsie to collapse into them.

'Oh, God... Oh, God,' she sobbed as Ruth led her to a chair. 'It's my Arthur,' she wailed.

'Arthur? What's wrong with him?' Sally gasped, feeling her heart thumping in her chest.

'He's going away, emigrating.' Their neighbour pulled at her hair in anguish adding, 'And I'll never see him again.'

'Now slow down and start at the beginning,' Ruth urged, rubbing her hands gently across her friend's bent shoulders.

Elsie drew in long shuddering breaths in an effort to compose herself, then raised pain-filled eyes. 'It's that Jenny's family. They're all emigrating to Australia and my Arthur's decided to go with them. Oh, I can't bear it,' she sobbed, fresh tears filling her eyes.

'I can't believe it,' Sally whispered.

'No, neither could I at first,' Elsie said, and with a trace of venom now evident in her voice, she added, 'I've never liked that bloody Jenny. She's a right flighty piece and I've tried to warn Arthur about her antics, but he won't have it, and now she's taking my son away from me.' She reached up, grasping Ruth's hand. 'Oh, what am I going to do? How can I stop him?'

Sally stared at Elsie's bent head as only her snuffling sobs filled the silence in the room. It was the first time she had ever heard her say a bad word about anyone, and was shocked at her opinion of Jenny. She fumbled in her mind for something to say, unable to think of any words of comfort. 'Perhaps he'll change his mind,' she stammered ineffectually.

'Yeah, Sally's right,' Ruth agreed. 'That family in the next street waited for over a year before they emigrated. Don't you remember, they had all sorts of formalities to go through first. Anything can happen in that time, Elsie.'

'I didn't see it in the cards,' the woman cried, her face twisted with anguish. 'There was nothing there, I'm sure there wasn't. Oh yes,' she nodded her head, 'I saw travel, but then that's to be expected when he works for his father.' Hope glimmered suddenly in her eyes. 'I didn't see a sea voyage – do you think that's a good sign, Sally?'

She shook her head. 'I don't know, Elsie. I don't believe in using the cards now, you know that.'

She jumped back in surprise when Elsie suddenly reared to her feet. 'Yes, you've made that perfectly clear, haven't you! You even had the nerve to tell my Ann that I'm being misled by the devil. Well, it isn't me who's being misled, miss. It's you!' She shook her head indignantly. 'How can you stand by and let your gran suffer so much pain when you've got the power to help her? Jesus healed the sick, yet you and your hoity-toity boyfriend seem to have forgotten that. I'll tell you something else, my girl. This is all your fault, and you needn't look at me like that. My Arthur has loved you for years, but you didn't want to know, did you? What's the matter – wasn't he good enough for you? And now look what's happened. Because of you he's going to bloody Australia.'

Sally was stiff with shock. How could Elsie blame her? She had never given Arthur any encouragement; in fact, she was always nervous when he came near her and avoided him as much as possible. She threw her mum an agonised glance before dashing out of the room, and was only halfway up the stairs when she heard Elsie's shout. 'Wait, Sally, please wait.'

Ignoring the call she stumbled into her room, slamming the door behind her, and finding her knees shaking as reaction set in, she slumped onto her bed.

'Please, Sally, can I come in?' Elsie begged, opening the door a few inches. 'Honestly, love, I didn't mean it,' she said, edging further into the room. 'I don't know what came over me. I'm ashamed of myself, I really am.' She sat down on the bed beside her. 'I had no right to use you as a scapegoat or to vent my anger on you.' She sighed deeply. 'Sometimes it's easier to blame someone else when things go wrong. Look, I'm really sorry. Can you forgive me?'

Sally nodded mutely, picking at a loose thread on her jumper as Elsie started talking again.

'You see, I've always had this dream that you and Arthur would marry one day. I'm so fond of you and it would have been wonderful to have you for a daughter-in-law. No, it's all right,' she said, stopping Sally's reply. 'It seems it just wasn't meant to be.'

'I'm sorry, Elsie.'

'No, love, it's me that's sorry. I know things haven't been right between us lately, and I must admit I think it's a shame that your spiritual gifts are being wasted.' She shook her head sadly. 'But it's your decision and I've no right to interfere.'

'I didn't mean it when I said that you're misled by the devil, Elsie. It's just that I was upset at the time and it sort of came out all wrong.'

'Come on now, let's forget it, shall we?' she said, squeezing Sally's hand. 'And who knows, perhaps I can bring Ann round too.'

Sally turned her head sharply. 'Oh, I hope you can, Elsie. I miss her so much.'

'I know you do, just like I'm going to miss my Arthur.'

They sat quietly for a while, each with their own thoughts, until Sally felt the mattress lift as Elsie stood up, her eyes brimming with tears again. 'Oh God,' she choked, as she left the room. 'How will I be able to bear it when he goes to Australia?'

The following morning dawned cold, but clear and bright. Sally was just towelling her hair dry when her mum called out that someone wanted to see her. She frowned, wondering who would call so early, and wrapping the towel turban-style around her head, went to the top of the stairs.

'Hello, Sally, I just popped round to see if you fancy walking to work with me,' Ann said, looking up at her from the bottom of the stairs.

'Yes, of course I would,' she told her, beaming with delight. 'Give me about half an hour.'

'Right,' Ann smiled back. 'See you later then.'

Sally rushed back into her bedroom and hastily pulled on a skirt and blouse, unable to believe that Elsie had managed to talk Ann around so quickly. Oh, it was wonderful, she thought, feeling a surge of happiness. She had her friend back.

She bolted her breakfast, listening with half an ear to the radio. Lonnie Donegan was belting out 'My Old Man's a Dustman' and her mum was obviously enjoying it as she sat opposite, humming the tune and tapping her feet.

'It's about time you and Ann came to your senses. Are you happy now, love?' she asked.

'Of course I am,' Sally grinned, scrambling from the table. Then throwing her coat on and tying a scarf around her neck, she said goodbye to her mother and went to knock on Ann's door.

At first as they walked along there was still a touch of constraint between them, but as they turned into Falcon Road it was dispelled when Sally asked Ann if her mum was any better.

'Not really. She cried nearly all evening and then started again as soon as Arthur came down this morning. Somehow I can't help feeling sorry for him. It's obvious he's really keen to go, but Mum is making him feel so guilty about it. His face was as white as a sheet when he left for work.'

'Will he marry Jenny before they emigrate?' Sally asked.

'No. Apparently their first priority is to save as much money as they can to take with them.

Jenny's not prepared to compromise on a big white wedding with all the trimmings and is prepared to wait until they're settled in Australia.' Ann snorted derisively. 'Though how she's got the cheek to get married in white I'll never know. She's had more blokes than I've had hot dinners.'

'It sounds like you don't think much of her, Ann.'

'No, I don't,' she said emphatically. 'I saw her once in the pictures with another bloke and you should have seen her face when she spotted me. She tried to give me some waffle about him being her cousin.'

Sally stared at her friend in surprise. 'What did Arthur say about it?'

'He believed her story and had a go at me for trying to cause trouble.' She shrugged. 'Since then I've kept my mouth shut.'

'I had no idea that Jenny was like that. Why would she go out with other men when she's got Arthur?'

''Cos she's a tart,' Ann retorted. 'God, I could kill her for taking my brother away.'

'You're all going to miss him so much,' Sally said sympathetically.

'I know, but I can't believe that he's really going. It's too much to take in, and I don't think it's hit me yet.'

Sally hooked her arm through Ann's. 'Yes, I know what you mean. It seems unreal somehow.'

They walked along quietly for a while in a companionable silence. Then Sally, feeling a surge of relief, squeezed her friend's arm, saying, 'Ann, I'm so glad that things are all right between us again. I've really missed you.'

'I've missed you too, but please, Sally, don't ever say anything about my mum again.'

'I won't, I promise.'

Ann smiled. 'Right then, let's put it all behind us and start again. Now come on, I know you got engaged, so how about showing me your ring?'

Taking off her glove, Sally held out her hand.

'It's lovely,' Ann whispered. 'But are you sure you know what you're doing, Sally? Are you sure he's the right one for you?'

'Look, let's make another pact. I've promised that I'll never say anything about your mum again. Now perhaps you'll agree not to say anything about John? He *is* the right man for me, and I love him. Please, Ann, can't you accept that?'

'All right, Sally, you win.' She heaved a sigh. 'If you really love him, I'll just have to make an effort to like him, won't I?'

'Oh Ann, you make him sound like a monster. He's wonderful, and once you get to know him a bit better, I'm sure you'll get along fine.'

'I hope so, Sally, I really do,' Ann said, but there was still a trace of doubt in her voice.

Chapter Twenty-Three

On Sunday Sally sat in her gran's room facing her across the fireplace, feeling overwhelmed by a strange sensation as she watched her twisting newspaper into firelighters. It felt as though this isolated moment in time had been imprinted in her memory and she would remember it for ever. Her gran took another sheet of newspaper, rolling it tightly from corner to corner to form a long neat tube, and flattening it from end to end between her fingers. She then folded it neatly in half, plaiting it, one piece over the other until it resembled a concertina. Fastening the ends neatly, her hands black with newspaper print, she threw it into the coal-bucket, unaware of her granddaughter's gaze as she grimaced and flexed her fingers.

'Are you in a lot of pain, Gran?'

'No, it's not too bad,' Sadie told her, smiling bravely. 'But I think I've made enough lighters for now.'

It was then that Sally felt a sudden surge of rebellion, recalling Elsie's words. Yes, she thought, Jesus *had* healed the sick and sent His disciples out to do the same. Surely John couldn't expect her to sit by and watch her gran suffer like this! How could easing her pain be evil? She closed her eyes, searching for words from the Bible, trying to remember all the tracts John had pointed out, but instead only remembered how Jesus had restored a blind man's sight and amongst other things, cured leprosy.

She stood up abruptly, her shoulders stiff with resolution. 'Gran, come on. I'll give you some healing.'

'What?' Sadie spluttered, her voice high with surprise. 'Are you sure, love? I don't want to cause trouble between you and John.'

'Yes, I'm sure. Elsie's right, you shouldn't be in all this pain when I may be able to help you.'

Will it work, Sally wondered, as she stood behind her gran, lifting her head in a silent prayer. She had been rejecting her spiritual gifts for so long, would she still be able to summon the help she needed? She inhaled deeply, controlling her breathing as Elsie had taught her and allowing herself to become a channel for the power that came through her hands.

'I can't believe it.' Her mum s voice penetrated her concentration.

She opened her eyes, startled to see her mother and aunt standing in the doorway, both looking flabbergasted. Glancing at the clock she was amazed to see that twenty minutes had passed.

Her gran stood up, smiling with delight. 'Oh Sally, it's wonderful, my pain's almost gone again!' she exclaimed.

Just then, there was a loud knock on the front door and they all looked at each other in surprise. 'I'll get it,' Mary said, hurrying back into the hall.

'No, no, go away!' they heard her shriek, and Sally saw her mum stiffen at the sound of a man's voice, urging Mary to let him in.

She followed as Ruth rushed into the hall, seeing her blanch with shock when she saw Ken, his shoulder on the door, trying to stop Mary from shutting it in his face.

'Ruth!' he shouted. 'I'm not here to cause trouble. I only want to talk, for Christ's sake.'

'Let him in, Mary,' she said, her voice flat.

'What, are you mad?'

'Just open the door,' she replied, her face set and cold as though carved in marble. Then stepping forward, she added unemotionally, 'There's nothing he can do to hurt me now. Let's hear what he's got to say.'

As Mary stepped back, allowing Ken into the hall, he removed his trilby hat, smiling softly. 'Thanks, Ruth, you're looking well, and surely this isn't little Sally,' he said ingratiatingly. 'Well, you've turned into a right little beauty haven't you?'

'Sally, go to your room.

She stiffened. 'No, Mum, the days when I had to keep out of *his* way are long gone. I'm not a child that has to be hidden away any more.'

'I want to talk to yer mother in private. Do as she says, Sally, and go to your room,' Ken demanded.

Ruth bristled. 'How dare you!' she snapped, colour returning to her cheeks. 'The time has gone when you could give us orders. No, Sally's right, you can say what you've got to say in front of all of us.'

Sadie had come out of her room, saying nothing until they had all gathered in the kitchen. Then, throwing a look of disgust at Ken, she said scathingly, 'Huh, bad pennies always turn up.'

'Nice to see you too, old girl,' he grinned, seemingly unconcerned.

'Just say what you've come to say, Ken,' Ruth snapped. 'And who said you could sit down?' she added as he pulled out a chair from under the table.

'Now then, Ruth, there's no need for nastiness,' he placated. 'Can I sit down?'

'No, you can't. Now what do you want?'

He puffed out his cheeks with exasperation, his eyes flicking around the room. 'You seem to 'ave done all right without me, gel.'

'Yeah, I have. When you left me it was the best thing you ever did,' she retorted.

'My sister's well rid of you,' Mary told him haughtily.

At the tone of her voice, Ken's manner changed. He straightened his shoulders and slowly turned to face her, saying with a sneer, 'Don't come the high horse with me, Mary. Your husband obviously decided to get his oats elsewhere too. I saw him with his lovely wife just recently.' He grinned maliciously at the expression on her face, adding, 'Yes, a lovely blonde piece he had on his arm. And their son – he's a smashing little nipper, and the apple of his father's eye.'

Sally saw the colour drain from her aunt's face, her eyes like saucers as she stared at Ken, but before she could respond Sadie moved forward, her face livid. 'You bastard!' she shouted. 'My daughters 'ave suffered enough. Now get out! Go on – get out of here!'

'All right, old girl, calm down,' Ken told her. 'Look, I'm sorry, Mary. I assumed you knew about Harry's new wife,' he lied.

'*I'm* his wife,' she snapped. 'We're still married.'

'According to Harry, you were divorced years ago. You've got a right one there. Not only a pervert, but a bigamist too.' Then, ignoring the impact his words had on Mary, he turned his attention to Ruth. 'While we're on the subject of marriage, that's what I've come to see you about. You've made it pretty obvious that you don't want me back, so I want you to give me a divorce.'

Sally watched in amazement as her mum's

214

hands balled into fists, her stance rigid as she squared up to him. 'Get out!' she screamed. 'You've got the nerve to turn up here after six years, upsetting my sister and asking me for a divorce. Well, you can go to hell.'

'Now come on, Ruth. I'll make it worth yer while,' he urged.

'I said get out!' she screeched, bright red with anger.

Ken's face tightened momentarily and Sally stiffened, remembering his violence. But he sucked in his breath and said, 'All right, calm down, I'll go. But you ain't heard the last of this. I'll be back.'

As he turned to leave the room, Mary seemed to shoot out of her chair. 'No, wait, wait!' she shouted, running across the room and grabbing his arm. 'Where did you see him?' she urged. 'Where did you see Harry?'

'He lives in the same town as me, as it happens.'

'Yes, but where? Please, Ken, please tell me.'

'Well now,' he drawled, his confidence back, 'that all depends on yer sister. If she's prepared to see reason...' His voice trailed off.

Mary turned to Ruth, still clutching Ken's arm, mute appeal in her eyes.

Seeing the expression on her sister's face the fight seemed to go out of Ruth, and slumping she said, 'All right, Ken. You win, you can 'ave your divorce.' She sniffed then, adding, 'In fact, I'll be better off without you. But only,' she stressed, 'if you tell us where Harry is.'

Ken grinned in triumph. 'It's funny really, because although I knew that like me, he lives in Blackpool now, I didn't have an address.' He strolled back across the room, pulled out a chair and sat down, smiling when this time, Ruth made no protest. 'However, as I was driving out of town one morning, I happened to spot him leaving a house on the edge of town, his pretty wife waving to him from the doorstep.' He flashed them a wide smile. 'Now, how's that for a bit of luck?'

When Ken left there was an aftermath of strained silence. It was as if both Sally and her gran didn't know who to sympathise with first. Strangely they all ended up sitting around the kitchen table, each with their own thoughts.

It was Sadie who broke the silence. 'Mary, I think it's time you told us what went on between you and Harry. I mean, how on earth can he be married to someone else, and with a child too?'

'He can't, Mum, at least not legally.' A child, she thought, it was unbelievable – and did the child's mother know that she and Harry weren't divorced? She felt bile rise in her throat. My God, he wasn't fit to be a father. Taking a deep breath she cast a glance around the table and seeing the worried expressions on their faces, nodded. 'Yes, perhaps the time has come to tell you about my marriage, but I'm afraid it's a long story.'

'Wait a minute, Mary, do you think Sally should hear this?' Ruth said worriedly.

'For God's sake, Mum. I'm not a child,' she protested.

'No, it's all right,' Mary intervened. 'Sally and I have already talked about it so there won't be any surprises for her.'

Ruth's eyes narrowed as she looked at her

daughter. 'Well, you're a dark horse. You kept that quiet.'

'That's because I talked to her in confidence,' Mary told her. 'And perhaps when you've heard what I've got to say, you'll understand why.' She took a deep breath before continuing, 'Now, I'll try to keep it as short as possible. You see, it started on my honeymoon...'

She saw the compassion in their eyes as she described her married life. 'Then, Mum, when you decided to live with Ruth, it all became too much. That was the start of my nervous breakdown. Not only was I washing my hands all the time, I became moody and obsessive, scrubbing the house day and night, trying to get it clean.' She shook her head, adding, 'No matter how hard I tried, it always looked dirty to me.'

'Oh Mary,' Sadie choked. 'I feel terrible. I would never 'ave left if I'd known how bad things were for you.'

'How could you have known, Mum? I've never been one to show my feelings and I kept everything locked inside. I must have been heading for a breakdown for years. Anyway, Harry couldn't cope with it, and things came to a head the day you found me.' She tightened her lips. 'You see, only that morning, he walked out on me.'

'But I don't understand. After what you've told us, weren't you glad to see the back of him?' Sadie asked.

'Yes, of course I was. But I hated myself more than I hated Harry. I blamed myself for what he had done to Sally.' Her voice low now, she murmured, 'And that's why I took those pills.'

Sadie, on the point of speaking, was silenced as Ruth asked, 'If you're glad he left, why are you so desperate to find him now? Anyway, if he's got a kid he must have had this woman on the side for a couple of years. Sod him, I say. He still sends you money every month and the rent gets paid on your house.'

'My God, Ruth,' Mary said, 'it's got nothing to do with money. Can't you see, I want him stopped? He's a paedophile, and my stomach churns with the thought of how many other children might suffer at his hands, as Sally did.' She drew herself up. 'But I may have got him now. I can't prove he's a paedophile, but if he really has married this woman, I can at least prove he's a bigamist.'

'Yeah, and if it's true he'll go down all right, and for a good few years I should think,' Sadie said. 'But how are you going to find out, Mary?'

'I'll confront him. I'll go to his house in Blackpool.'

'Not on your own, you won't.' Ruth reached out and placed her hand on top of Mary's. 'I'm coming with you. I'd like to see that bastard get his come-uppance too.'

They smiled at each other, closer now than they had been in years. 'And what about you, Ruth? Are you upset about divorcing Ken?' Mary asked.

She snorted. 'You must be joking. No, good riddance to bad rubbish,' and winking at her sister, she added, 'In fact it might be nice to be young, free and single again.'

'Well, free and single, yes, but I don't know about young.'

'Here, watch it. We're in our prime ... well, almost,' Ruth laughed.

Sadie's thoughts drifted as her daughters bantered together. She had been overwhelmed with guilt when Mary had attempted suicide, berating herself for not realising how unhappy she was. When David had been killed during the war, followed soon afterwards by Charlie, the pain had been so intense that she hadn't wanted to live either. Instead, for a long time, she had closed down emotionally, shutting herself off from the girls.

Now, watching them, she realised that Ruth had always been her favourite daughter, even though she had refused to acknowledge it. Mary had always been so self-sufficient, and even as a child had been distant and independent, rarely crying. Unlike Ruth, who from the start had been a needy child, wanting lots of hugs and kisses.

It was a relief to see her daughters laughing together now, despite what life had thrown at them, and Mary on the road to recovery at last.

Turning her head she looked at her grand-daughter, and saw Sally grinning as she listened to the banter between her mum and aunt. Touching her arm, she said, 'Look, love, with all that's happened I never got the chance to thank you for giving me some healing. It's wonderful to be almost pain-free again.'

'Blimey,' Ruth said. 'Yeah, I almost forgot. Thanks for helping your gran. I know you're seeing John later. Are you going to tell him?'

'I'll have to, Mum, I can't deceive him.' She stood up. 'I had better go and get ready. He'll be here soon.'

Sadie frowned as her granddaughter left the room. Mary and Ruth had made bad mistakes with their husbands and she wasn't happy with Sally's choice either. The girl kept insisting that John was wonderful, but despite that there was something about the boy that made her skin crawl. Yes, he was nice-looking and seemed a proper gent, so why couldn't she take to him? What was it that made her suspicious?

Sally rifled through her wardrobe, settling at last on the blue sheath dress that John had chosen. She was feeling strangely lethargic and instead of looking forward to seeing him, she was filled with dread. How was she going to tell him?

'Sally, John's here,' her mum called.

'I won't be a minute,' she shouted, frantically back-combing the top of her hair to give it some height. Glancing in the mirror she frowned, knowing that she looked less than her best.

'Hello, sorry to keep you waiting,' she said, sensing the strained atmosphere as she walked into the kitchen. John was standing by the window looking immaculate in a light grey mohair suit. He fastidiously straightened his tie as he moved across the room towards her, a smile on his lips that failed to reach his eyes.

'Never mind, you're ready now,' he said stiffly.

As their eyes met she looked away, feeling a flush of guilt. 'See you all later,' she mumbled, picking up her coat and following him out of the front door.

'Have you styled your hair differently, Sally?' he

asked as they walked down the Lane. 'I'm not sure that I like it.'

'Sorry, darling, but I had to get ready in a rush. My stepfather turned up unexpectedly today.'

'Really!' he said, turning to look at her. 'I was going to suggest that we go dancing at the Hammersmith Palais, but perhaps you'd like to go for a drink instead. You look a little upset.'

'Yes, I'd like that, John.'

'Right, we'll go to that pub by the river in Chelsea and you can tell me all about it.'

Arriving at the pub, they sat at a window table, dazzled by the setting sun reflecting on the dark surface of the River Thames. Vivid shades of red, purple, and orange glowed like molten glass on the water, the illusion of beauty only marred by the cheerless silhouette of Battersea Power Station on the opposite side of the Embankment.

'It must have been a bit of a surprise when your stepfather turned up, Sally. Is he going to stay?' John asked as he sipped a gin and tonic.

'No. He came to ask my mother for a divorce,' she told him, putting down her glass of lemonade.

'I see,' John said, a slight frown on his face. 'Has your mother agreed?'

'Yes – after the initial shock, I think she's quite relieved really.'

'Oh dear, I'm not sure if I approve of that. Marriage vows are something that shouldn't be taken lightly. Till death us do part and all that,' he told her.

'John, how can you say that? My mother had a terrible life with him. He was very violent, and you know he ran off with another woman.'

'I'm not condoning that, Sally, but after all it must have been very hard for him to come home after the war to find that his wife had been unfaithful.'

'Yes, I agree it must have been awful for him, but that's no excuse for the way he treated us.' She cast her eyes around the room, knowing that somehow she had to bring the conversation on to her spiritual healing.

'How's your aunt?' she asked. 'I saw that she was in pain again yesterday.'

John stared into his glass. 'She's a bit better today, but I'm worried about her, Sally.'

'I think you should encourage her to go to the doctor's, John.' She drew herself up, adding, 'Look, I don't know how to tell you this and I know you'll be annoyed, but please try to understand. You see, ever since I was a small child I've been able to see auras, and even though I've stopped using my psychic powers, they're still visible to me.'

'Yes – go on, Sally,' he urged, his voice quiet, giving her some encouragement.

'I've ignored them, John, really I have, but when I saw your aunt was in pain ... well, I sort of couldn't help it – I looked at her aura.'

'And?' he said, his eyes narrowing.

'I could see an illness, and she really should see a doctor, John. There's something else I must tell you,' she said on a rush, not giving him time to speak. 'My gran's arthritis has been getting steadily worse, and it's awful to see her in so much pain. So ... I ... I gave her some healing.'

'You what!' he exploded. 'Sally, how could you?'

'I just had to. Oh John, please try to understand. I just couldn't bear to see her suffering.'

'It's not for you to make that decision, Sally. We've been over this so many times. What happens in life is God's will.'

'But Jesus healed the sick – you can't deny that.'

'I don't, but that doesn't make it right for you to use psychic healing. Please, Sally, promise me that you'll never do it again.'

She closed her eyes, shaking her head in despair. 'I can't, John. I'm not going to stop helping my gran and ... if... if you can't accept it, perhaps the only thing we can do is to break off our engagement.'

He sat quietly for a while, then turned towards her, a pained expression in his eyes. 'No, Sally, I'm sorry – I can't accept it. It goes against all my beliefs.'

Hearing the finality in his voice, her stomach lurched. She didn't want to lose him and part of her wanted to back down. But as tears pricked her eyes she knew that it would be impossible to see her gran in pain again, and do nothing. Unable to bear it, she stood up. 'I think it would be better if I went home, John. Perhaps we both need time to think about this.'

'Sally, don't be silly, sit down and let's talk,' he begged.

'What is there to talk about?' she choked. 'You can't accept that I'm going to use my healing gifts, and I can't agree to stop.'

'All right – perhaps we do both need some

breathing space. Come on then, I'll walk you home,' he said stiffly.

'No, it's all right, I'd rather go on my own,' she whispered, hurrying out of the pub, a hard knot of pain in her chest.

Oh, what have I done? she thought. I've lost him. It's over – he'll never agree to my use of spiritual healing. But I can't let gran suffer, I can't.

John, John, she agonised, the tears now running down her cheeks and blinding her as she fled along Chelsea Embankment.

John followed Sally out of the pub, watching until she was out of sight, and feeling utterly deflated. Pushing his hands into his trouser pockets, he walked slowly towards Albert Bridge, head lowered and deep in thought. It was unbelievable! How could she go back to doing that dreadful spiritual healing after all he had taught her. Frowning, he remembered what she had said about his aunt, and shivered. She had seen something wrong in Lottie's aura ... was it possible?

'Lottie, it's me,' he called as he entered the flat, making his way to the sitting room. 'How are you feeling?'

'Not too bad, dear. I've taken a couple of aspirin and it's eased the pain. What are you doing home so early?'

'I'll just make us a drink and then tell you all about it. What would you like?'

'A cup of cocoa, please, then I'll have an early night.' She followed him into the kitchen, watching as he measured milk into a saucepan. 'What's wrong, John? Have you had a row with Sally?'

He sighed deeply, turning slowly to face her. 'She's been doing that awful spiritual healing, Lottie.'

'No – I can't believe it!' she gasped.

'I'm afraid it's true. She admitted it to me, and what's more she's going to carry on with it.'

'Oh dear, what are you going to do?'

'I don't know,' he answered, pouring hot milk into the mugs and passing one to Lottie. 'She said that if I can't accept it, our engagement is off.'

'Sally said that! What on earth has come over the girl?'

'It seems that she's no longer prepared to see her grandmother in pain without trying to help her.' He shrugged. 'Maybe she's right. She threw it at me that Jesus healed the sick, and that's something I can't deny.'

'John, you know our church is strictly against the use of psychic powers.'

'Not all denominations feel that way, Auntie. Some churches have healing services.'

'Yes, I know they do, darling.' She shook her head. 'Well, come on, we had better put our heads together and decide what to do.'

They returned to the sitting room and sat side by side on the sofa as they sipped their cocoa.

Lottie then reached out and stroked his hair. 'Are you still going to marry her, John?'

'Of course I am. We agreed that she's perfect. A lot of suspicions at work have been allayed since we got engaged and there's even a whisper of promotion.'

'Oh, how wonderful, darling,' Lottie enthused. She tipped her head to one side, a thoughtful expression on her face. 'How about bending a little, allowing Sally to use spiritual healing on her gran, but not on anyone el...' She paused, clutching the pit of her stomach.

'You're in pain, aren't you? Please, Auntie, I really do think you should see the doctor. In fact, I'll make you an appointment in the morning.'

'Don't fuss, my dear, I'm sure it's nothing. I'll be fine after a good night's sleep.' She swallowed the last of her cocoa and stood up, leaning forward slightly as though to ease the pain. 'Good night sweetie, I'll see you in the morning.'

John's eyes followed his aunt as she left the room, worry creasing his brow. Sally had said she could see something in her aura, and he had to admit that Lottie did look worse. He shook his head worriedly, determined to make an appointment for her to see the doctor, despite her protests.

For the first time he faced the thought of his aunt's mortality. She had taken him on when he was seven years old, after his parents had been killed in a bombing raid during the war. He had been evacuated to Devon at the time and still had vivid memories of the day Lottie had turned up to break the news. He swallowed. She had become his rock: his mother, father, and friend.

When at eighteen he had plucked up the courage to reveal his secret, she had accepted it without judgement, offering her help and support. Oh Lottie, he thought, what would I do without you? Please God, please let Sally be wrong.

Lottie, clenching her teeth against the pain,

climbed into bed. John's marriage to Sally couldn't go wrong now, it just couldn't! She was desperate to see him settled before the end, which she knew was inevitable.

She thought about her mother, and how she had died when John was just four years old. It hadn't taken Lottie long to recognise that her symptoms were the same, and remembering her mother's agony at the end, she prayed that God would give her the strength to endure it.

Although they weren't close, it had been a shock when her father died just six months later, almost as though he couldn't live without the woman he had been married to for over forty years. She remembered how she had felt then at losing both her parents; although an adult, she had felt like an orphan.

Her thoughts turning to John again, she shook her head in despair. She had to protect him, to hide her illness from him for as long as possible. How she treasured their relationship, a relationship that had come about so unexpectedly when her brother and his wife had been killed.

There had been nobody else left to claim John, just her, and she would never forget how she felt when she went to collect him from the farm he had been evacuated to in Devon. Those feelings had left her plagued with guilt, a guilt that would never go away, no matter how hard she tried to assuage it.

Another sharp pain made her gasp and she closed her eyes, praying inwardly. Please God, please give me a little more time.

Chapter Twenty-Four

Sally hardly slept on Sunday night. She tossed and turned, wondering if she had done the right thing, yet what choice did she have? Her gran needed continual healing and she had to help her. Oh John, she agonised, why can't you understand?

She finally drifted off to sleep in the early hours of the morning, waking to her mum's shout that it was time to get up, and ineffectually tried to cover the dark circles under her eyes with Pond's cream and face powder.

Her head was thumping, and as she thought about John, tears constantly threatened. How could she go to work? Not only would she have to face Lottie, but worse was the thought of seeing John, knowing that their relationship was over.

She put off going downstairs until the last moment and kept her head lowered as she walked into the kitchen, relieved to find that only her mother was up.

'Are you all right, Sal? You look awful.'

'I've just got a bit of a headache, Mum, that's all.'

'Well, you had better get a move on or you'll be late. I've made you some toast.'

Hurriedly swallowing a cup of tea and unable to face any food, Sally went out into the hall and shrugged on her coat. Then, just putting her head around the door, she called, 'Bye, I'm off.'

'Sal, wait! What about yer breakfast?'

She heard her mother's shout but ignored it, rushing out of the door. Ann was leaving her house at the same time, and after one look at her friend's face, she said, 'Heavens! What's up?'

'Oh, it's nothing, just a headache.'

'Well, looking at the state of you, it must be a right thumper. Are you sure there isn't anything else wrong?' Ann asked, her eyes narrowed with suspicion as she gazed at her.

Anxious to avoid any more questions Sally shook her head, fumbling in her mind for something to distract Ann. 'My aunt's going to Blackpool on Saturday with my mum. They're determined to sort my uncle out.'

'Oh, when are they coming back?'

'They're staying overnight and travelling back on Sunday.'

'I wish I could be there when they knock on his door,' Ann said, grinning widely. 'I'd love to see the look on his face.'

'Yes, I know what you mean, but I can't help thinking about the woman he's living with. If she thinks they're legally married, how is she going to feel, and what about their little boy?'

'I hadn't thought about that,' Ann said, the smile leaving her face. 'Oh, the poor things.'

As they approached Arding & Hobbs, Sally's footsteps faltered; she was dreading the prospect of facing John's aunt. But when she reached her department she found Lottie absent, her place taken by a temporary assistant from another section.

The morning dragged by, and only her concern

for Lottie forced Sally to the canteen at lunchtime. She had to face John; it was the only way to find out what was wrong with his aunt.

She found him sitting at their usual table, her heart leaping when he looked up, smiling softly. 'Hello, darling, sit down,' he urged.

Sliding onto a chair beside him she found her hands were trembling, and she clenched them in her lap. 'Why is Lottie absent today, John? Has her pain worsened?'

'I took your advice and made an appointment for her at the surgery. She may be back to work this afternoon; it depends what the doctor says. But listen, darling, I want to apologise for my behaviour last night. Will you forgive me?'

Sally gawked, unable to believe her ears. 'But what about my psychic healing?' she asked, her voice high.

He sighed, shaking his head slowly. 'I can't say I agree with it, Sally, but I do understand the dilemma you're in. I've given it a great deal of thought and I wondered if we could come to a compromise. Would you agree to confine your healing to your gran and not use it on anyone else?'

'Oh John, of course I will,' she cried, relief flooding through her body and her eyes filling with tears of happiness. She hadn't lost him. Oh, it was wonderful.

It was two days before Lottie returned to work. The doctor had sent her for several tests at St Thomas's Hospital, and now she was waiting for the results. She looked tired and drawn, and Sally tried to help her as much as she could, rushing to serve the customers when they approached the counter. Throughout the day she furtively studied Lottie's aura, worried by the dark places she could clearly see.

It was when there was a lull in the late afternoon and she could see pain etched on Lottie's face, that she plucked up the courage to speak. 'Are you all right?' she whispered, standing close to her side.

'I'm not too bad, Sally,' Lottie answered softly, 'but I won't be sorry to go home.'

'Please, would you let me help you? I'm sure I could alleviate some of your pain with spiritual healing.'

'No! How could you even suggest it, Sally? You know how I feel about using psychic powers. It's wrong, very wrong,' she said angrily.

'Oh, please don't get upset. I'm sorry, I just wanted to help you, that's all.'

'I suggest that you keep to your agreement with John and confine your activities to your grandmother, and in future, Sally, I don't want to hear another word about it. Now please go and sort the records out in that rack; they're in an awful muddle. Put them in alphabetical order, please.'

Sally nodded, knowing by the dismissive tone in her voice that it would be useless to argue, and for the following hour the atmosphere between them was strained.

It was a relief to go home, and as she stepped into the kitchen, Sally was surprised to see her aunt busily laying the table. 'Hello,' Mary said, smiling

231

a greeting. 'Dinner won't be long.'

'Where's Mum?'

'I'm afraid she's in bed with a shocking cold and it feels like she's got a temperature.'

'Oh no, I thought she sounded a bit hoarse this morning. I'll just pop up to see her.'

'All right, my dear, and perhaps you could ask her if she'd like something to eat.'

Quietly opening the bedroom door, Sally found her mum propped up in bed looking distinctly sorry for herself. 'How are you feeling?'

'Bleedin' awful and my head's swimming,' Ruth complained.

Sally laid a hand across her forehead, surprised at how hot she felt. 'Well, you're in the best place. Have you taken anything?'

'Just a Beecham's Powder.'

'Why don't you try Gran's cure-all?'

'I would, but we ain't got any whisky,' she said dolefully.

Sally smiled inwardly at the hint. 'I'll pop down to the off-licence to get some. If anything will put you back on your feet, it'll be Gran's concoction.'

'What about you? Can't you give me some of your healing?'

'Oh Mum, I can't cure a cold,' she said, shaking her head. 'By the way, Aunt Mary wants to know if you'd like something to eat?'

'No thanks, me throat's too sore.'

'All right, Mum, get some rest now. I'll pop up again later.'

She rushed to buy the whisky before dinner, despite her aunt's complaints that it would be ruined, and now watched her gran mixing up her

232

famous recipe. A good measure of whisky, mixed with honey, lemon, and a couple of teaspoons of Galloway's cough syrup, all topped with boiling water. 'There,' she said, handing it to Sally, 'that'll do the trick. Make sure she drinks it while it's hot.'

On Friday evening Sally sat beside her mum, surprised that her cold was still raging. Her temperature was down, but she was still feeling poorly. 'You won't be able to go to Blackpool now, Mum.'

'I know,' she croaked. 'I feel awful letting your aunt down, but she's so determined to go, I couldn't persuade her to wait.'

Sally frowned; she didn't like the thought of her aunt going to Blackpool on her own. 'Mum, I could go with her. I've got the day off tomorrow.'

Mary stepped in the room, just in time to hear Sally's offer. 'Oh, that would be smashing,' she said.

'I don't think it's a good idea,' her mother said worriedly. 'What if Harry turns nasty?'

Mary smiled sardonically. 'There's no chance of that, Ruth. Harry runs away from trouble. He's a coward.'

'Yeah, but even so, I don't like the idea of Sal...' A fit of coughing suddenly shook her, leaving her drained.

'Don't worry, Mum, we'll be fine. Have you booked somewhere to stay for the night, Auntie?'

'No, I'm afraid not. But don't worry, the summer season's well over now, so we'll easily find a little B and B.'

'I think I'll pop next door,' Sally said, allaying any further protest from her mother. 'I'm sure

Elsie won't mind keeping an eye on you and Gran while we're away.'

'Of course I'll make sure they're all right,' Elsie said. 'Though I'm surprised your mum's allowing you to go.'

Sally grinned. 'Yes, I know what you mean, but she's too poorly to put up much of a fight. She still treats me like a child, doesn't she, and forgets that I'm all grown up now and engaged to be married.'

'Sally, you're an only child so she's bound to be more protective,' Elsie said, adding with a grin, 'and as for being grown up, I reckon you've got a good few years to go before you get the key to the door.' She glanced around quickly then as Arthur walked in. 'Hello, son,' she said.

Arthur smiled at his mother, then turned his gaze to Sally. 'Hello,' he said softly. 'You look nice.'

'Thanks,' Sally said, feeling herself turn pink. Why did he always have this effect on her? It felt as though her stomach was full of butterflies. Like his father Bert, he seemed to fill the room with his presence and looked incongruous standing beside his mother, his six foot two height dwarfing her.

'Sally and her aunt are going to Blackpool in the morning to sort that Harry out,' Elsie told him.

Arthur frowned. 'Will you be all right, Sally? Would you like me to come with you? I could drive you both up there.'

'Thanks, Arthur, it's very kind of you to offer, but we'll be fine. I'd better be off now. Thanks again, Elsie. Bye, Arthur.'

As she left the room, Elsie turned to her son. 'You're making it a bit obvious, love. You still like her, don't you?'

'Yes, I do. I'll always have a soft spot for her. But we're both engaged now and I'm happy enough with Jenny.'

Elsie touched his arm. 'Are you sure you know what you're doing? Australia is a long way away, son.'

'Don't start again, Mum. We've been through this so many times. Yes, I've made the right decision,' he told her, marching swiftly out of the kitchen.

Elsie twisted the tea-towel in her hand as she heard the door slam. I've driven him out again, she thought. Yet she couldn't help nagging him. The thought of never seeing him again was unbearable. Oh, if only he and Sally could have got together, Arthur would never have thought of emigrating then.

Chapter Twenty-Five

The following day, as Sally stepped off the Black-pool train feeling tired and dishevelled, a blast of cold blustery wind whipped around her legs. She shivered as she turned to her aunt. 'I wonder if Harry's house is far from the station.'

'Let's hope it isn't, dear,' Mary answered, struggling to tie a scarf around her hair. 'Come on, we'll get a taxi.'

They handed the driver Harry's address, sinking into their seats; pleased to be told it was only a ten-minute journey.

'What are we going to do if he's out, Aunt Mary?'

'I don't know. We'll cross that bridge when we come to it.' She removed her scarf and ran a comb through her hair. 'I don't want to turn up on his doorstep looking a mess. Daft isn't it, but it will make me feel at a disadvantage.' Digging in her handbag and taking out a compact, she peered into the mirror, powdered her face, and applied a fresh coat of pink lipstick. 'There,' she sighed. 'Ready for battle.'

Sally reached out to grasp her hand and gave it a gentle squeeze. 'Are you sure you don't want to leave it until the morning?'

'No, I just want to get it over with,' she answered, as the taxi pulled into the kerb.

Paying the driver, they turned to look at the neat row of terraced houses. 'Come on, Sally, it's this one,' Mary whispered, her face drawn.

Sally stood behind her aunt as a pretty blonde woman, a toddler at her side, opened the door. 'Yes, can I help you?' she asked.

'I've come to see Harry. Is he in?' Mary said curtly, nerves making her voice high.

'No, he's just popped into town for a few things, but I'm expecting him back shortly.' The little boy began to whimper and she swung him up into her arms, asking, 'Why do you want to see my husband?'

'*Your* husband?' Mary said sharply. 'That's a good one, considering he's still married to me.'

The woman's face stretched into an expression of utter disbelief, and clutching her son closer to her chest, she said, 'No, he can't be, you must be mistaken.'

'I can assure you there's no mistake. I have it on good authority that my husband lives at this address, and I'm not moving from here until I see him.'

'But Harry divorced his first wife,' she paused, her face turning ashen. 'Is ... is your name Mary?'

'Yes, it is, and despite what he's told you, we aren't divorced. I'm still legally his wife.'

The woman swayed, her voice a whisper, 'Not divorced? But ... but that would mean we're not married. No, no, I can't believe this.' Holding the child with one arm, she clutched the stanchion.

'Are you all right?' Mary asked, stepping forward with concern.

'Yes, I just felt a bit dizzy for a moment.' Standing aside, she added, 'It might be better if you came in. I'm sure we can straighten this out when Harry comes home.'

They walked into a sitting room strewn with children's toys, the woman gesturing them to a sofa. After sitting down they looked up at the little boy sheltered in his mother's arms, his thumb stuck in his mouth as he stared down at them. Sally gave him a cheeky wink and was rewarded when he removed his thumb, giving her a wide, wet smile.

'There, Daniel,' the woman said, putting him gently down onto the floor. 'Play with your toys, darling.'

He tottered across to a wooden train, squatted down and grabbed it in his chubby hands. Rising unsteadily he stumbled towards Sally, dumping it on her lap. 'Choo, choo,' he gurgled.

Sally picked up the toy, chatting to Daniel in an effort to fill the strained silence, and getting chuckles in reply.

The door opened and they all turned their heads as Harry walked in, followed by a little girl. 'Bloody hell – Mary!' he exploded. 'What are you doing here?'

'Isn't it obvious?' she said sarcastically. 'Aren't you going to introduce me to your other wife?'

'Harry, tell me it isn't true! Tell me you aren't still married to Mary?'

He lowered his eyes guiltily. 'Sheila, I...' His words were cut off as with an anguished wail, she ran from the room. The little girl moved to follow, but Harry put a detaining arm around her shoulders, and she flinched at his touch.

Oh, no! Sally thought, her stomach churning. The little girl's eyes met hers, and – in that moment – she knew.

Jumping to her feet, unaware of her actions and acting purely on instinct, she flew across the room. 'Don't touch her,' she screamed, grasping the child's arm and pulling her out of his reach.

Daniel began to howl, his little face bright red, lower lip trembling. 'Mama, Mama,' he sobbed, his arms held out.

It was Mary who came to the rescue. Bending down she swooped the child up, throwing a puzzled look at Sally as she left the room, saying, 'I'll take him to his mother.'

White-faced, Harry stumbled towards a chair and almost fell into it, while the little girl edged closer to Sally.

Seeing the distress on her face, Sally crouched down, and taking her in her arms, she could feel her thin body trembling.

Mary came back into the room then, staring at Harry distastefully. 'Your so-called wife is putting your little boy to bed.' She turned to look down at Sally, her eyes widening as comprehension dawned. 'No ... oh no! He hasn't, please tell me he hasn't!' she cried, her voice rising hysterically.

Standing up, Sally placed an arm around the girl's shoulders.

'Please, calm down, Auntie. Can't you see how upset she is?'

'I'm sorry, it's just so awful,' Mary gasped, struggling to compose herself.

'I'll take her out of here and you can talk to *him*,' Sally nodded her head in Harry's direction. Then, turning her attention back to the child, she asked, 'Where is your bedroom, darling?'

Finding her room, Sally sat down beside the little girl on the bed, saying softly, 'My name's Sally. What's your name, sweetheart?'

'Linda,' she whispered.

Seeing that she was still shaking, Sally reached out and took her hand. 'Listen darling, I promise that Harry will never touch you again.'

Linda's eyes were like saucers as though unable to believe what she was hearing. She gave a small cry, throwing herself into Sally's arms as a dam of pent-up emotions burst from her lips. 'He ... he...' she stammered, struggling to speak through her wracking sobs.

'Shh ... it's all right,' Sally whispered, her own eyes full of tears. 'I know, sweetheart, but you're safe now.' She rocked her back and forth, reliving her own experience at her uncle's hands, realising it had been nothing – nothing compared to what this child might have been through.

As she stroked Linda's hair, the child's sobs slowly turned into soft little hiccups that finally stopped altogether. Then, laying her gently back onto the pillows and covering her with an eiderdown, Sally sat quietly beside her, relieved when she fell into an exhausted sleep.

Closing the door softly she stepped onto the landing, coming face to face with Sheila. Feeling her anger flare, she hissed, 'I want to talk to you about Linda.'

With a puzzled look, Sheila gestured them into another room, and seeing a double bed dominating the space, Sally's mouth curled in distaste.

'You said you wanted to talk to me about Linda?' Sheila asked.

'Yes I do,' she snapped. 'Your little girl's in a terrible state. Don't you know what Harry's been doing to her? Couldn't you see?'

'See what? I don't understand.'

'My God, you must be blind. Harry's a paedophile and he's obviously been interfering with your little girl. Surely you suspected something?'

The colour drained from Sheila's face. 'No ... no, you must be mistaken. Harry loves Linda, he would never do anything like that.'

'I can assure you I'm not mistaken. You see, as a child I had personal experience of his sick perversion.'

Sheila collapsed onto the side of the bed. 'Oh, this is too much,' she wailed, bending forward as though in pain. 'First I find out that my husband is still married to someone else, and now you're trying to tell me that he ... he ... oh God, I'm going to be sick.' She rushed out and soon afterwards, Sally heard dreadful retching sounds from the bathroom.

The anger she felt began to dissipate, leaving her feeling drained. It isn't over yet, she thought tiredly. There's still Harry to sort out. She tentatively approached the bathroom. 'Are you all right?' she asked.

Sheila was leaning over the sink, splashing her face with cold water. She grabbed a towel from the rack and roughly dried her face. 'I don't think I'll ever be all right again,' she croaked. 'Please, leave me alone. I must go to my daughter.'

Sally made her way downstairs, hearing raised voices as she approached the sitting room. She paused in the narrow hall; there was a telephone on a small table. Picking up the receiver, she dialled 999.

The next morning, sitting on the train on their way back to London, Sally turned to her aunt who appeared both mentally and physically exhausted.

'Thank goodness it's all over,' she said.

'No, my dear, I'm afraid it isn't. There will be many more questions and the trial to face yet.'

'I still don't know if we did the right thing, Auntie. Maybe we should have told the police that Harry's been interfering with Linda.'

'Darling, I know how upset you are, but it's her mother's decision – and anyway perhaps she's right. The child has been through enough and dragging her through the courts would be a dreadful ordeal.' She sighed. 'I can't help feeling sorry for Sheila. The poor woman's all alone in the world without parents or other relatives to offer their support.'

Sally, remembering the venomous look Harry had thrown at her as the police led him away, shivered. Her aunt hadn't noticed, she had been too busy comforting Sheila, and instead of bitterness and hatred, Sally had seen a closeness developing between the two women. It had been well past midnight when Sheila insisted that they stay; telling them it would be impossible to find a B&B at that time of night.

The morning had brought fresh tears when Sheila had gently questioned her daughter, finding her worst fears realised. It appeared that Linda might have suffered abuse for quite some time, but she was reluctant to tell them, obviously still in fear of Harry.

Then when Mary warned that Harry might be let out on bail, Sheila had frantically insisted on packing his suitcases, throwing them out onto the doorstep with her mouth set in a grim line. 'He'll never set foot in this house again,' she told them, determination in her voice and the set of her shoulders.

'Sally, do you remember when not long after I came to live with you, we had our little talk about Harry?' her aunt asked now, breaking into her thoughts.

'Yes, of course I do. It was when you told me he was a paedophile,' Sally answered.

'I noticed the way you looked at him yesterday,

242

and there was so much hatred in your eyes. No, don't interrupt me, my dear, let me finish,' she urged. 'I don't blame you for hating him, I do too. But I'm still worried about how his abuse may have affected you.'

'Don't worry, I'm all right,' Sally assured her. 'It only happened once, don't forget. I didn't suffer over a period of time like Linda.'

'I know, my dear. Oh, that poor child, how will she ever get over it?'

'I don't know, Auntie. Perhaps Sheila will get her some professional help.'

They both fell silent then, Sally still thinking about Linda, and hoping the child's life wouldn't be ruined as they feared. Her thoughts then turned to herself, and for the first time she faced up to her own abuse and how it had affected her. Yes, it had made her frightened of men, but they weren't all like Harry, she realised that now. Take John for instance, he was so gentle and kind, and for the first time she didn't flinch at the thought of what would happen when they were married. It would be all right, she was sure. John was wonderful, so caring, and she was sure that with his help, she would be able to overcome her fears.

As the train swayed, Sally glanced at her aunt and saw that she had fallen asleep. Her own eyes grew heavy, and behind closed lids she once again found herself thinking about her uncle. He's got away with it again, she thought. Yes, he would get a prison sentence for bigamy – but what about when he got out?

Chapter Twenty-Six

Sally was standing on a chair, stretching out to remove the paper-chains that festooned the ceiling. Her mother was busily sweeping up pine needles that had fallen from the Christmas tree, complaining as she did every year that they were lodged into every nook and cranny.

Climbing down, Sally gazed around the room, finding it bare now that it had been stripped of decorations. The house felt empty too since her aunt had returned to her own home in Tooting. Still not totally recovered from her depression, but without an income from Harry, she had gone back to work, finding a job as a receptionist in a doctor's surgery.

It had been a dreadful few months and they still couldn't believe that Harry had only been sentenced to eighteen months in prison.

He had a good lawyer who had enlisted the sympathy of the judge when her aunt had given evidence. In the witness box she appeared cold and hard, and under cross-examination had been forced to admit that the marriage had never been properly consummated. Only those who were close to her knew how much Mary was suffering, her demeanour just a front, hiding her real feelings.

Both her aunt and Sheila's humiliation had increased when the national newspapers got hold of the story. The women had been besieged by reporters, the Blackpool bigamist making the front pages. Yet they had united in their shared adversity, becoming close friends. Now, for a few more weeks, Sheila and the children were in London, staying at Mary's house, and Sally hoped that 1960 would be a better year for all of them.

She glanced at the clock. John was due soon, and they were going to visit his aunt in hospital. 'Can you manage now, Mum? I had better get myself tidied up.'

'It's all done now, love, you go and get ready.' Ruth grinned, nodding her head towards Sadie, asleep in a chair by the fire. 'Look at the state of that – she'd sleep through a hurricane, wouldn't she?'

'Oi, I heard that, you cheeky mare. I was only having forty winks. Now then,' Sadie added, smacking her lips hopefully, 'a cup of tea would go down a treat.'

'Bleedin' hell, Mum. Don't you know that slavery's been abolished?' Ruth admonished, yet unable to hide her smile.

'Of course I do, but don't forget I'm a poor old lady who needs looking after,' she replied, with a sly wink at Sally.

'Old lady, my foot,' Ruth retorted. 'You're still a spring chicken, Mum.'

'More like an old broiler,' Sadie chuckled. 'Now come on, how about that cup of tea.'

Laughing, Sally left the room. What a pair, she thought fondly, as she mounted the stairs.

Sally's heels tapped on the pristine floor as she

and John entered the ward, making their way to Lottie's bedside. She was lying on stiff white pillows, her face, devoid of make-up, looking pale and drawn.

'Hello, children,' she whispered.

'How are you, Auntie?' John asked, placing a bunch of yellow chrysanthemums on the bed.

'Not too bad, darling. Thank you for the flowers, they're lovely but we'd better move them in case Matron comes round. Honestly, the woman's an absolute dragon and she keeps everyone on their toes.' Picking up the flowers she turned to Sally. 'Would you mind asking the nurse to put them in water for me?'

Sally nodded her assent and approached a nurse sitting at her desk in the middle of the ward, handing her the chrysanthemums. Her uniform – blue dress, crisp white linen apron, drawn in at her trim waist by an elastic belt and fastened with a gleaming silver buckle – made Sally smile in admiration. She loved her white linen hat too; resplendent with crisply starched pleats fanned around the edge.

The ward was quiet with only the gentle hum of voices as Sally made her way back to Lottie. 'Mission accomplished,' she said. 'When are you having your operation?'

'Tomorrow morning, I think.'

Sally couldn't resist looking at her aura, frowning when she saw that the dark area had increased in size. Glancing up she saw John's eyes on her, one eyebrow raised quizzically. She reddened, quickly engaging Lottie in conversation, relieved when the bell rang, signalling that visiting time was over.

Sally was glad to get home; a thumping head-ache drove her to bed early and a full moon cast a luminous glow across her face as she lay snuggled under the blankets, her thoughts on Lottie and the operation she was having tomorrow. She closed her eyes, offering up a prayer.

At work the next morning the time seemed to drag by. Stocktaking was in progress and writing the endless lists made Sally's eyes ache. Now, pleased to see that it was lunchtime, she hurried to the canteen and joined John at their usual table, happy to find that they had it all to themselves.

'Are you all right, darling?' she asked, noticing that he seemed distracted.

'What? Oh sorry, Sally, I was miles away. I can't help worrying about Lottie. She must have been down for her operation by now and the thought of it keeps going round and round in my mind.'

'You don't have to apologise, John. Of course you're worried. I am too, but I'm sure she'll be fine,' she said, trying to reassure him.

'God, I hope you're right,' he answered, his lunch still untouched on his plate.

For once his appearance was less than immaculate. A slight stubble was evident on his chin, and there were dark shadows below his eyes. Reaching out, Sally touched the back of his hand. 'Try to eat something,' she urged.

'I'm not hungry,' he said, hands trembling as he picked up his cup of tea.

Sally found herself unable to eat her lunch either, and as John was obviously not in the mood for talking, they sat quietly for the rest of their break.

His eyes were still clouded when they had to return to their departments, and Sally was reluctant to let go of his hand. 'I'll see you later, darling,' she whispered as they parted on the stairs, watching as he walked away, his head bent.

Now, she glanced across at Ann as they strolled home from work, neither saying much, each busy with their own thoughts. 'What's wrong?' Sally asked finally, sensing that her friend had something on her mind.

'Arthur passed his medical and it won't be long now before they get their departure date. I'm worried about Mum. She still hasn't accepted that he's going and is refusing to talk about it.'

'He may still change his mind,' Sally said hopefully.

'No, we've got to face it. He's determined to go.'

Sally felt a pang of sorrow. Arthur had lived next door since she was ten years old. She remembered how he had looked then, a scruffy and naughty schoolboy, who took great delight in tormenting his sister. Smiling ruefully she recalled how he looked now – tall and ruggedly handsome, yet with a gentle smile. Jenny was a lucky girl, she thought.

Noticing that Ann's eyes were brimming with tears as they stood outside her front door, she said, 'I've got to go to the hospital with John later, but if I can get back early, would you like me to come round?'

Ann dashed the tears from her eyes, nodded, and with a tremulous smile, hurried indoors.

Pausing for a moment before going inside, Sally wished there were something she could do to comfort both Ann and John. She felt powerless. John's aunt was in the hands of a surgeon, and now it seemed obvious that nothing was going to stop Arthur from emigrating.

That evening, Sally and John stood by Lottie's bed, staring worriedly at her ashen face. Her eyes were closed and she groaned softly, turning her head on the pillow.

A nurse came to stand beside them, and seeing their expressions, said, 'I'm afraid she was late going down for her operation and is still under the effects of the anaesthetic.'

'Is she going to be all right?' John asked anxiously.

The nurse removed Lottie's notes from a clip at the foot of the bed, scanning the pages. 'The operation went well, but other than that there isn't much more I can tell you.' She smiled reassuringly. 'Don't worry, she'll look a lot better when you see her tomorrow.' Then, replacing the notes, she moved on to the next bed.

Seeing how desolate he looked, Sally pulled out a chair, urging John to sit down. He took Lottie's hand, a tear running down his cheek. 'Oh Sally,' he choked, 'she looks awful.'

She took his other hand. 'I know, darling, but I'm sure she'll look a lot better once she comes round.'

They sat quietly beside the sick woman for

about another half an hour, and even when the nurse came to take her blood pressure, there were no further signs of her regaining consciousness. John stood up, and with a small sigh, said, 'Come on, we might as well go home.'

Whilst sitting beside Lottie, Sally had looked at her aura and couldn't wait to tell John what she'd seen. Once they were outside the hospital, although slightly worried about his response, she said hesitantly, 'Listen, darling, there's no need to worry about Lottie. She's going to be all right.'

'Oh, I do hope so, Sally.'

'John, I looked at her aura and there's no sign of any illness now. She really is going to be fine.'

'Really! Are you sure, Sally?'

'Yes, I'm sure.'

He shook his head, running his hands through his hair. 'I feel like a hypocrite. I know I should be annoyed with you for using your psychic powers, yet I can't help feeling relieved. You were right about her illness, so I'm going to dare hope that you're right now.'

They walked hand in hand to the bus stop and Sally was relieved to see that John's face looked a little lighter. He yawned, saying apologetically, 'Do you mind if I go straight home, darling? I hardly slept last night and I'm absolutely exhausted.'

'No, of course not. Anyway, Ann was a bit upset today and I'd like to spend some time with her.'

Sally knocked on Ann's door, her face flushing when Arthur opened it. Their eyes locked and they stood gazing at each other. It was Sally who broke the spell. 'Is Ann in?' she asked.

He stood back, gesturing her inside. 'Yes, come on in.'

As she passed him in the narrow hallway, their bodies brushed together and she heard his quick intake of breath. She too felt strange, and walking into the kitchen she was once again wondering why Arthur always had this effect on her.

Elsie was sitting at the table, the Tarot cards spread out in front of her, obviously giving a reading for Nelly Cox who was perched opposite.

'Hello, Sally,' Nelly smiled, her top dentures falling. 'Bloody things,' she complained, pushing them up with her tongue. 'Elsie's reading the cards for me.'

'Yes, I can see that,' Sally told her.

'Ann's having a bath, dear, but she won't be long. Sit yourself down,' Elsie urged.

Sally sat by the fire, glad of its warmth and unable to hide a smile when Arthur popped his head around the door, giving her a cheeky wink. 'I've told Ann you're here,' he said, before turning to his mum. 'Right, I'm off out now, see you later.'

'Cheerio, son. Don't be late.'

'Mum, I'm a big boy now. Don't you think it's time you stopped telling me that?' he joked as he went out.

'I'm sorry, Nelly, I just can't seem to concentrate,' Elsie said, as the door closed behind him. 'The thought of never seeing my Arthur again seems to be blocking all my powers,' she added sadly.

'That's all right, Elsie. Nothing is likely to happen in my life anyway so I don't suppose the cards could 'ave come up with much.' Nelly then levered herself to her feet. 'Well, I'll be off now. Are you popping in to see me soon, Sally?'

'Yes, I'll be round after work tomorrow,' she assured her.

As Nelly went out of the room she left a strong smell of urine in her wake which made them both wrinkle their noses. 'She's getting worse, isn't she? I thought it was only her house at first, but she's let herself go too,' Sally said worriedly.

'She's an old lady, love, and lost without George.' Elsie's face fell. 'I know how she feels. I'm going to be lost too when Arthur goes to Australia.'

Before she could answer, Ann shouted that she was out of the bath, and as Sally left the room to go upstairs, she smiled at Elsie, wishing there was something she could say to comfort her. Yet what could she say? All Elsie wanted to hear was that Arthur was staying in England.

Chapter Twenty-Seven

Sally was thrilled with her seventeenth birthday present from John; she held out her arm, admiring the pretty charm bracelet on her wrist, surprised when he dropped another present into her lap. She grinned up at him before opening the small box, puzzled as she lifted out a key.

'A flat has come up in the house next to ours,' John told her, his face alight with excitement. 'They rarely come up for rent so I grabbed at the

252

chance. It's perfect for us, darling.'

'But, John, we aren't getting married until I'm eighteen. That means we'll be paying rent on it for a whole year. How on earth will we be able to save up for furniture and things?'

'That's just it, Sally. We could bring the wedding forward. Now that I've been promoted we can easily afford the rent and Lottie has offered to help us out with some furniture. She's giving us a double bed and the wardrobe and dressing-table from my bedroom.' He crouched down by the side of her chair, an earnest expression on his face. 'I've had a look inside the flat and the last tenants have left carpets and curtains. There's even a cooker. It's old, but in good working condition.'

'We'll need more than that, John,' Sally told him, doubt evident in her voice.

'Darling, anything else we need we can get on hire purchase. Please say yes, Sally,' he urged.

Sally nipped her lower lip with her teeth, wondering if her mum would agree to them bringing the wedding forward. 'When do you want us to get married, John?' she asked.

'Well, it's February now, so how about in May? That'll give us three months to get the flat ready. It needs a lick of paint in some of the rooms, but that shouldn't take long to do. Come on, Sally!' he cried, jumping up. 'Get your coat on and I'll take you to see it. You'll love it, I know you will.'

Sally gazed around the light and spacious sitting room and had to agree that the flat was lovely. The kitchen, though small, was adequate and the double bedroom and bathroom would look fine once they had been freshly painted.

'Well, what do you think?' John asked.

'You're right, darling. It's perfect for us,' she told him.

'Then can we bring the wedding forward?' he asked hopefully.

She threw herself into his arms. 'Yes, John, let's do it. Let's get married in May.'

He pushed her gently away and stepped back. 'We had better go and tell Lottie. I know she's waiting anxiously to see if you'd agree. Then after that we'll have to tell your mother, and she'll probably hit the roof.'

Hurt that John had rebuffed her again, Sally hung her head. He reached out and lifted her chin with his forefinger, looking at her with the crooked smile on his handsome face that she always found irresistible. She opened her mouth to speak, but he grabbed her hand.

'Come on, darling,' he urged, laughing as he pulled her out of the flat. 'Let's go.'

Unable to resist his enthusiasm, she pushed the doubts to the back of her mind. It'll be different when we're married, she thought, as she tripped along in his wake.

Lottie smiled at them with delight when they told her the news. Of course she and John had discussed it, so it was no surprise really. Her only worry had been that Sally might refuse to get married so early. Yet one look at the adoration on her face as she gazed at John, made her realise that her fears had been groundless.

Sometimes she felt a twinge of guilt at using the

girl. But John was such a lovely young man, and despite everything, would make Sally a wonderful husband.

She had become very fond of Sally since she and John had been courting, pleased with the way she had progressed; her diction was good now and in some ways it felt as if she was gaining a daughter.

With luck, Sally would never find out – but even if she did, knowing her problem it was almost certain that she wouldn't mind. That was why she had picked her for John, and with them living close by, it would be like having an extended family.

Lottie still felt that a miracle had happened when her tumour had turned out to be benign. When the surgeon told her that her biopsy was clear she had stared at him in disbelief. It was as though their prayers had been answered and she had been granted another chance at life, an opportunity to do some of the things she had always wanted. One of these was to have a go at selling her paintings, and who knows, she thought dreamily, if they actually sold well, maybe they could all go travelling together – visit Paris, Italy and all the other wonderful places she wanted to see.

Rushing across the room she pulled Sally into her arms. 'Oh, my dear, I am so happy for you both,' she cried, overcome with emotion.

Sally returned her hug, then pulled back, smiling with delight. 'The flat's lovely, Lottie. Aren't we lucky that one came up?'

'Yes, you certainly are. This is a lovely part of Battersea, and like me, you'll have a view of the park.'

'Oh Lottie, with all that's happened I almost forgot. Thank you for my birthday present, it's lovely and as you can see I've got it on already,' Sally said, turning to give a twirl, her arms outstretched.

'Yes, it's a nice blouse and I'm glad you like it.'

'I'm sorry to break this up, girls,' John interrupted, 'but we had better go and face the dragon.'

'Dragon! What on earth do you mean?' Lottie laughed.

'I mean Sally's mum,' he answered, grinning widely.

'Hey, my mum's not a dragon, John,' she protested.

'Well, she certainly breathes fire when I'm around. You wait and see.'

'No,' Lottie protested. 'I'm sure she'll be as delighted as I am. Goodbye, Sally. I'll see you tomorrow, my dear.'

But John was right; her mother's face was red with anger. 'What do you mean, get married in May? That's only three months away.' Ruth shook her head. 'No, Sally, it's far too soon. You told me you'd wait until you were eighteen.'

They told her about the flat, watching as she huffed and puffed with agitation, suiting John's description.

After much persuasion she finally calmed down, looking almost ready to give in, and saying, 'But how can we prepare for a wedding in such a short time, Sally?'

'Mum, we don't want any fuss. Just a quiet wedding, and perhaps a small tea-party afterwards with family and a few close friends.'

'But I've always dreamed of seeing you in a lovely white dress with a long veil, flowers in yer hair and...' she trailed off, her eyes dreamy.

'We can't afford a big do, Mum, and a wedding dress would be a waste of money. I thought a nice cream suit and perhaps one of those pretty pillbox hats.'

'At least tell me it'll be a church service,' she said hopefully.

John, after a quick glance at Sally, smiled reassuringly at her mother. 'Yes, Mrs Marchant. I'll have a word with our vicar. I'm sure he'll be happy to perform the ceremony.'

'Hmm, that's something, I suppose. I wouldn't 'ave wanted you to get married in a registry office.'

'But, Mum, you never go to church – why is it so important to you?'

'I dunno, Sal, it just seems more real somehow. Yer dad and me got married in a registry office and it was over so quickly I didn't 'ave time to draw breath. I just want something better for you, that's all.'

'Ken isn't my father,' Sally reminded her.

'I know that,' she snapped. 'And you won't 'ave anyone to give you away either.'

Sally's thoughts raced. 'I could ask Bert.'

Her mother flopped onto a fireside chair. 'Yeah, Bert would do it,' she murmured.

'Please, Mum, say yes,' Sally begged.

Drumming her fingers on the wooden arms of the chair, Ruth stared into the fire, finally heaving a sigh and saying, 'All right, Sally. If this is what you really want, I won't stand in yer way.'

Chapter Twenty-Eight

The weeks seemed to fly past. March turned into April and Sally's wedding was only a month away. She had found the perfect outfit in Oxford Street, a cream suit with a Chanel-style box jacket and straight skirt ending just below her knees. She had even managed to find a matching pillbox hat decorated with a wisp of net that just covered her forehead.

Changing the heavy shopping bag over to her other hand and panting with exertion, she hurried to the flat. Nelly had been having a sort-out and had given her a lovely tea-set, insisting that she never used it, along with an unused pink quilt, still in its wrapping. She pictured it on the bed and knew it would fit perfectly with the décor. John had painted the walls magnolia and the colour blended well with the pink chintz curtains left behind by the last tenants. Now she was anxious to put the quilt on the bed and to hang the freshly washed curtains, before John turned up later to finish decorating the bathroom.

The smell of fresh paint was strong as she let herself into the flat, hurrying along the hall, a happy grin on her face as she anticipated John's surprise when he saw the finishing touches to the bedroom. She flung open the door, the smile still on her lips, and froze.

At first she couldn't comprehend the sight that

met her eyes. There were two heads on the pillows, two bodies, their limbs entwined amongst the jumble of sheets on the bed. What were they doing? *No, no, this can't be,* her mind screamed. Bile rose in her throat and she dropped the shopping bags, covering her mouth as she stared at the scene in horror. Two faces stared back over their shoulders – both male.

'Sally, wait!' John shouted as her legs unfroze and she bolted back down the hall. 'Let go of me, Larry, I must go after her,' she heard him cry in agitation.

She was going to be sick; she had to get out of there. Wrenching open the door in panic, she ran wildly down the stairs, her heel catching on a piece of loose carpet, twisting her foot painfully. Losing her balance she toppled forward, hands flailing as she tried to grab the banister, her scream cut off abruptly as she hit the hard hall tiles.

Sally regained consciousness feeling confused and lethargic, aware of a sharp pain every time she drew breath. Slowly she realised there were people in the room, talking softly, and it was Lottie's agitated tone that penetrated her clouded mind.

'We've got to keep her quiet, John. If this comes out you'll be ruined.'

'Calm down, Auntie. I'll make up some sort of excuse – I'm sure I can handle her.'

'Don't be ridiculous, John. She might be young and sexually inexperienced, but she saw what was going on. This isn't something you can just explain away. My God, all the years we've spent building an image of respectability will be wiped out.'

'Oh Lottie, do stop worrying. Now please, just let me think, will you!'

Sally squeezed her eyes shut, listening to his footsteps as he paced the room, her mind a jumble of pain, hurt and disgust. How could I have been so blind? she berated herself. It was obvious now that John had never loved her; he had just used her to cover up his homosexuality. They were talking again ... discussing her.

'I've got an idea, Lottie,' John said. 'I'll tell her that Larry's an old friend and we both had too much to drink. It was very late and he was in no condition to drive, so rather than disturb you, we bunked down in the flat.'

'Yes, it might work. But what exactly did she see when she barged in on you?'

It was too much for Sally and she sat up, gasping at the stabbing pain in her ribs. They were in Lottie's bedroom, she realised in confusion, wondering how she had got there.

'Sally, don't get up, the doctor's on his way. You've had a nasty fall,' John said, rushing to her side.

'Don't touch me!' she recoiled. Then moving painfully to the other side of the bed, she eased her feet to the floor and yelped, quickly raising her left leg.

'Sally, you must sit down. Your ankle is terribly swollen and it might be broken,' Lottie admonished, taking hold of her arm.

'Leave me alone,' she sobbed, trying to stand again, but finding it impossible. Oh God, she cried inwardly, sinking back onto the bed. Please help me; please get me out of here.

As if in answer to her prayer the doorbell rang. 'That'll be the doctor,' John said, hurrying to answer it.

After an examination the doctor arranged for her to go to hospital. John and Lottie stood side by side on the pavement as Sally was put into the ambulance and driven away. She refused to let them accompany her, despite their appeals.

In Casualty they found two broken ribs, but another X-ray showed that her ankle wasn't fractured, it was just a nasty sprain. Binding both her ribs and her ankle tightly, the nursing staff assured her that she was lucky; other than extensive bruising, there were no serious injuries, and she could go home.

Lucky? Sally thought. How can I be lucky when it feels as though my heart's been broken? Tears threatened again and she fought to hold them back, stifling her sobs when she rang Elsie.

Bert said he'd come to pick her up, and when the car arrived she wasn't surprised to see her mum and gran sitting in the back. The painkillers had taken effect, making her drowsy, and using this as an excuse she managed to avoid most of their questions, just saying that she had fallen down some stairs. She closed her eyes then to avoid their probing.

When they arrived home, Bert carried her upstairs, where after being tucked into bed solicitously by her mother, she fell into an exhausted sleep.

The room was dim when Sally awoke, hearing voices on the stairs. She tensed: it sounded like

John. 'Go away,' she whimpered as he approached the bed, her mother hovering behind him.

'Mrs Marchant, may I talk to Sally alone, please?'

'No, Mum, please don't go,' she begged. Then, trying to keep her breathing shallow, she steeled herself, fighting to quell the tears that lay just below the surface. 'John, I said go away and I meant it. If you don't leave right now, I'll tell everyone what I saw.'

'No, Sally, you were mistaken,' he said urgently. 'Larry and I–'

'Don't bother to lie to me, John,' she interrupted. 'I heard you concocting your story with Lottie.' She shook her head. 'It wouldn't have worked, you know. You see, I saw what you were doing.'

'Sally, please,' he begged, eyes flicking towards her mother, his colour high, the panic on his face showing how frightened he was of exposure.

Oh God, she had loved him so much, but he had used her, lied to her. Worst of all was the pain of realising that he had never really loved her in return. No wonder he rejected my embraces, she thought bitterly, I was the wrong sex. Tears threatened again and unable to cope she turned to look at her mother. 'Mum, please get him out of here.'

'Come on, John,' Ruth said firmly. 'You heard my daughter. I'll see you out.'

Sally lowered her head, unable to bear the appeal in John's eyes, before he turned and walked out of the room.

In no time her mother was back and standing

by the bed. 'Well, what was all that about?' she demanded.

'Please, Mum. Not now, I don't want to talk about it.'

'Am I to take it that you've broken up with him? Is the wedding off?'

'Yes, it's over,' she told her, the finality of the words causing the long-held tears to flow.

'Oh Sally, don't cry,' Ruth appealed, sitting down beside her on the bed. 'Why don't you tell me what happened. Who's this Larry, and what was it you saw?'

Hearing the questions, her tears turned into sobs, the pain in her ribs agonising. She wouldn't be unable to speak coherently, even if she wanted to; she could hardly breathe.

'Come on now, calm down or you'll make yourself ill. Look, I'll go and get you a nice cup of tea.'

A cup of tea, Sally thought, fighting hysteria. Her mother's cure-all for everything that life threw at you. Oh God, if only it was as easy as that.

'Well, he didn't stay long,' Sadie said acidly as soon as Ruth walked into the kitchen. 'What's going on?'

'Sally's called the wedding off,' Ruth told her, whilst filling the kettle with water.

There was a stunned silence as Sadie digested her words. That had shut her mother up for a few minutes, Ruth thought, spooning tea into the pot. It was terrible to see Sally so upset, yet she couldn't help feeling relieved that the relationship was over.

The silence didn't last long. 'Why has she

called it off?' Sadie asked.

Ruth sighed with exasperation. 'I don't know. Sally won't talk about it, and to tell you the truth, I didn't like to push her. She's in a bit of a state.'

Sadie poked a stray wisp of hair back into her hairnet and pushed herself out of the chair. 'I'll go and 'ave a word with her.'

'Don't force her to talk about it, Mum. She'll tell us when she's good and ready.'

'There's no need to lecture me, Ruth,' Sadie said indignantly. 'I ain't a complete fool, you know.'

As she was about to leave the room, Elsie popped her head around the back door. 'I've just come to see how Sally is, and to ask if she's up to a visit from Ann.'

'Come to think of it,' Sadie mused, returning to her chair, 'it might be better if Ann talks to Sally. She's more likely to confide in her than me. The days when she used to run to me with her problems are long gone.'

'Confide in her about what?' Elsie asked. 'I know she's had a nasty fall, but has something else happened?'

'Yeah, you could say that,' Ruth answered. 'The wedding's off, and before you ask, I don't know why.' She paused, brows drawn together. 'Mum's right though, she might tell Ann.'

'I'll go and get her,' Elsie said, scurrying out of the back door. 'Pour out the tea, I'll be back in a jiffy.'

Ann placed Sally's cup on the bedside table, and smiling sympathetically, asked, 'How are you feeling?'

'As if I've been hit by a train,' Sally answered. 'But it's just a couple of broken ribs, a sprained ankle, and I'm black and blue with bruises.'

'It sounds like you were lucky. From what I've heard it was a nasty fall and you could have been seriously injured.'

Lucky? Sally thought, closing her eyes in despair on hearing those words again. She shifted slightly in the bed and then turned to look at her friend. 'I suppose Mum's told you that I've broken up with John.'

'Yes, she did, but she didn't say why. Have you had a row?'

'Something like that,' she murmured.

'Don't worry, you'll make it up with him. It's probably just pre-wedding nerves.'

Sally picked at a fingernail; she needed to talk, to get it off her chest, the scene of John in bed with a man still vivid in her mind. She couldn't face telling her mum, it was so awful; she felt safer confiding in her friend. 'No, Ann,' she finally said, 'it was more than just a row. You see, I went to the flat, and...'

Stumbling over the words, she watched the growing horror on Ann's face. When her story came to an end there was a moment of stunned silence before Ann, taking a deep breath, said, 'Sally, I know how awful this must be for you, but I think in a way you've had a lucky escape. I mean, what sort of marriage would it have been?'

Sally knew her friend was right, but the pain of John's rejection was hard to bear. 'I had no idea he was homosexual, Ann. How could I have been so blind? What a little fool I've been.'

'Oh Sally, how could you have known? He didn't go around with a label on his forehead. None of us realised that he was a queer so don't blame yourself for not catching on.'

'But he never wanted to touch me – to hold me, or kiss me.' She wrung her hands together. 'Do you know, I once discussed it with Nelly Cox and she told me how lucky I was to have a man like John, a man who was prepared to wait until we were married.'

'Huh, lucky. I don't think so,' Ann said, a scowl on her face.

Sally suddenly looked hard at her friend. 'You never really liked him, did you? Come on, be honest.'

'No, you're right, and if you want me to be totally honest, I didn't like the way he controlled you.'

Sally digested Ann's words. Yes, in a way John *had* controlled her; he had moulded her, changed the way she dressed, the way she spoke and even the way she thought. And I let him, she admitted to herself at last, and all because I never felt good enough for him. Sinking back onto the pillows and feeling emotionally drained, she berated herself again for being such a fool.

Ann looked at her with concern. 'You're exhausted. I'll go now, you need to rest.' She paused at the door. 'That lot downstairs are bound to ask me what happened. Is it all right to tell them?'

Gathering her thoughts, Sally realised that they would have to be told eventually, although she dreaded their reactions. Still, it would probably be better to get it over and done with. 'Yes, you can tell them, if you're sure you don't mind. But please, would you ask them to keep it to themselves? It isn't something I want made public. I feel humiliated enough as it is.'

'All right, but don't worry, I'm sure they won't say anything.'

When the door closed, Sally turned painfully onto her side, struggling to plump the pillow under her head. It was still difficult to breathe normally, but finding that she did feel a little better after talking to Ann, she eventually drifted off to sleep.

The room was in darkness when she awoke, slowly becoming aware of a presence. A familiar glow started to form and she relaxed — suddenly remembering that she didn't have to push the entity away now. It was as though a great weight had been lifted from her shoulders and she felt a wonderful sense of freedom. A glorious feeling of exhilaration filled her as she realised that once again she could stretch her wings and fly. Smiling, she reached out her arms to the golden shimmering light.

Chapter Twenty-Nine

'Well, what did she say? Did you convince her to keep quiet, John?' Lottie asked, pacing the floor in agitation.

'I didn't get a chance to say much. She

wouldn't let her mother leave the room.'

'Oh, John. What are we going to do? If she opens her mouth, you'll be ruined.'

'She may not say anything, Auntie. We'll just have to keep our fingers crossed.'

'Don't be silly. We can't leave it like this! Why on earth didn't you insist on speaking to her alone?'

'I did, but she wouldn't have it. She was very upset.'

'Well, of course she's upset. Can't you imagine how awful this must be for her? Seeing you with Larry must have been a dreadful shock. Perhaps I should go to see her – she might listen to me.'

'Yes, you could give it a try, I suppose.' He sank back in his chair, sighing heavily. 'God, I've really made a mess of things, haven't I?'

'You weren't to know she would turn up at the flat, darling. But taking Larry there was a rather silly thing to do. Oh, by the way, he left this note for you.'

He took the note eagerly, ripping open the envelope and scanning the contents. Lottie saw his face blanch, then leaning forward he covered his face with his hands.

'What is it, darling?' she asked anxiously.

John looked up, his eyes wet with tears. 'He doesn't want to see me any more. He says it's too risky now, and he has his reputation to think of. Huh, I expect he's frightened that his wife will find out about us.'

'Reputation – *his* reputation – what about yours?' Lottie said indignantly.

John ran a hand over his forehead. 'Oh Lottie, I thought he loved me,' he whispered brokenly.

'Obviously not enough to stick by you now,' Lottie retorted. Then seeing the depths of John's pain, she rushed to his side. 'I'm sorry, that was cruel of me. Oh darling, you look exhausted. I think we're both too tired to think straight. Why don't you get yourself off to bed and we'll talk again in the morning.'

He nodded, rising slowly from the chair. 'Perhaps if you can persuade Sally to keep quiet, Larry might change his mind,' he said hopefully. 'Good night, Auntie.'

'Good night, my dear, and try not to worry too much. I'm sure she'll listen to me.'

Sally awoke the next morning to the sound of raised voices, and recognising one of them as Lottie's, she called out urgently, 'Let her in, Mum, I want to speak to her.' Pulling herself up onto the pillows and catching her breath painfully, she ran her fingers through her hair. There were things she wanted to say to Lottie, and it might as well be now.

'I don't know why you want to see the likes of her,' was her mum's caustic remark as they stepped into the room, and folding her arms across her chest, she stood by the bed like a sentinel.

'Sally, may I talk to you alone, please?' Lottie asked.

'No, you bleedin' well can't,' Ruth snapped. 'Anything you've got to say, you can say in front of me.'

Ignoring Ruth, Lottie looked at Sally propped up in bed. 'Please, Sally,' she begged.

'My mother already knows about John's homo-sexuality, if that's what you're worried about,' Sally told her, seeing her eyes widen.

'Oh no!' Lottie gasped. 'Please, I beg you, please don't tell anyone else. Don't you realise that homosexuality is illegal? If the authorities find out, it could ruin John's life.'

'Huh, I like that,' Ruth spat. 'John's life will be ruined. What about my Sally?'

'Mum, can I have a cup of tea, please?' Sally asked, knowing it was the only way to get her mother out of the room. Seeing the doubt on her face, she added, 'It's all right, I'll be fine.'

'Yeah, all right then. But don't go upsetting my daughter. You and yer bleedin' nephew 'ave done enough damage,' Ruth told Lottie, giving her a hard look as she left the room.

'How *could* you, Lottie! How *could* you let John use me like that!' Sally asked, as soon as her mother was out of earshot.

'We didn't mean to hurt you, Sally. Really we didn't. You see, I noticed that you seemed fright-ened of men and when I thought you wouldn't be interested in ... well, that side of marriage ... you seemed the ideal match.'

'Ideal match?' Sally retorted, her voice high. 'How can being married to a ... a *queer* be ideal? All right, I admit I'm afraid of sex, but I could have got over that – and what if I had wanted children?'

Lottie stared at Sally, her face pale. 'Oh, I am so sorry, my dear. I didn't think, really I didn't. I just wanted to protect John and I honestly thought you would be happy together.'

Looking down at her hands, Sally suddenly

realised that she was still wearing John's ring, and slowly pulled it off. She held it clasped in her fist momentarily, intending to hand it back to Lottie, but was surprised when she suddenly saw a vision flash in front of her eyes. 'My God,' she gasped. 'This ring, John said it belonged to his mother.'

'Yes, it was my sister-in-law's engagement ring,' Lottie answered, her voice suddenly wary.

Sally's brow creased and she clenched the ring tightly, closing her eyes. Seconds later they flew open. *'You're* John's mother,' she said. 'This ring belongs to *you.*'

Lottie staggered and held onto the post at the foot of the bed. 'No, no, you're wrong!'

'No, I'm not,' Sally insisted. 'I saw a vision of you wearing it. It's definitely yours.'

At that point, the fight seemed to go out of Lottie. 'Can I sit down, please?' she whispered, just as Ruth came back into the room holding a cup of tea in her hand.

She looked from her daughter to Lottie, and seeing their expressions, demanded, 'What's going on? Are you all right, Sally?'

'Yes, I'm fine, but Lottie's had a bit of a shock. Could you get her a cup of tea too, Mum?'

'Christ, what do you think this is – a café,' she retorted crossly. 'I ain't a bleedin' waitress, you know.'

'Please, it's all right. I don't want anything,' Lottie said, as she lowered herself onto a chair.

'Mum, would you leave us alone, please,' Sally asked, and seeing Ruth's expression, added, 'Just for five minutes.'

'All right, but five minutes and no longer,' she

snapped, puffing loudly with indignation as she left the room.

As soon as the door closed, Lottie leaned forward in the chair. 'All right, Sally. I suppose I owe you the truth. You're right, I am John's mother, but he must never find out.'

'Why? I don't understand.'

'Oh, my dear. It's still a stigma now if a girl gets pregnant before marriage, but it was even worse in nineteen thirty-six.'

'But what happened? Why didn't you get married?'

'I was jilted, Sally. When I was just two months' pregnant my fiancé ran off with another girl.'

'I still don't understand. If your brother and his wife were killed during the war, why does John think they were his parents?'

Lottie heaved a sigh. 'To all intents and purposes they were, Sally. You see, when my father found out that I was pregnant, all hell broke loose. He went absolutely mad and threatened to throw me out. It was my brother who came to my rescue, and he took me to stay with him and his wife. When John was born, they offered to adopt him.'

'But why did you let them?'

'What choice did I have, Sally? I was a young woman, on my own. Where could I go with a baby son? How could I support him?'

'Yes, all right, I can see that. But I still don't understand why you haven't told John the truth.'

Lottie sighed, her eyes pools of anguish as she gazed at Sally. 'Guilt, that's why I haven't told him. I suppose you could call it my penance.'

Seeing Sally shaking her head in obvious confusion, Lottie continued, 'You see, I wasn't a very religious person then, only going to church for the usual weddings and funerals. But after giving John up I missed him so much. Night after night I used to lie in my bed, praying to God to give him back to me. To somehow make it possible.'

'And you got him back,' Sally whispered, her eyes wide.

'Yes, I did. But at what cost? The death of my brother and his wife.'

'But that wasn't your fault,' Sally protested. 'You have no need to feel guilty.'

'Oh, but I do, Sally. When they were killed, do you know what my first reaction was? No, I can see that you don't. It was joy. Yes, joy! I couldn't wait to get John back and was on the first available train to Devon. Even before their funeral.'

Sally averted her eyes, shocked by what she was hearing, yet unable to feel anything but pity for Lottie.

'I've been paying the penance for it ever since, Sally. I go to church twice a week, help as much as I can in fund-raising events. And I vowed never, ever, to tell John the truth. It's the only way I can assuage my guilt.'

As Sally was about to speak the door opened, and her mother walked in. Seeing her expression, Lottie rose to her feet. 'I'll go now, Sally. Thank you for seeing me. It seems I'm leaving you with two secrets now. Will you keep them both?'

Sally looked at the woman she had been prepared to hate, and searching her feelings realised that all the anger she felt had drained away, to be replaced by compassion. Lottie was punishing herself, and had been for many years. Yes, she had used her, but like any mother, she had just been trying to protect her child.

'Your secrets are safe with me, Lottie, if you promise me just one thing?'

'Yes, whatever you ask,' Lottie said eagerly.

'Will you promise me that you won't encourage John to marry another young woman.'

'Oh yes, my dear. Now I've seen the hurt it can cause, I realise how misguided I was. All I can do now is to pray that the law will change and it will no longer be illegal to be homosexual in this country. If that happened, there would be no need for them to marry to cover up their sexuality.'

'Do you think the law will be changed?'

'I doubt it, Sally. There is so much prejudice, you see.'

'Yeah, and I should think so too,' Ruth said harshly. 'It's disgusting, that's what it is. Now if you don't mind, my daughter needs to rest.'

'See what I mean, Sally?' Lottie said, turning to leave. 'Prejudice, so much prejudice. Goodbye, my dear, I hope you recover from your fall soon.' Then, giving her a tremulous smile, she turned to Ruth. 'Thank you for allowing me to see your daughter, Mrs Marchant.'

Her mother just stared at Lottie, giving no answer, and with her mouth set in a grim line, she escorted her downstairs.

In what felt like minutes, she was back, standing by the side of the bed again, her arms folded across her chest. 'What was she on about? What two secrets?' she demanded.

'You already know that John's a homosexual,

Mum, but I can't tell you the other secret. I promised Lottie I would keep it to myself. But don't worry, it's nothing that affects us, it's something personal to her.'

'Huh, typical. You always was a dark horse,' Ruth said huffily, and turning to leave the room, she hissed, 'I hate secrets.'

Sally stared at the door as it closed. Her mother called her a dark horse, yet she was one to talk. It had taken her thirteen years to find out that Ken wasn't her real father.

Chapter Thirty

The catalyst came for Sally three weeks later, when she woke up to what would have been her wedding day. She climbed slowly out of bed, her injuries almost healed, and opening her wardrobe door, she looked at her cream suit. Tears filled her eyes, and grabbing the suit from the hanger she held it clutched to her chest. 'John, oh John, why?' she agonised as she had done so many times whilst confined to bed.

Her sobs increased, her stomach sore as she drew in deep shuddering breaths. Then, throwing the suit away and onto the floor, she went into the bathroom, splashing cold water onto her face.

How much longer can you go on like this? she asked herself, staring into the mirror. She suddenly found herself thinking about her relationship with John, finding that instead of getting emotional again, for the first time she was analysing her feelings. Yes, she had felt safe with him; there had been no fear of passion, or sexual advances. But now she began to wonder if she had really loved him as a woman should love a man. She had admired him, and had to admit to being in awe of him. He always looked so perfect, and had been instrumental in changing her own diction and appearance, always wanting her to act and dress perfectly. His good looks, immaculate manners, gentleness and kindness couldn't be denied – but had he ever raised any *real* feelings in her? But if she hadn't really loved him, why was she so hurt? What was causing this pain?

Slowly she began to realise that it was the deceit that hurt the most. Both Lottie, to whom she had become very close, and John, had used her. It had all been a sham, a pretence; they hadn't really cared about her at all.

As the weeks went by Sally gradually began to recover, finding that she was feeling relieved, not only that she had discovered John's secret before they had married, but relieved too that she could now do what she wanted, wear what she wanted, without fear of censure.

When her injuries were completely healed she decided not to go back to Arding & Hobbs. She couldn't face the thought of seeing John each day or of working alongside Lottie.

It was Ann who was instrumental in finding her a new job, having seen it advertised. Though some distance away, in Wandsworth, she had to admit she had fallen on her feet. Sidney Jacob's small haberdashery shop was a decade out of date: a mishmash of old and faded dressmaking patterns, wool, zips, and a hundred and one other miscellaneous goods, all jumbled in a myriad of wooden drawers that stretched from floor to ceiling behind the old-fashioned, glass-fronted counter.

When she went for the interview, Sally and Mr Jacob took to each other on sight. Mr Jacob's wife had died several years ago and he had lost interest in the business. When he'd found difficulty in climbing the ladder to reach the top shelves, he reluctantly reached the conclusion that he needed an assistant.

Sally was now climbing down this old wooden ladder, a drawer clutched precariously in her hands. She was gradually bringing the shop into a semblance of order, but there was a long way to go yet. Placing the drawer on the counter, she couldn't help grinning at the contents as she pulled out a selection of men's woollen long johns, yellow with age. Counting them and entering the amount in the stock book she had devised, she added them to the growing pile of items waiting to be sold off in a clearance sale.

The door at the back of the shop opened and Sid came shuffling towards her, wearing his baggy old cardigan despite the lovely late August weather. 'Are you all right, Sally?' he asked. 'I'm sorry I ain't bin down this morning, but I knew you could cope.'

She smiled affectionately at the man she had become so fond of in just a couple of months. He was only five foot four inches tall, and wore his sparse grey hair brushed over to one side, attempting to cover the fact that he was balding. Sid wasn't exactly fat, but he had a rotund stomach and wore his trousers hitched up high with ancient braces. Of course, this caused them to look too short, and they flapped around his ankles, showing off his battered black shoes.

'Do yer fancy a cup of tea, gel?' he now asked.

Sally knew this was her cue to go up to his flat above the shop. She would make them lunch every day, usually something simple like soup or salad, with nice fresh crusty rolls from the baker's shop across the street. As soon as the food was ready he would turn the shop sign to *Closed* and join her upstairs for a leisurely half an hour break, which if they got engaged in conversation, sometimes stretched an extra fifteen minutes.

She sliced the tomatoes, thinking once again how lucky she was to work for Sid, who in a very short time had handed most of the responsibility of running the shop over to her. She was determined to bring the stock up to date and only yesterday had spotted some wonderful new styles in the latest dressmaking catalogue.

'Sid, lunch is ready,' she called.

Watching him tuck into the salad with obvious relish she tentatively raised the subject of stock. 'I was looking at the new catalogue and I er ... I wondered if it would be all right to order a few new patterns, just to see how they sell.'

He held his hands out, palms up and shrugged, saying, 'My life, Sally, just do what you think is best. When my Rachel was alive she used to order all the stock.' His rheumy eyes clouded for a moment and then he sighed. 'Just get what you think will sell, but don't go mad. I ain't made of money, you know.'

Sally smiled. It was a small start, but one she hoped would eventually bring in more customers.

At five thirty, locking the shop door behind her, she made her way to the bus stop. It had been a productive day and she was pleased with her achievements. All the drawers had been sorted and catalogued, and now she could concentrate on the shelves in the back room, piled high with old rolls of dressmaking material.

It was Thursday evening and she would be joining Elsie at the Spiritualist Church later for a healing service. She hurried along, perspiring slightly, anxious to get home for a bath. After rummaging around in so much dusty old stock she felt distinctly grubby.

It had been six months now since she had broken up with John, and Elsie had advised her to offer her services at the church. There were two other healers and they had been so welcoming, encouraging her gift and helping her to develop other psychic abilities that were gradually growing in strength.

She was glad to arrive home, and stepping into the hall, called, 'Hello, it's me. What's for dinner, Mum? I'm starving!' Her smile faded as she walked into the kitchen, immediately picking up the atmosphere and realising with a sinking heart that something was dreadfully wrong.

Her mother was sitting by the empty fireplace, Elsie opposite, her face wet with tears.

'What is it, what's the matter?' she asked anxiously.

'Arthur's got his departure date,' Elsie sobbed. 'He's sailing in three months.'

Sally ran across the room and crouched by her side. 'I'm so sorry,' she cried, realising there was nothing she could say to ease their neighbour's pain, and finding that she too was devastated by the news.

'I've got to accept it now, haven't I?' Elsie said dolefully. 'He really is going, and before Christmas too.' She rubbed an already sodden handkerchief over her face. 'Do you mind going to church on your own tonight, Sally? I don't think I can face it, and anyway I'd be no use to anyone in this state.'

'No, of course not,' she assured her, and putting an arm around Elsie's shoulders, gave her a quick hug before going upstairs for her bath.

A few weeks later on a Sunday morning, Sally and Ruth were once again attempting to arouse Elsie's interest. They had tried everything to snap her out of the lethargy that had gripped her since Arthur had received his departure date, but so far with little success.

'Elsie, I've had a couple of funny experiences,' Sally told her.

'Have you, love?' she answered distantly.

'Yes. I've found that if I hold a piece of jewellery, I get a sort of vision about the person who owns it.'

'Clairsentience,' she murmured.

'How does it work, Elsie?' Sally asked.

The woman looked up, her eyes dull. 'It's a form of divination,' she answered tiredly. 'I'm not surprised that you have the ability to use it.'

'Perhaps I should develop it and use it more often. Will you help me?'

'Oh, not now, Sally. I'm just not in the mood. Anyway, I think you should concentrate on your spiritual healing.' She stood up. 'I'd better go now. I told Bert I'd only be popping round for a little while, but do you know, I dread going back.' She walked across to the back door. 'I know he's taking Arthur's departure badly too, but he won't talk about it and it's driving me mad. If I so much as mention it, he leaves the room.'

'Men never seem to talk about their feelings, Elsie. It must be their way of dealing with them,' Sadie told her.

'Yeah, maybe, but it isn't just that he won't talk to me. I resent it that he hasn't once tried to persuade Arthur not to emigrate.' She sighed deeply. 'I'd better go, I'll see you tomorrow.'

'Poor Elsie,' Ruth said as the back door closed. 'It's hard to know what to say to comfort her.'

'There ain't nothing we can say,' Sadie shrugged. 'The only thing she wants to hear is that her Arthur isn't going. And I can't see that happening now.'

They were surprised when only a couple of hours later, Elsie came round again, scuttling through the back door with a sense of purpose.

'I've been thinking, and I've decided to throw a farewell party for Arthur, I know it's short notice, but I'm here to recruit some help – any offers?' she asked, looking at them appealingly.

'What brought all this on?' Ruth wanted to know.

281

'An argument. I know, daft isn't it, but it brought me to my senses. You see, I was having a go at Bert and he was shouting back, when Arthur came in. Oh, you should have seen his face, he looked devastated. My great big strapping son actually had tears in his eyes and I suddenly realised how selfish I've been. Not only that, I'm making his last weeks at home absolute hell.'

Seeing that Elsie was close to crying, Sally jumped in, saying lightly, 'I think a party's a great idea. What do you say, Mum, shall we give her a hand?'

Her mother, taking her cue, said, 'It depends on what the hourly rate is. How much are you paying, Elsie?'

'Go on, you daft pair,' she said, a small smile appearing on her face. 'Now, are you going to help me or not?'

Sally and Ruth exchanged a quick glance, relieved to see Elsie looking a little more cheerful. 'Of course we are, yer silly bugger, and we'd better get a move on. He sails in about eight weeks.'

'Yes, I know.' Elsie hung her head for a moment, then looked up with a strained smile on her face. 'Come on then, let's make a list. I want this to be a party Arthur will never forget.'

The list of food grew longer and longer: sandwiches, pork pies, sausage rolls and amongst other things, Elsie insisted she wanted seafood. Cockles, winkles, mussels and whelks were added. 'They're my Arthur's favourites,' she told them, 'and I bet he won't be able to get grub like this in Australia.'

'We'll never be able to manage this lot,' Ruth

told her in exasperation. 'It's no good, Elsie, we'll 'ave to recruit more help.'

'How about Aunt Mary?' Sally suggested. 'I know she'd be glad to muck in.'

'Yeah, good idea. There's Nelly Cox, Peggy Green, and a few others too who would be glad to lend a hand. And what about old bossy boots Joan Mason.'

'Please, spare me that,' Elsie begged. 'That woman should be in the army, she'd make a perfect Sergeant Major. Have you seen the way she marches up the street, arms swinging, and her back as stiff as a ramrod? She probably wears her corsets so tight that it's impossible for her to bend over.'

'Yeah, I know what you mean,' Ruth laughed, 'but she's great at organising things. Look how well the Coronation street-party went in 1953.'

'Christ, you've got a memory like an elephant. That was over seven years ago.' Elsie grinned widely. 'Do you remember her twins winning the fancy-dress competition? I think the judges were too frightened to give first prize to anyone else. And what about when her husband got drunk and flirted with that blonde piece who lives opposite Nelly?'

'How could I forget,' Ruth laughed. 'It was the one and only time I've seen a woman lay her husband out – and with just one punch.'

'Crumbs, it sounds like Ann and I missed all the fun,' Sally complained. 'If I remember rightly, we weren't allowed to stay up for the adult party.'

'You were too young, Sal, and it's just as well that you were in bed. The language that issued from

Joan's mouth was enough to turn the air blue.'

They were all laughing as Sadie came in from her room. 'What's all this then?' she asked, a grumpy expression on her face.

Sally smiled, knowing her gran hated missing out on anything.

'We're organising a party, Mum,' Ruth told her.

'Oh yeah, and what are we celebrating?'

The smile dropped from Elsie's face and there was a strained silence. 'It's a going-away party for my Arthur,' she answered. 'But somehow I don't think I'll be celebrating.'

'You 'ave to let them fly the nest, love,' Sadie told her. 'He'll come back one day, you wait and see.'

Elsie looked at her sadly. 'No offence, Sadie, but I wish Sally had said those words to me. Then I'd know my son was definitely coming home again.'

When they had finished making all the arrangements, Sally left them, deciding to go next door to see Ann. She stuck her head round the back door, surprised to see Arthur sitting by the fire, gazing into the flames.

'Hello, is Ann in?' she asked him.

Startled, he looked up. 'Yes, she's upstairs. How are you, Sally?'

'I'm fine, Arthur. I hear you'll be off to Australia soon.'

'Yes, not long now.' His face darkened, brows drawn together. 'I was just sitting here thinking about it, Sally. I hope I'm doing the right thing.'

She advanced further into the room, his words making her feel strangely disturbed. 'Are you having second thoughts? Is that it, Arthur?'

'Not exactly. But it's hard to see my mother in such a state. Have you noticed how much weight she's lost?'

'Yes, but don't worry. She looks a lot more cheerful now, and I think she's finally accepted that you're going.'

'Do you think so?' he asked eagerly.

'Yes,' she whispered, lowering her eyes. It was obvious to see how relieved he was, and she suddenly realised how much he must love Jenny to follow her to the other side of the world.

'It's strange really, Sally. You only live next door, but we hardly ever get the chance to talk, do we?'

'No, I suppose not.'

'Have you got over breaking up with your boyfriend?'

'Yes, it was nearly six months ago, and I'm fine,' she told him, feeling her face growing hot. As far as she knew, Arthur had no idea that John was homosexual. What could she say if he asked her why they had broken up?

He stood up, walking towards her and seeing the expression on his face, her heart began to thump. Smiling softly he touched her arm, his voice tender as he said, 'Sally, I–'

'Hello, I thought I heard your voice,' Ann said, bouncing into the room, totally unaware of the tension between her brother and Sally. 'Come up to my room, Sal, I've got something to tell you.'

Sally tore her eyes away from Arthur's and followed Ann upstairs, unable to understand why her knees felt so weak. 'Right, what have you got to tell me then?' she asked, pushing the strange feelings aside.

'I've got a date with Billy,' Ann told her, with a wide smile.

'So you managed it at last.'

'Yep,' Ann said, squirming with delight. 'Do you remember when I first saw him, Sally? He was choosing a record to play when we went to the youth club. How old were we then – fourteen, fifteen?'

'Coming up to fifteen, I should think, and how could I forget? You've talked about him often enough.' Sally sat on the side of the bed, her own memories flooding back. She flushed, remembering how she had run out of the club because Arthur had put his arm round her, and the many times since when she had been frightened by the way he looked at her.

'We're going to the pictures tonight. Oh, I can't wait,' Ann said.

Sally hardly heard her; she was remembering Arthur's expression as they gazed at each other downstairs. It was the same look, but this time she hadn't been frightened. It wasn't fear that she felt – it was something else. The feelings Arthur evoked were so different to what she had felt for John. That relationship had been based on some sort of childish crush, almost hero-worship, and she realised that now.

Chapter Thirty-One

Sally, realising that there was nothing else she could do, managed to avoid Arthur as much as possible. Now that Ann was courting, and out most evenings with Billy, she rarely went round to Elsie's.

She threw herself into her work at the shop, polishing, dusting, and tidying up constantly. Now, as the bell above the door rang, she looked up as a customer came in, the woman's eyes scanning the interior in amazement.

'I can't believe it's the same shop,' she said. 'Have you taken it over from old Sidney Jacobs?'

'No, I just work here,' Sally told her, smiling with pleasure at the woman's obvious appreciation of all her hard work. She had to admit the shop did look lovely now. The mahogany drawers had been polished back to their former glory, revealing the beautiful patina of the wood, enhanced by the brass handles that gleamed after an application of Brasso and a lot of elbow grease.

Sally was standing behind the shiny glass-fronted counter that now revealed neatly arranged balls of wool on the interior shelves. Knitting patterns in large books were on display on top, alongside a rotary rack holding a good selection of buttons.

'Well, it looks a treat. Just like it did when Mrs Jacobs was alive,' the customer said, slowly walking forward. 'My daughter's having a baby so can I look at some wool please – four-ply if you've got it.'

Quickly showing her a selection, Sally managed to sell her a knitting pattern too, along with some pretty buttons, and ribbon to thread through the booties of the pram-set pattern she had chosen.

As she left the shop, Sid came in from the back room. 'You've increased sales already, Sally,' he said. 'Now go on, get yourself home. I know you've got a party to go to. A going-away do for your neighbour's son, ain't it?'

'Yes, but it's only four o'clock,' Sally said, surprised by his offer.

'It doesn't matter. After all your hard work you deserve some time off, and I can manage on my own for an hour or so.'

'You will be careful if you've got to climb the ladder?' Sally said worriedly.

'I won't need to. You've made sure that it's only spare stock in those top drawers, so anything I'm likely to be asked for is within reach. That was a good idea of yours – I don't know why I didn't think of it myself. Now go on home before I change me mind.'

Sally pulled her coat on, and wrapping a thick woolly scarf around her neck, said, 'Well, if you're sure, I'll be off. See you on Monday, Sid.'

'Cheerio. Have a good time,' he called as she left the shop.

Sally hurried down Wandsworth High Street, hands stuffed in her pockets and head bent against the sharp wind. Have a good time, Sid had said. She shook her head sadly, knowing that

288

it would be impossible.

Later that evening, Sally sat on one of the hard wooden benches lined around the wall, a glass of gin and lemon clutched in her hand, watching Arthur dancing with his girlfriend. When the music came to an end and they crossed the floor, she noticed that Jenny looked pale, swaying slightly, despite the fact that Arthur was holding her around the waist. She suddenly clamped a hand over her mouth and made a dash for the toilets, leaving him to stare after her. Smiling ruefully he ambled across to Sally, sitting down beside her.

'Is Jenny all right?' she asked.

'She's had too much to drink and feels sick,' he answered, raising an eyebrow quizzically as he studied her appearance. 'You look a bit down in the mouth. Is something the matter, Sally?'

'No, I'm fine,' she assured him, hoping that her feelings were well hidden.

'Would you like to dance?' he asked. 'Come on, it might cheer you up.'

'No, oh no,' she told him, a slight edge of panic in her voice. She couldn't dance with him – she couldn't. It would give the game away.

'Sally, why do you always look so frightened when I come near you? You've been doing it for years. Crumbs, love, I only asked you to dance, yet you act as if I'm going to rape you.'

'I'm sorry,' she whispered, unable to tell him that it wasn't fear she was feeling now. She looked up and saw Jenny returning to the hall, her black mascara streaked, and an inane grin on her face as she stumbled towards them.

'Look at her,' Arthur grinned. 'I think I'd better take her home. See you later, Sally. If you see my mum, will you tell her I'll be back soon?'

She nodded, rising to make her way yet again to the makeshift bar at the back of the hall. For the first time in her life she was feeling decidedly tipsy, and knew, though it didn't stop her, that she was drowning her sorrows with drink.

As the evening wore on, Sally's head was spinning. The music blared and couples jiving before her became a blur of swirling skirts, colourful petticoats and the occasional flash of stocking-tops and suspenders. She stood up dizzily, deciding to make her way outside, hoping that the fresh air would revive her.

She was leaning on the wall when Arthur approached. 'Are you all right?' he asked.

Tears stung her eyes as she looked at him. How could she tell him the truth? It was too late. She felt drained, emotionally vulnerable, and knew that if he held out his arms she would fall into them. Closing her eyes she fought to hold back the overwhelming urge she felt to blurt out her feelings. Why, she thought, oh why has it taken me so long to realise that I love him?

'Sally, please, what is it?' he murmured, his voice gruff with concern.

Unable to help herself she swayed forward and as his arms went around her, holding her tightly, she buried her face in his jacket. 'Come on,' he said huskily. 'You're freezing, let me take you home.'

As they walked the short journey her head was

still swimming, and when they arrived at her house Arthur had to take the key from her shaky hand. He opened the door and they stepped into the small hall, turning towards each other in the dim light. Their eyes locked and Sally took an involuntary step forward. With a gasp Arthur wrapped her in his arms, murmuring her name.

Sally knew she was drunk, yet it was this very drunkenness that stripped away her inhibitions. Taking Arthur's hand, she turned, leading him upstairs to her bedroom.

It had happened, the thing she had feared for so long, and it had been wonderful. Strangely she felt sober now as she gazed at Arthur lying beside her, his eyes closed. She looked at his bare chest, unable to resist reaching out and running her fingers over the dark hair. Still with his eyes closed he grasped her hand, lifted it to his lips and kissed her palm.

'Are you all right?' he asked softly.

'Oh, yes. Thank you for being so patient with me, Arthur.'

'I wish I'd known before, Sally. I always wondered why you acted so skittish every time I came near you. God, I'd like to get my hands on your uncle.'

'I'm sorry I was so nervous at first.'

'Well, that's understandable, and thank God you told me why. Are you sure it was all right?' he asked again worriedly.

'It was wonderful,' she told him, her eyes flicking to the bedside clock. 'Arthur, look at the time! The party will be nearly over. Quick, you must go.'

He lazily turned his head and peered at the dial. 'Christ!' he yelped, leaping out of bed and hopping around the room on one foot as he hastily thrust one leg into his trousers. The other followed, then he stuffed on his shoes and dragged his shirt on over his head. Grabbing his coat he rushed over to the bed. 'We must talk, Sally,' he husked, leaning over and giving her an urgent kiss. 'I'll be round in the morning.'

Smiling, she watched him as he ran out of the room, and it wasn't long before she heard the back door slam. Faintly in the distance she could hear singing, and as the sound increased Sally recognised the voices of her mum and gran. Jumping out of bed, her eyes quickly scanning the room, she saw Arthur's tie slung across the back of a chair. Picking it up hastily and rolling it into a ball, she thrust it into the back of a drawer. Then, flinging a nightie over her head, she scrambled back into bed, frantically pulling the blankets into some semblance of order.

It wasn't long before the bedroom door opened. 'Are yer ashleep, Shally?' her mum slurred.

Keeping her eyes tightly closed she didn't answer, relieved when her mother didn't advance any further into the room.

'Yeah, ashleep,' she heard Ruth mumble as the door closed.

Sally snuggled down in the bed, a soft dreamy smile on her face. Arthur had been so kind and gentle, and though she had been frightened, he had patiently removed her fears.

She felt a surge of guilt, thinking about Jenny.

Arthur wouldn't be going to Australia now – he loved her, just as much as she loved him. Poor Jenny, how would she take it?

Sally awoke to the sound of someone banging on the front door. Blinking rapidly, she glanced at the clock. It was only just after seven – who could be calling so early on a Sunday morning?

She clambered out of bed, slung on her dressing-gown, and padded softly downstairs. There was no sign of movement from her mum and gran and she wasn't surprised. They had both sounded pretty drunk last night. What was it they were singing at the top of their voices as they came down the Lane? Oh yes, that was it, she thought, as she ran the tune over in her mind. It was one of Gran's old favourites – 'My old man said follow the van'.

The song died abruptly in her thoughts as she opened the door. Jenny Jackson was standing on the step looking dishevelled and tight-lipped. She thrust her way inside and marched into the kitchen, Sally following in her wake.

'I may 'ave been drunk last night, Sally Marchant, but I ain't blind,' she snapped, standing stiffly in the centre of the room, her arms folded across her chest. 'I was in our front bedroom, and I saw my Arthur coming in here with you before the party was over. What was going on?'

'I ... I ... didn't feel well,' Sally stammered, unable to get her thoughts into any coherent order. 'Arthur just walked me home.'

'Well, that's funny isn't it, 'cos I saw him come in with you ... but he never came out again.'

Sally stared blankly at Jenny, relieved when an answer popped into her head. 'That's because he went out the back way.'

Jenny narrowed her eyes suspiciously and began to pace the room. 'I know Arthur fancies you, Sally, I've seen the way he looks at you – but you can't 'ave him!' She stopped pacing and turned, a look of triumph on her face. 'You see, there's something he don't know yet. Something I'm gonna tell him today.'

'What doesn't he know?' Sally asked, but somehow she already knew what Jenny was about to say, and her heart sank.

'I'm pregnant, ain't I?' she crowed, swaggering across to stand in front of Sally, fixing her with hard blue eyes. 'I'm 'aving Arthur's baby.'

Sally looked down, hiding her feelings, then putting on a dismissive act she shrugged her shoulders, saying, 'Well, you haven't got anything to worry about from me. Now if you don't mind, I'd like to get dressed.'

'All right, Miss High and Mighty – I'm going. And I can't wait to see my Arthur's face when I tell him,' she gloated.

There was a hollow pain in her midriff as Sally went back to her room, and resting her hands on the windowsill, she stared with unseeing eyes at the Lane below. Only last night she had been so happy, and now it had been snatched away. It was over – over before it had really begun. There was no way she could come between Arthur and Jenny now. A baby needed both parents. She knew from personal experience what it was like to be without a father's love, and how could she inflict that on an innocent child?

Now, as she flung herself on the bed, she wondered why she didn't have any warning. Why can I foresee the future for other people, she agonised, but not for myself?

It was three in the afternoon before Arthur knocked gently on the back door. Sally glanced at her mum and gran snoozing in their chairs as they always did after Sunday dinner. Quickly grabbing a coat she opened the back door, putting her fingers to her lips as she stepped into the yard.

Arthur's face was white and drawn. He ran both hands through his hair in agitation, staring at her and shaking his head helplessly as though unable to speak.

Sally was overwhelmed with love for him. She had thought long and hard about what she was going to do, and though it would be hard, she knew it was the only way. If she could pull it off, hide her feelings, Arthur would go to Australia with no idea how much she loved him.

Drawing her shoulders back, and feigning impatience, she said, 'I'm a bit busy at the moment, Arthur, is there something you wanted to see me about?'

He looked puzzled by her attitude, but then shook his head as though to clear it, saying, 'It's about last night, Sally. Something's happened. Jenny came to see me this morning and she said–'

'Yes, I know,' she interrupted. 'Jenny came to see me too. She was a bit jealous when she saw us together.' She shrugged nonchalantly. 'I told her I'm not interested in you and that you just walked me home. After all, there's no need to let on about our drunken little fling, is there?'

'Drunken fling?' he whispered. 'Is that all it was to you?'

'Of course it was, and I'm sure it was the same for you. It serves us both right for drinking too much.' She saw the pain in his eyes and had to turn away.

There was a stunned silence and Arthur's face flushed. 'I see. Bloody hell, what a fool I've been. I should have known better – after all, you've been shunning me for years.' He reached out and gripped her arm. 'Did Jenny tell you about the baby?'

'Yes, she did – and congratulations,' Sally answered, trying to sound flippant.

He looked at her with disgust. 'Christ, and there I was, worried about how to tell you.' He let go of her arm and slumped against the wall. 'I was worrying about nothing, wasn't I? Thank God I didn't tell Jenny about us.'

'There is no us, Arthur.'

'Yes, you've made that pretty obvious.' He shook his head and stood up, his voice firmer now. 'I've told Jenny not to tell anyone about the baby. Mum's upset enough about me going, and if she knew Jenny was pregnant she'd be heartbroken at not seeing her first grandchild. I'll write and tell her as soon as we get to Australia. Will you keep it to yourself until then?'

'Yes, of course I will. Now I must go in, Arthur,' she told him, feeling her legs starting to cave under her. She couldn't keep up this façade much longer, and turned hurriedly away.

'Wait! Sally, just give me one last chance to–'

'See you later,' she managed to blurt out, cutting him off mid-sentence. Wrenching open the door she dashed inside, her head drooping despondently when she heard the back gate slam. That's it, she thought. He's sailing in five days' time, and I'll never see him again.

Chapter Thirty-Two

Sally was feeling the strain of hiding her feelings and her veneer was beginning to crack. The days leading up to Arthur's departure had been bad enough. She had managed to avoid him, yet all the time screaming inside to see his face, just once more. Now it was here, the day she dreaded but knew was inevitable, the day he departed for Australia.

Standing at her bedroom window she watched as they piled into the car, all going to see him off: Elsie looking like death, Bert long-faced and Ann already crying into her hankie. Her stomach lurched – there he was, a suitcase in each hand. *Arthur, Arthur!* she cried inwardly.

'Sally, come on, they're going. Ain't you coming down to say goodbye?' her mum called.

Oh God, she thought, I can't do it I can't. I'll break down.

'Sally, come on!' her mum called again.

She took several deep breaths, realising that it would arouse their suspicions if she didn't say goodbye. Then drawing herself up to her full height, pulling back her shoulders and praying for strength, she walked slowly downstairs.

'Are you all right, Sal?' her gran asked. 'You don't half look pale.'

She didn't answer – she couldn't. Her legs were shaking so badly that it took all her concentration just to put one foot in front of the other.

Stepping out into the Lane she kept her head lowered as Arthur turned, aware that if their eyes met he would see her agony.

Her mother rushed in front of her, thankfully postponing the moment, and reaching up she flung her arms around his neck, saying, 'Bye, lad – have a safe journey. Don't forget, you promised to write.'

'I won't forget, Ruth. Will you keep an eye on Mum for me?'

'Yes, of course, we all will,' she answered, indicating other neighbours who were waiting to say their goodbyes.

'Thanks. I'm going to miss you all,' he said, his voice strained with emotion.

Sally's breath caught in her throat. He had stepped forward, was moving towards her. She had to stay calm, *had* to – so many people were watching.

'Goodbye, Sally,' he said softly.

She knew she had to raise her head; it would look odd if she didn't. Oh God, this was too much. Looking up, she focused on his chin. 'Goodbye, Arthur. Good luck,' she said, her voice coming out in a croak.

'Sally,' he whispered.

'Take care of yerself, Arthur,' her gran said, moving to stand beside them and touching his sleeve.

'I will, old girl,' he said, covering her hand with his.

Using this moment of distraction, Sally turned quickly away, fighting to hold back her tears. Ann was staring at her strangely from the back of the car, her hand flat on the window as she leaned forward. Sally waved distantly in her general direction then rushed back indoors, seeking the sanctuary of her bedroom.

Arthur sat in the front seat, next to his dad, his mind in turmoil. He had hardly seen Sally during the time leading up to his departure; she had obviously been avoiding him, but why? He had tried to talk to her just now when she came to say goodbye, but her gran had interrupted them. How could he have been so wrong? The night they made love he'd been sure that she returned his feelings, and he had made up his mind not to go to Australia.

It had been absolute hell the next morning when Jenny came round and told him she was pregnant. He had stared at her in horror, unable to believe his ears, sure that he had always pulled out in time. Thankfully she had prattled on about how wonderful it was and asking if they should tell everyone before they left, giving him time to pull himself together. He had got rid of her as quickly as possible, telling her to keep the news to herself for the time being.

After that he'd sat in his room for hours, his thoughts spinning. What could he do? Finally he came to realise that he had no choice. He couldn't break up with Jenny now – she was carrying his child!

Grimacing, he remembered how he'd agonised about how to tell Sally. Christ, what a fool he'd felt when he went to see her. Their lovemaking had meant nothing to her, nothing. He went over and over it in his mind, thinking about what she had told him about her uncle. She had been a virgin, he was sure of that, so how could she dismiss what had happened so flippantly?

'Jenny and her family only left about fifteen minutes before us, Arthur. We may be able to catch them up,' his dad said, breaking into his thoughts.

'Yeah, right,' he answered, trying to shut his mind to the snuffling sobs coming from the back of the car. He hadn't wanted his family to come to the docks to see him off, dreading how painful it would be. But they had insisted, and now he wondered why he hadn't put his foot down.

There was only sporadic conversation for the rest of the journey and it was a relief when they reached Southampton. It took them some time to find Jenny and her family in the crowd, and when they did, the Jacksons were anxious to board the ship.

Arthur drew in a deep breath; and turning to face his mother, he found the pain in her eyes agonising to see. 'Bye, Mum,' he whispered, taking her small plump body in his arms.

'Oh, son, son,' she sobbed.

He had to pull away, had to, it was too painful. He gave Ann a quick hug, feeling her face, wet with tears, against his. Then, after giving his

300

father's hand a quick shake, he turned quickly to leave. But his father pulled him back, and Arthur found himself gripped tightly as Bert's huge arms wrapped round him. 'Bye, son. If you don't settle, if you change your mind, don't be too proud to write and tell us. You can always come home,' he choked, his voice strangled with emotion.

Arthur wrenched himself out of his father's arms. He had to get on the ship, he couldn't stand any more. 'I must go,' he gasped, trying to hide his feelings as he stepped onto the gang-plank, boarding the ship that would take him to a new life.

Chapter Thirty-Three

'Sally, what's worrying you?' Sid asked, joining her behind the counter. 'You ain't been yourself for weeks now.'

'Nothing, I'm all right,' she told him, and turning away pulled out one of the drawers, fiddling with the contents.

He shuffled over to the door and putting the latch down, said gruffly, 'Right, it's half-day closing time. Come upstairs, please.'

She looked at him nervously; he sounded annoyed. Was he going to sack her? Yet how could she blame him if he did? Her heart hadn't been in the job since Arthur's departure.

Following him upstairs she knew that it wasn't just her job, she had lost interest in everything lately – every day had become like a burden to be got through. Arthur was constantly on her mind. When she fell asleep at night she saw his face and when she woke up in the morning, he was her first thought. Her unhappiness was like a hard knot of pain in her stomach.

'Talk to me, Sally,' Sid said as she stepped into the room, indicating that she should sit opposite him.

Sally looked into his eyes, finding them full of sympathy, not anger – and suddenly found that all her pent-up emotions rose to the surface as she sobbed out her unhappiness, crying for the first time since Arthur's departure.

Silence filled the room when she finally managed to bring herself under control. Sid, saying nothing, went over to the old butler sink in the corner, filling the kettle from the cold tap. After putting it onto the gas stove he returned, and sitting down leaned forward, his elbows resting on the table. 'Do you know something, Sally, when my wife died, I wanted to die too. She was a wonderful woman, my Rachel, and we were together for over forty years.'

Sally just stared at him and he smiled softly.

'What's the silly old fool going on about, I expect you're thinking. No, it's all right,' he said when she started to protest. 'All I'm trying to say, Sally, is that time is a great healer. You'll get over the loss of your young man. I know it doesn't feel like it now, but it does get easier.'

She shook her head, a denial on her lips as he continued.

'Just give it time,' he said gently. 'Perhaps

you've been trying too hard to put on a brave front. My Rachel was a wise woman. She used to say that tears are the best medicine for unhappiness, and I'm sure she's right.'

Oh, it was too much – the sympathy was too much, Sally thought guiltily. Sid thinks I'm putting on a brave face, but in truth I'm a coward. I'm afraid to let anyone know how I feel about Arthur, especially Elsie. She would never forgive me if she knew I might have been able to stop him from emigrating.

Christmas Day had been awful. They were invited to Elsie's for dinner, and it had proved a disaster. Seeing how much they were missing Arthur had added to her guilt, and though her mum and gran had tried to cheer everyone up, it was a relief when the day came to an end.

Talking to Sid had made her take a good look at herself, and to admit her feelings for the first time. Perhaps crying had helped, for she realised now that she had to accept that Arthur had gone – gone for ever. Somehow she must get on with her life without him.

She stood up, determined now to make an effort. 'Right, I think I'll pop across to the baker's and get us a couple of nice crusty rolls. If I don't make lunch before I go, you won't bother to eat, will you?'

'That's the ticket, Sally. How about a nice bowl of chicken soup to go with them?'

After Sid had eaten his fill, he leaned back, patting his tummy contentedly. 'The shop's done really well, Sally. Those Christmas lines you ordered 'ave nearly all gone, especially the sewing

303

baskets. We've hardly got anything left to put in a January sale. But come on now, it's time you went home, you're wasting your half-day off.'

'All right. I'll see you tomorrow then,' she told him, making her way back down to the shop, gratified that the new lines she'd tried had been a success.

A quick glance around showed her that everything was neat and tidy, so putting her coat on she left the shop, locking the door behind her.

The sky was laden with dark, heavy rainclouds, and as she walked home, her spirits dropped again. The determination she had felt to make an effort diminished as her thoughts turned, yet again, to Arthur.

Elsie stared at the Tarot cards, unable to make any sense of the spread. The only thing that leaped out at her was that she was going to get a letter. She shook her head impatiently; she didn't need the Tarot cards to tell her that. After all, Arthur had been at sea for six weeks now and must be due to land in Australia soon.

Something was going to happen, she had been sensing it for days – but what? Impatiently gathering the cards together and wrapping them in a silk cloth, she put them back into their wooden box. The room looked so bare now without the Christmas decorations, yet she had been glad to take them down. Their first Christmas without Arthur had been awful – they were all pining. Bert was still refusing to talk about his feelings, only commenting that *Jones & Son* would never be painted on the side of his removal vans now.

She had invited Ruth, Sally and Sadie around for Christmas dinner, which she soon came to realise was a mistake, because it had ended up spoiling their Christmas too. Poor Sally had been dreadfully subdued and Elsie guessed that she was intuitively picking up on their unhappiness.

The door opened and she looked up in surprise when Bert walked into the room, almost as though her thoughts had conjured him up. 'Hello, love, what are you doing home so early?' she asked him in surprise.

He yanked his cap off, pulled out a chair, and sat down, gazing at her earnestly. Elsie shivered intuitively. He was going to tell her something – something very important.

'We've got three vans now, love, and may need another one soon. As you know, I can't do any more lifting, so I spend most of my time in the office and going out to give estimates. When I looked at the accounts last week it made me realise how the business is thriving.'

'Yes, Bert, you've done really well, but what is this leading to?'

'Think back to the day we moved into this house. What did I say to you?'

'How can you expect me to remember that? It was nearly eight years ago.'

'Well, I remember, Elsie. I've never forgotten the look on your face when you saw this house. You put on a brave front, but I knew you hated it.'

'I must admit I didn't like it at first, but we've been happy here,' she told him, picking at the tablecloth, before adding, 'until recently, that is.'

Bert nodded, his eyes clouding momentarily.

'The day we moved in, I told you that if things went well with the business, we wouldn't be here for long.'

'Yes, you're right, you did say something like that.' Elsie smiled. 'It's lucky I didn't hold you to it though.'

He smiled back ruefully. 'You can hold me to it now, love. In fact, that's why I've come home early. I've been to give an estimate for a couple moving to a smaller property, and from the moment I walked into their house I fell in love with it. So come on, get your coat on and I'll take you to see it. If you like it – well, I'm going to buy it.'

She gawked at her husband, unable to believe her ears. This had come like a bolt out of the blue. 'Wait a minute,' she begged. 'Give me a chance to take this in, Bert.'

'We've got to leave now, Elsie. I told the couple I would bring you back to see it and they're expecting us.'

She rose to her feet, her thoughts still racing. She knew the business was going well, but to own their own house, it was like a dream. Grabbing a comb, she quickly tidied her hair and after applying a dab of lipstick, grabbed her best coat out of the cupboard. 'Right, I'm ready,' she told her husband, following him out of the door.

It's beautiful, Elsie thought, as they pulled up outside the house. Bert was right – and even without seeing inside, she loved it. Driving here she had felt her excitement mounting, realising that they were heading for Wimbledon, and to Elsie that was like coming home.

As they got out of the car she gazed with delight at the wide, tree-lined avenue. Blossom trees, bare now, would be beautiful in the spring, she thought, picturing their froth of pink and white flowers. She turned to look at the semi-detached house again, loving the deep red bricks, mullioned windows and gabled roof, realising that it would look even better in the summer when the wisteria twined along the walls was in full bloom. 'Oh Bert, it's wonderful,' she whispered, turning to smile at him.

He took her arm and they walked through the gate leading to the front door. Mature shrubs bordered the path, some evergreen, others, including roses, neatly pruned.

'I can't wait to see inside,' she told him, feeling a quiver of excitement.

As the elderly couple escorted them around the ground floor, Elsie fell more and more in love with the house. From the moment she saw the oak panelling in the hall, to the time she stood on the red flagstones on the kitchen floor, she thought it was perfect. 'Ann will love it too, Bert,' she told him.

'My husband will show you the bedrooms. I'm afraid I'm having difficulty with the stairs,' the genteel lady told them.

'Oh, is that why you're moving?' Elsie asked.

'Yes. We've found a lovely little bungalow in Bournemouth, and though we'll be sorry to leave this house, living by the coast will be some consolation.'

Elsie smiled gently, sensing her sadness, before following her husband upstairs. The bedrooms were spacious and looking out of one of the windows, she was amazed to see that the back garden was over a hundred feet long. It was mostly laid to lawn at the moment, but she was already picturing it planted out with a profusion of summer flowers.

'Well, love, shall I make them an offer?' Bert asked, coming to stand behind her.

'Yes! Oh yes, it's perfect,' she answered, turning to give him a quick hug.

Back downstairs, Elsie gazed around the lovely big sitting room again, while Bert negotiated the asking price with the couple, thrilled to hear them accepting his offer almost immediately.

'I can't wait to move in,' she told him as they returned to the car.

'If we find a good solicitor, and there are no hitches along the way, we could be living here in just over a month or so.'

It was only as they were driving back to Battersea that Elsie's thoughts turned to her friends. She would miss the Marchants so much. They had become like an extended family, and the thought of moving away lowered her mood.

'You've gone quiet all of a sudden, what's the matter?' Bert asked.

'I was thinking about Ruth and Sally, Sadie too.'

'Now then, Elsie, we're only moving to Wimbledon, not the other end of the country. You'll be able to see them often enough.'

'It won't be the same though, will it?' she said doubtfully.

'You'll soon get to know the neighbours here,'

he answered.

Yes, but will they be as friendly? she wondered, shaking her head in doubt. The Avenue had been practically deserted. No curtains twitching at windows, no children playing in the street, and somehow Elsie couldn't imagine poking her head round their back doors to ask if the kettle was on.

She twisted in her seat, looking back for a last glimpse of the house before they turned the corner. Oh, it was lovely – more than lovely, it was beautiful. How can you compare it to Candle Lane? she thought, chastising herself for being silly. Bert was right, she would make new friends. It just might take a little longer, that was all.

'I'm going back to the yard for a little while,' Bert told her as they arrived home and he pulled into the kerb.

'All right, love,' Elsie said, her thoughts still distracted. 'I'll see you later.'

She had just taken her coat off and put the kettle on the hob, when the back door opened.

'And where 'ave you been, all dolled up in your best bib and tucker?' Ruth asked, grinning at her as she came into the kitchen.

'You don't miss much, do you?' Elsie said, forcing a smile. 'I'm just making a cuppa, do you want one?'

'Can a duck swim?'

Elsie smiled at Ruth's quip, and as she poured boiling water into the teapot she took a deep breath, deciding to tell her friend straight away. 'Bert took me to see a house.'

'What did he do that for?'

'He wants to buy it, love,' she said, turning to see a stunned look on Ruth's face.

'So you're moving then?' she whispered.

'Yes, in about a month or so. Look, Ruth, it's only in Wimbledon so we can still see each other. I'll come to visit you every week and you can come to me. There's no need for us to lose touch.'

Ruth nodded, her smile tremulous as she said, 'I'm happy for you, really I am. It's just come as a bit of a shock, that's all. I don't blame you for wanting to move away from this area; it's really gone to the dogs. A lot of people from the Lane have gone and it ain't the same now, is it? Joan Mason's been given one of them new flats the council 'ave built.' She grimaced. 'Though what on earth has possessed her to move into one of them is beyond me. They're an eyesore and look like a pile of bleedin' matchboxes.'

Elsie could see that Ruth was being brave for her sake; only the fact that she was unconsciously wringing her hands betrayed her agitation. She kept the description of the house down to a minimum, her delight diminishing again in the face of her friend's distress.

Later, when Ann came home from work, her reaction was contrary to Elsie's expectations too. Instead of being thrilled, she was horrified at the thought of leaving Battersea. She didn't want to move away from Billy, and the journey to work would take ages, she complained, stomping up to her room in a sulk that was so out of character, it left Elsie reeling.

When Bert came home that evening, he was obviously bewildered by the atmosphere as they

310

sat round the table, eating dinner.

'What's the matter with everyone? Why all the long faces?' he asked innocently.

Ann scowled as she cut into her pork chop. 'I don't want to move, Dad,' she told him.

Seeing him stiffen, Elsie caught her daughter's eyes, shaking her head reproachfully. 'You'll just have to get used to the idea, Ann. It's a wonderful house and we've already agreed to buy it.'

'I'll stay here then. I can find a bedsit to rent,' she said belligerently.

'No, you won't,' Bert said, his voice a dangerously quiet growl. 'You're not old enough to leave home yet, my girl.'

'I'm seventeen, Dad, and I'll be eighteen in March. You can't stop me leaving home if I want to.'

Elsie was startled to see her usually mild-mannered husband rear out of his chair.

'If you leave home, that's it!' he roared, his voice resounding in the small room. 'I'll wash my hands of you. First my son buggers off to Australia and now you're making threats. Hasn't it occurred to you that your mother and I need a fresh start, a chance to get away from this stinking area?'

Ann's face crumbled, and as she ran from the room, Elsie held out a restraining hand. 'Wait, your father didn't mean it.'

Shaking off her mother's touch, she bolted for the stairs while Bert, looking utterly deflated, sank onto his chair. 'I'm sorry, Elsie, I don't know what came over me. Perhaps I had better go and talk to her,' he said worriedly.

She shook her head. 'Leave her, love. She'll

come round. We're all still missing Arthur and it's making us a bit touchy.'

And, as predicted, after about fifteen minutes Ann walked sheepishly into the room, her eyes red from crying. 'I'm sorry, Dad,' she whispered. 'I don't know what made me act like that. Of course I won't leave home.'

Elsie smiled as Bert reached out and grasped Ann's hand, his relief evident. 'I'm sorry too, darling. Anyway, how could you leave your poor old dad?'

'Well I can't can I? If you're that old, you'll need me to look after you,' she replied, half-laughing and half-crying.

Elsie sighed; they'd be all right now. And perhaps Bert was right – they did need a fresh start.

Chapter Thirty-Four

A week later, just as Sally was about to leave for work, Elsie came rushing in waving a letter. 'It's from Arthur,' she cried excitedly.

'How is he?' Ruth asked.

'He says it's very hot and they've all been put in a hostel until they find their own accommodation. His job isn't too bad, but there's no unemployment out there so he might look around for something better.' She frowned, scratching her head. 'It doesn't sound like he's enjoying it much, does it?'

'Blimey, give him time. He's only just arrived,'

Ruth told her.

Sally listened to the conversation, waiting for the news about Jenny, surprised when Elsie just rattled on about how Arthur said he'd been seasick on the journey and how glad he was to get off the ship. 'What else has he got to say?' she asked, glancing anxiously at the clock.

'Nothing really, just that he misses us and hopes we're all well. Are you off to work now, Sally?'

'Yes,' she answered distantly, her thoughts confused. 'I'm just going – see you later.'

Hurrying down the Lane to the bus stop, she wondered why Arthur hadn't told his mother about Jenny's pregnancy. Was it because he was going to wait until they got married?

Her thoughts drifted to Ann, dreading it when she moved to Wimbledon. God, she would miss her so much, Elsie too. They had been living next door for over seven years; she and Ann becoming like sisters, and though they had consoled themselves by arranging to see each other as much as possible, it wouldn't be the same.

She just made it by nine o'clock and unlocking the door, rushed into the shop. There was no sign of Sid, so hanging her coat in the back room, she returned to the shop, grabbing a duster and running it over the counter.

'If you polish that glass much more it'll fade away,' Sid chuckled, appearing in the doorway and handing her a cup of tea. 'I've put two sugars in it, Sally. Drink it while it's nice and hot, it'll warm you up.'

'Thanks,' she said gratefully, taking a gulp of the strong tea. Almost immediately she paled,

313

clamping a hand over her mouth as her stomach heaved. 'Oh God, Sid, I feel sick,' she cried, running from the shop and into the toilet, just making it in time.

Afterwards, staring at her distorted reflection in the cracked mirror above the sink, she wondered why she had been sick again. Still feeling slightly nauseous she splashed cold water onto her face, hoping it would revive her. It was then that the penny dropped and she clutched the side of the wash basin, her knuckles white. She hadn't had a period last month and now realised that she'd just missed another one. Oh God, she thought, I'm pregnant. She swayed, her heart thumping with fear. What would her mother say? How could she tell her?

'Sally, are you all right?' Sid called from outside the door.

'Yes, I'm just coming,' she croaked, roughly drying her face.

When she returned to the shop Sid gazed at her, a question in his eyes. 'You don't look too good, Sally. Maybe you should go home.'

'No, no, I'll be all right,' she told him, an edge of panic in her voice. How could she go home? Her mother would want to know what was wrong.

'Sally, do you know why you're being sick?'

She stared at Sid, surprised by the intuitive question, and flushing, she grabbed the duster again, polishing the counter as she mumbled, 'I expect I've eaten something that's upset my tummy.'

'No, gel, you've been sick for three mornings on the trot now – and I think you know why.'

Rubbing the glass vigorously she ignored his

question, but he grasped her arm, turning her gently round, his eyes deep with compassion. 'You're having a baby, Sally. I can remember when my Rachel suffered from morning sickness too.'

Her shoulders slumped. 'Are you going to give me the sack?' she whispered.

'No, of course not, but you'll be leaving to get married, won't you?'

'No, I won't be getting married. The father's in Australia.'

'Oh, my life, Sally. What are you going to do?'

'I don't know,' she admitted. 'My mum will go mad when she finds out.'

Sid shook his head, obviously worried by her dilemma. 'Well, you won't be able to hide it from her for long, Sally.'

That evening, making her way home, Sally thought about how understanding Sid had been and prayed her mother would be the same. And her gran, how would she take it?

She arrived home, finding them discussing Elsie's move again, both deeply affected. 'We'll never get neighbours as good as them again,' her mum was saying as she walked into the room. 'Hello, Sally, you look frozen, dinner won't be long,' Ruth gabbled, turning back to the subject of Elsie. 'I'm pleased for her, really I am, but I wish she was staying.'

Sadie smiled at her granddaughter, motioning her over to the fire. 'Come and warm yerself up, love,' she invited, before responding, 'I know what you mean, Ruth. They've been bloody good to us over the years.'

Sally sat down, staring at the fire, and only dimly hearing the conversation in the background. Her thoughts raced. She had to tell them, there was no choice, but she quivered with fear at the thought.

Her eyes were fixed on the flickering flames, and she became mesmerised as a picture began to form. Was it her imagination – was that really Arthur she could see standing on the prow of a ship, gazing out to sea? She blinked, startled as her mum's voice intruded, the vision disappearing.

'Come on, Sally, I said dinner's on the table. Blimey, you were miles away.'

She joined them at the table, where she sat gazing at her plate, piled high with braised steak and mashed potatoes. Her mouth was dry with nerves, and picking up her fork, she stabbed half-heartedly at a piece of meat.

'Are you all right, Sal? You look a bit pale,' her mother said anxiously.

Putting her fork down, the piece of steak uneaten, Sally braced herself before saying, 'I've got something to tell you both.'

'Yeah. Well spit it out then.'

Looking at her mother and gran across the table, Sally struggled to find the words, but her throat was constricted and she ended up just shaking her head in despair.

'Have you got the sack, is that it?' Ruth asked sympathetically. 'Don't worry, you'll soon get another job.'

'Oh Mum, I ... I'm...' she gasped, her eyes filling with tears.

'What's the matter? It can't be that bad, surely.'

The sympathy was almost too much, and finding herself still unable to speak, she turned to look at her gran. But it was no good, the words just wouldn't come, and she lowered her head.

A hand covered hers, the fingers gnarled with arthritis and skin freckled with age. 'Come on, Sally, tell us what's wrong. As the saying goes, a trouble shared is a trouble halved,' her gran urged.

Oh Gran, she thought as her hand was gently squeezed again, you're going to be so ashamed of me. Yet she had to tell them, she had no choice. 'I'm having a baby,' she finally blurted out, feeling her face flame.

Silence – there was utter silence. Raising her face she saw both her mum and gran sitting frozen like statues, staring at her in disbelief.

'No, you can't be,' her mother finally gasped. 'It takes two, Sally, and you ain't had a bloke since you broke up with John. How can you be pregnant?'

'Are you sure, Sally? I mean, how far are you gone?' her gran asked.

'I haven't had a period for two months,' she whispered.

Her mother's eyes narrowed calculatingly. 'That was about the time of Arthur's going-away party, and if you met a bloke there, you've kept it bloody quiet.'

Sally jumped as her mum suddenly slammed her fist on the table, shouting, 'Whoever it is, you'll 'ave to marry him, my girl – and quick too!'

'Calm down, Ruth,' Sadie intervened, 'Now, Sally, tell us, who 'ave you been seeing?'

She shook her head. 'I haven't been seeing

anyone. I don't know who the father is,' she lied.

'Don't know? You don't know!' her mother screamed, jumping up and pacing the floor. 'You must know, you soppy cow. Or are you gonna tell us yer the Virgin Mary?' She added sarcastically.

'Wait a minute, Ruth,' Sadie urged. 'There must be some explanation.' She leaned forward. 'Sally, did a man force himself on you? Were you raped – is that what happened?'

'No, no!' she exclaimed. What could she say? How could she hide the truth from them? 'It was the party – I had too much to drink. There was someone, but I don't remember who it was.'

Her mother marched across the room and Sally winced as she grabbed her arm painfully. 'You're telling me you got drunk, had sex with someone, but you don't know who it was? You're a slut, Sally Marchant, a filthy, dirty little slut!'

'Stop it, Ruth!' Sadie cried, 'Shouting and bawling ain't gonna solve anything. We need to think, decide what to do.'

Ruth's eyes were like venomous slits. 'Well, to start with she'll 'ave to go away. Can you imagine the field day our neighbours would 'ave if they found out? Bleedin' hell, there's enough scandal in the Lane as it is. Don't you remember how everyone reacted when Judy Wilson got pregnant without getting married! Christ, her mother walked around with her head down for ages, she was so ashamed.' She threw a look of disgust at Sally. 'Bloody hell, how could you do this to me?' she spat.

'I'm sorry Mum.'

'Sorry? You're *sorry*? My God, I could kill you.'

318

'Ruth, that's enough!' Sadie shouted. 'I'm ashamed of you, talking like that. Who are you to throw stones? Have you forgotten what you got up to during the war? Were *you* any less of a slut?'

Ruth gave an agonised gasp and dropped onto a chair. She folded her arms on the table, laying her head down on them as her shoulders started to shake with sobs.

Sadie got up to stand by her side, stroking her hair gently. 'I'm sorry, but it had to be said. You've put your daughter on a pedestal, and when you do that it's always painful when they fall off. Now come on, it's not the end of the world. She's not the first girl to get into trouble and she won't be the last. We'll work something out.'

They were quiet then, waiting for her mum to calm down, the dinner congealed on their plates. Sally hung her head, deep in thought. Mum had said she would have to move out, but where could she go?

It was her gran who finally came up with a solution. 'I've got an idea. She could go and stay with Mary.'

Ruth raised her face, dashing away the tears with her fingers. 'Yeah, she could do that, and we can tell people she's got a new live-in job. But what about when she's had the kid – what then?'

'We'll cross that bridge when we come to it, but for now I'm going to give Mary a ring and ask her to come round. I'm sure Elsie won't mind if I use her telephone.'

Sally stood up; they were talking about her as if she wasn't there, as if she had no say in the matter. 'I'm going upstairs,' she told them, quietly leaving the room, unable to bear the pain in her mother's eyes any longer.

Mary arrived an hour later and looked absolutely dumbfounded when Sadie told her that Sally was pregnant. 'I simply can't believe it,' she said. 'When you rang and asked me to come round, this was the last thing I expected. Who's the father?'

'We don't know and that's why we needed to see you,' Sadie told her daughter.

'What do you mean, you don't know? Won't Sally tell you who it is?'

'No,' Sadie answered shortly.

'But I don't understand. This isn't like Sally – there must be a reason.'

Ruth spoke at last, a scowl on her face as she said, 'Oh, there's a reason all right. She got drunk and had it off with a bloke, but can't remember who it was.'

Mary's face stretched into an expression of disbelief. 'No, I'm sorry, I just don't believe it. I know Sally – she wouldn't do a thing like that.'

'Huh, well I can assure you she did. Your precious niece opened her legs to a stranger and she's got a bleedin' bun in the oven to prove it.'

'All right, Ruth, there's no need to be coarse,' Mary snapped, her lips curled with distaste.

'Oh, I beg yer pardon, I forgot what a little prude you are.'

Jumping to her feet, Mary pulled her gloves on. 'I don't have to listen to this. I came round because Mum said you needed to see me urgently. I didn't come here to be insulted.'

'Wait, love,' Sadie urged. 'Take no notice of

Ruth. She's in a bit of a state, and surely you can understand why.'

Mary sighed with exasperation. 'All right, Mum. I suppose you have a point.' She sat down again, crossing one leg over the other and swinging her foot impatiently. 'Now then, what are you going to do about this situation?'

'We wondered if you'd let Sally stay with you?' Sadie told her.

Mary blinked rapidly, obviously surprised at the request, but after a short pause answered, 'Yes, all right. But how does Sally feel about it?'

'She'll do as she's bloody well told,' Ruth snapped.

'Wait a minute though, have you thought this through? Yes, coming to stay with me will hide the fact that she's pregnant, but when she's had the baby, what then?'

'I dunno, it's come as such a shock that I can't think straight. I suppose she could 'ave it adopted.'

'That's Sally's decision, Ruth, not yours' Sadie said tartly.

'Well, she ain't bringing it back here, so she won't 'ave much choice.' Then, pushing herself out of the chair and walking to the bottom of the stairs, Ruth yelled, 'Sally, get down here!'

Sally agreed to their arrangements, happy to go to her aunt's. They had worked it out that she could continue to work by getting the bus each morning, but then things became heated again when they raised the subject of the baby.

'You'll 'ave to get it adopted, Sally,' her mum spat.

'No, never, I won't do that. I'll look after it, save

as much money as I can while I'm working, and then, well...' she floundered.

'Yeah, that's stumped you, hasn't it, my girl? You ain't got any choice – you can't keep it. Adoption is the only solution.'

'There must be another way!' Sally cried desperately.

'Well, you can't bring it home to Candle Lane. How are we supposed to explain you turning up with a child and no husband – answer me that?'

Sally couldn't stand the poison in her mother's voice and felt her eyes brimming with tears. It was her aunt who intervened. 'I think we should worry about this later, Ruth. Let's just sort things out one step at a time.'

'Yeah, all right. I've had enough for one night anyway and me head's splitting,' she said, looking at Sally reproachfully.

'Can I go back to my room now?' Sally whispered, unable to stand much more.

'Yeah, go on, get out of my sight,' her mother said unkindly.

The next day Sally found it just as hard to tell Elsie and Ann. It was useless trying to hide it from them, the atmosphere at home would soon give the game away. Her mum was stiff with repressed anger and barely talking to her.

She hung her head in shame as she broke the news, but although they were shocked they responded with compassion. The worst part was lying about the father. They looked horrified when she told them she didn't know who it was, but unlike her mother, they were still kind.

'Drink can do terrible things,' Elsie said sadly. 'I could see you weren't yourself at the party and guessed you were still upset about John.' She sighed. 'These things happen and though it's a bit late, I expect you've learned your lesson.'

Sally bit her lip painfully. John, she thought. Elsie thought she was upset about John! She wanted to scream, to shout, that it was Arthur she loved, not John.

'Are you sure you want to go to your auntie's?' Elsie asked. 'You could come to stay with us in Wimbledon.'

'Yes, do come, Sally,' Ann urged.

She was overwhelmed by their kindness. 'Thank you, I'd love to, but all the arrangements have been made now. I'm to go to Tooting in about a month's time. Mr Jacobs said I can carry on working for as long as I want and even said he'd keep my job open for me.'

'He's a good man,' Elsie mused, 'but I don't know how you'll be able to carry on working when you've had the baby.'

'Mr Jacobs said I can take it to work with me.'

Elsie shook her head doubtfully. 'It might work, I suppose, but it won't be easy.'

No, Sally thought, it won't – and where will I live? Her mother had been adamant that she wouldn't have her back home with a baby.

'Do you know, I saw in the cards that I was going to get news of a baby, and there I was thinking it would be from my Arthur,' Elsie said, breaking into her thoughts.

'Give them a chance, Mum, they aren't married yet,' Ann said.

Sally had to bite back the words that wanted to spring from her lips, almost telling Elsie that she would get news of another baby soon, that Jenny was pregnant too. She stood up quickly, afraid that she would break down. 'I had better go, but when you move can I still come to see you in Wimbledon?' she asked hopefully. 'I'll understand if you'd rather I kept away.'

'Of course you can, Sally. Crumbs, you haven't got the plague, love, you're having a baby,' Elsie told her, reaching out to grasp her hand. 'If you need us, please don't hesitate to let us know.'

Ann put an arm around her shoulders as they walked to the door. 'I'm so sorry, Sally. It must be awful for you.'

'I'll be all right, don't worry. Bye, Ann, bye, Elsie,' she choked, as she hurried out.

Chapter Thirty-Five

Sally's eighteenth birthday in February came and went with little to mark the occasion. Elsie was moving on Saturday and her mother, already upset about her pregnancy, was now deeply unhappy about her friend's imminent departure.

'I think it's about time you went to yer aunt's, Sally,' she said irritably, staring at her daughter's stomach.

'But I'm hardly showing yet, Mum.'

'Yes you are. Look, I can see a bump already.'

'Blimey, Ruth,' Sadie spluttered, 'surely there's

no need to make her go just yet?'

'I ain't having the neighbours tittle-tattling, Mum,' Ruth said decisively. 'If I can see it, you can be sure other people will notice too. You can go to Mary's on Sunday, Sally.'

'Yes, all right,' she answered dully. What difference does it make, she thought. And perhaps it would be better to be away from her mother's constant carping. 'Do you mind if I pop round to see Ann? I said I'd give her a hand to sort her room out.'

'No, I'll be glad to see the back of you,' Ruth said spitefully.

'Stop picking on the girl,' Sadie intervened, jumping to Sally's defence. 'I know yer upset about Elsie moving away, but you shouldn't keep snapping at Sally like that.'

'I'll talk to her how I bloody well like,' Ruth shouted. 'She's my daughter, not yours, and I wish to God that she'd never been born.'

'Shut up!' Sadie retorted. 'I'm sick to death of the way yer carrying on, and saying that is the final straw.' Levering herself up from the chair, she threw a look of disgust at her daughter. 'I'm going to me own room, and I don't think I can stand to be in the same house as you for much longer.'

With a stricken look at them both, Sally scurried out. Argue, that was all they did nowadays, and it was all her fault.

'Are you all right?' Elsie asked as soon as she stepped into her kitchen.

'Yes,' she said, blinking her eyes to stem the tears that Elsie's concern had brought to the surface.

'Give it time, Sally. Your mum will come round.'

'No, I don't think she'll ever forgive me.'

'Of course she will. Once you've had the baby she'll love it, darling. She won't be able to resist her first grandchild.'

'Do you really think so?' Sally asked hopefully.

'You wait and see. Somehow I just know that everything is going to be all right for you.'

'Oh, I hope so,' she whispered.

'I've sent a letter to Arthur to give him our new address,' Elsie said now, changing the subject as she sat down, 'but I'm worried about him, Sally. We've only had that one letter from him, and that was just after he arrived in Australia.'

Sally frowned. Arthur and Jenny must be married by now; after all, she was probably about six months' pregnant. Why hadn't he written to tell his mother?

'Perhaps he's still trying to move out of the hostel and is waiting until he gets a permanent address,' she offered, unable to think of any other explanation.

'I suppose that's possible,' Elsie said doubtfully, 'but something's telling me that it's more than that.'

Seeing that Elsie was close to tears and hoping to divert her mind, Sally said, 'With all these crates piled up I can see you've nearly finished packing. I came round to give Ann a hand.'

'Oh, she isn't in, love, she's gone out with Billy. Her head's in the clouds these days and she must have forgotten about it.'

'It doesn't matter, it wasn't a firm arrangement,' Sally assured her, dreading the thought of return-ing home. 'I'm going to my aunt's on Sunday, and as she's on the telephone I'll be able to ring you occasionally.'

'Don't just ring us, Sally. Come to see us in Wimbledon as often as you like. I'm going to miss you, love.'

'Thanks, Elsie, I'm going to miss you too,' and feeling a lump in her throat she turned hurriedly to leave. 'I'd better go now, I'll see you tomorrow,' she said huskily.

'Bye, love. And keep your chin up.'

As Sally stepped out into the yard, she paused to look up at the sky. No stars were visible through the polluted atmosphere, but she could just see a misty crescent moon, and couldn't help her thoughts turning to Arthur. Was the sky above him blue, the sun hot? His face floated into her mind, the gentle smile when he looked at her, the love she had seen in his eyes. A dog suddenly barked, snapping her out of her reverie. Cut it out, she berated herself. You've got to stop thinking about him. He's gone, gone for ever.

It had been hard saying goodbye on Saturday morning. The removals van had left, driven by Bert's partner, but Elsie and Ann had stood hovering on the pavement, their expressions stricken as they gazed from the empty house to Ruth, Sally and Sadie, waiting outside to see them off.

Other neighbours came out to wish them luck, amongst them Peggy Green and Nelly Cox – and even old bossy boots Joan Mason looked sad as she said goodbye.

There had been tears, and hugs, until Bert finally ran out of patience and ushered his wife and daughter into the car.

And now I'm leaving too, Sally thought, as she loaded her cases into a taxi, sent courtesy of her aunt on Sunday morning. She climbed in, closing the door and giving a small wave to her mum and gran. The Lane was deserted as the taxi drove off, looking bleak and cold in the early morning light – as bleak as her feelings as she wondered what the future held.

After that awful parting, her aunt's welcome had been surprisingly warm, lifting Sally's spirits a little.

She soon became addicted to television, having only seen it on the odd occasion before. Now she watched it avidly every evening. *Dixon of Dock Green*, *Emergency Ward Ten* and *I love Lucy*, they all took her into another world where she could forget her troubles for a while.

There was a slight softening in her mother's attitude when she came to visit, and just lately she seemed jealous of Sally's easy interactions with her aunt.

Now Sally was staring out of the window, her eyes scanning the street. It was Sunday morning and she was expecting her mum and gran. There they were, walking slowly along, her gran limping slightly. Time to give her some healing, she thought as she went to the front door to let them in.

Her mum as usual avoided looking at her stomach, but her gran gave her a wide smile. 'How are you, Sally? Yer showing a bit more now.'

'Fine, but my legs are swelling up. Sid's put a

stool behind the counter and insists I sit down as much as possible. He clucks around me like a mother hen,' she added fondly.

'Huh,' was all her mother said.

Mary came in carrying the tea tray and Sally smiled when her gran gave her a grin, guessing what was coming. She still took great delight in winding her eldest daughter up and was now looking with glee at the biscuits piled on a plate.

Sally masked a smile; her gran was in for a shock. Since living with her aunt she had discovered her hidden sense of humour, and knew she had something planned for today.

'Here you are, Mum,' Mary said, handing her a cup of tea. Then with a quick sly wink at Sally she sat down, and taking a biscuit from the plate promptly dunked it into her own cup, before raising it to her mouth and slurping into it with relish.

The look on Sadie's face was priceless. Her eyes popped and her jaw dropped as she stared at her daughter. 'Cor blimey, I never thought I'd see the day,' she gasped.

Sally was bent double with laughter, holding her stomach as she rocked with mirth. It was her mother who broke the mood and made the laughter die in her throat as she spoke, her voice ringing with authority. 'Right, my girl it's time we talked about this baby again. I've given it a lot of thought and as I said before, I'm certain that the only thing to do is to 'ave it adopted.'

'No, Mum, I've told you. It's my baby and I'm keeping it.'

'Don't be bloody daft, girl. How can you keep

it? You ain't bringing it home with you, and that's final.'

'Hold on a minute, Ruth,' Mary intervened. 'I've been giving this a lot of thought too, and I think I've come up with a solution.'

'Oh yeah? Well, let's hear it then,' Ruth said coldly.

'Why don't you move? You don't have to stay in Candle Lane. Then when Sally's had the baby, who's to know she isn't a widow?'

'Don't be daft, she's a bit young to 'ave lost her husband, ain't she? Christ even new neighbours won't swallow that,' Ruth told her sister scathingly.

'Tell people the baby's yours then,' Mary suggested.

Ruth gawked. 'Mine? Pretend it's *mine?*' she spluttered.

'I think it's a good idea,' Sadie said. 'You know you're not happy since Elsie moved away.' She turned to look at Mary. 'The new neighbours are awful. Four kids they've got and they're a right little bunch of hooligans.'

After thinking about it, Ruth slowly nodded her head. 'Yeah, it could work. I suppose I could ask the council for a transfer. Mind you, it won't happen overnight. It could take some time before they offer us anything.'

'It doesn't matter. Sally's welcome to stay with me until you get something sorted out,' Mary told her.

They're doing it again, Sally thought. They're talking about me as if I'm not here. She stared down at her swollen ankles, feeling helpless as she heard all the arrangements being made. It didn't seem right that her mum was going to pretend that the baby was hers. A thought struck her and she reared up, unable to stop herself blurting out, 'No, no, it isn't fair! My baby will grow up thinking I'm its sister.'

Her mother looked at her through narrowed eyes. 'Do yer think we don't know that? Fair? You talk about fair! Christ, you're an ungrateful little madam. Here we are, trying to sort things out for you, and do we get any thanks? No, all you do is whine. Now listen to me. Yes, I'm prepared to say the kid's mine, but you needn't think I'm looking after it. That's your job, miss. I've got enough to do working fulltime in the grocer's shop.'

Sally stared at her mother, her thoughts racing. Maybe they were right, maybe it was the only way to keep her baby, and at least she would be looking after it, that was something. But never to hear the child call her Mummy – how would she be able to bear it? Oh Arthur, Arthur...

Chapter Thirty-Six

The sweat was running down Arthur's face as he made his way home from work. Christ it's hot, he thought, thinking longingly of a nice cold beer. They were still in the hostel, but Jenny and her parents would be moving into their own place in a couple of days. They had offered to put him up but he had refused, hoping that by putting a distance between himself and Jenny, it might improve matters.

Things weren't working out too well between them and they seemed to be constantly rowing. It had started on the ship only a week before they arrived in Sydney, and he scowled, remembering how Jenny had told him that she wasn't pregnant after all. It had been a false alarm, she said. There was something in her eyes when she told him that, a look he couldn't quite fathom, almost like triumph, and it had preyed on his mind ever since.

It had been strange when soon after arriving in Sydney, they had spent Christmas Day on Bondi Beach, having a picnic. God, how he had missed his family, but Jenny couldn't understand his unhappiness and had moaned at him for being miserable.

He should write to his mum again, he knew that, but what could he tell her? That he was happy, when in reality he wasn't? Oh, there was nothing wrong with Australia, it was a great place, with a vibrant economy, no unemployment, and plenty of opportunities for those prepared to work. The people were great too, friendly and open, and other than the occasional jokes about 'whingeing poms' he got on really well with them. So what was the matter? Why couldn't he settle?

Now, arriving back at the hostel, he had a cool shower, ignoring the letters waiting for him, somehow unable to face reading news from home.

He sat on the edge of his bed, deep in thought. He and Jenny had agreed not to see each other tonight as she wanted to wash her hair. But her parents would be out as they were going to take another look at the house, so should he pop round to see her? Perhaps if they talked, tried to work things out, their relationship could be rescued.

I'll surprise her, he thought, take her out for a meal – she would like that. His mind made up, he went over to the married quarters, and knocking softly on the door before opening it, called, 'Hello, love, fancy going out for a–' He paused, his sentence unfinished, not able to comprehend the sight that met his eyes. She was with another bloke, wrapped in his arms.

'Arthur!' she gasped, stepping quickly away and struggling to button up her blouse.

'You slut!' he yelled, and as he stared at her a rage built up inside him. He had to get out of there; if he didn't, God knows what he might do. Turning and slamming the door behind him, he headed for the nearest bar. He needed a drink, a stiff one.

'You all right, mate?'

Arthur tried to focus on the voice and finding himself swaying, managed to clutch the edge of the bar. 'Yesh,' he mumbled.

'Don't tell me – you're English,' another voice said, thick with sarcasm. 'What's the matter? Homesick, are you?'

'Yesh,' he answered, feeling a nudge in his side that made him stagger.

'Leave him alone,' someone protested. 'He'll settle down, it's hard at first.'

Arthur, feeling his legs going from under him, managed to lean on the bar again, the voices around him coming in waves, loud now and angry.

There was some sort of row going on, but his head was spinning and he felt detached, not part of it.

The noise increased, and there was a crash as a chair was thrown. Some section of his mind told him that he should get out of there, and pushing himself up, his eyes bleary, he made for the door, staggering dizzily.

Almost falling outside, his fuddled mind registered that it was dark. He saw headlights – then there was nothing.

Arthur woke up to find himself in a hospital ward. A nurse, seeing that he was conscious, rushed to his side. 'It's all right,' she told him. 'You've had a bit of an accident, but the doctors had a look at you and you're going to be fine. No bones broken or anything.'

'How long have I been here?' he croaked.

'You came in last night.'

'Can I have some water?'

The nurse filled a glass and after helping him to sit up, held it to his lips. He drank gratefully, gulping the cool liquid.

'Hello, how's our patient?'

'He's just woken up, Doctor.'

'Hmm, well, let's have a look at him then.'

The curtains were drawn around the bed and Arthur submitted to the doctor's gentle examination. A light was shone in his eyes, questions were asked, until finally the doctor, after scribbling on his notes, went on to the next patient.

As the nurse drew the curtains back, Arthur was surprised to see Jenny's mother standing at the foot of the bed, a scowl on her face.

'Awake at last, are you? It's about time. I can't stay long, we're moving into our house tomorrow and I've got a lot to do. I'm only here because of Jenny.'

'Jenny? I don't understand.'

'She asked me to give you this,' the woman told him, holding out an envelope.

'But how did you know I was in here?'

'A bloke came knocking on our door last night. We weren't too pleased to be woken up at one o'clock in the morning, I can tell you. He said you'd had a bit of an accident, but that it wasn't serious.'

Arthur moved his body cautiously, wincing as he did so. 'Why hasn't Jenny come to see me herself?' he asked, looking at the envelope.

''Cos she's too bloody upset, that's why. Now I've got to go,' Mrs Jackson said curtly and walked hurriedly away.

Arthur fingered the letter, feeling something bulky inside. He tore it open, his eyes quickly scanning the contents, and then holding the envelope upside down, he tipped out the ring.

So it was over. What did he feel? Nothing, he had to admit, except anger that he'd been made a fool of – and perhaps relief too, he realised. The funny thing was, Jenny was blaming him. It was his fault, she wrote. He was so bloody miserable it was spoiling her new life in Australia.

Sinking down onto the pillows he closed his eyes, and at some point must have dozed off, waking to the sound of a voice. 'Hello, mate, feeling better are you?'

Arthur opened his eyes, frowning at the man

335

who stood by the bed. He didn't know him from Adam.

'You don't recognise me, do you? I'm not surprised, you'd had a pretty good skinful last night.'

Arthur stared at the tall figure without comprehension. 'I'm sorry, I...'

'The bar – we met for a few minutes in the bar, just before all hell broke loose. I followed you outside and managed to pull you back when you stumbled into the road, but I wasn't quick enough and the wing of a car clipped you. I didn't think you were badly hurt, but you passed out, so I brought you to the hospital just in case.'

'Christ, I don't remember anything,' Arthur told him. 'But thanks for helping me.'

'Nah, mate, that's all right. Before you left the bar you said you were homesick and I guessed that's why you were drowning your sorrows.' He grinned widely, adding, 'My name's Joe, by the way.'

Arthur found himself smiling back. There was something about this bloke that he liked. 'I'm Arthur Jones, pleased to meet you, mate.'

'So how long have you been in Sydney?' Joe asked.

'Since just before Christmas.'

'No wonder you're feeling a bit down. I suppose you left your family behind?'

'Yeah, I came out with my girlfriend and her parents.' Arthur smiled ruefully, 'Though I've just been given a Dear John,' he added, pointing to the letter on his locker.

'Bad luck, mate. Strewth, I picked a good time to visit you, didn't I, but to tell you the truth I won't be around after today. I'm not sure where I'm going, probably Melbourne.'

'But surely there's plenty of work in Sydney?'

'You're right, there is, but I fancy a change of scenery. I've been here for a while now and I've got itchy feet. I fancy seeing a bit more of the country.'

'Well, I can't say I blame you. It's a big place, that's for sure.'

'What are you going to do now, Arthur?'

'I dunno, but I don't fancy staying in Sydney. I suppose I could go back to England, find out how much it would cost to book a berth. The money I saved before coming out here might cover it.'

'No, mate, you shouldn't go back yet. Give Oz a chance, or you'll always regret it. You'll be left wondering if you could have made a go of it here.'

Arthur pinched his bottom lip between his fingers. So much had happened that his thoughts were jumbled. He had no sense of direction, no idea of what to do.

'Hey, Arthur, I've got an idea. How do you fancy coming with me? I could do with the company,' Joe suggested eagerly.

As he stared at Joe, his mind racing, a nurse came to stand by the bed. 'The doctor said you can be discharged, Mr Jones,' she told him.

Arthur's eyes widened; it seemed like an omen somehow. What did he have to lose? He only knew Jenny and her family in Sydney, and now they'd broken up there was nothing to keep him here. He looked at Joe and somehow felt they could become good friends. Making a snap decision, he grinned. 'Yeah, I'll come with you. What time are you leaving?'

'In about two hours. I tell you what, I'll pick you up at the hostel.'

'So it was you who told Jenny I was in here?'

'Yeah, I found the address in your pocket. I hope you don't mind, mate. It seemed the right thing to do.'

'No, of course not,' Arthur told him, liking Joe more and more. It had been good of him to take the trouble.

When Joe left the ward, Arthur got out of bed, dressing as quickly as he could. He ached a bit, and had a terrible hangover, but nothing he couldn't cope with, and he was soon on his way back to the hostel.

It didn't take him long to pack, and stuffing the unopened letters from home in the pocket of his suitcase, he left the room to the sound of Joe's horn, honking at him from outside.

Climbing into the truck, he grinned at his new friend, and as they drove off, he didn't look back.

Chapter Thirty-Seven

Sally was sitting with her feet up when she heard the telephone, but before she could get up, her aunt answered it.

'Sally, I've got a bit of a problem,' Mary told her, her face drawn with anxiety as she returned to the sitting room. 'That was Sheila on the phone.

Harry's been released from prison and has been round to her house demanding to see his son.'

'Oh, no! I hope she called the police.'

'She's frightened, Sally. Apparently Harry has changed dramatically. He was very abusive and almost violent. Yes, she called the police, but by the time they arrived he'd gone. She wants me to stay for a while, just until she sells the house and can move away.'

'Oh, I didn't realise the house was hers. I assumed it was rented.'

'She inherited it from her parents, and as she and Harry weren't legally married, he hasn't got a claim on it.'

'When are you going, Auntie?'

'I can't leave you on your own.'

Leaning back in her chair, Sally's eyes closed in thought. Her aunt had to go to Sheila's, the poor woman must be out of her mind with worry. And what about Linda? The child must be terrified, having to face Harry again. 'You must go, Auntie. I'll be fine on my own,' she assured her.

'Sally, you're over six months' pregnant, and I have no idea how long I'll be away. No, if I go someone will have to come to stay with you.' She paused, frowning worriedly, then her eyes lit up. 'I know, what about Ann?'

'Yes, good idea, I'm sure she'll agree. I'll go and give her a ring now.'

Her aunt looked up hopefully as Sally came back into the room. 'All arranged. Bert's going to bring her over and they should be here within an hour.'

Sighing with relief her aunt stood up. 'I'll give Sheila a ring to tell her I'm on my way, then I'd better pack. Now are you sure you don't mind, Sally? I feel awful leaving you like this.'

'Of course I don't mind. Sheila hasn't got anyone else to turn to, and as for poor Linda, she's probably only just started to get over Harry's abuse. God knows what effect this will have on her.'

Ann settled in happily. Tooting was closer to Billy's home in Battersea and she went out with him twice a week. Tonight they were going dancing at the Hammersmith Palais.

Sally turned her head as Ann came into the room. 'How do I look?' she asked, twirling around to show off her pretty dress.

'Great,' Sally told her.

Smiling happily, Ann threw herself onto the sofa. 'Billy won't be here for about another half an hour. Does my hair look all right?'

Sally smiled gently. Even though Ann's eyes were perfectly straight now, a slight cast only showing when she was tired, she was still uncertain about her appearance. She had backcombed her dark brown hair into a bouffant style that gave her added height. 'Your hair is fine,' she told her. 'That style really suits you.'

'What about my make-up?'

Sally studied Ann's face. 'It's fine,' she assured her. 'You always look nice. By the way, has your mum had another letter from Arthur yet?'

Ann's face fell. 'No, and she's getting more and more upset. Honestly, I could kill him, worrying her like this. She even tried writing to Jenny, but she hasn't replied either, and–' She paused, hearing a knock at the door. 'That'll be Billy,' she said, jumping to her feet.

'Will you be all right, Sally?' Ann asked as she led him into the room. 'We could stay in if you like.'

'Don't be daft, I'm fine. I know I look huge, but I've still got another eight weeks to go yet,' she assured her.

'Well, if you're sure. I'll see you later then. Come on, Billy,' she said, grabbing his arm.

The door had only just closed behind them when the telephone rang. Sally heaved herself off the sofa, waddling into the hall to answer it.

'Hello, how are you?' her aunt asked.

'I'm fine. Is everything all right? Harry hasn't been round again, has he?'

'No, not a sign of him. The court injunction seems to have done the trick.'

'Oh good. How's the sale of the house going? Has Sheila found a buyer yet?'

'Yes. A couple came to view it yesterday and have put in an offer.'

'That's great.'

'Sheila and I have decided to rent a place together. She wants to invest the money from the sale of the house to give her an income. If we find a place with a reasonable rent we can split it between us, saving us both money.'

'That's a good idea,' Sally told her. 'But have you decided where?'

'Yes, in London, but it's got to be somewhere that Harry can't find us. And we've decided to change our surnames to make it harder for him.'

Sally laughed. 'How clever of you. So have you

any idea when you'll be coming home?'

'No, not really. As soon as the sale of the house goes through, I expect. Now, how's your pregnancy coming along? Any problems?'

'I've still got swollen ankles, but it was my last day at work today so I'm hoping they'll go down. I wanted to carry on working a little longer, but as my blood pressure is up, Sid insisted that it's time for me to stay at home. He was wonderful, paying me a month's wages, and giving me a lovely present too, a complete baby layette.'

'Oh, that was kind of him. He's going to miss you, Sally.'

'I think he'll be all right. He takes a lot more interest in the shop now, and I finally persuaded him to advertise for another assistant.'

'What if you want to go back after you've had the baby?'

'That's just what Sid said. But I don't know if it would be practical taking a baby to work, and I wouldn't be able to afford a childminder. I just couldn't give him a firm answer, Auntie. Anyway he needs an assistant now, he really can't cope on his own.'

'Yes, I suppose you're right. Now, has your mother been down to see you this week?'

'She's coming with gran tomorrow,' Sally told her.

'Well, that's all right then. Give them my love. I had better ring off now, darling. I'll talk to you again next week.'

'All right, Auntie. Give my love to Sheila and the children.'

'I will, my dear. Goodbye.'

The house was quiet, and after making herself a hot drink, Sally settled in front of the television. She looked down at her tummy, thinking about her baby. Would it be a girl or a boy, she wondered, resting her hand on the large mound. A wave of loneliness swept over her and once again she found her thoughts turning to Arthur. Jenny must have given birth to her baby by now, so why hadn't he written to his parents? It didn't make sense.

God, she still missed him so much. Was he happy? Did he ever think about her? She had tried so hard to put him from her mind, knowing that she would never see him again, but sometimes when she was alone, it was impossible.

Stop it! Stop thinking about him, she admonished herself, shaking her head. The baby kicked and she stroked her tummy again, swivelling sideways to put her legs up on the sofa. They looked awful, she thought, swollen and ugly.

There was the sound of a key in the lock, footsteps across the hall, and she looked round as the sitting-room door opened. 'Hello, forgot something, did you?' she asked, expecting to see Ann. Her breath caught in her throat. It wasn't Ann standing on the threshold. 'No, oh no,' she gasped.

'Hello, Sally,' Harry said, with a menacing smile as he dangled a set of keys. 'It was a bit remiss of Mary not to have changed the locks, wasn't it?'

'What do you want? Why are you here?' Sally whispered, feeling her heart thudding with fear when she saw the look of utter hatred in his eyes.

'I came to see you, of course,' he said, advancing further into the room.

'You'd better go, my friends will be back in a minute,' she told him desperately.

'Don't bother to lie. I've been watching the house and saw them leave. It was easy enough to follow them and they boarded a bus ten minutes ago.'

Feeling as though she was moving in slow motion, Sally managed to stand up, but could feel her legs trembling. 'What do you want?' she asked again, backing away as he moved slowly towards her.

'You ruined my life, Sally – do you know that? I had everything once. A wife and daughter who loved me – a beautiful son. But now, because of you, I've got nothing. Nothing!' he spat.

'I ... I didn't ruin your life,' she gasped, and as he almost reached her, she edged sideways, trying to aim for the door.

He moved too, blocking her path, standing right in front of her now. Then looking down he eyed her stomach, and with a sardonic smile on his face, said, 'So you're pregnant. How nice, and how would you like it if your baby was taken away from you?'

She felt her heart jolt at the implied threat. What could she do? How could she get away? 'Look, I know you're angry,' she placated, 'but I don't see how you can blame me.'

'You don't see!' he yelled, making her jump in fear. 'Let me tell you, I've thought long and hard while I was in prison. After all, I had plenty of time. I soon realised that Sheila would have forgiven me for marrying her without divorcing Mary. She loves me and I could have talked her

344

round. Your aunt was a cold fish, and becoming as mad as a March hare. She wouldn't have given me a divorce, just out of spite, and I'm sure I could have convinced Sheila of that.'

'But you didn't ask her for a divorce,' Sally protested.

'No, because I knew what her answer would be. But let's talk about what *you* did, shall we? You told Sheila that I was molesting Linda,' he spat, eyes narrowed in anger. 'And now she won't take me back. She even reported me to the police, and obtained a court injunction to keep me away from my son.' He shook his head, his voice rising again. '*And* she's got Mary staying with her. Mary, of all people! All because of you and your big mouth.'

'But I had no choice! Surely you realise that?'

'I wasn't hurting Linda. I love her, and she loves me.'

She felt a wave of nausea. He must be mad, she thought, turning her head and desperately looking for a means of escape.

'And I loved you too, Sally,' he continued. 'I didn't hurt you, did I? Like Linda, you enjoyed it.'

At that her temper flared. 'My God, you're disgusting,' she cried. 'Of course I didn't enjoy it! You nearly ruined my life. I was terrified of men after what you did to me.'

'Oh, don't give me that. You're pregnant, for God's sake. You girls are all the same, crying that you don't like it, when all the time you love it really. But now I'm going to make you pay for what you've done to me,' he snarled.

Sally recoiled. She tried once more to make a

345

dash for the door, but he grabbed her arm, yanking her violently back. She screamed then – screamed in terror.

'Shut up,' he hissed, holding his hand over her mouth. 'If you scream again you'll be sorry. Now I'm going to take my hand away, but I'm warning you – keep quiet. Do you understand!'

She nodded her head frantically, and as he removed his hand she staggered away from him.

'You've got to be punished, Sally. You do realise that, don't you?' he said, his voice heavy with menace as he moved towards her again.

She backed off until she could go no further, feeling a chair against her legs. He was almost level now, and she could see madness in his eyes. Oh God, my baby, she thought, clutching her stomach protectively. 'Leave me alone, please! Leave me alone!' she cried.

'You've been a naughty girl, Sally,' he told her, a cold smile on his face as he reached out.

She collapsed onto the chair, feeling the room spinning. I'm going to faint, was her last thought, as the room tilted.

'You're all right now, miss. Come on, wake up.'

Sally opened her eyes, and feeling a wave of nausea, clamped a hand over her mouth.

'Can you tell us who the man was?'

Sally's vision cleared and she looked at the policeman crouching by the side of the chair. 'Harry, it was Harry,' she gasped. Then, unable to hold it, she leaned forward and was violently sick.

'Perhaps we should call another ambulance.'

The voice came from behind her, and turning she saw a second Constable. Wiping a shaking hand across her mouth, she protested, 'No, please, I'm all right,' and as her eyes frantically scanned the room, she cried, 'Has he gone?'

The two Constables exchanged looks, one shaking his head slightly. Sally's brow creased. They were hiding something, but what?

She tried to stand up, but finding that her legs wouldn't support her, she slumped back down again.

'You shouldn't be on your own, miss. If you won't let us call an ambulance, is there someone we can contact?'

'My mother isn't on the telephone. Could you call Elsie Jones? Her number is on the pad in the hall. But, please, will you tell me what's happened?'

'All in good time, miss. Now, are you up to answering a few questions?'

'Yes, but I need to go to the bathroom, and could I have a drink of water?'

The policeman nodded and leaning forward, he helped her out of the chair. Sally averted her eyes from the vomit on her aunt's rug and slowly made her way upstairs, her mind racing. Something had happened. The police were there, but how?

She was away for some time as not only using the toilet, she ran water into the sink and washed her hands and face. Reaching for a towel to dry herself, she gagged at the foul taste in her mouth and grabbing a toothbrush, brushed her teeth.

When she returned to the sitting room, her nose wrinkled at the smell. 'I must clear this mess up,' she told the policemen. It was easier to think of practical things, to turn her thoughts away from Harry.

'Leave it for a minute, miss,' one of them insisted. 'Please sit down, we need to get a few things clear.'

As Sally reluctantly took a seat on the sofa, he sat beside her. Then, pulling a notebook from his top pocket, he licked the end of his pencil and asked, 'Was the man attacking you?'

'Yes, sort of,' she whispered.

'Could you explain what you mean by "sort of".'

Sally stared at him. How could she explain? No, as far as she could remember, he hadn't actually hit her. It was more the implied threat, the look in his eyes that had terrified her. 'I ... I thought that he was going to hurt me,' she stammered. 'He was so angry, and he stopped me when I tried to run out of the room.'

'How did he do that, miss?'

'He ... he grabbed me, and when I screamed he put his hand over my mouth.'

'What happened then?' the policeman asked, scribbling in his pad.

'I don't remember, I think I must have passed out.'

'I see. Now you said it was Harry – do you know his full name?'

'Yes, it's Harry Taylor, he's my uncle.'

'Why was he attacking you?'

The second policeman reappeared in the room, and as he held out a glass she looked at him gratefully. Taking sips of the water she gathered her thoughts, then taking a deep breath she told

348

them what had happened, and why. 'Did you catch him?' she asked tremulously.

'In a manner of speaking, miss.'

Sally frowned as she looked at him. What did he mean?

There was a screech of tyres outside, the sound of car doors banging, and then Elsie was in the room, Bert behind her. 'Oh Sally, Sally, are you all right?' she cried. 'What's been going on here?' she snapped, glaring at the policemen.

The Constables glanced at each other, then one of them gave a small nod, after which his colleague spoke. 'We had a call from a neighbour to say she could hear screaming coming from this house. When we arrived we endeavoured to apprehend a man who tried to run off. This young lady tells us it was her uncle, a Mr...' He looked at his notebook, scanning the page, 'Harry Taylor.'

'No!' Elsie gasped. 'Oh my God. Sally, what happened? Why was he here?'

'He said it was my fault that Sheila wouldn't let him see his son.' Sally turned to the policemen. 'Tell me, did you catch him?' she asked again.

'I'm afraid there was an accident,' one of them replied. 'While our colleagues were in pursuit, Mr Taylor ran into that block of flats on the corner and made his way up to the roof.' He hesitated, rubbing his hand around his chin. 'We think he must have panicked, miss. You see, he climbed onto the parapet and then – well, he fell.'

Sally's jaw dropped. What did he mean? Surely Harry hadn't fallen off the roof. 'Is he all right?' she asked in confusion.

'No, miss, I'm afraid he's dead.'

She slumped, unable to stop the surge of relief that flooded through her, but then almost immediately felt overwhelmed with guilt.

Elsie came over, and sitting down between her and the policeman she took her hand. 'Sally, where's Ann?'

'She's out with Billy,' she told her, finding that her whole body was beginning to tremble. 'Someone will have to ring Sheila, she'll have to be told. Oh God, my aunt too.'

'You're shaking like a leaf, love. Calm down and leave it to me – I'll tell them. Now listen, you've had a terrible shock and when Ann comes back you're all coming home with me.' She stood up then, and with her arms folded across her chest, she addressed the officers. 'I hope you're finished with your questions. I'm sure you can see that she's had just about enough.'

'For now, yes, but if the young lady is going to stay with you, I will need your address, Mrs Jones.'

Sally felt exhausted. She heard Elsie talking to the policemen, Bert too, but the voices washed over her. At one point she became aware of the smell of disinfectant, and the sight of Elsie scrubbing the rug. Then she was being led to Bert's car and found herself sitting in the back with Ann, who was holding her hand, her face drawn with concern.

'I'm calling a doctor as soon as we get home, Sally. You don't look at all well. Are you in any pain?'

Sally shook her head. No, she wasn't in any pain. She just felt numb.

Chapter Thirty-Eight

Sally had seen the emergency doctor, who examined her, frowning when he took her blood pressure. He had insisted she stay in bed, and now three days later, she pushed at the blankets impatiently. Elsie had given her a lovely room overlooking the back garden, which was alive with a profusion of summer flowers. There was a trellis below the window entwined with honeysuckle, the heady perfume drifting into the room. She knew she should appreciate it, but hated its confinement. Ever since her childhood, being forced to stay in a room made her feel trapped.

'The police are here to see you,' Elsie said, poking her head round the door.

Sally hastily tugged the blankets up again, looking at them warily as the same two Constables approached the bed. 'Hello, miss. Sorry to bother you again, but we just need to clear up a few more details.'

What can I tell them that they don't know already? she thought. How many times had she been over her statement? Sheila and Ruth had travelled back from Blackpool, as shocked as she was by what had happened. They too had been questioned and were now, like her, waiting to attend the inquest into Harry's death.

Now, answering their questions, she went over the same things yet again, sighing with relief when they rose to leave. 'Can you tell me when the inquest will be?' she asked.

'No, I'm afraid not. We're conducting an internal investigation, and the inquest will follow, but it could be some time yet.'

Sally closed her eyes momentarily, still full of guilt, not only about the relief she had felt when told of Harry's death, but the fear that she might have caused it. Had she over-reacted? Had she imagined the madness in his eyes? If she hadn't screamed, the police wouldn't have been called, and her uncle would still be alive. It weighed heavily on her mind, causing her sleepless nights.

'We'll be off now, miss. I don't think we will need to question you again.'

'Thank you,' Sally murmured as Elsie escorted them out.

A few minutes later she pushed the blankets away again, and throwing her legs over the side of the bed, stood up gingerly, only to hear Elsie's voice, a hint of chastisement evident. 'Now then, Sally. You know what the doctor said. You've got to stay in bed for at least a week.'

'But I'm fine,' she said as Elsie advanced across the room, carrying a tray.

'You don't necessarily feel ill with high blood-pressure, and until it goes down you must rest. Now come on, I've made you a sandwich.'

'I'm not hungry.'

'You've hardly eaten in days, Sally. Think of the baby, darling.'

Sighing, she got back into bed and Elsie placed the tray across her lap, saying, 'It's ham, a nice bit of honey roast. And I've made you a glass of lemon barley water too.'

Sally half-heartedly bit into a sandwich while Elsie started to bustle around, tidying up the already tidy room, moving things around on top of the dressing-table.

'We had better think about your antenatal appointments, Sally. When is your next one due?'

'Sometime next week, I think. But I'm booked into St George's hospital in Tooting and it's a long way from here.'

'Yes, it is. And too great a distance to travel when you're in labour. I tell you what, where's your appointment card? I'll give them a ring and see if we can change hospitals.'

Sally frowned, trying to recall when she had seen it last. 'I can't remember. Ann unpacked for me – is it in one of the drawers?'

Elsie rummaged. 'No, there's no sign of it.'

'You could try looking in my bag,' Sally suggested.

Picking it up, Elsie looked inside. 'I can't see it in here. Hang on, there's a pocket on the front, isn't there.'

As Elsie's words sank in, Sally reacted, her voice loud as she cried, 'No, Elsie, no, don't look in there!'

It was too late; she had found it, her face puzzled as she drew it out. 'What are you doing with this?' she asked, her fingers stroking the material. 'This is Arthur's tie. I recognise it because he spilled hair oil on it just before we went to the hall for his going-away party. Look, you can still see the residue.'

Sally's mind went blank. What could she say?

She shouldn't have kept it, but when she packed to go to her aunt's she'd found it in the back of her drawer. Remembering how Arthur had left it behind the night they made love, she had clutched it, holding it to her nose, trying to breathe in his scent. It was all she had left of him, and she couldn't bear to part with it.

'What's the matter?' Elsie asked, her voice concerned.

Sally just shook her head, unable to speak.

After moving the tray, Elsie sat on the bed. 'Talk to me, Sally. I thought there would be a simple explanation, but if there is, I don't know why you look so worried.'

It was no good, she couldn't do it, couldn't lie any more. Elsie had been so kind, taking her in, looking after her, when all the time she had deceived her. The baby kicked against her ribs, as if sensing her fear. 'Oh Elsie, you're going to hate me,' she burst out.

'Hate you? Why on earth would I hate you?'

Taking a deep breath, Sally said, 'I lied when I said I didn't know who my baby's father is. I do know.' She paused, lowering her eyes, cringing at what was going to happen next when Elsie heard the truth. 'It's Arthur's baby,' she whispered, too terrified to look up.

If she could have imagined Elsie's response, she would have expected her to explode with anger. Instead, bending hastily forward, she pulled Sally into her arms.

'Oh Sally, Sally,' she cried. 'You're having my Arthur's baby! I can't believe it. Why didn't you tell me? Why have you kept it to yourself?'

'Because Jenny's pregnant too. In fact, she must have had her baby by now.'

'What! Jenny's had a baby?' Elsie's brow creased. 'I don't understand. How do you know, Sally?'

'Because she told me she was pregnant before they left for Australia. How could I ask Arthur not to go then? I knew the baby would need its father.'

Elsie drew back. 'None of this makes sense. If what you say is true, Arthur would have told me.'

'He was supposed to write and tell you as soon as they arrived in Australia.'

'Well, I did have a letter from him then, the only one I've received, but there was no mention of Jenny being pregnant. And anyway, if it's true, why didn't he tell me before they left?'

'He didn't want to hurt you. He said you were upset enough about him going to Australia, without finding out that you wouldn't see your first grandchild.'

'Oh son, son,' she groaned.

'I'm sorry, Elsie.'

'No, love, there's no need to be sorry. I don't blame you – after all, you only did what you thought was for the best. But if Jenny's had a baby I just can't understand why Arthur hasn't told us. There's something wrong out there, I just know there is, and I'm worried sick.'

After a few moments Elsie heaved a deep sigh, then pulling Sally briefly into her arms again and giving her a gentle pat on her back, she stood up. 'I still can't take this in, really. You're actually having my grandchild.'

'What do you think my mum will say, Elsie?'

'I don't know. But she'll be here this evening so we'll soon find out. Your gran's still got bronchitis so she's coming on her own. Bert's going to pick her up.'

Sally closed her eyes, nervous at the thought of her mother's reaction. 'I'm dreading telling her.'

'Leave it to me, love. I'll tell her. Now come on, you look exhausted and I think you should have a little nap.' With a small smile, she added, 'Try to stop worrying, Sally, everything will be all right.'

As the door closed behind Elsie, Sally's taut nerves snapped. All the pain of losing Arthur, all the guilt she felt at Harry's death, rose to the surface. She tried to hold back the tears, squeezing her eyes tightly shut, but they oozed out of the corners, running down her cheeks and soaking the pillow. She didn't see the glow forming in the corner of the room, didn't see the translucent shape, and only when she felt a feathery touch on her cheek, did her tears stop.

'Hello, how's Sadie?' Elsie asked when Ruth arrived that evening.

'A bit better, but she was up half the night coughing. How's Sally?'

'She's still not eating a lot, and she's nervous about the inquest.'

'Are you sure you don't mind having her? She could come home with me now. You look surprised, Elsie, and I don't blame you, but I've been wracked with guilt since Harry's death. I can't bear thinking about what he might 'ave done to her if the police hadn't been called. Christ, Elsie, if I 'adn't made her leave home, she'd 'ave been safe. And *why* did I make her go? Because I was worried about the bleedin' neighbours!' She hung her head. 'I've been a rotten mother, Elsie.'

'Don't be silly, of course you haven't. Most single girls who get pregnant are shunted off somewhere. And anyway, I don't mind Sally staying here. You've got enough to do at the moment looking after Sadie.'

'Well, maybe she can come home when her gran's a bit better.'

'We'll see. Now I'm going to make you a cup of tea. Don't go upstairs to see Sally just yet. I've got something to tell you, Bert too,' she added as he came into the room.

'Oh yeah, come up on the pools, have we?' he joked as he sat down.

'It depends on how you look at it, Bert. Now I've had time to think about it, to me it's better than winning the pools.'

Elsie smiled to herself as she hurried out of the room, not giving them a chance to ask any questions. It was true: once the news had sunk in she found she was filled with joy. A grandchild, she was going to be a gran! Sally would still be unmarried, they couldn't change that, but at least Ruth would know who the father was now. She was hoping that after the initial shock, like her, Ruth would be pleased. It was funny really; with Arthur being the father it made her feel that in some way they were related. Oh, son, why don't you write? she thought for the umpteenth time.

Carrying the tea tray through to the sitting room she passed the cups around, before quietly breaking the news.

357

'What!' Ruth exploded, choking on her tea.

'I'll bloody well kill him,' Bert growled.

'Calm down, love. You'd have a job to do that, considering he's in Australia.'

'But to run off and leave the girl when she's pregnant,' he said in disgust.

'No, Bert, he didn't know Sally was pregnant when he emigrated. Sally didn't know herself until January. Anyway Jenny was already pregnant when they left.'

'I don't believe this!' Bert roared, jumping to his feet.

Elsie took a deep breath. This was harder than she'd predicted. Bert was pacing the floor like a caged animal and Ruth was looking stunned, her cup halfway to her lips. 'Sit down, Bert, and I'll start at the beginning,' she urged.

It took her some time to explain it all to them, but at least they were quiet, waiting for her to finish. She glanced at Ruth now and saw that tears were running down her cheeks. 'Don't cry, please don't cry,' she begged.

'It's all right. I think they're tears of relief really. It was awful not knowing who the father was, and I just couldn't believe it of Sally. Oh the poor kid, when I think of all the awful names that I called her.'

'I'm so sorry. I too can't believe it of my Arthur,' Elsie told her.

Ruth gave her a watery smile. 'I can't take it in really, it seems unbelievable, your son being the father. If it wasn't so tragic it would be funny. Here we are, best friends, both going to be grandmothers, and sharing the same grandchild.'

'Oh, I'm so sorry,' Elsie said again.

'Christ, it's a rotten mess, ain't it?' Ruth said, pausing and biting her bottom lip. Then with a deep sigh, she added, 'Well, we'll just have to make the best of it. Sally will still be a single mum, but she'll 'ave us to help her, won't she?'

'Of course she will,' Elsie assured her. Then, turning to Bert, she asked, 'Haven't you got anything to say?'

He growled low in his throat, his hair standing on end where he had raked it through with his fingers. 'What do you expect me to say? I'd still like to get my hands on my son. Making one mistake is bad enough, but two...' He shook his head in disgust.

'I just wish he'd write, Bert. We've only had one letter from him since he went to Australia. I just don't understand it.'

'I don't either,' Bert told her, turning his head as the door opened.

Sally stepped nervously into the room, clutching the front of her dressing-gown ineffectually over the mound of her stomach.

Elsie was surprised at the speed with which Ruth got to her feet. She appeared to fly across the room. 'Oh Sally, I'm so sorry, darling,' she cried, throwing her arms around her daughter.

Chapter Thirty-Nine

Arthur climbed out of the truck, wiping the sweat from his forehead. Holding up a hand to shade his eyes from the sun he gazed at the flat landscape. Just dark red earth, as far as the eye could see, miles and miles of desert, and he marvelled at how alien it looked.

Taking a swig from his canteen of water, he turned to look at Joe, and seeing that he had the map spread out in front of him covering the steering wheel, asked, 'Where are we heading for now?'

'Well, I dunno about you, Arthur, but I don't fancy going any further into the interior. How about we make our way down to Adelaide?'

Arthur shrugged his shoulders. They had been travelling for months, drifting as the mood took them, picking up the odd bit of casual work here and there. Canberra, Wagga Wagga, then skirting along the Murray River for a while until Joe got the whim to go further into the interior. But now it seemed it had lost its thrall and he was itching to get back to the coast. Arthur nodded. It didn't matter to him where they headed for. 'Yes, Adelaide sounds all right to me.'

'Jump in then, and we can put a few miles in before dark,' Joe urged, and pointing at the map, he added, 'with any luck we may reach Broken Hill.'

As the truck bumped along, Arthur was deep in thought. He enjoyed travelling with Joe, but somehow the sense of adventure had worn off. He was tired of drifting from place to place, though Joe looked happy to carry on indefinitely. He never seemed short of money, spending it like water despite the small amount they had earned. Arthur tried to keep his expenditure down to a minimum, but was worried about his dwindling funds. Should he settle for a while in Adelaide, try to find work?

'Are you all right, mate?' Joe asked, breaking into his thoughts. 'You seem a bit down in the mouth today.'

'Yeah, I'm fine. Just a bit fed up with travelling, that's all,' Arthur assured him.

'Have you got that girl of yours out of your system now?'

'Who, Sally?'

Joe took his eyes off the road as his head snapped round. 'Sally, who's Sally? I thought you said her name was Jenny.'

'Er, yeah, Jenny. Sally was a girl I knew back home in England.'

'Oh, I see. Nice, was she?'

'Yeah, gorgeous,' Arthur told him as a picture of her rose in his mind. I wonder how she is, he thought, closing his eyes against a sudden wave of homesickness.

'Are your parents dead, Arthur?' Joe asked.

'No, of course not. What makes you think that?'

'Sorry, mate. It's just that you never talk about them. Whenever I try to bring up the subject of England, you clam up.'

Arthur had to admit that Joe was right. He couldn't bear to talk about home; in fact, he avoided thinking about it as much as possible.

'Are you still homesick, Arthur?'

With a deep intake of breath, Arthur turned to look at his friend. 'Yeah,' he sighed.

The light was starting to fade as they reached Broken Hill, and finding the mining town had a boarding-house, they rented a room and sank onto their beds gratefully.

After a short rest, Arthur pulled a clean shirt out of his now battered case, deciding to have a bath. As he reached into the back pocket for his shaving gear, his hand touched the old letters from home, and for the first time, instead of ignoring them, he pulled them out.

'I'm going for a beer,' Joe said. 'Coming, Arthur?'

'No, mate, I'll join you later,' he told him, sitting back down on the side of the bed. He fingered the envelopes then flipped them over, looking at the addresses on the back. One was from his mum, the other from Ann. Taking a deep breath he threw down Ann's and ripped open the one from his mum. Quickly scanning the contents, his eyes widened. So they were going back to live in Wimbledon. Dad must be doing really well, he thought. He read on, smiling at all the gossip, his expression changing when he came to the last page. Raking his fingers through his hair he shook his head in disbelief. Sally was pregnant.

His face darkened with anger. Christ, he'd only been in Australia for about six months and she'd already found another bloke, *and* got herself in the club. Sinking back on the bed, he saw Sally's face behind closed lids. He had tried so hard to put her out of his mind, still unable to believe her change of attitude. She had been like a chameleon, loving him one minute and then totally dismissing him the next. How could he have got it so wrong? Yet look what a mug he'd been with Jenny. She had certainly made a prize fool out of him, so why not Sally?

Drearily picking up the letter, intending to read it again, his eyes suddenly fixed on the date. Bloody hell, what an idiot, it had been in his case since February! Something clicked in his mind and his thoughts raced. He'd left England in November and by February his mother wrote that Sally was pregnant. Screwing shut his eyes, he tried to work out the dates. Was it possible?

Sitting up abruptly, he burst out aloud: 'It's mine, I'm sure it's mine! Oh, Sally,' he moaned. When would she be having it? Think, come on, *think*. He counted the months again. Bloody hell, it was due in August, she'd be having the baby in August and it was already the first week in June. He had to get home and quick, he just had to. But how?

It didn't take him long to realise that it was impossible. He just didn't have enough money. The only thing he could do was to find work, well-paid work, and save every penny. All right, it would take a while, but what choice did he have?

'Joe, I want to go back to Sydney.'

'Christ, you must be joking. Why?'

Arthur rested an arm on the bar, thinking

363

furiously whilst rubbing his forehead with his other hand. Should he tell Joe, explain the situation? But if he did, he knew that his friend would offer to drive him back and that didn't seem fair. Finally he said, 'After all the places we've seen, I've decided that I prefer Sydney. It's time I settled down. I can't drift around for ever and I need to make some real money.'

Joe scratched the stubble on his chin. 'Well, if that's how you feel, I won't argue – but are you sure you don't want to see Adelaide first?'

'Yeah, I'm sure. Look, Joe, you don't have to come with me. I can get a train from here to Sydney.'

'I know that, mate, but I'll miss you. We've had some good times, haven't we?' he said, taking a swig of beer.

Arthur smiled at his friend. Yes, they'd had some good times. It was strange really, neither of them had talked much about their past. He knew Joe was from England too and had been in Australia for about eighteen months. His parents lived in Sussex, somewhere near the South Downs, and he had a younger brother who was at University, but other than that he knew little else.

'Fancy another beer, Arthur?'

'Yeah, why not,' he answered.

It was late by the time they staggered back to the boarding-house, but thankfully they could still get in, the landlady just smiling indulgently as the two men, holding each other up, fell inside the door. Arthur slumped onto his bed, too drunk to undress, and almost immediately passed out.

Joe sat looking at his mate. Although he'd had a good few pints, he wasn't as drunk as Arthur, and was still puzzling over his reasons for going back to Sydney. It didn't ring true somehow. Yes, he could accept that he was a bit tired of travelling, and that he needed to make some decent money, but what was the matter with Adelaide? It was a big place and sure to have plenty of job opportunities, so why go back to Sydney?

He stood up, intending to switch off the light, when he saw the letter on top of the chest of drawers. Walking stealthily across the room he picked it up, returning to sit on his bed. Was this the answer? Was there something in this letter?

When Arthur woke up the next morning he sat up slowly, groaning at the pounding in his head. It took him a few minutes to register that Joe wasn't in the room, and another couple to realise that his friend's belongings had gone too. Standing up, unsteady on his feet, he saw a note propped on the empty bed.

In capital letters Joe had written: BYE MATE. HAVE A SAFE JOURNEY HOME. Arthur glanced at his watch; it was nine thirty. He couldn't believe it. Why had Joe left like this, without even waiting for him to wake up?

Unable to take it in, he shook his head. Joe was fine last night and had wished him well on his journey back to Sydney and he hadn't been upset, he was sure. They had both been pretty drunk, he knew that, and even a bit maudlin at times. Had something else happened that he couldn't remember?'

He hurried downstairs, finding the landlady in the kitchen. 'Excuse me, could you tell me what time my friend left this morning?'

'Yeah, it was real early, just after six o'clock. He paid for the room, and said you'd be leaving later.'

'Did he say anything else, or leave me a message?'

'No, love. He just paid the bill and went.'

'All right, thanks,' Arthur said, returning to his room none the wiser. He had a quick wash, and as all his gear was still in the suitcase, he shoved in his dirty shirt and shut the lid. With a last glance around he made his way downstairs and after handing in the key, headed for the station.

He plodded along, still unhappy that Joe had left so abruptly without saying goodbye. When he finally reached the station, he reached into his back pocket for his wallet. Bloody hell, he thought, feeling its bulkiness and gawking when he saw the thick wedge of notes inside. Where had all that money come from? There was a letter stuffed in with it, and pulling it out, he found his answer. Joe had given it to him.

Scanning the note, his eyes widened. Joe admitted to reading his letter and realised that Arthur wanted to go home. He went on to say that he hadn't come to Australia on an assisted passage, but had paid his own fare out of money he'd inherited from his grandparents. Unhappy with his home life because of a bad relationship with his father, the money had given him the freedom to travel and he had come to Australia for a good look round, with the intention that if

366

he liked it, he would eventually buy a farm.

The breath left Arthur's body with a whoosh. Bloody hell, what an idiot I've been, he thought. All the clues were there, but I didn't see them. Joe never seemed short of money, his truck was almost new and must have cost a pretty penny. And I never even thought to ask him about it.

How could he accept all this money? But how could he find Joe to give it back? With no transport, Arthur soon realised that it would be impossible. Joe could be anywhere by now, and in a country this big, it would be hard to find him. Yes, he had said he was heading for Adelaide, but that didn't mean he'd end up there. Many times they had been aiming for a place when Joe decided to veer off to somewhere else, just on a whim. He looked at the cash again. Joe had given him the opportunity to go home, and silently thanking his friend, he decided to take it.

He boarded the train, and after stowing his case, slumped in a seat. He should have read his mother's letter before, and answered it. And why hadn't he? Because he was too proud to admit that Jenny had made a fool of him, and too proud to admit that he had made a mistake. They had tried to warn him, but he wouldn't listen.

Should he try to find their telephone number, and tell them what had happened? No, he decided. It was too complicated a story and explanations could wait until he got home. For now he had this long train journey to face, and when he got to Sydney he had no idea how long it would take him to find a berth on a ship. Would he be able to make it home before Sally had the baby?

Chapter Forty

Sally found the following weeks somewhat surreal, and she felt that she was in some kind of crazy dream. Everything appeared to have gone topsy-turvy. Her mother's attitude to her pregnancy had changed completely. Ruth was now excited about the baby, and talked about it endlessly when she came to visit.

Elsie had gone into a frenzy, buying a pram, cot and baby clothes, while Bert, instead of getting cross about her expenditure, just smiled indulgently as she showed him each new purchase. There was still no news of Arthur, and though Elsie tried to hide it, Sally knew she was desperately worried about him, guessing that shopping was, for her, some sort of compensation.

But now it was Ann who was acting hostile, hardly talking and avoiding her as much as possible. This had taken Sally by surprise; Ann was the one person she thought she could count on.

As she was thinking about her, the bedroom door opened and Ann herself walked in carrying a cup of tea. She plonked it on her bedside table. 'Mum asked me to bring you this,' she said coldly, turning swiftly to leave.

'Ann, wait. Please, can't we talk?'

Her friend spun around, her voice clipped. 'It's a bit late for that now, isn't it? I can't understand why you didn't tell me, Sally.'

'I couldn't tell anyone – surely you can understand that.'

'No, I can't. I thought we were friends. And not only that, I think it's awful that you kept it from us. He's my brother, for God's sake, and the baby you're carrying will be my niece or nephew. How could you do it?'

'Ann, I thought both you and your mum would hate me. I realised I loved Arthur before he left for Australia, and I think he loved me too, but when Jenny told me she was pregnant, what could I do? I know you and your mum would have wanted me to convince Arthur to stay, but I couldn't do that.'

'Why not? If you love him, how could you let him go?'

Unbidden tears flooded her eyes. 'Ann, I never had a father, and I've longed all my life to know what it's like to have a father's love. How could I inflict that on their innocent baby?'

There was a strained silence, then with a small sob Ann ran back across the room. 'Oh Sally, I'm sorry. I've been so awful, I didn't think,' she cried, throwing herself onto the bed.

'No, it's me that's sorry.' Sally sniffed, struggling to pull herself together. 'I realise now that I made a mistake, a big one. I should have told you all, should have trusted you.'

'Looking back now I could kick myself,' Ann said. 'I remember thinking how strange you became leading up to Arthur's departure, but I was stupid enough to think you were still upset about John. When you came out to say goodbye to him the day he was leaving for Australia, I was watching you from the back of the car. You looked awful, so white and drawn. Why didn't I see it – why?'

'Because you weren't meant to. I knew you thought I was still upset about John, and I let you go on believing that.'

'If I hadn't been so wrapped up in Billy, I might have worked it out. I can't believe I accepted it when you said you didn't know who the father was. I should have known better.'

'Ann, please, can we just forget it now, get back to how things were between us?'

'Yeah, of course. Anyway, how do you think "Auntie Ann" sounds?'

'Great, and you'll make a lovely auntie.'

'And Arthur would make a lovely dad. Oh no, I'm sorry, I shouldn't have said that. Me and my big mouth,' Ann gasped. 'Why do I keep doing that, speaking without thinking first! You're upset enough as it is.'

'It's all right,' Sally assured her, trying not to let Ann see how stricken she was. 'As I told your mum, Jenny must have had her baby by now, so Arthur already has a child, and at least one baby will have its father.'

'I don't get it, Sally. Why doesn't he write? And I'll tell you something else: he knows you're pregnant. I mentioned it in my letters and I think mum did too.' She shook her head. 'Of course, he doesn't know it's his though.'

Sally sank back onto her pillows. Arthur knows, she thought, he knows. Of course they would have told him – why hadn't she thought of that?

But would he work it out, or would he think she had met someone else? 'Ann, have either of you written to Arthur again since you found out the baby's his?'

'No – well, at least I haven't. I don't know about Mum. Why do you ask?'

'I just don't know if we should tell him. Can you imagine how it will affect him, Ann?'

'Oh, I don't know about that, I think he has a right to know.' Ann glanced at the clock. 'Look, I'm sorry but I've got to go or I'll be late for work. We'll talk about it again when I come home.'

'Yes, all right,' Sally whispered distantly, her mind still on Arthur.

The following day Sally dressed slowly, frowning at her appearance in the mirror. I look awful, she thought, staring at her huge stomach and badly swollen legs. The doctor allowed her to get up now, but only if she rested as much as possible with her feet raised. He still wasn't too happy with her condition, and though her blood pressure had gone down a bit, he was now talking about the dangers of eclampsia. There was a possibility that she would have to go into hospital, and to avoid that she made sure that she followed his instructions.

She made her way slowly downstairs, her hand held in the crook of her back. Aunt Mary would be here soon with Sheila and the children, and like her, they had been summoned to the inquest on Monday.

Just as she had taken a seat in the sitting room, with her legs up on a pouffe, the doorbell rang.

'Hello, Sally. How are you, my dear?' Mary asked as she came into the room, Sheila and the children behind her.

'I'm fine, Auntie. Linda, aren't you coming to give me a kiss?' she asked, holding out her arms.

Linda stepped forward, staring at Sally's tummy. 'You're awfully fat,' she said, making them all burst into laughter.

Bert came into the room, and as soon as Linda saw him she ran back behind her mother. Seeing her reaction, he quickly left again, returning with their latest acquisition, a basket of kittens courtesy of the cat that had adopted them soon after they moved in.

Unable to resist them Linda stepped forward, and with Daniel, was soon kneeling beside Bert on the floor, her fear of men temporarily forgotten as she gazed mesmerised at the tiny squirming bodies. Just then Treacle, the mother, turned up, pushing her way into the basket and lying on her side for the kittens to fight for a teat.

While Linda was distracted, Sheila sat beside Sally, talking quietly. 'How do you feel about the inquest?' she asked.

'I dread going. I still feel so terribly guilty.'

'Don't be silly. You have nothing to feel guilty about.'

'But if I hadn't screamed, the police wouldn't have been called.'

'Oh, my dear, I'm glad they were. I can't bear to think what might have happened otherwise. When Harry turned up at the house in Blackpool we were so frightened of him. He was like a different man, and I thought he was bordering on madness.'

'Yes, I must admit I was terrified of him. He used to be so mild – how can someone change so much in such a short time?'

'I don't know. But if you're feeling guilty, take a look at Linda. You saw the way she reacted to Bert. It will probably take years for her to get over her fear of men, if she ever can. I know it sounds an awful thing to say, but in a way I'm glad that Harry's dead. At least he won't be able to damage any more children.'

Sally sat quietly, thinking about what Sheila had said, and in some ways it did alleviate her guilt. She watched now as Bert picked up a kitten, Linda staring at him in wonderment as he placed it gently in her arms. But when he stood up, she reared back nervously, the kitten mewing as fear made her squeeze it too tightly. He tried to reassure her by bending down again, but Linda dropped the kitten, hastily scrambling back across the room to her mother.

Bert quietly left the room then, his face reflecting his sadness, and shortly afterwards Elsie came in carrying a tray, piled with an assortment of cakes and sandwiches. Daniel, who was still absorbed with the kittens, soon abandoned them when he saw the coconut pyramids.

Sally watched him as he eagerly took one, biting the cherry on the top off with relish, a small smile on her face. Then, turning to her Aunt Mary, she asked, 'Are you going to stay in your flat now?'

'Yes. It's close to the Common which is nice for the children, and I'll be able to keep my job on at the surgery.'

Sally nodded, her thoughts returning to the inquest, wondering what the procedure would be. She knew she would have to give evidence, and cringed at the prospect.

On Monday morning Sally climbed nervously into Bert's car, Elsie beside her in the back as they made their way to the Coroner's Court. On arrival they stared at the large building that looked forbidding, despite the sunlight that shone on the brick-faced edifice.

Bert left them to go inside while he went to park the car, and Sally stepped tentatively into the large entrance hall. She saw her aunt and Sheila perched on a long bench and quickly joined them, Elsie behind her.

'When do we go in?' she whispered.

'We're next,' her aunt hissed back.

'Why are you whispering?' Elsie asked.

They smiled wryly at her, then a silence descended on them. Sally gazed around the hall. There were two policemen looking their way and she recognised them as the Constables who had been called out on the night of Harry's death. She had to bend over slightly then, annoyed that she had indigestion again; all she had eaten for breakfast was some toast and marmalade.

'Sally, sit down,' Elsie ordered. 'Honestly, I think this is disgusting. Here you are, nearly due to have your baby, and you're called to attend this inquest. You should be resting, you know what the doctor said.'

'I'm all right, please don't fuss,' she said, irritable with discomfort.

The hall then appeared to be filled with people, all making their way outside. 'The last inquest must have finished so it won't be long now,' Elsie said.

It seemed an age before they were finally called in, and Sally, perspiring heavily, followed the others through the doors. She looked around in surprise; the place was nothing like she'd expected. It wasn't like a courtroom at all. There were lines of wooden chairs, a desk at the far end, with another small table and a chair alongside it.

'It's different from what I expected,' she whispered to Elsie.

'It's not a criminal court, that's why.'

The room fell strangely silent as the coroner came in, most eyes on him as he took a seat behind the desk. Sally hardly noticed his entrance; she was too busy trying to get comfortable on the hard wooden chair, thinking that this was the worst bout of indigestion she'd ever had.

The proceedings began. They were there, they were told, to ascertain the cause of death of the deceased, Mr Harold Taylor. Sally tried to listen to the evidence, hoping it would distract her mind from the pain, but most of it washed over her.

The post-mortem results made her grimace. God, she had no idea that they even examined the contents of the stomach.

The policemen were called next, each giving their evidence clearly and concisely, but by now Sally was hardly listening. The perspiration was running off her, the indigestion gripping her tummy. It was only when her aunt gasped, that she pricked up her ears, listening to what the coroner was saying. 'Yes, you say you saw Mr Taylor fall from the roof. But were you close enough to be sure that it was accidental?'

'Yes, sir. I was only about three feet away at the time, and I clearly saw him lose his balance. He didn't jump, I'm certain.'

Sally's brow creased. Why was the coroner asking if it was an accident? Surely he didn't think that Harry had deliberately – no, it didn't bear thinking about. She winced as another pain shot through her abdomen, relieved when at last the policeman left the chair, and she was called to give her evidence.

She answered the questions; told them that Harry had threatened her, all the time just wishing it were over. The coroner was patient when she stumbled over some of her answers, and at one point asked her if she was all right.

At last he seemed satisfied and she returned to her seat, just managing to sit down as she was gripped by another sharp stab of pain. Hardly aware of anything else, she was relieved when the coroner finally announced his verdict.

'I have heard the evidence that suggests the balance of Mr Taylor's mind may have been affected in the time leading up to his death. However, I have listened to the account given by the police, and am satisfied that the deceased did not deliberately take his own life. I am therefore recording a verdict of Death by Misadventure.'

Sally heard the scraping of chairs, the rustle of paper, and then Elsie's voice in her ear. 'Come on, love, we can go now.'

She stood up, leaning forward slightly, trying to ease the pain.

'Are you all right?' Elsie asked anxiously.

'Yes, it's just a nasty bout of indigestion,' Sally told her.

'Oh dear, I remember suffering with that towards the end of my pregnancies too. Never mind, we'll soon be home and I'll give you a glass of liver salts.'

Sally smiled wanly, just glad to be sitting in the car again and away from the ordeal.

As soon as they arrived back in Wimbledon, Sally sank onto the sofa. Elsie brought her a glass of salts and she gulped it down, hoping it would relieve the pain.

'Why don't you go and lie down, love?' Elsie urged. 'You look worn out.

'Yes, I think I will,' Sally told her, heaving herself up and groaning with the effort.

Sitting on the edge of the bed and kicking off her shoes, she held her back. God, it was aching. It must have been that uncomfortable chair in the Coroner's Court that had caused it. Wet with perspiration, she pulled off her maternity dress and eased herself down on top of the blankets, closing her eyes. She tried to sleep, but it was impossible. Every time she felt herself drifting off, the pain in her back jerked her awake.

Finally, unable to stand it any longer, she sat up. The toilet, she needed the toilet. Clutching her stomach she waddled across the room and was about to open the door, when her waters broke. Without a shadow of doubt, she knew then that the baby was coming.

Opening the door and stepping onto the landing, she called, 'Elsie! Elsie!' as another wave of pain had her bending forward.

There was a flurry as Elsie ran up the stairs, smiling widely. 'Well, it's about time my grandchild decided to be born,' she said. 'Come on, let's get you back to bed and I'll call the midwife.'

'I'm sorry, Elsie. My waters broke all over your carpet,' she told her, groaning as another contraction ripped through her stomach.

'Sod the carpet,' Elsie laughed. 'Now then, have you timed the contractions?'

'No, but I think they're about every five minutes,' she gasped as Elsie helped her back into bed.

'I'm glad you decided to have the baby at home, I'll be able to see it born. Now, are you all right while I pop down to the telephone?'

Sally nodded. 'Don't be long though, Elsie.'

'I won't, but I had better get the rubber sheet to put under you too.'

When Elsie returned, Sally had to get off the bed again while she pushed the protective sheet under the linen one. She sat in a chair, clutching her tummy. God, she had had no idea it would be as bad as this. It was excruciating.

'Elsie, I'm scared,' she whimpered as she heaved herself back onto the bed.

'You'll be all right, darling. In no time you'll be holding your baby in your arms and it will all be worth it.'

Elsie stroked her forehead as another contraction shot through her, and Sally gripped the edge of the mattress, her knuckles white.

'Oh, it hurts, it hurts,' she cried.

'I know, love. I know,' Elsie soothed.

Sally tossed her head in agony as the pain came in waves, growing worse and worse, until she barely had time to gasp before another ripped through her. It went on and on, never-ending, and she lost all track of time.

She screamed now, as another contraction gripped her, and after a while it felt like she'd been screaming for hours. The midwife must have arrived, but she had no memory of it, only becoming aware of her voice as she issued instructions.

'Mum, I want my mum,' she croaked.

'She'll be here soon. I've sent for her,' Elsie promised.

Oh God, it was agony, unrelenting. When would it stop? Please someone make it stop! She could hear voices, as though from a distance, muffled and indistinct. 'Ambulance', she thought she heard the word 'ambulance', and struggled to speak.

Her mother's voice – was that her mother's voice? 'Mum, Mum,' she whimpered.

'Shush, love, you'll be all right. I'm here now. Hold on, darling, please hold on.'

When had her mother arrived? How long had she been there? Pain again, all she was aware of was pain, filling her whole body and tearing her apart. Other sounds momentarily penetrated – a door banging, shouts, and was that laughter?

Then another voice. No, it couldn't be. She knew then that she was hallucinating.

'Sally, Sally, I'm here, darling,' the voice whispered, close to her ear.

She turned her head. She could see him. 'Arthur?' she husked.

'Yes, Sally, it's Arthur. My boy's come home,' Elsie sobbed, tears streaming down her face.

Sally tried to smile, tried to reach out to touch him, unable to believe that he was real, but she felt strange, and there was a loud ringing in her ears.

There was another voice, someone shouting, 'Oh God – no, she's haemorrhaging!'

Was that her mother screaming, her voice sounding hysterical as she cried, 'Please do something – you must do something! Stop the bleeding! For God's sake, stop the bleeding!'

'Sally, don't leave me, please don't leave me,' she heard Arthur pleading.

Then a final pain, a slithering, rushing sensation, and a chorus: 'It's a girl, a lovely little girl.'

'Sally!' her mother screamed.

She was suddenly cushioned, floating, the pain gone. A golden light was forming and she drifted towards it, arms outstretched. Her friend had come. 'Angel, my angel,' she whispered.

Then there was nothing, just darkness...

'Oh thank God, thank God,' she could hear someone sobbing, the voice penetrating her mind. Opening her eyes she saw her mother, tears rolling down her cheeks.

'You're gonna be all right now, Sally. You're gonna be all right, darling.'

380

For a moment she was bewildered. What had happened? She had vague memories of floating through a tunnel, a wonderful feeling of peace, a light in the distance, something she had experienced before, a long time ago. She struggled to remember, but then a hand gripped hers and she turned her head.

Arthur was sitting beside her, his face full of joy. 'Look, Sally. Look, here's our daughter.'

'You're here, you're really here,' she whispered, her heart flooding with happiness and her eyes lowering to see the beautiful baby nestled in his arms, a wisp of red hair visible.

'Yes, darling, I'm here, and I promise I'll never, ever leave you again. Oh Sally, I love you so much.'

'Jenny?' she managed to whisper.

'It's over, Sally, and she wasn't pregnant after all.'

She managed to smile, feeling weak and exhausted, yet so happy as Arthur looked down at their baby, his face full of tenderness and love.

'The ambulance is here, you've got to go to the hospital,' her mother said.

But Sally barely heard her; she was too busy gazing at her daughter as she was placed in her arms. 'You've given her a beautiful name, darling,' Arthur said softly.

She raised her eyes, puzzled. 'Name, what name?'

'Why Angela, of course. You called out her name as soon as she was born, and stretched out your arms to hold her.'

Sally smiled softly as her daughter nuzzled into her breast. 'Angela,' she whispered. 'My angel.'

The publishers hope that this book has given you enjoyable reading. Large Print Books are especially designed to be as easy to see and hold as possible. If you wish a complete list of our books please ask at your local library or write directly to:

Magna Large Print Books
Magna House, Long Preston,
Skipton, North Yorkshire.
BD23 4ND